Frederick William Robinson

Milly's Hero

Fourth Edition

Frederick William Robinson

Milly's Hero
Fourth Edition

ISBN/EAN: 9783337214067

Printed in Europe, USA, Canada, Australia, Japan

Cover: Foto ©Andreas Hilbeck / pixelio.de

More available books at **www.hansebooks.com**

MILLY'S HERO.

BY

FREDERICK W. ROBINSON,

AUTHOR OF

"WOMAN'S RANSOM," "UNDER THE SPELL," "WILDFLOWER," ETC.

"Equality is no rule in Love's grammar."
HEYWOOD.

FOURTH EDITION.

LONDON:

CHAPMAN AND HALL, 193, PICCADILLY.

MILLY'S HERO.

BOOK I.

WHEAL DESPERATION.

CHAPTER I.

A LUCKY FELLOW.

"Gentlemen, I need not detain you any longer with my remarks. The health, gentlemen, of Mr. Laurence Raxford."

"The health of Mr. Raxford." "Mr. Raxford, your health, Sir." "Here's your good health, Mr. Raxford." "Your very good health *and* happiness, Sir!"

Mr. Raxford bowed and smiled in every direction; he was gratified at all these good wishes; more, he felt them at heart, and was grateful for them, for they *were* good wishes, and not the effervescent result of a good dinner and plenty of wine.

This was a dinner-party with a dash of novelty in it; it took place under peculiar circumstances, and there were peculiar people facing the gentleman whose health had been so heartily drunk.

The dinner was given by Mr. Jonathan Fyvie, senior, in honour of his new partner, Mr. Laurence Raxford, who had made his first appearance in that capacity at Wheal Desperation that day—coming from London and the Royal School of Mines to accept the honours of partnership with two of the richest men in Devonshire, Mr. Jonathan Fyvie, senior, and his son, also called Jonathan, and rather objecting to the cognomen.

1

It was a five o'clock dinner, and those who sat down to it were simply the partners in that copper-mine, a clerk or two fixed to the premises, and about a dozen mining captains —men at the heads of their respective "gangs" above and beneath the surface; men who had travelled and seen life— especially mining life—in many quarters of the world; men who knew their business well, and were paid well for it; hard-featured, keen-eyed, horny-handed men, with some sense in their looks, and with opinions on business matters which were worth consulting, and which opinions had, at one time and another, put many thousands of pounds in the pockets of Fyvie and Fyvie.

One of these captains, a harder-featured, keener-eyed, and more horny-handed man than the rest, leaned across the table with more energy or confidence than his compeers, and exclaimed,

"I knew your father, Sir—I was here when he and Mr. Fyvie had this counting-house all to themselves, and lived here night and day, and prayed for more copper and less slag."

"Ha! ha!" sang out the captains, after some furtive glances in the direction of the senior partner, whose features had relaxed at the remark of the last speaker.

"Ah! and it was Mr. Fyvie's mine then, Athorpe—not Wheal Desperation," said Mr. Fyvie, senior; "you all know the story of the new christening—and I'll tell my young friend going home. So we save time, and give Mr. Raxford an opportunity to make a longer speech."

The mining captains laughed again; Mr. Fyvie, junior, looked up and smiled at the new partner; Mr. Laurence Raxford hastened to disclaim any intention of taking up the valuable time of the gentlemen assembled round him by any long or elaborate speech. He had, in the first place, to thank them all for drinking his health,—he spoke with a rapidity of utterance and a slight nervousness of demeanour natural to a young man facing his seniors; and in the second place, to assure them all that he had not come down to Devonshire as a sleeping partner, but to work with them and be one of them, above the surface, or beneath it, till he thoroughly understood the working principles of mining, and felt that he could be of service to his partners. He was grateful for the honour those partners had done him—to the unexpected honour, he might say, by adding his name to the proprietary of Wheal Desperation ; he would study to deserve his promotion, and, at least, he entered upon his career with his heart in his work—with a heart full of gratitude, too, for the kind hands that had set such work before him, and made' him partner in so prosperous an undertaking. I think he added that this was the happiest day of his life—he had tried very hard to dodge that phrase, but it came upon him at last, and he expressed it by way of peroration. But he meant what he said, also, for he was a happy, as well as a lucky fellow, and he entered upon a fair and rich estate at two-and-twenty years of age.

A few lines of description—the fewer the better—will serve in this place for the partners in Wheal Desperation. Long-winded descriptions of characters, we take it, do not assist a story much in its outset.

Laurence Raxford, then,—the gentleman on his legs,—a good-looking young fellow enough, despite the absence of all classicality of feature ; a fresh-coloured, hazel-eyed, chestnut-haired man, above the middle-height, with a face unmasked by whisker or moustache ; rather a clever face, we might say, and a good-tempered one certainly, although he did not always look so pleased as on this particular day in May, when we find him rising to return thanks for the handsome manner in which his health had been proposed by his friend and partner Mr. Fyvie, senior.

And Mr. Fyvie, senior—tall and wiry—a man drawn out to no end of inches—a grey-haired, grey-eyed old gentleman, with a face of many wrinkles, a pair of gold-mounted spectacles, across a long, straight nose ; a white, thin hand, just then clutching a pointed chin—a well-dressed, well-"got-up" individual, who might have worn a less extensive shirt collar, without losing caste in society. Still, a long throat carried his head above the plenitude of linen, over which his head craned now and then in giraffe fashion, watching the world before him very vigilantly yet, and evidently a man not to be done by it.

Mr. Fyvie, junior.—Not quite so tall as his father, but five feet eleven, for all that. Something like his father in figure, being narrow-chested and spare, but having a face all his own—a handsome face, bright as a woman's, and with almost a womanly expression thereon—a soft, simpering,

1—2

shy—his enemies said "sly"—expression, that detracted from his good looks, and was not toned down in any great degree by his long fair moustache and "weepers."

These three men, the ruling agents from that day forth of Wheal Desperation—we shall learn more of them, and estimate them at their proper worth, before all the pages of this book are written.

Mr. Laurence Raxford closed his speech, and sat down amidst much hammering of knives and forks upon the table ; the conversation became general after that, savouring a trifle too much of "the shop," which was natural to a dozen men who had studied mining operations all their lives. It may be remarked here, that Captain Athorpe—the man who had startled Laurence by the mention of his father's name— had less to say now than the rest, and seemed making amends for his former impulsiveness by the assumption of a taciturn demeanour.

Laurence glanced more than once at this man in the intervals of conversation with the captain on each side of him, and wondered why Athorpe looked at him so hard, and whether the fierceness of aspect was natural to him, or attributable to the sherry, or to his own presence there. He felt that he had dropped unceremoniously into the midst of these mining people, and might not be exactly welcome yet. In good time he would understand them all, and they would understand him, he hoped, and take to him. Everybody had taken to him, he thought, with a little self-gratulation at the reminiscence ; it was his good luck to be liked ; and looking back upon his past career, he could not pick out one enemy upon the road. A lucky fellow, yes !—a man whose rise in life had not brought him one envious rival, but increased the host of well-wishers round him. He was thankful for this, as well as proud of it ; he had certainly endeavoured to make himself agreeable to all those with whom he had come in contact, and he had been rewarded by the success which waits, as a rule, upon all honest attempts to gain men's esteem. In every sense of the word, a lucky fellow, then. He owned it in his speech—he confessed it to himself.

Life so smooth with him—cast, as it were, in such "pleasant places" already, that even the stolid aspect of a mining captain perplexed him, and rendered him a little restless

—fidgety even, lest he should have given that man offence, or the man should have taken offence without just cause.

Captain Athorpe sat and watched him, evidently with a fierce expression of countenance—preferring to regard him in this lugubrious fashion to helping himself from the decanter at his elbow.

"Get on, Athorpe, you're licensed to be drunk on the premises to-day," said a fellow captain in his ear. "We'll excuse it—your wife will excuse it—Mr. Fyvie will excuse it."

Mr. Fyvie caught the full meaning from the last words, which had arrested his attention.

"To be sure I will," he cried laughing; "he who spares the wine to-day insults my butler, and doubts the genuine nature of the vintage. Athorpe, your glass is empty"

"And will keep empty, Mr. Fyvie," was the blunt but not rude answer. "I did not know it was so strong. I'm not used to wine drinking."

"You—a traveller, too!"

"I've been drinking long enough. Hold hard, Peters!" he cried, as Peters attempted to fill his glass surreptitiously, and was rewarded for his pains by nearly having the decanter knocked out of his hands—"when I say a thing I mean a thing—don't you know that by this time?"

"Well, dorm it, you needn't ride rusty about it," said Peters in an aggrieved tone, wiping some splashes of sherry off a pair of white trousers that he had donned for the occasion, "or make this mess. Just look here, now."

"I don't want any more wine. I've had more than enough already," grumbled Captain Athorpe, turning his back upon his persecutor.

"Very well, then. Perhaps you'll give us a song," said Captain Peters sharply, at which suggestion there was a roar of laughter at Captain Athorpe's expense, and at which Athorpe himself condescended to smile grimly.

"He who has seen me drunk has heard me sing," said Athorpe.

"Athorpe has not sung since his marriage," cried a new voice from the remote end of the table, and the joke went against the fierce man again, who shrugged his shoulders, and tried to smile—this time with an evident effort.

The presence of the principals had evidently no depressing

effect on these men; they were quite at home there, ready with their jests, quick with their answers, loud voiced, hilarious, and free spoken. They were all equals in that long, low room, the windows of which looked upon the mining-grounds, and there was nothing in the manner of the masters to damp the spirits of the general community. Once a year, in the middle of the month of May, Mr. Fyvie and son dined with their leading men, and there were feastings and revelry, in lieu of figures at the office—once a year, in commemoration of the birth of Wheal Desperation. Masters and men, all "hail-fellows well met" on that special occasion, however much at arm's length for the remainder of the year—liberty, fraternity, and equality, and nobody the worse for the alliance.

Presently there was considerable tobacco smoke, Mr. Fyvie and his son indulging in long clay pipes with the rest—Laurence and Captain Athorpe alone remaining non-consumers.

"You don't smoke, then?" cried Athorpe across the table to the new partner, with a suddenness that was startling.

"Very little," responded Laurence, with a laugh, "and never before supper."

"You're better without it altogether. It's a nuisance, as well as a bad habit. Your father never smoked."

"Indeed!"

"Not but what he was a poor weak fellow enough, for all that," affirmed Captain Athorpe; "you're like him about the eyes. I have been trying to think all this time where the likeness lay. Like him, Sir, about the eyes," he repeated, addressing the senior partner of the mine.

"Who's that?—like whom, Athorpe?" asked Mr. Fyvie, with characteristic sharpness.

"I'm thinking that the young master here is like his father, after all, across the eyes—so," and Athorpe drew his horny hand sideways across the bridge of his nose.

"Yes, there's a faint likeness," said Mr. Fyvie—"I see it; why you should, I don't exactly make out. You were not six months with us then."

"*His* father discharged me—I offended him; he did not like to hear the truth, poor man."

"Yes, yes, yes, I remember now," answered Mr. Fyvie

quickly; "you offended him—exactly. You had a habit of offending people when you were younger; but you've grown out of that, thank God! I'll take a glass of wine with you, Captain Athorpe."

Captain Athorpe reddened very much at the compliment, hesitated, finally stretched out his hand sideways for the decanter, keeping his eyes fixed upon his employer.

"What are you groping after, Captain?" asked Peters, ironically.

"Sherry," growled the other—"Mr. Fyvie drinks wine with me."

"Oh! I thought when you said a thing you *meant* a thing," said Captain Peters, as he passed the wine to him.

Athorpe filled his glass in silence, raised it, met his patron's glance, bowed, and drank his sherry—drank it off at one gulp, as though in defiance of his late resolution, or the taunt of his friend. When Mr. Fyvie passed his hand over his thin nose and mouth an instant afterwards, as though to repress an effort to smile, the man whom he had especially favoured was still staring at him intently.

"I believe he did it on purpose," grumbled Athorpe to his left-hand neighbour.

"A joke of his, very likely," replied the man addressed, an old and white-haired Nestor of the mines; "he was a rare fellow for his jests once. I mind him forty-five years ago at Wheal Fellowship, in Cornwall, as full of mischief as a monkey."

"Ah! you always knew more than anybody else," said Captain Athorpe, brusquely; and having succeeded in disturbing the equanimity of the gentleman on each side of him, he thrust his hands into his pockets, and was isolated for the remainder of the feast.

The feast was at an end by seven o'clock, and there was a general rise as the great clock struck in the corner.

"An hour behind time," said Mr. Fyvie, to his new partner. "What will the ladies say to us, Laurence?"

"They will forgive us, I hope, in consideration of the special character of this festivity," was the reply.

"Well, they should do so—and we'll make atonement for our sins of omission, lad. Jonathan, you return home on that wild horse, I presume, instead of accepting a snug corner in your father's carriage?"

"Well, I must get him home somehow, Sir," said Jonathan, with a laugh.

Mr. Fyvie turned to his head clerk, a portly gentleman, who had also grown grey in the service, as most men might, if it pleased them and their God, after once working for Wheal Desperation.

"It has been a general holiday here, Waters?"

"Of course, Sir."

"All going on well?"

"As well as ever, Mr. Fyvie. Everything slow and sure," he added, rubbing one hand over the other, "but going on well—everything."

"And where's everybody?"

"Eh, Sir?"

"What are they all doing with themselves to-day in the village—holiday-making?"

"And love-making, Sir," added Mr. Waters, who was evidently a bit of a wag, considering his years.

"Ah ha! and love-making. Love and idleness together. You hear that, Laurence? Nothing like hard work to dissipate the frivolities."

"You'll not escape an ovation, I'm afraid, for all the idleness, Sir," said Mr. Waters.

"Eh!—what's that? Why shan't I?"

"They've been coming up from the village the last two hours to see you off, Sir. I think we have all the hands upon the ground again."

"Put them all to work, the lazy rascals and idle hussies, who ought to know better," cried Mr. Fyvie. "Where's the carriage? Let me escape the clamour of the mob. Captains, good-evening. Come, Laurence."

"Good-evening, Sir, good-evening. A happy year to you, Sir, until we meet again."

"Meet again! Why, I may be here to-morrow. You have not got rid of me for twelve months. You fellows, don't think that. I shall be down upon you like an avalanche this year, so keep straight, and to the mark. Good-night."

They were echoing his good-night when he was outside the brick house that was built on his estate; they were following him with their good wishes, when he and Laurence found themselves the centre of six or seven hundred men and women, of all ages, but of one degree, all bustling round the carriage and pair, and waiting to catch a glimpse of "the master."

The keen face took a new light from the interest which it had awakened; much of the sharpness, or the worldliness, vanished away at the sight of the many dependants, ranged in two long rows from the counting-house to the carriage-steps, all anxious to see the principal, who seldom troubled them, and who was like a king to them.

"Glad to see you—glad to see you all," he cried, in cheery accents, "well and strong, and so bravely dressed that I fancy I must be paying every one too well here."

"Oh! noa, Sir," laughed the men, and simpered the women, and a flutter of delight at the master's words vibrated like an electric current through the crowd.

"Where's Jonathan?" he said to Laurence.

"The young master rode off at once on the black horse, Sir," a man volunteered to inform Mr. Fyvie.

"Ah! he don't like deputations—too fussy for him," remarked Mr. Fyvie, in a lower tone. "And here's another young master for you, to look after your interests, and fight your battles when I am gone. He has come here to take a little of the hard work off my shoulders, and let me rest a little more!"

This was a jest, but no one saw it, or received it as a jest. They regarded Mr. Laurence Raxford with intense veneration, as another demigod coming from heaven to watch over them, and give them wages.

"So the world goes round, you see, and the old men give place to the young. Good-night to all of you."

"Good-night, Sir, good-night," was echoed from all sides, and one "God bless you!" rang out sweet and silvery from the midst of the crowd.

The blessing did not fall unheeded on the old man's ears, and he turned very quickly in the direction whence the words had issued.

"Ah! are you there, Milly?" he said, nodding his head towards the last speaker, and laughing; "it wouldn't have been quite complete without you and your greeting. Here, Laurence, this is the prettiest girl in Devon."

"Oh! Sir," cried Milly, disappearing at this compliment, and shutting out the fair prospect to which Mr. Fyvie had directed the attention of his junior partner, who met with a host of gaping and laughing faces instead.

"Off like a lapwing. Now, Laurence, let us follow her example."

The carriage was entered, and the doors closed. The coachman lashed his pair of thoroughbreds, and amidst a humming of women's voices, a waving of hands and handkerchiefs, and an English cheer from the men, that woke the sleepy echoes of the Dartmoor hills, the proprietors of Wheal Desperation were whirled away from business.

CHAPTER II.

THE STORY OF WHEAL DESPERATION.

Mr. Fyvie with his face, and Mr. Laurence Raxford with his back to the horses, ensconced themselves in snug corners of the carriage.

"Jonathan will be home with that brute an hour before us," said Mr. Fyvie; "an *avant courier*. Well, what do you think of my captains?"

"An honest and a hearty set of men," said Laurence, immediately.

"You will get on with them very well—they're an independent lot; but you're no more likely to upset their good opinions of themselves and their styles of going to work, than Jonathan or I are."

"No, Sir. Not likely."

"You come fresh from the Royal School of Mines, full of book knowledge and running over with experiments—you will find my captains pay respect to your learning, and to all the theories with which you may be acquainted; but you will not lure them easily and without sound reasons from the beaten track."

Laurence laughed.

"Not Captain Athorpe, at all events."

"No, not Captain Athorpe," was the dry response; "he has the very finest opinion of his abilities—I can't say I like the man, or his manners, and I am thankful that I see little of him. A fellow of an excellent memory, Laurence."

"Evidently, Sir."

"I don't envy you the next six months—and really, though I admire your principle of seeing for yourself everything around you, it is scarcely necessary to become so *bonâ-fide* a working partner."

"Oh! yes, it is, Mr. Fyvie," answered the other, with enthusiasm; "I don't want to play the fine gentleman here, but to work for my share of the profits, just as I intended to work for the sake of experience, before you surprised me with your kindness—your generosity."

"Pooh! pooh! my forethought, if you looked at the matter in the right light, Laurence; for the mine wouldn't get on with my sleepy-headed son to manage it. There's no fire in that youth—and Wheal Desperation would go back twenty years. You, I have been watching."

"Ah! yes—thank you," answered Laurence.

"There, we'll have no more expressions of gratitude," said Mr. Fyvie, almost tetchily; "I object to grateful people —I like people to act their good feelings towards me, and sink the demonstrations. You come here and fall in love with my daughter—like your impudence," added the old gentleman; "and I suppose my daughter fell in love with you—like her forwardness, and the thing being settled, everybody looks to me for marriage portions. A very good joke—but at my expense, eh?"

"I did not ask you for a marriage portion, Sir—I did not expect one."

"Exactly—and you have not got one. I constitute you partner in the mine—you will for the present take but a small portion of the profits; when you are married, a larger share; when I am dead, one half."

"May that——"

"Yes, yes; but I suppose I shall die some day. I don't care much about it at present, and therefore we will not dwell on that topic. You're a lucky fellow, a great many think, to drop into a partnership so easily, and ensnare—so easily, too—Jonathan Fyvie's daughter; but I think"— laying his hand suddenly on the young man's knee—"that I am the luckier fellow of the two, for everything that your mother and I have planned together, like a couple of old

conspirators, has come true to the very letter of our scheming. My dear Laurence, I never was more happy."

" It *was* your wish, then—as well as hers ? "

" Certainly it was. I didn't want a rich son-in-law—or a
proud one—some inanity with a title and a lisp, who would
pocket my savings, and then look down on the connection.
I simply looked out for Laurence Raxford, and waited
patiently for him."

" All this for my sake, Sir—how can I ever thank you ! "

" Partly for yours, for I saw that you were a steady young
man—partly for my own—partly for my son's, for he needs
a counterpoise—and partly for the sake of my dead friend."

" My father."

Mr. Jonathan Fyvie's face assumed a shade more gravity
of expression.

" Yes, your father. He and I, two orphan boys, began
life together as clerks at a Cornish mine—worked on together—became partners in the mad scheme of sinking a
shaft or two on the Dartmoor ground, where we have dined
to-day."

" Is this the story which you promised to tell me this
evening ? "

" Exactly. Now, keep your mouth shut, Laurence, whilst
I run through it as briefly as I can. I shall have finished
in five minutes."

He looked at his watch, and then darted into his subject.

" Your mother is aware of the story, or the greater part
of it; but it was a promise between her and me that I
should have the telling of it, somewhat after this fashion,
and, if possible, under these very circumstances. All
mapped out like a book, you see, and all coming true, not
after the fashion of books, by any means, and there the advantage lies with us. To have known this story in your
youth would have rendered you discontented, morose, selfish
—at all events, seeing more selfishness in others than they
were endowed with, perhaps. Well, we are beginning with
a windy preface, and I am terribly loquacious."

" Not at all, Sir."

" And I so fidgety under other people's talk, too—egad !
another good joke. I hope that sherry has not been a trifle
too much for me."

He laughed pleasantly, and then grappled with his subject in earnest.

"Your father and I were unsuccessful; we spent nearly all our money on rash ventures; we found our judgment at fault, and our bankers grumbling at the smallness of our accounts—poor things! Small accounts are great troubles to everybody, you see. We two young men, who had started in life with fair legacies, were reduced at last to three thousand pounds between us. Your father grew nervous—he was not a strong man, and he thought that I was a very rash one. So I was. Sleepy Laurence was right enough; I was very desperate just then. I wanted to sink everything in the mine, and make another dash for copper in a new direction. Your father was despondent, and 'caved in.' We dissolved partnership—he went abroad, and left me to make shift with fifteen hundred pounds; and I came here one night—one bitter night it was to me!— and looked at the mine, and at the wreck of good intentions that were scattered about, significant of my ruin, and your father's. Well, looking at that wreck, with the Dartmoor hills frowning at my misfortunes, I made up my mind to go on with the scheme from which your father had withdrawn. I was annoyed with him, poor fellow, and I was a young man, hot headed and obstinate. I looked upon fifteen hundred pounds as valueless to me with my ambitions; and I made up my mind to let it all go after the rest, and then pitch myself down the deepest shaft, or slip out of the world in some fashion or other, when the last penny was sunk. To tell you the truth, I was in love, too—in love with Hester's mother, who was a woman of position, and whose family was so high that it looked down upon heaven —and so I was mad at all points. Everybody said so— I knew it myself—but I sank my money like a fool, and was rewarded, as fools are sometimes in this world of ours, and for wiser purposes than we wot of. When I had only twenty-three pounds in the world—it was twenty-three pounds, twelve and sixpence, for I counted it in my bed-room at the hotel, and *felt the edge of my razors* afterwards—by Heaven, Sir!" he cried enthusiastically, "we came to copper—as fine a vein of copper as any in Devon, and I was rich from that day. That's the story of Wheal Desperation, Laurence, and now you know what a pig-headed father-in-law you are likely to be blessed with."

"I admire your courage, Sir."

"It was simply despair," said the senior partner; "I did not hope for riches, Hester's mother, anything, when my luck came. I was content with fishing up lumps of quartz and grains of copper, and losing by every truck-load that was drawn to the surface. It was dogged despair that brought me a fortune— I hold my breath now when I think of it, for I might have been at this very hour licking out my wooden bowl of skilly in the union, if I had had the weakness to live after my loss. *But*—I should have died."

Laurence believed that, noting how the old man's lips compressed, and the brow contracted. Yes, Mr. Fyvie had been a desperate man in his youth, and had gone to work in a desperate way, seldom rewarded by such good fortune in the end as his had been.

"Your father, Laurence, made a thousand or two abroad; he came back to England, married, and died, seeing his old friend at the very last, not before, for he was jealous of my prosperity, poor fellow! He left your mother and you just enough to live on, and I looked after you both in due course. Then I told your mother what I wished to make of you— just as I told your father on his death-bed what I intended to do—what I felt bound to do for the sake of the old partner who had first ventured with me, and whose sunken money was, after all, but the prelude to my greatness. Then, Laurence, your father understood me better."

Laurence looked down, and his lip quivered a little. He understood the old man better also ; he felt that for that man he must work and sink self, and try to deserve his good fortune, as he did not deserve it yet awhile.

"You have been very kind," he murmured.

"Tut, tut ; I have been very wide-awake," was the answer ; "I have been making a partner after my own heart for the last ten years, and if you had not turned out well in the casting, I should have set you aside as a flawed and valueless article—kicked you out of my sight with a beggarly income, Laurence."

Laurence laughed.

"Oh ! I do not believe that now. I read your character very clearly,"

"Do you ?" was the sharp reply—"you're a wiser man than your contemporaries, then. Do you see that I have talked myself into a comatose state, and am going to take my usual afternoon nap ?—seeing that, don't disturb me by any more loquacity."

Mr. Fyvie tilted his hat over his eyes, which he closed at once ; and Laurence, respecting his wish, sat very silent in his corner of the carriage, wistfully regarding the patron, guardian, and friend, and thinking once again of the luck that had fallen to his share. He was very grateful, too, for only a little while ago he had been perplexed about his future, and half angry with his mother for thinking so little about it. He had been a poor young man, with some-what high notions for his position, and his mother. had rather fostered them than otherwise, till at one and twenty they had begun to prey upon him. He had fancied that he should be a clerk, or a manager, in Mr. Fyvie's service —earn three or four hundred a year in due course ; but that prospect had hardly contented him, and two months ago he had gone down to Mr. Fyvie's house just a trifle discon-tented with himself and his chances, and aggravated by his mother's complacency.

Even as a guest of his father's old friend, he had been unsettled, for he was a sensible young man for his age, and it had struck him that this new sphere was artificial, and did not belong to him, or suit him. All very pleasant—far too pleasant—but likely to make the future very dull when the fine house, and all this fine company, became a retro-spect. It made him ambitious and envious, he thought ; he was sure, even then, sitting in a corner of the carriage, looking back upon his past sensations, that he had been am-bitious, and almost inclined, to scheme for that position which had actually been determined upon when he was a boy at school. That made him ashamed of himself, and he hoped that no one had seen his efforts to ingratiate himself into the favour of the Fyvies, male and female, whom he had met at the great house. He had only striven to render himself agreeable to everybody, and that was natural enough in Laurence Raxford ; but he fancied that he had striven a little too eagerly, because the Fyvies lived in a great house, and could advance his interests in the world,

He was sure that he felt small—exceedingly small—and that after that day he must work with a great effort for the interests and the happiness of those who would be his relations as well as his partners.

"By George!" he said to himself, "how I will work! they shall never regret giving me a lift in the world."

He muttered many protestations of this kind—this young man with his heart full, and with a wild and unguessed life before him—causing Mr. Fyvie to open his eyes once or twice with a jerk, and regard him attentively.

"Aren't you well, Laurence?" he asked at last.

"Well, Sir—but full of soliloquy."

"Ah! that's the potatoes—hard bullets of things—I would swear Waters cooked them—the old potterer! Where are we?"

"Not off the moor yet."

"Confound it, another half hour's ride!" said Mr. Fyvie, "and my long legs full of cramps already! Don't soliloquise any more—there's a good fellow. It's a bad habit, and can't do anybody good. Oh, dear!"

And Mr. Fyvie yawned and stretched himself, and finally went off to sleep again, leaving his more wakeful companion to look out upon the dark landscape.

So on for another half hour, a descent down hill, a turn out of the main road, a sharp curve to the right through a pair of open lodge-gates, at which a man was standing with a lantern — and then Mr. Fyvie was awake for good.

"Home at last," he cried, letting down the window suddenly; "I'm glad of it, though I wish the house, *entre nous*, was less full of company for once. I would be in bed before another hour struck, and now I've to dress—ugh! that's aggravating after a mining dinner."

A long carriage-drive ending in a noble mansion, its windows full of light and life that May night. A man darted from the house before the equipage had stopped, and opened the carriage door, erect and obsequious as six feet of stature and a tight suit of Fyvie livery could make him.

"Hang it! I can hear myself creak as I walk," said the master, getting out of the carriage very gingerly. "Here, Laurence, your arm, or I shall be saying my prayers on this gravel. Mr. Jonathan's home, I suppose, Ranwood?" he asked of the domestic.

"No, Sir—not yet."

"Not yet, eh?—why, where the deuce has he got to? Well, thank the Fates that I am at home, at any rate!"

~~~~~~~~~~~~~~~~~~~~~~

CHAPTER III.

A HOUSE FULL OF PEOPLE.

HALF an hour afterwards, Mr. Fyvie and Laurence Raxford were in the drawing-room of Tavvydale House. A large drawing-room, that "cost money." That was the first thought which rose to the mind of a person entering the state room—one was not so struck with the elegance or the grace of the furniture and its surroundings, as with the money that had been lavished there. It was an apartment that appealed to your sense of costliness, and though it was neither garish nor vulgar, yet the impression seized you on the threshold that it was the room of a man who had not been rich all his life, and who, with money at command now, was letting the world see what a show he could make.

The furniture was as rich, choice and *new* as an upholsterer with a *carte-blanche* could set there; there were some thousands of pounds' worth of ornaments about the room and on the mantelpiece; the carpet had taken one of the first prizes at an International Exhibition; the lace curtains, sweeping from the gilded cornices above the windows, had been copied for an engraving in an Art Journal, and the piano, in its marqueterie work case, had not its equal in all England.

A young lady was sitting at that piano when Mr. Fyvie and Mr Raxford entered the room—a fair-haired, tall, and graceful girl, somewhat too pale, perhaps, to please all tastes, and whose features might have been considered a trifle too sharp—too much of the Jonathan Fyvie cut about them—to have stamped their owner as a beauty infallible. Still she was a pretty, if delicate-looking girl, with a figure fit for a duchess, and a straight nose, like her father's, that touched

2

the susceptibilities of the aristocrats, who wanted straight noses all to themselves.

Hester Fyvie looked round with a smile of welcome at the new comers, but continued to dash on with her symphony—and catching that smile, as you and I, reader, pass into the room with the partners, we can judge how sweet was its expression, and what a character—soft and womanly and beautiful—it gave to the whole face. Yes, this Laurence Raxford was a very lucky fellow !

The room was full of company ; Mr. Fyvie had found means to fill his house, though London was beginning its season, and fashionable people were as thick as thieves in London streets. Mr. Fyvie had met with no difficulty in finding friends to accept his kind invitation—gentlemen in his position seldom are troubled and vexed by kind regards and compliments, but regret the inability, &c. There was plenty of first-rate wine to drink, plenty of horses to ride, fine shooting and hunting in their seasons—in fact, at Tavvydale House a man or woman was always happy.

It is not our task to sketch all the guests assembled at Tavvydale House that year—but there are a few whom we cannot pass over in silence, who have their big and little parts to play in future pages.

Mrs. Fyvie cannot be overlooked in the first place, though it was her misfortune to be overlooked a great deal in real life. A tall woman, like the rest of the Fyvies, " very high in her notions," it was said, as befitted that high family to which the senior partner of Wheal Desperation had already alluded, but sitting there in her lounge chair the picture of meekness and placidity—a white-faced, languid lady, in black silk and diamonds. Evidently a lady with not much will of her own, and who found "company-keeping" a somewhat hard task for her that evening—she looked so unutterably weary.

By her side, Mrs. Raxford, mother to our hero—for Laurence is as much of a hero as the reader will catch sight of in the progress of *this* history. Mrs. Raxford, short, plump and prim, with a rosy pair of wrinkled cheeks and a shower of silver ringlets on each side of a face that was a very motherly and kind one, despite a set expression thereon at that juncture, suitable for the grand folk assembled about her. She also smiled her welcome to the

senior and junior partners as they came into the room, and
looked a little disappointed when the latter was button-holed
by a wiry-haired individual, on his way across to her.

Then there were the Llewellyns—branches of the great
family whence Mr. Fyvie had plucked that languid lady in
black silk—four of them present in the flesh to overawe and
chill the rest of the community. Mrs. Llewellyn, an elder
sister of Mrs. Fyvie, by a year and a half, also a tall woman,
with an inflexible back, a carroty head of hair, and a
quantity of jingling little gold ornaments in her carrots, an
iron-featured woman, with washed-out eyes and high check-
bones, who, in a blue serge jacket and short skirt, with a
basket of fish at that inflexibility already hinted at, would
have represented a Newhaven fish-wife to the life. Mr.
Llewellyn, short, but stiff and starchy, with one of the
largest white ties ever seen out of a pantomime—a first
cousin to his wife, and rather sorry for it, perhaps—stood
with his back to the mantelpiece, his hands behind him, and
his feet planted firmly on the hearth-rug, a man who, in his
own opinion, evidently did honour to Tavvydale House by
his presence, and deserved a testimonial, a vote of thanks,
or something in that line, for leaving his post and his snug
room in the Treasury, to patronise his relations at that time of
year. At his side Miss Llewellyn, tall, like her mother, and
almost as upright and carroty, but with a meek and pasty
face, that evinced less decision of character. Scattered
about on chairs, couches, and ottomans, possibly a dozen
more people—a great gun and his wife from Plymouth, the
first-named also in the mining way ; a fourth Llewellyn, the
eldest son of the inflexibility, a young man who has but
little to do with us, and who had been seized with the
natural idea that if his uncle had wanted a partner, he
might have sent for him—therefore a gentleman who loved
not Laurence Raxford ; the family solicitor and his son ;
a London physician, and the gentleman who had pounced
on Laurence as he entered, and who, having a place in this
book, is entitled to an outline sketch with those who have
preceded him.

A wiry-haired man, of Laurence's height, and Laurence's
age, wearing spectacles, a swarthy man, with a high, broad
forehead, and large, bony hands, which opened and shut with
suppressed excitement when there was nothing in them, or

2—2

to catch hold of in reach. A man of good family, and considerable property into the bargain, therefore one of the few
whom the Llewellyns could take to their bosoms, but, alas!
one of the many who fought shy of the Llewellyns, and a
man who had his private opinions as to the desirability of
their acquaintance.

"Mr. Raxford," he said, fastening on to the lappels of our
hero's dress-coat, before he had made four steps into the
room, "did you ask about that for me?"

"About what, Mr. Engleton?" asked the forgetful
Laurence.

"Why, good gracious, Sir, you have never forgotten all
about it!" exclaimed his disappointed *vis-à-vis.*

"Oh! I beg pardon, yes, I have. You see, it was rather
confusing for me to-day, and, after all, there is plenty of
time. Why, to-morrow I shall have all day to think of it,
or, better still, you can come over to the mines with me, and
make your own inquiries."

"It's no good my coming over," said Mr. Engleton, leaving
go one lappel to bite the tips of his fingers nervously. "I
have made all my calculations, and I only want you to verify
a few of the figures."

"I'll ask one of the captains to-morrow," said Laurence.
"Let me see, what am I to ask, now?"

"God bless me, what a memory you have, and what an
interest in the social condition of the mining classes! Sit
down a bit, please, and we'll run over these papers again.
I have them all in my pocket."

"Oh! have you?" said Laurence. "Very well, we'll go
into them in a minute or two. My mother is beckoning
me, I think, just now."

"I beg her pardon," said he, politely bowing in Mrs.
Raxford's direction, much to her sudden confusion. "You'll
not be long, then?"

"Not very long, I hope," replied our hero, effecting his
escape at last.

Mrs. Raxford welcomed her son with a true mother's
smile, and gathered her skirts closer to herself, to make
room for him on the couch at her side, an invitation which
he did not accept, however.

"So the day of inauguration is over, Laurence?"

"Yes, and I have been formally introduced at the mines

as the junior partner. I got over the whole affair better than I expected, almost gracefully, mother, by George ! "

" Hush, dear, don't swear, they may think it low," said Mrs. Raxford, looking rather nervously round her.

Laurence laughed.

" Oh ! they'll forgive me—at least, a few of them will. What have you been doing all day ? "

His mother told him. There had been walking in the grounds, a drive out with Mrs. Fyvie, a dinner, and then a gathering together of social atoms in that drawing-room.

" It's very nice, of course, all this, very genteel ; but "— dropping her voice into a frightened whisper — " oh ! Laurence, dear, I shall be so glad to get home ! "

" Bustling about that little quiet place, and flourishing the inevitable duster—to be sure you will. We shall all be glad to settle down again."

" And when I have arranged everything, how delightful to come back to another little quiet place near here, and take care of you, dear," said the mother, archly. " That was the dream you had once, before Hester and you understood each other."

" What a rare conspiracy it has all been for my rise in life," he replied, smiling : " and I, the victim, have cause to rejoice at it. But——"

" But what ? " asked the mother.

" Well, I don't know that there's a ' but ' in the case," he answered, quickly, " not even a crumpled rose-leaf anywhere. Why, I never expected this good fortune, and I don't believe that I deserve it."

" You deserve everything, my dear boy, for you have been always to me——"

" Yes, yes," he interrupted ; " but don't turn my head with my own amiabilities just at present. I am as perfectly aware that I am the best son that ever lived—of course I am !—as that you are the best mother, spoiling me a little with your praise, as mothers with only sons always do."

Mrs. Raxford made a clutch at his hand, which he laughingly withdrew from hers.

" Society," he cried, with harmless satire, " this high-bred and exquisite society. If the Llewellyns should see us ! "

" Oh ! they are dreadful people," exclaimed the mother, with a glance in the direction of Mrs. Llewellyn, sitting in

an erect position, and with a basilisk stare in their direction.
"But sit down, Laurence, I haven't had a long chat with
you for a week."

"My dear mamma, I have not spoken to Mrs. Fyvie or
Hester yet. Monopoly at Tavvydale is impossible."

"Well," with a sigh, "I suppose so. But I shall come
to your room to-night—just for a little while—to wish you
joy of—of all this!" spreading out her hands suddenly, as
though the drawing-room furniture was included in that
day's good luck.

"Very well, then I'll not turn the key on visitors until
you bid me good-night."

"There's a dear boy!"

Laurence was allowed to withdraw after this promise;
he steered his way through the guests, a man at his ease
there, a man thoroughly at home, and secure of his position.
He stopped to speak to Mrs. Fyvie *en route*, bringing a smile
to her pale face more than once by his remarks on passing
things; he dodged Mr. Engleton very cleverly, and with
apparent innocence, round a settee on which three dowagers,
with voluminous skirts, had placed themselves. He was at
last by the side of Hester Fyvie, coming in at the end of
the symphony in very good time, so that, as she rose from
the music-stool, she and her betrothed were face to face together. Nothing more natural than than that they should
walk away together, and sit down, a little apart for a
while, from the rest of the people.

"In at the death, Hester," he said.

"Meaning that I have been murdering Beethoven, Sir?"
was the playfully reproachful answer.

"No—you have buried him with becoming grace," replied
Laurence. "Not that I admire symphonies much at any
time—they're such long-winded affairs!"

"And you so great a Goth, Laurence! There, I do not
believe that you like music at all."

"I could exist without it," was the dry answer; "at all
events, without concertos, and symphonies, and all three
volume harmonies. Now 'Home, Sweet Home's' first-
rate."

"That implies that you are tired of Tavvydale House,
Laurence."

Hester Fyvie was very quick in her replies. There was

a Fyvie sharpness in her answers as well as in her features; but there was a crispness—sweet and melodious, too—that rendered her responses very pleasant at that time.

" Do you think so ? "

" I don't know what to think of you sometimes," she replied. " I don't believe, Sir, that you are aware yourself what a strange and restless being you are."

" No—upon my honour, I am not aware of that."

" And I should like to know, Laurence—very much like to know—what you were thinking about this morning before you started with papa and Jonathan for the mines ? "

" Thinking ! " said Laurence, very much surprised ; " I don't remember. How do you know that I was thinking— at all ? Why, I never think—upon my honour, I am the most thoughtless being under the sun."

" Thoughtless of sunstrokes, for I longed to come out and pelt you with that ugly felt hat which you had left in the hall."

" Pray be good enough to explain—this is becoming interesting. Sybil of Tavvydale, I conjure you to speak ! "

" You don't remember sitting in the full blaze of the morning's sun, on the lawn beyond there "—pointing to the drawing-room window—" staring and thinking—think- ing and staring—down at your feet, like a—like a great goose ? "

" It is the habit of geese to think and stare in that manner, perhaps," he laughed ; " but upon my word, Hester, I don't remember it."

" Upon your word and honour ? "

" Upon both those valuable perquisites."

" There, that makes my words out. You *are* strange, odd, and restless. To fall into a syncope for three-quarters of an hour this morning, and not remember anything about it. Now, Laurence, I really don't——"

" Don't believe me—after pledging no end of good faith to convince you. Thank you—so the fair sex doubt all honourable protestations. I might have sat down for a moment—very likely ; but I don't try to remember every time I sit down."

" If it were not for Aunt Llewellyn looking at us, I should box your ears," she cried, raising her hand a little way, and then letting it drop again, nearer to him, half hidden in the folds of her dress, where he found it, and pressed it in his own for a moment, bringing the blushes to her face, and the light to her eyes.

"Don't, Sir," she gently remonstrated ; "let my hand go."

"It *was* only for a minute, then ? "

"It was for three-quarters of an hour."

"Consider yourself my prisoner of war, until you confess to a gross exaggeration of the facts."

"I defy you ! "

"Show me the seat whereon I sat dreaming—thinking of you, perhaps. The window is ajar, and one step takes us both into the moonlight, Miss Juliet."

"Thank you, Romeo ; but I can't neglect my father's guests for the sake of catching cold, and looking at a garden-seat. And if you don't let go my hand—somebody will see you."

"Hester, my dear," exclaimed Mrs. Llewellyn at the same instant, "can I speak to you for a moment ? "

"Certainly, aunt." And Hester rose at once, and, with a comical little glance at Laurence, vanished from his side.

"If ever there was an aggravating old woman—I suppose such a phenomenon has occurred once or twice—it's that red-haired ogress of an aunt," muttered Laurence to himself; "and I was feeling so comfortable, natural, and genuine. Really I believe she does it to aggravate me. I wonder what I have done to offend her."

He looked after Hester ; he noticed that she sank gracefully down by the side of her aunt. He wished that he could hear what they were talking about ; and had he heard it would not have made much difference in his opinion of the one or the other just then.

"Hester, my dear," said the grating voice of Mrs. Llewellyn, "I really *do* wonder how you can behave so. An engagement is all very well, and proper under most circumstances—but you, educated with my own Jane, too, should show a little more respect to society, even a little more attention to your friends here, who have a right to consider—I think I may add a right—that there is some one else in the world worthy of notice besides that young man opposite."

Hester took this reproof very good-humouredly

" Why, aunt, I have not spoken to Mr. Raxford all day before this."

" You would have sat there all night," was the sharp answer.

" No, I should not," was the quiet reply.

A trifle too quiet—for Hester's face began to assume a grave expression, as though the last remark had somewhat disturbed its owner.

" And you will pardon me, niece—but——"

" And you will pardon me, aunt," was the rapid interruption here, " but I really don't admire any remarks upon my behaviour—you know how hasty I am—and how I object to any one, except papa and ma, calling me to account. I can take their scoldings humbly enough—but oh ! I get so cross if any one else attempts."

" Your papa and mamma have completely spoiled you."

" Well, I think that they have sometimes."

" They give you entirely your own way."

" Bless them both—I am very grateful for it."

" Now, Jane——"

" Who is flirting desperately with Mr. Engleton, aunt. Only look at them," she cried with a mock alarm, that must have been rather irritating to Mrs. Llewellyn, " taking no notice of the general company, but screwed up in a corner like turtle-doves in a nest. Shall I ask Jane to play our old duet over ? "

" Oh ; no more music—no more of that wretched thumping—four hands at once on a grand piano, good gracious ! " exclaimed Mrs. Llewellyn, " you may get up a whist party, if you will, and I'll make one, only don't let me have that weak-minded Mrs. Raxford for a partner—she trumps everything right off, whether she can follow suit or not, it makes no difference. Jane and Mr. Engleton," she added, returning to the old subject, " have been only sitting there a moment—I never saw them together before, that I remember."

" Well, I'll not disturb them. My dear aunt," sinking her voice to a whisper, " I should be very, very glad to see Cousin Jane and Charles Engleton make a match of it—but oh, dear ! I don't think that they would ever agree."

" I am sure that *we* need not discuss those probabilities at present, Miss Fyvie," said Aunt Llewellyn with dignity ;

"my Jane is a good and obedient girl, and I do not see any-thing antagonistic, as it were, in Mr. Engleton."

"He's one of the best little fellows living," said Hester, "but very excitable over his crotchets, and if you are not excited also, he takes it as an insult. Now, I cannot re-member, aunt," said the niece with her fau to her lips in a reflective manner, "when I saw Cousin Jane excited last."

Mrs. Llewellyn again glanced at the couple, to whom her attention had been drawn very unnecessarily a short while since. No, certainly not an excitable girl ; Jane was sitting bolt upright, a rigid and stony lay figure—something in the style of that Saxon king effigy, which may be seen any day in the North Nave of the Crystal Palace—the longest backed statue in the world.

"I don't admire girls betraying emotion at every fri-volous incident in life," was the lofty comment to Hester's last remark.

"But, aunt, a girl may betray a little emotion at the pros-pect of being married, I hope."

"Hester," was the solemn answer, "your sad habit of catching up people's words and turning them into un-seemly jests, grows upon you, and deteriorates from those good qualities which you inherited from *us*. In your father, it is not pleasant at all times—but in you, Hester, it is absolutely terrible."

"Do I 'catch up?'" asked Hester. "Well, that is unami-able, and I'll try and break myself of the habit, though it's my dear old father's—or it used to be, before he had every-thing his own way in this world."

"If he had let me have my own way in this last affair——"

"What affair's that?"

"There you go again," cried Mrs. Llewellyn, "that's just what I say. I'm sure it's so great a mercy to be al-lowed to get through a sentence in this house that one ought be grateful for the privilege. I meant, of course your en——"

"Aunt, I wouldn't speak of that again, please. It is un-necessary—really it is."

"But as one of the family, surely I have a right?"

"No, you haven't," said Hester. "There, don't look so scared, aunt," in a softer tone, "but I don't think that you have, now it's all settled, and I love *him*—though I don't tell him so, for fear of making him conceited—as I love no one else, not even myself."

" Good gracious !—how immodest ! "

" And I fight his battles with all the Fyvie sharpness, and with all the Fyvie *pluck*."

Away started Hester from her aunt's side, after this in-elegant and unladylike peroration, leaving Mrs. Llewellyn gasping for breath. When she had recovered from her astonishment, she exclaimed:

" I never did like that rude girl—never."

" What girl's that, Charlotte ? " inquired Mrs. Fyvie in her ear, that languid lady having found strength to cross the room to her sister.

" Dear me, Hester, how you startle one ! " said Mrs. Llewellyn, peevishly ; "why, Miss Bonnyrook, to be sure—we were talking of her just now, Hester and I. You re-member Miss B.—she was governess here once."

" Poor thing, yes—I didn't notice any rudeness in her manners."

" But I did, Hester."

That being conclusive, the subject was dropped ; and Mrs. Fyvie feeling rather faint, and wishing that she had not taken the trouble to cross the room, sat and sniffed at her smelling-salts.

" I asked Hester to make up a rubber at whist," said Mrs. Llewellyn ; "but she has forgotten my request—her head's full of nonsense just now."

" Dear Hester ! " murmured Mrs. Fyvie ; " if ever a girl deserved to be happy, Charlotte, it is she."

" Ah ! yes—very likely. There's Mr. Engleton off."

" Off!—off where ? "

" My dear woman, how should I know ? "

Mr. Engleton, looking suddenly up from his corner, had seen for the first time that Mr. Raxford was no longer absorbed by the fascinations of Miss Fyvie. He sprang to his feet with a half apology for curtailing his own story, to which Miss Llewellyn had been listening, and the instant afterwards was at Laurence's side.

" My dear fellow, I'm sorry to have kept you waiting," he said, producing a handful of papers from his pocket; " but I had become a little disturbed over my pet grievance

—the social condition of the masses, and failed to notice that Miss Fyvie had left you.   Here are all the calculations that I have made."

"Oh! indeed," said Laurence, drily; "if you'll pass them over, I'll run through them in my own room."

"You're very kind—thank you," said Mr. Engleton, after pausing for an instant to consider that new proposition; "I knew you were a fellow that did not mind a little trouble for a good cause.   And this is a good cause—a something that wants looking into."

"What is that which requires looking into, in Devonshire, Engleton?" asked Mr. Fyvie, senior, from the opposite side of the room, where the loud tones of Charles Engleton's voice had reached him; "is it a secret?"

"On the contrary—it requires your co-operation, Sir—the co-operation of the best men in the place."

"What does?"

"Drains, Sir."

"The nasty man!" ejaculated one of the dowagers before alluded to; "what an excessively filthy subject, to be sure!"

"I consider, Mr. Fyvie," cried Engleton, leaning towards his host, with both hands extended, and full of papers, "that the drainage of the whole place is defective, and that in the village near your mine, there is not even an apology for a drain amongst—let me see, how many houses?—I have it here somewhere."

"Yes, yes—exactly—I see," said Mr. Fyvie, seeing also that he had mounted Mr. Engleton on a very odd hobby for a drawing-room assembly; "we'll look into that matter to-morrow."

"And as for a good, practicable sewer——"

"Ah! we'll look into that too—or I'll get somebody to look for me, as the prospect is not very inviting.   Will you have any tea, Engleton?   here are the cups coming round."

"Thank you—in due course, Sir.   And as for the village itself—which I have studied now for two months incessantly and at which I may say I have worked night and day—for I want to get my book out on 'The Masses,' by the autumn—why, Sir, it's a sink of abomination."

"Drains—sewers—sinks!" murmured Mr. Llewellyn, still on the hearth-rug, with his hands behind him; "to think that a man of good family should be putting his nose into things of that description !   It's very odd."

"His nose, or the idea of the thing ? " inquired a facetious guest near him.

Mr. Llewellyn never allowed liberties of this description.

"The idea, Sir, *is* odd," he said fiercely.

"It's the cleanest village in Devonshire," affirmed Mr. Fyvie, ruffled in the slightest degree at Mr. Engleton's new charge.   He had had a hand in the formation, and had given more than one opinion as to the construction of his miner's cottages : he was the landlord of half Tavvydale, and therefore he did not like the last remark of Mr. Engleton, and protested against it.

"And that's not saying much, you know," said Engleton, launching himself into this new branch of an old subject. "I appeal to any one who has seen this Tavvydale village to answer me if it is not an unhealthy, horrid settlement. Two or three thousand people at the bottom of a hill, instead of the top, all crammed into houses like sardines into a box, stewing in their own oil—with no delicacy as to the sleeping accommodation—not a bit of it.   I counted myself thirteen persons of one family of the name of Simmons in a two-roomed house, the head of that family, Sir, actually kept pigs, and what is more, my opinion is that the pigs slept with the children, or were made pillows of by the senior members.   Sir, it's a gross abuse—it lowers the masses—and the whole subject requires ventilation."

"Like that last house you visited," said Fyvie laughing ; "but I did not know about the pigs.   Egad! my dear," turning to his wife with a little dismay, "didn't we buy a pig of Simmons, just to help him with the rent—or some bacon—or something ? "

"You want twice as many cottages, Mr. Fyvie," cried Engleton, " three times as many cottages before the work of purification — outwardly and inwardly, morally and physically—can be proceeded with.   And then you require an inspector—that is my idea of the case—to visit house after house."

"And be kicked out of door after door—exactly."

"Sir, don't make a jest of a thing so serious as this," cried Engleton, now very warm and energetic, "you should think of these classes—working classes—herding together like brutes almost."

"But, bless me, Sir!" exclaimed Fyvie with a stamp of his foot, "it's as moral a village as any in England. No drinking, except water-drinking — no swearing — never heard a bad word in my life there. The whole thing is an absurd exaggeration, Mr. Engleton, and you are wasting valuable time over a foolish theory. Very creditable to you to take all this trouble, but it can't possibly answer."

"I'll keep on at it for all that."

"Nothing like perseverance," said Mr. Fyvie; "and by the way, about those new refuges—on that excellent principle of soup and psalm-singing alternately—you carried *that* out, I suppose, last year?"

Mr. Engleton looked somewhat crest-fallen at this.

"It was certainly tried, Mr. Fyvie," he said spasmodically; "my idea was, ladies and gentlemen," he added, perceiving that he was the centre of attraction at that moment, "that the waifs and strays of great cities might be taught to sing an evening hymn or so after supper— softening imperceptibly thus, and acquiring here and there a taste for music that might be of use to them in after life."

"Howling about the streets all the blackguard melodies in fashion," said Mr. Fyvie.

"I was speaking of hymns — teaching these poor creatures *hymns*, Sir," said Engleton very severely, "not secular melodies, blackguard or otherwise. Well, Sir—after supper——"

"I should have made it—No song, no supper," observed the gentleman whose first facetious remark had been quenched by Mr. Llewellyn.

"Sir, I have no doubt you would have managed things a great deal more cleverly," retorted Engleton, who was inclined to lose his temper—good-tempered fellow as he was naturally—beneath all this polite badgering; "but hungry and cold people are not inclined to sing hymns after a day's tramp, as a rule."

"Well?" said Fyvie interrogatively.

"I have nothing more to say, Sir," replied Mr. Engleton; "we will dismiss the subject, if you please."

And Mr. Engleton folded his arms one over the other, and surveyed the carpet stolidly.

"But, Mr. Engleton," said Hester, "you have not told us why these poor people did not sing after supper, out of very gratitude?"

Mr. Engleton still remained silent, until Laurence reminded him that a lady was addressing him.

"It's a very uninteresting subject, Miss Fyvie,—not worth mentioning again, but—if you wish it—if anybody really wishes it——"

"Certainly we all wish it," said Mr. Fyvie, "we are all anxious for the sequel."

"Oh! very good, then," remarked Charles Engleton. "They would not sing out of gratitude, at all events. A few tried to sing—but the rest complained of the soup having inflated them too much for musical purposes."

This was too great a trial for the gravity of the masculine portion of the community, and a roar of laughter, that disturbed the sensitive nerves of Mr. Engleton, woke up the echoes of Tavvydale House. The narrator glanced round very fiercely at his tormentors, and then burst forth into a hearty laugh himself.

"Well, it was ridiculous," he assented; "I didn't see it in that light before. Laugh away, gentlemen, it's a very good joke after all. After that failure, I left the refuges to people better versed in such things."

"Just as I would leave the cottage question," said Mr. Fyvie, "for everybody's very comfortable, Engleton, I can assure you."

"I shall go in for statistics, and make every inquiry, at all events," said Mr. Engleton. "Why, there's only one decent little cottage within twenty miles of this house."

"Indeed! whose cottage is that?" asked Mr. Fyvie.

"I know," cried Hester. "Milly's cottage."

"It's a cottage in Wind-Whistle Cleft," explained Mr. Charles Engleton. "A pretty little place, perched half-way up the slope of the hill, with a background of rock and ivy. The cleanest place, too, as well as the prettiest—just big enough for one. Now, why can't cottages be built apart from each other, like this; nice one-roomed cottages for young single people of either sex?"

"It is not well for man to live alone," quoted Mr. Fyvie.

" She's happy enough, I know. In such a spot she **must** be happy."

" Oh ! you have seen her, then ? " said Fyvie.

" Certainly I have seen her. I have been sketching the cottage, and its proprietress comes home from work sometimes whilst I am studying the artistic."

" Take care," said Hester, laughing. " Milly's very pretty."

" Really ! I have not noticed that," said Engleton, earnestly.

" And you an artist, and a young man ! " cried Fyvie. " Ah ! it may be true ! "

" I have but seen her at a distance," explained Engleton ; " she is very shy, and makes a long circuit to avoid me. And there again is a proof of the modesty which— which——"

" Which follows isolation," concluded Mr. Fyvie. " Not exactly a proof, for Milly has lived in the village, and was just as modest there. Her father built that cottage, with my permission ; he was a miner, and as honest a fellow as ever breathed. When he was killed in my service, poor fellow, I gave Milly the cottage for life, rent free. And she clings to the place like a young hermit, and at the mines or at home she always seems as happy as the day is long, the jade. We all like Milly Athorpe."

" Athorpe ? " said Laurence.

" A niece of the man who dined with us to-day, Laurence. Captain Athorpe rose in life, and his brother did not."

" Why don't she live with her uncle ? " asked Mr. Llewellyn, suddenly intruding upon the conversation.

" Well, he hasn't asked her, perhaps, or she's too independent—I don't know ; do you, Hester ? "

" Oh ! yes."

But Hester did not condescend to explain the reasons for Milly's solitude, on the contrary, turned the conversation, which became less general. Half an hour afterwards, when Laurence had pocketed all Mr. Engleton's papers, the head of Jonathan Fyvie, junior, suddenly peered round the drawing-room door.

" Oh ! here you are at last," exclaimed his father ; " come in. Where have you been ? "

"To Colonel Jarvis's—I have had a long ride. I'm very tired—good-night."

And before his good-night could be responded to, the head had disappeared.

Later in the night still, when Laurence had gone up to his room, after a whispered injunction from his mother to leave his door open for a while, as she must come and congratulate him more heartily before she went to sleep that night, he found Jonathan Fyvie the younger sitting before his empty fire-grate, complacently smoking a cigar.

"What, Jonathan!" he exclaimed.

"Ah! shut the door, old fellow. I have been waiting here no end of time for you."

CHAPTER IV.

CONGRATULATIONS

LAURENCE RAXFORD, thus adjured, closed the door behind him, opened the window to allow the egress of a little of the tobacco smoke, drew a chair towards his friend and sat down facing him.

"Light up, old fellow," suggested Jonathan, whose father we shall hereafter term Mr. Fyvie, for the sake of distinction, "and then we shall be on an equality."

"I did not think of smoking to-night—I have an insufferable headache."

"This will soothe you."

He tendered an elaborately-worked cigar-case to Laurence, who opened it, and took therefrom his Havannah. Presently both young men were doing their best to render the atmosphere of that spacious sleeping-chamber as poisonous as possible.

"I thought that I would not go to my room, Laurence, without offering you my congratulations on becoming a partner in the old mine—without seeking an opportunity for a quiet chat with you about the future."

"You are very kind, Jonathan."

3

"Most men in my position would have grumbled a little with the senior partner at the introduction of a third to the concern; but I knew the mine could afford it, and I never was, you know, a selfish fellow."

"No," assented Laurence, who, however, knew but little concerning him.

"Your father and mine were old friends and old partners together before we were born, so the matter was square enough. I did not enter into the story—it's not my way to worry myself concerning details—there was a promise and all that, no doubt."

"No promise, Jonathan. I am indebted to my position entirely to your father's generosity."

"Ah! it doesn't matter—here you are a partner, at all events, and I congratulate you. I think that I have cause to rejoice, for you're a good-tempered fellow, full of energy, and just the man to look after everybody—which I never was. Candidly, I am not partial to supervision of subordinates, supervision of accounts—or anything in that line. Give me my share of profits, and let me rest, that is all; there are sure to be heaps of profits, and, as junior partner, you will see that they're not frittered away in working expenses. You take a load off my mind, Laurence, and I'm content."

He lay back in the capacious arm-chair that he had selected for himself before our hero's entrance, crossed one leg over the other, and puffed complacently at his cigar. Laurence looked at his handsome, sleepy face, and read at once that no fair share of work would be borne on the shoulders of Jonathan Fyvie, junior. Just enough, no doubt, implying every confidence in him, and therefore indirectly flattering him, but still objectionable in a way that Laurence could not explain, even to himself.

"I'll work for the two of us with all my heart," he said at last, almost by way of reproof to that sense of opposition which had instinctively crept into his thoughts.

"Oh! I know that — we all know that," asserted Jonathan; "you bring harmony into the council, and there was a split in the cabinet—a little one—before you turned up. My father don't care for work now any more than I do, and has been worrying me the last six months about my neglect of the mine, as if there were any necessity for

crawling over there four or five times a week, when everything was going on well without me. If things had not
been going on well, that would have been a very different
affair, of course. Then I—I should have looked into it at
once, no doubt."

"It seems necessary to me that the principals should
visit the mines very frequently," said Laurence.

"They're all honest people there ; and if they're not, I
can't help it," said Jonathan ; "if they had been robbing
us by wholesale, I should have never found them out, so
what was the use of my visits there ? Have another
cigar ? "

"No, thank you," said Laurence, "I am not half through
this one."

"You don't mind me keeping you up ? "

"Pray don't mention it."

"Then I'll light up again. What do you think of these
weeds, Raxford ? "

Raxford thought that they were very good ones

"I should think they were," he cried, with an energy
that was strangely at variance with his previous indolence,
"they cost me ninepence a piece, first hand, and I bought
a hundred pounds weight of them. The only weeds worth
fighting after, and I was determined no one else should
have them. They cost me two journeys to Liverpool, but
—ha ! ha !—I secured them at last."

"They're very good cigars," repeated Raxford, for the
want of anything else to say at this juncture.

"I'm glad you like them. I'll send over half a dozen
pounds in the morning to that queer crib of yours at
the mines. You'll find them serviceable in the even-
ings."

Laurence Raxford would have entered a protest at this,
had not Jonathan interrupted him.

"They'll be too dry before I get through them, so it's
quite a favour to accept this little present from me. They
will be capital companions for you—the only ones you'll
get at Wheal Desperation, unless you try a little flirtation
with the mining girls."

Jonathan Fyvie laughed very heartily at this — it was
his own joke, and therefore to be patronised.

Laurence shook his head.

3—2

" I don't think that I shall adopt that latter suggestion, Jonathan."

" l'm hanged if there are not some of the prettiest girls in Devonshire amongst them, Laurence," his partner affirmed. " Of course they're ignorant, and clumsy, and shy, and mutton-fisted many of them ; but it's astonishing how a little attention turns their heads, and draws them out. Astonishing ! "

Jonathan had tilted back his chair, and was looking up at the ceiling, or he would have noticed a sudden contraction of Laurence Raxford's brow. It disappeared as rapidly as it had presented itself, however, and Laurence said,

" Ah ! you are jesting ; it is neither my habit nor yours, I am sure, to experimentalise on the vanities of these country wenches. What do you think your sister will say to you, for recommending me this odd indulgence for my leisure ? "

" You don't tell my sister everything, Laurence," he replied, with a meaning shake of the head. " I am a man of the world, and understand human nature. And I know that you—shut up in that odd box amongst the Dartmoor Hills — will not die of the horrors if you can help it. And if I find you out, Laurence — and upon my soul I have my suspicions of this extraordinary energy of yours—why, I'll—I'll say nothing at head-quarters."

" You are welcome to say anything you please," said Laurence, trying very hard to change the conversation ; " and I hope that you will find me out now and then there, and help me on with my studies."

" How long do you mean to stick there ? " asked Jonathan.

" Until I am married."

" It will be a long journey to Tavvydale House. I presume your studies will not interfere with your courting in this direction."

" No, I hope not."

" You can have a look at Wind-Whistle Cleft by the way ; there's some pretty scenery about there."

Laurence anticipated another allusion to a pretty girl—to the Milly whose name had been already mentioned twice that day ; but the locality indicated did not appear to suggest one of its inhabitants. Jonathan smoked on very placidly after this, until Laurence said,

"We have been speaking of Wind-Whistle Cleft this evening."

"Have you?" said he quickly. "Who has?"

"Mr. Engleton."

"Ah! what a bore that fellow is; he's always hanging about that Cleft, I hear—sketching Milly's cottage, isn't he?"

"Yes, he told us so."

"He's a sly humbug—after Milly himself, I'll wager. Whenever I hear a man preaching about the elevation of the working classes, or the reformation of this and that abuse, I write him down a humbug."

"You must make a few mistakes in your judgment at times, Jonathan."

"And Milly, I dare say, encourages him—looks out of the corners of those big eyes of hers, I'll lay twenty pounds."

"Why, I hear a capital account of this girl."

"Oh! she's a favourite of the family—a pensioner, and Heaven knows what—and that makes her proud and stand-offish from her class. Then her uncle looks after her like an ogre, and her aunt attends to her morals, and her religious duties—but for all that, my opinion of Milly is that she is as vain, as sly, and as much of a woman, as any girl in Devon."

"I am afraid that you have formed a very poor estimate of the sex, Fyvie."

"I have formed a correct one," was the conceited answer. "I don't believe in the virtues of either sex—we're all alike —I don't believe in you!"

Laurence laughed with him at this naïve assertion—they were still laughing when Mrs. Raxford opened the door softly, entered, and then went back a step gasping and coughing.

"Oh! dear, the smoke!" she cried. "Oh! I beg pardon, Mr. Jonathan, I was not aware that you were keeping my Laurence company."

"Just for a few minutes," said Jonathan rising, "to congratulate him, and all that kind of thing. Pray, don't let me send you away."

Jonathan bade good-night to his partner and departed. Laurence's mother took the seat which the late visitor had vacated.

"How long has Mr. Jonathan been with you, Laurence?" asked Mrs. Raxford.

"I found him in possession of this room when I arrived."

"Do you like him, dear?" asked the mother anxiously.

"He's an odd fish," was the evasive answer; "I can't make him out exactly."

"He always appears to me a quiet—I may say an extremely quiet young man in company. Has he—has he much to say to you? He was laughing very heartily when I came in."

"He launched out a little to-night, mother," answered Laurence, "and astonished me with his facetious side."

"A very good-tempered young man—don't you think so?"

"Probably—very good-tempered."

"And gentlemanly—extremely gentlemanly."

"Y—es," was the evasive answer.

"Laurence, dear," said the mother anxiously, "don't you —oh! I'm afraid you don't—like young Mr. Fyvie? May I ask you in confidence?"

Laurence laughed at his mother's solicitude.

"My dear mother, I can only repeat my former statement—I can't make him out exactly. He's a riddle to me, and I was never fond of riddles. I shall solve him in due course, *sans doute.* Whether I admire him or not in the future, we shall agree together all the same, for I quarrel with no man."

"Yes," said the mother, "of course you will agree with him. And now, my dear boy, let me congratulate you with all my heart; I haven't had an opportunity before to say how happy—really and truly happy I am!"

The good mother left her chair to take the manly face between her hands, and kiss it long and tenderly, and with motherly love. He was an only child, and, though she had disguised her feelings well, she had been anxious concerning his future—even till the eleventh hour—despite Mr. Fyvie's promises. For she was a nervous woman, who had met with many bitter disappointments.

"And to think that it is all finished, and that you will be a rich man."

"Without working honestly towards riches, in the first place," replied Laurence. "Ah! how a man must value himself and his position, if every step upwards has been hewn by his own hands."

"Why, Laurence—not dissatisfied?"

"No—it would be ungrateful to grumble," replied Laurence; "everybody has been very kind and generous to me, and I have met with more than my deserts. But——"

"But!" repeated Mrs. Raxford, wondering.

"But it has all been knocked up in so great a hurry," he said, hurriedly himself; "that I am dazed, as it were. I have not settled down yet—I do not realise all the blushing honours that have been heaped upon my head. I am a lucky fellow—I know that. I should be very happy, mother, I feel that, but——"

"But, again!" exclaimed Mrs. Raxford; "my dear Laurence, what *is* the matter with you to-day?"

"Heaven knows!" answered Laurence, almost sadly; "I feel that I have done my best to be grateful, to please every one, but I have scarcely been a free agent in all this. I *was* very grateful for the lift—for Mr. Fyvie's generosity I even took his hint, and yours, concerning your mutual wishes, and proposed to Hester."

"Laurence, Laurence, but you loved her. You have never been so——"

"So great a brute as not to love her!" concluded Laurence; "I hope not so bad as that. I should have preferred a longer courtship, less impulse in the proposal, and more steady consideration of my heart and hers—how do I know that she loves *me*?"

"You may be sure of that."

"She's a dear, amiable girl, and I am very much in love with her now, naturally. There, hurry or no hurry, everything is over—I am a partner in Wheal Desperation—I am engaged to Hester Fyvie, and all before me, around me, far ahead of me, is bright with sunshine, mother."

"Thank God for it!" cried the more grateful woman.

"Amen!" echoed Laurence Raxford.

Then followed fresh congratulations, and Mrs. Raxford composed herself for a long talk, crying with very joy over

Laurence's future.　Laurence introduced no further "buts" into his discourse; he was light-hearted and joyous, as befitted his position; and when his mother left him there was not the shadow of a cloud to mar her rejoicing.　She was going away to-morrow—going to London to look after her little house property, and to arrange a plan for disposing of the same when the marriage day was fixed between Miss Fyvie and her son.　After that, to come to Devonshire, and settle near those two who were to take each other for better for worse, and live happily ever afterwards.　Hester Fyvie was dear to her already as a daughter—Hester had fallen easily and naturally in love with "her boy," and that was a compliment to the mother as well as to the son.

"You will see me to the station to-morrow, Laurence?—and you will write to me every post when I get back to town?"

"Every time I have news to communicate, at any rate."

"I shall think something has happened if you don't write."

"I'll write twice a week."

"There's a dear lad," said Mrs. Raxford; "and let them be nice long letters, telling me how you prosper.　And you'll mind and not go too near the machinery—those fly-away wheels have people's heads off before there's time to get them out of the way.　Good-night, Laurence."

"Good-night."

She came back again to whisper that she was so happy, and then fluttered out of the room, leaving Laurence in sole possession of his bachelor chamber at last.　When he was sure that she was gone, he locked himself in for the night, took off his dress-coat, and then changed his position for a seat by the open window, looking out across the country, bright with the moonlight, and shadowed but in the distance by the sullen range of the Dartmoors.　He found that his cigar had gone out, when he was sitting alone there.　He half rose, as if with the intention of re-lighting it; then he abandoned that idea, and let Jonathan Fyvie's favourite brand drop from his fingers into the garden below.　Finally, he crossed his arms upon his chest, bravo fashion, and went off into that vague, misty, speculative dream-land, wherein his eyes were open, and he was conscious of sitting there, staring at the moonlit scene ahead of him.

He gave way to no soliloquy, such as had disturbed Mr.
Fyvie's after-dinner nap—such as a reader has a right to
expect from a hero in a thoughtful mood, sitting at an open
window gazing at the moon. On the contrary, he compressed his lips together, as though frightened lest a secret
should escape him, or a terrible doubt or two find voice to
betray him. His face assumed a graver, sadder expression ;
it was not like the face of a man who had had his fortune
made for him, and who had been lucky in his loves. It was
the same perplexed face which Hester Fyvie had noticed
once before that day. We can only speculate as to the train
of thought which kept the young man so long at the open
window, and gave a tinge—just a tinge—of dissatisfaction
to his looks. Whether we are right or wrong in our sur-
mises, we must leave to after chapters to decide.

Was he still thinking of the haste with which everything
had been concluded—his partnership in Wheal Desperation
—his engagement to its proprietor's daughter ? Had both
been thrown a little too persistently in his way, and had
he been too full of gratitude, and not full enough of that
circumspection which his prior training had warranted ?

Or was he thinking more of the future than the past ?—
of the life at the mines—the life that he was sure that he
should like, that he had sought, in the first instance, without
dreaming of a partnership ; of the partners, father and son,
with whom he was allied ; of Fyvie, junior, in particular,
with his free-and-easy notions, his lax principles, his carelessness and his good-humour ? Or of the wife that would
be his, and the task that would be ever before him to make
her as happy as she deserved ?

Before he left for Devonshire he had pictured to himself
somewhat of an uphill life, and felt all the brighter and the
stronger for the prospect. He had told his mother, with a
swelling heart, how he would work his way upwards, caring
for no barriers in his way ; and he had wondered, without
suspecting anything, at the strange smile with which his
mother had responded to his eloquence ; for she had known
Mr. Fyvie's secret all along, and had kept it in an unwomanly spirit, bursting, as she had been, with the intention
for years. So it had all come suddenly on Laurence Raxford,
and, from the first intimation of Mr. Fyvie's wishes, he had
been confused and unlike himself.

He had said strange things, and done strange things ; he had been very grateful, and he considered himself a very lucky fellow. Half a dozen times a day he told himself *that*, as well as his friends, but it was a thoughtful, almost a gloomy face that looked from the window at the night.

One more supposition, and then the curtain shall be rung up on our story proper. Had Jonathan Fyvie's cigar been too much for Laurence Raxford ?

CHAPTER V.

WIND-WHISTLE CLEFT.

LAURENCE RAXFORD went fairly at the working partner ship on the following day. Long before luncheon at Tavvy-dale House he had escorted his mother to the railway station, received her manifold injunctions and blessings, seen her start for London, returned in Mr. Fyvie's carriage to Mr. Fyvie's mansion, wished good-bye to all friends—and enemies, if he had any—took a more tender adieu of Hester in the garden, promising everything that was necessary and proper in a favoured suitor,—to write regularly when business was brisk, and to stroll very frequently to Tavvy-dale House when his services were not required at the mines —and then he had settled down to thoughts of Wheal Desperation.

If he were thoughtful still—as he was being driven in a light gig to the old battle-ground of the Fyvies, the new battle-ground for him from that day—his reveries were not of yesternight, or at least they gave a more pleasant expression to his countenance. In the bright sunshine he could once more exult at his good fortune, and promise himself that he would deserve it, if ever energy and perseverance deserved good fortune yet.

He had even said to Hester, in an interval of eloquent and fervid leave-taking,

"You must not blame me, Hester, if I have my business on my mind too much—for a while, even if Wheal Desperation be almost first in my thoughts. I am going to work in earnest!"

"That is what papa wishes, too. No, I shall not blame you; and if I am now and then just a trifle jealous of this mine you shall never know it."

"Ah! but I would rather know that—you shall not keep even one little grievance to yourself, if I can help it."

"Which you cannot," she said, laughing; "I shall be very secretive over my wrongs, and until they master me you shall not take your share, Laurence."

These words, and the loving look with which they were accompanied, to keep him company on the long road towards the mine, and then before one o'clock of the day at work in earnest.

Laurence was a man who wished to know his ground, and to take his place upon it as speedily as possible. One fault of our hero's might be that what he desired to do earnestly he did at times too hurriedly—darting at his task, or his desire, with a precipitancy that once or twice in life he was sorry for afterwards. But he was anxious to be of service in his new estate, to test the many theories which long study had engendered—to understand practically, and at any sacrifice, the whole art of wrenching money from Mother Earth.

An hour after his appearance on his property he was many fathoms below the surface, in a miner's dress, and with a candle in his cap. Before work ceased that day he had astonished a few of the hands by his superfluous energy.

Possibly a few had shrugged their shoulders, and laughed quietly to themselves. Energetic young men from the School of Mines had turned up before at Wheal Desperation, taking their share of work, and earning, with no small labour, their experience; but they had tamed down wonderfully after the first week, and taken the affairs of mining life with great composure. It would be the same with the junior partner, no doubt. But at the end of the week it was not exactly the same with him. He was working, if anything, harder than ever. His theories had gone wrong, or he had gone too quickly at them; the mining captains, as Mr. Fyvie had prophesied, had listened to the ideas based on his book knowledge, the lectures he had heard, and the experiments he had witnessed, but they had not helped him much, and

Captain Athorpe had objected to be put too much out of his way, and at last to be interfered with, so far as the men under him in his own particular level were concerned. Laurence, considering that he had lost time, did his best to make up for it, and succeeded, as he deserved. At the expiration of one clear week he knew his mine, at least, every inch of ground therein, and half the faces of the men and women in his employ He began to hope that *he* was beginning to be appreciated too, for he had exerted himself to win everybody's esteem ; he was naturally kind in his way, and free with his good words, and with those bright smiles, which go so far to win the hearts of subordinates. He was like a clever and genial schoolmaster, ruling well, and exacting discipline and obedience, but winning, also, respect and affection unto himself—a conquest which many men miss all their lives, and wonder how it happens so.

Laurence took an interest in his workpeople as well as in their work, and they were simple-minded, honest folk, with whom a good word went a long way. In time he should know every man and woman by name and sight ; he should not feel thoroughly at home till he was acquainted with this large family. He knew the mine well now ; he should know everybody on it presently.

There were larger mines in the vicinity than Wheal Desperation, but few richer, and none more busy for its size. It was a mine worked solely by water power—therefore, a little old-fashioned and cumbrous in its machinery, here and there. The river flowing on through the Dartmoor country had been seized in its progress, twisted from its course, bent to the purpose of crafty men, made to run in divers intricate channels, to serve as shafts, to wash the metal from the dross, and to turn wheels of monstrous size, that had cost their owners many thousands of pounds, and were like wheels of another age, when Titans lived ; to cross and recross itself, running in many grooves—a net-work of water, black and dense at last with its metallic surcharges ; and after doing all the service in its power, and all the dirty work, dismissed, slave-like, to force its way, as best it might, towards a purer life. It found it in the sea, seventeen or eighteen miles away—scarcely before, for Tavistock folk grumbled at their poisoned fish, and the rocky banks of the river five miles hence glittered with specks of copper ore.

Wandering now and then above ground, where the Tavvy did good service for the mining folk, Laurence, full of interest in his pursuit, was content enough. So far as peace and rest constitute happiness, he looks back still at this first week of his life in earnest, and fancies it was one of the happiest weeks of his existence; for it was free from storms, and he was content with himself, his present, and his future. Women and children, to the number of three hundred, perhaps, worked above the surface till six in the evening, and Laurence, watching them at times, wondered, with a listless wonderment, born of an oft-repeated name, which was Milly Athorpe amongst that number there. He did not ask the question, for he was not curious enough, and he knew that in good time she would cross his path with the rest.

There were many pretty faces bent shyly away from him as he took stock of his servants; any of them might belong to Milly, who was a pretty girl, he had heard. But they were faces all of one pattern, he thought, and all of one expression, for what he could see to the contrary; rosy faces, most of them, buried in extraordinary limp bonnets, or headgears of a bonnet-like construction, that hung far over the head, and flapped about with every movement of their owners. Women at unfeminine vocations, as is customary in mining districts, and where labour is cheap; women in circles, with a centre of copper ore—ore in the rough—at which they pounded incessantly with long, heavy hammers; women pushing truck-loads of ore from the mouth of the shaft to these centres; from these centres to others, where the ore was finer, and fit for washing, or for sending off presently to capitalists, who had bought largely of the precious stuff, and would deal with it as it suited them, and the markets; women under long open sheds, doing their metallic washings cheerfully; women everywhere, a few overlooking the others in some departments, but the majority overlooked by the Captain Peters with whom we dined in our first chapter; women in short blue skirts, and thick boots, and with mufflers and leathern gloves round those mutton-fists to which Jonathan Fyvie had alluded, and of which fists most of them were careful. Amongst these specimens of the softer sex a sprinkling of children, and a few old and feeble men, who had done their best in life, and were of no more use than children in the mines, and had but children's wages; whole generations of one family here working in the interests of Fyvie, Fyvie, and Raxford.

A bustling scene till sundown, and then a stillness over everything, that was almost depressing ; the miners away in their village, a mile distant from the property ; the clerk, Waters—an old bachelor, with old bachelor-like habits of going to bed in his room over the clerk's office, at 8 P.M. precisely—left in possession of Wheal Desperation, with Laurence and a deaf old woman officiating as housekeeper, cook, and general maid-of-all-work.

Laurence's room was on the upper floor of this office, a long, low-ceilinged room, tolerably furnished, with windows looking back and front, and sideways over the property, and draped with heavy moreen curtains, that gave an air of "stuffiness" to the chamber. This had been Mr. Fyvie's room in the old times when he lived upon his estate, and was a desperate man. There was a great F scored on the wooden mantelshelf, thirty years old, at least, and it appeared to have been done by a savage gash or two, when the mind of the carver was beset by strange thoughts. This room was "the queer crib" at which Jonathan Fyvie had laughed a week since, and in this room it was the wont of the new partner to rest after the fatigues of the day, to write his letters to his mother and Hester, to dive into accounts, and pore over the books—matters which he wished to understand as thoroughly as the mining business—occasionally to smoke one of his friend's favourite cigars, half-a-dozen pounds of which had been sent, according to promise, and in all faith and friendship, by special messenger from Tavvy-dale House.

In this room, then, exactly a week after his appearance as a partner there, Laurence was sitting, staring at the blackness of the night, and speculating as to whether it would be fine enough to-morrow to dine at Mr. Fyvie's, and go courting for the first time since he had entered energetically upon his duties at the Wheal. He had been for a stroll along the broad road that crosses the moor, and had been glad to get back again, the wind being sharp and cold, and inclined to be boisterous with any one in reach that evening. On his return he had looked at the account-books for a few minutes, along with Mr. Waters, stayed also for a few minutes' chat with the old gentleman, who was one more who had taken a fancy to Laurence, and then at the respectable hour of 9 P.M. he was considering the expediency of turning into his large four-poster for the night. He was the last person up in the house; the old woman was snoring in the distance somewhere, and Mr. Waters, in the room to the left, had been fast asleep one clear hour by the eight-day clock.

Laurence was falling easily into the new habit of retiring early to bed; he had been a student in his day, wasting midnight oil over his researches, and latterly, at Tavvydale House, keeping late hours there, for fashion's sake; but he dropped readily enough into his new habit—accepting it as a phase in his new life, and feeling the better for it already. He liked his life, for he was gaining knowledge in it, and he did not give himself much time to think of the monotony of after-business hours, with only old Waters for company. He was content, and he felt that a visit to Tavvydale House, and the enjoyment of Hester's company, was to be indulged in with more zest, looked forward to, and back at, with more pleasure, for duty keeping him six days out of seven apart from her society. He was content, then, with his position; nay, he must have been happy, we reiterate, for he was singing away in his room, not too loudly,—lest he should intrude on Mr. Waters's slumber,—and not with much soul in his music, for, as already intimated, he was speculating if it would be fine enough for a long walk to-morrow afternoon.

His whistling, and his speculation in one direction, were suddenly brought to a full stop by a handful of small stones rattling with sharp precision against the glass.

"Holloa!" said Laurence, startled in spite of himself, "Here's a visitor, for a change, and Jonathan Fyvie—for a sixpence."

Laurence opened the window, and looked out, drawing his head precipitately back again, as a second shower quitted the hand of the person below.

"Oh, I beg your pardon," said a strange voice beneath the window. "I was in a hurry, and afraid that I had not made you hear. No damage, I hope?"

"Not much," answered Laurence, as the last handful of missiles spread themselves over the carpet of his room. "You've made a nice mess in here, that's all.

Why didn't you come round to the door and knock, if you wanted anything ? "

"I thought I might alarm the house; and seeing your light, I took the liberty of arresting your attention," piped the shrill voice below; "but I sincerely hope that I haven't inconvenienced you in any way ? "

"All right," said Laurence; "no occasion to apologise, as there's no glass to pay for. May I ask what you want on the premises ? "

"I fear I am trespassing," said the polite individual below; "but the fact is, I have been stupid enough to lose myself. I have passed this place once before to-night. This is the Wheal Desperation, young man, I think ? "

"Yes, Sir. Where do you want to go to ? "

"I want to find Wind-Whistle Cleft. I thought I knew every step of the way—I ought to have done so, by this time—but the night is terribly dark, and, in try-ing to make a short cut by the bridge, I lost myself and got round here again somehow. Perhaps, if it's not inconvenient, you'll come down, and put me in the right way. I can't be walking about here all night, you know," he concluded somewhat peevishly. "I shall meet with an accident before I have finished."

Laurence leaned further out of window, to inspect the in-truder, who had thus coolly asked his services. He could make out but dimly the figure of a man, evidently of short stature, and with a hat on the back of his head—a man with long white hair, he fancied, as he strained his eyes into the darkness. Laurence was considering the stranger's invita-tion, as he looked down, when the shrill voice said again,

"Of course, you needn't come if you don't like—I wouldn't press you for the world, against any inclination you may have to the contrary. But you are a young man, and I am an old one; and if you have been taught to honour grey hairs, or entertain any reverence for your seniors, you'll not leave me out here. But if you won't come, why take this."

He stooped so suddenly towards the ground that Laurence's first idea was that another handful of stones was coming in his direction; but, to his surprise, a large, and apparently heavy, carpet-bag was held aloft.

" Shall I try and pitch it through the window, Sir ? I'll call for it in the morning, if you'll wait a moment, and allow me to get my night-shirt out."

" No, no, don't pitch anything more. What a fellow you are for pitching things ! " exclaimed Laurence. " You have lost your way, you tell me, and want to find Wind-Whistle Cleft ? "

" Precisely so."

" I'll come down, and put you in the way."

" Sir, I am extremely obliged to you."

The old gentleman set down his carpet-bag, and then raised his hat politely, putting it on afterwards still further at the back of his head. Laurence closed the window, went down stairs softly, took the key from the lock—a large key, weighing about a pound and a quarter—and then let himself quietly out of the house, and went round to the back of the premises, where the old gentleman was waiting for him.

" Sir, I am indebted to your courtesy. Will you carry this carpet-bag a little way, or shall I take my turn first ? " said the stranger, elevating his hat once more.

" Well," said Laurence, doubtfully, " I think that I will have the first turn at it."

" You are very kind. Perhaps you will be good enough not to shake it too much, for there's a bottle of port wine in it, and I dare say the crust is very much disturbed already."

" I dare say it is."

Laurence was amused with the coolness, or self-complacency, or whatever it was, of the old man ; he was interested in his adventure, and inclined to prosecute it to the end. He looked intently at the stranger, when he was face to face with him ; despite the night's darkness, he could make out that the face was very deeply lined, and the thin mouth shadowed by a long and heavy white moustache ; that the figure of the man was far from robust, and shook a little at the knees ; that the dress-coat which he wore was as short for his arms, as the tight-fitting black trousers were for his legs. An old man, with a dash of the scarecrow in him, thought Laurence,—what did he want at Dartmoor at this hour of the night?

4

"You will excuse me, but is it necessary to go through the Cleft to-night?" asked Laurence.

"Not entirely through it—only to my niece's cottage there."

"Is your name Athorpe?"

"My name is Whiteshell—at your service," and off went the gentleman's hat again.

"Oh! thank you—I don't think I shall require your services just at present," said Laurence, drily; "now, if you are ready, Sir, I'll try and put you in the way."

"*Try* and put me in the way!" echoed Mr. Whiteshell; "are you not a native, then?"

"No, I am not."

"But—bless my soul, Sir, you know your way about here, I suppose?"

"I have been a week at the mine—a month or so in Devonshire. I know Wind-Whistle Cleft by name well enough—by sight, tolerably. I have been twice close upon it, in an evening stroll lately, and I fancy that I can find it in the dark."

"Yes—I fancied that too, and I haven't a bit of skin on my knees. I have been tumbling about here an hour—I dare say I have broken that bottle of wine, for the bag has been a terrible nuisance—I think now that we had better turn back and leave it at your place till the morning."

"I never turn back," said Laurence, striding on with the bag; "this way, Sir. You don't object to my walking fast?"

"The faster the better, Sir—I am an excellent walker," said Mr. Whiteshell, who had already begun to trot, to keep up with Laurence's sharp swinging pace.

They walked and ran on in silence together for several minutes. Mr. Whiteshell was the first to break silence, by gasping forth,

"I—I hope that I am not hurrying you too much, Sir?"

"Not at all," said Laurence, in reply; "we will go on faster if you wish it."

"Not on my account—certainly not, thank you," answered the man; "I—I really don't see any pressing occasion for this haste, upon second thoughts, now."

"We may have the rain down—it's a good mile to the Cleft."

"We leave the Tavvydale village on our left, I think?" said the traveller.

"Yes."

"Bearing off suddenly by Captain Athorpe's cottage, which used to be, I fancied, at the mouth of the Cleft—keeping guard over my Milly, as I used to say."

"You are then——"

"Miss Athorpe's uncle—on the mother's side. Do you know my niece?"

"I have not the pleasure."

"You are holding some genteel situation at the mines, Sir?"

"Yes."

"Very good situations in the office, I dare say, and decent wages, for the country! And you have not seen Milly?"

"I am not certain. There are some hundreds of girls at surface work, and I have been here a week."

"Hum!—I should have fancied that she would have been pointed out to you before this—as beautiful a girl as ever breathed, and, though I say it myself, as good as she is beautiful."

"I have heard her praises sung before. She appears to be a favourite in these parts?"

"She *is* a favourite, Sir. She's a kind of forewoman and overlooker of one of the divisions on the mine—not a common mining girl, you know."

"Indeed."

"A very clever girl, Sir—intensely clever, I may say, and quick as lightning. Her mother—my dead sister, Sir—was a beautiful and clever woman—she married for love, poor soul, and made a mull of it. She married one of the Athorpes, and by this time you are probably aware what an Athorpe is like?"

"I know Captain Athorpe very well by this time."

"A good man in his way—a pious and upright man, I have no doubt—but no gentility, Sir, no evidence of breeding, no respect, in fact, for anybody's opinions but his own. Not generally admired, I fancy?" he added, interrogatively.

Laurence did not venture to express an opinion upon this, and Mr. Whiteshell continued,

"I only fancy, of course. I have not the pleasure of an intimate acquaintance with Captain Athorpe, who is rather above his brother's wife's family, and likes to show it. Merely his manner, perhaps, or a little honest pride concerning his worldly possessions, but not pleasant, for all that. The truth is, Sir, though I am about the meekest man on the Middlesex side of the water, he and I never agree for five minutes together. In trying to avoid his cottage—to make a *détour*, in fact—I lost my way, and got down a wrong turning, and nearly off a precipice, or something. Shall I take the bag now?"

"I'll go on to the Cleft with it, Mr. Whiteshell."

"Thank you," raising his hat again, "you are exceedingly kind. James Whiteshell is for ever indebted to the courtesy of a stranger. Whenever chance leads you to Milk Street, Westminster, Sir, I shall be happy to repay the obligation. Across here?"

"Yes, this cuts off Captain Athorpe's cottage, you see."

"Exactly—that white house. They were singing hymns together—he and his wife—an hour ago. Very praiseworthy employment, although they need not have made such a noise over it. This is the way I came—are you sure that you are going right?"

"Quite sure."

"It's very odd. I can't make out how I managed to lose my way—down here, too? Why, I came down here with a run."

"At the bottom of this slope we shall find the Cleft, I think."

"Oh! you only think," said Mr. Whiteshell, ruefully.

The bottom of the hill was reached, and the traveller and his guide were standing at the entrance of a narrow glen or ravine, black as Hades in the dark night, with heavy, full-leaved trees hanging about its entrance, and above the rocks that lowered gaunt and ominous on either side of them.

"There—all this is what I particularly object to in the country," said Mr. Whiteshell, suddenly, "so depressing—such a cut-throat element about these rural back-slums. If it were not for Milly, I'd never set foot out of town—it does me a deal of harm, for I am naturally nervous. Here's a place for a murder now, and nobody a bit the wiser till a fellow is as green as grass. Oh! Lord, what's that?"

"That's a rabbit, probably, scouring through the brush-wood, more frightened than you are. I presume that you know your way now, Mr. Whiteshell?"

"You need not presume anything of the kind," he said, half fretfully, "for I can scarcely believe it's the Cleft at all —it has altered very much since I was here last—and the thing they call a path is worse than ever. I hope, Mr.— Mr.——"

"Raxford," said our hero.

"Thank you, Mr. Raxford—that you will not think of leaving a distressed traveller at the beginning of his difficulties. I am very thankful for the trouble you have already taken—but as you *are* out—and not a bit nervous—and used to these kind of holes—it would be adding materially to the obligation conferred, by accompanying me the rest of the journey. If you be still firm, Sir, why, I must bow to your decision, and proceed on my way alone."

Dark as it was, Laurence could see that the old gentleman drew himself up haughtily.

"Come on, Sir. I am your cicerone—hang it, if you put it in that light, what can a fellow say? But," he added, to himself, "you are an unconscionable old beggar for all that."

Laurence and Mr. Whiteshell went on through the Cleft, following the tortuous curves of a footpath, or sheep-track, or splash of gravel on the green hillside, as well as the darkness permitted, occasionally straying from the track, and pausing to consider their whereabouts.

"Well, it certainly is black enough," commented Laurence, "and the trees grow all manner of ways here. This must be a glorious place in the day time for a pic-nic."

"Or a suicide. Mind your head, Sir—you're a little taller than I am, I imagine, and here's a ridiculous tree coming straight out of the rock like the top of a finger post. Yes, I came this way—I remember that tree—I slipped on the other side of the place, and went down there ever so many feet where you hear that miserable gurgling of water. It's a mercy that I wasn't drowned—only came up stunned a bit, and walked all the way back again to Wheal Desperation. Shall I take the bag now?"

"I have just changed hands—all right, Sir."

"It's very selfish of me not to press the question, but the

fact is, I am feeling my way along with both hands—and you seem used to this scrambling, or have been more accustomed to carry parcels than I. A kind of messenger at the mines, perhaps?"

"No," answered Laurence, who was determined not to satisfy the gentleman's curiosity.

"Not a messenger—junior clerk, perhaps? There used to be a junior clerk at the office three years since—Simpson."

"Don't remember him, Mr. Whiteshell."

"Very likely not. He died down here—found all of a heap at the bottom of some hill or other—missed his way in the fog, and came to grief. Where are we now, Mr.—Mr. Raxford?"

"Really, I cannot say. I have never attempted the Cleft before. Is your niece's cottage on the left or on the right?"

"On the left here—half way up the hill where the Cleft widens. We shan't miss it if we look out for a light."

"And we talk less, for talking *is* a distraction just now. I nearly lost your bag a moment since."

"Good gracious! Keep a still tongue in your head, then, Sir, for the present. What's that?"

"That is the rain coming down. This is an awkward adventure, Mr. Whiteshell."

"Oh, its a miserable place," groaned that gentleman, tripping at the same time over a mass of bramble which shot out from the bank, and across the path. "I don't think that I will ever come again. It's only my love for the dear girl that brings me here at all. I have no right to come—I'm not in a position to afford it—it is a piece of extravagance which infallibly concludes with the horrors. Where are we now, Mr. Raxford?"

"More in the dark than ever, under these trees. But the Cleft widens, I fancy, further on. Steady here, Sir—the water below us is evidently deep in this place."

"Then pray walk cautiously. I don't see what is to become of me if you fall over."

"No—you would never get the bag back," was the dry response.

"The rain's coming through the trees now, like a cataract," said Mr. Whiteshell. "How I hate these clefts and valleys, and other nonsense, to be sure! Shall we run for it, Mr. Raxford?"

"Run—where?"

"Well, I don't know. Run into the open, if we can find any, and look out for a light on the left. She said that every night this week, she would put the candle in the window until half-past ten—she winds up her studies punctually at that time."

"Studies—what studies?"

"Oh, all kinds of studies that that stupid fellow Athorpe encourages her in—for the sake of the family, and so on. I don't despise education—I had an education myself, and it has been of use to me—but Milly was quite scholar enough for this place, Heaven knows! Where are we likely to be now, Mr. Raxford?"

Mr. Raxford did not reply. He was tired of his adventure, and the heavy rain that was now descending, he considered an unpleasant wind-up thereto.

There was a long journey back to Wheal Desperation, and the prospect even soured his naturally easy temperament. He had not done a wise thing in guiding this gabbling, conceited, selfish old gentleman through the valley; he had been extremely charitable, and received but little thanks for the sacrifice. Let him console himself with the thought that Mr. Whiteshell would have killed himself in the dark without his assistance.

The Cleft was wild and tortuous—the stream below them took strange curves and plunges; and Raxford could imagine that an immense rush of water in old times had torn through the Dartmoor Hills after the fashion of the stream below, and rent this gap in them. In the bright daylight, with the sunshine struggling in amongst the leaves above, making a wealth of fantastic shadowing and colour, this must be a lovely spot, he thought. He would test its beauties in the daylight presently; come here some quiet morning or evening, and slide down to the water's edge, just as huge boulders had slid before him, making islets of themselves in the stream, which split into rippling falls thereby, for ever after tinkled with sweet music. Raxford was a bit of a poet in his heart—his first dream, his boy's dream, was to make his mark in verse—and discontented as he was then, and savage with the motive which had brought him forth that night, he could not refrain from a promise to come again in search of beauty here, and to form in this place a dreamland of his own, where he could drop off into his characteristic "maunderings," with not even a Hester Fyvie to reproach him for his reveries.

"Mr. Raxford, I certainly see a light. It can't be a glowworm—no glowworm would be so excessively absurd as to come out this wet night. There, to the right—up the hill."

"Yes—you are right."

"Thank you—I generally am. This way, Sir," cried Mr. Whiteshell, suddenly adopting the initiative. "It's fine walking up this grass, and no pitfalls for the feet of the inexperienced. This way, Sir, if you'll be kind enough to follow me."

Laurence stood amazed for an instant at the sudden development of energy in Mr. Whiteshell. That gentleman, who had plodded wearily behind him for so long, now darted into the front with extraordinary agility, skipped up the hill like a fawn, turned, pirouetted, beckoned to Laurence, took two or three amazing leaps, for no purpose whatever, and was under a thatched porch, rattling away at the latch of a cottage door, a full three minutes before Laurence, weary and heavy-laden, and anathematising the old gentleman's frivolity, had toiled up the ascent after him.

By that time the cottage door was opened, a stream of light had issued thence, casting its bright pathway on the grass, and on a girl of eighteen years of age who was embracing very heartily the withered form of Mr. Whiteshell.

"My dear Uncle James, you have come, then, at last, to see your Milly!"

"My dear Milly, it's worth all the danger of the journey to hear your voice, and to find this hearty welcome here. Come along, Sir,"—turning to his late companion—"as quick as you can with that bag, Mr. Raxford."

CHAPTER VI.

MILLY.

Mr. Raxford made all the haste that he could towards the cottage—not out of respect for the adjuration of Mr. Whiteshell, but simply from an anxiety to get out of the rain, descending more fiercely and heavily in this spot of open ground.

Milly looked anxiously towards him as he came into the light.

"Why, it's—it's the new master!" she exclaimed; "it's Mr. Raxford!"

"Yes, it's part of him," he replied; "all that the rain has not washed away, at any rate. May I wait up for the shower a little?"

"Certainly, Sir. You are—you are very welcome—will you step this way, please?"

Milly was very embarrassed at this sudden appearance of so great a planet in her little sphere; she ran into the house to set her chairs in order, to whisk several books from the table into an inner room, to glance in a half-scared manner round her neatly furnished parlour, for any evidence of disorder which might unintentionally have got there, and then stood, blushing very much, fidgeting with the corners of her apron, and looking down on the red-tiled floor.

Laurence Raxford set the odious carpet-bag in a corner, and looked hard at the girl whose praises he had heard sung more than once lately—the favourite at Tavvydale House—the heroine of the Cleft whose name was to meet him, as he met her on that night, in strange places, and under strange circumstances of life.

Yes, Mr. Fyvie was right. She was, at least in Laurence's estimation, as well as in his senior partner's, the prettiest girl in Devon. It was a face that startled him with its beauty, with its expression, which was still more beautiful, for it was pure, and full of thought, and still so womanly. Richly endowed with a face that Murillo might have copied

for his angels, Milly stood there as if oppressed by her own
beauty—conscious of it, perhaps, but certainly finding it in
the way, and disturbed by the admiration, voluntary and in-
voluntary, of which it was the cause. Will the readers of
this book believe Milly—or her biographer speaking for her,
with his hand on his heart—when we assure them that her
one regret was that she was not a trifle more plain, more
commonplace, more like the every-day girls in Tavvydale?
It was an odd regret; but then Milly was a girl with some
odd thoughts of her own, and living alone in the Cleft had
helped to foster them more than she was aware. Milly, it
may be added here, was a "character;" people said so,
beyond the Cleft, and as a character worth, let us hope, a
little analysis, she makes her bow upon this stage. A pretty
girl, then, or, rather, a beautiful girl, with rich brown hair
—some shades darker than Hester Fyvie's—and with large
almond-shaped brown eyes. A lithe figure, full of grace of
movement—slight, ethereal, and almost childlike, that contrasted strangely with the buxom lasses amongst whom she
found herself at Wheal Desperation, or in the chapel on
Sundays in the village. Laurence marvelled that he had
not been struck with the contrast before; but then she had
buried herself in one of those odious limp bonnets—half
sun-shade and half night-cap—and with her back towards
him, she had probably passed for a miner's girl of thirteen
or fourteen years of age. He had never met Milly Athorpe
face to face before, he felt assured; and he did not wonder
now at the heroine—the heroine under protest, so far as she
herself was concerned—that she had become within fair
range of Wind-Whistle Cleft.

He should have to relate an adventure to-morrow at
Tavvydale House, and to add his opinion on Milly Athorpe
with the rest. He should tell Hester that this Milly was
very beautiful, and that it was fortunate for Hester—that is,
if he were of any value in her estimation—that he had
never met with a Milly in his own sphere before his late engagement. This would give rise to one of those smart inter-
changes of words—verging on *repartee*, he was inclined to
think conceitedly—which tended to render Hester so charming, naïve, and lovable. He should have quite a history to
relate to Hester after dinner. Laurence Raxford was a man
quickly at his ease, and always anxious to put others in the

same position. He noted the embarrassment—intense and painful—of Milly Athorpe at his presence there, and he made an effort to alter the position of affairs.

"Don't let me put you out, Miss Athorpe," he said, speaking very rapidly, "by my intrusion here—I'll only wait for the first outburst of wrath from these elements, and then effect my escape, chancing a wet jacket. Your uncle, Mr. Whiteshell, had strayed from the beaten track, and I thought it but fair—but Devonshire politeness—to set him in the right way as well as I could."

"And very much obliged to you I am," said Mr. Whiteshell, taking off his hat, and putting it on a little side-table near the window-sill, on which a host of plants was blooming; "what I should have done without you, I cannot readily conceive. An estimable young man this, Milly," he said, turning to his niece; "one who pays respect to grey hairs, however low the path on which their wearer plods his way."

"And however heavy the carpet-bag of the plodder!" added Laurence. He was half inclined to say "the potterer," but corrected himself in time very politely.

"Ten thousand thanks from me for your assistance in that quarter, Mr. Raxford," he said, "and ten thousand thanks from you for being full of health and strength to bear the burden lightly."

"Amen, with all my heart, Sir," cried Raxford, cheerily, as this oddity turned, with some degree of dignity, to him, and spread out both hands, cased in shabby and crinkly black gloves, seemingly made from the hide of a rhinoceros.

"Uncle, this is Mr. Raxford—one of the proprietors."

A sweet and musical voice to add to Milly's dowry from nature, touched just a little with that Devonshire burr, which will not appear—unless on very necessary occasions—in these pages, a promise for which the reader will tender his best thanks, we hope. The introduction of the real accent into novels of locality adds not materially to the interest when well done, and when badly finished off, the saints have mercy on the reader! Take it for granted, then, that here and there lingered the faintest twang of the Tors in the speech of this Devonshire rose, and that in a few characters, less self-trained and regulated, whom the reader may meet—even in Captain Athorpe, who did not study accents—there was more than a twang, which, to commit to print, would be superfluous and heart-rending.

"One of—the *what?*" asked Mr. Whiteshell, taken a little aback.

"One of the masters of Wheal Desperation—the new master," she added, dropping a curtsey to Laurence as she spoke.

"I tender an apology,"said Mr. Whiteshell, stiffly ; "and I consider myself still further indebted for the assistance proffered me. I was not to know—it was beyond my province to know—your state in life, without any information tendered me on your side, Sir. Mr. Raxford, I have to thank you now for your great condescension."

Mr. Whiteshell sat down, very red in the face, and pulled at his long white moustache with a nervous hand, from which he had removed now the wild-beast skin. He was annoyed, it was evident ; and he was inclined to think that in some way or other he had been the victim of an imposition. He did not see how, certainly ; but there was a matter of grievance somewhere—this young man had evidently been making a jest of him, and enjoying the ignorance that had been evinced throughout.

"Really, upon my honour, Sir," he added, quite warmly, as he detected a smile hovering round the corners of Laurence's mouth, "I see nothing to laugh at in indigent old age. We are all of one degree, Sir, after all, and in my way, and in my own fashion, I stand on my position."

"My dear Sir, do you think that I pride myself on mine, or would be foolish enough to smile at yours ? Why, Sir, I am an upstart myself, and indebted to the kindness of others, rather than to any exertion of my own, for the place I occupy just now. Hang it ! pray do not set me down for a proud man, Mr Whiteshell."

The heartiness of Laurence Raxford's protest softened Milly's uncle, who put his dignity into his pocket along with his last glove. The tetchy old gentleman rose and extended his hand to our hero across the table.

"Mr. Raxford, I appreciate your *bonhomie*—you are a true gentleman, at any rate, and acting as host for the nonce, I thank you for your presence and bid you welcome, in my niece's name."

"We are honoured——" began Milly.

"Tut, tut!" interrupted Mr. Whiteshell, "we are all equal in the sight of the Lord, and we'll talk no more of being honoured by Mr. Raxford's company. The gentleman himself does not wish to play the master here, and so the gentleman is welcome. What is for supper, Milly?"

Raxford sat down on a chair by the door, which opened, without any preliminary apology for a hall, upon the green slope up which he had recently climbed. He could hear the rain hissing and rattling on the porch under which he had first seen Milly Athorpe, and he was not sorry for the excuse that held him there a prisoner. He wished to understand the two beings before him there, and he was vexed at Mr. Whiteshell misunderstanding *him*, even after he had lugged that heavy carpet bag all the way from Wheal Desperation.

Milly bustled about and spread the supper-cloth upon the table, placing thereon some cream cheese and bread, tripping in and out of a little pantry facing the inner room—into which she had launched the *débris* of her studies—with a rapidity and grace of movement that her slight figure had already warranted.

The blushes had not died out of her face yet; they came and went rapidly whenever she felt that the gentleman— "the new master"—was looking within two yards of her direction, and Laurence perceived that she was relieved when she could turn her back towards him, and felt that she would be intensely grateful for the rain to cease and allow of his departure. He regretted Milly's nervousness, and looked no more towards her, on the contrary, opened the door once or twice, as if intensely hopeful of the rain's abatement,—and hopeful he was not just then, having to make a stand against false appearances.

Mr. Whiteshell unlocked his carpet-bag, and took therefrom a wine bottle, which he placed with emphasis upon the supper-table.

"Port wine is the right thing with cheese, I believe, Mr. Raxford," he said, with a chuckle, "when I was better up in the fashion of the table—and, ha! ha!—better up in the stirrups, it was considered so."

"Pray, do not open a bottle of wine for me," cried Laurence, "I am going in an instant, rain or no rain."

"Sir, we can have no more fitting occasion to drink wine

in this house," said Mr. Whiteshell, politely, "and it was brought here to drink, and not in any way for ornament. You will share our humble meal with us, I hope? Why, Milly—only *two* plates, girl?"

"Oh! I did not think the gentleman——"

"Could be so humble as all that," concluded Laurence, determined to dispel the illusion of his loftiness at once, "that is a good joke, when I'm as hungry as a hunter, Milly."

He tried the effect of her Christian name; evidently she had not been called Miss Athorpe in her life before, and he had noticed that *that* at least had quenched every atom of whiteness in her complexion. He must be one of them heart and soul; it was very odd if he, who prided himself upon his knowledge of character, could not suit himself to his company for half an hour.

"Here goes," he muttered to himself, "we'll have no airs and graces here."

He turned up the cuffs of his coat, made a dash at the loaf which was close to him, and flourished the first handy knife over it.

"Crust or crumb, Milly?—crust or crumb, Mr. Whiteshell?" he asked, without waiting for Milly's answer—thereby sparing her fresh confusion. "I'm afraid that we are keeping late hours here for the Cleft, and two of us at least have early work at the Wheal. Can you manage that corkscrew?—it was lucky we did not smash the bottle in the dark—there was good packing before you left London, Sir. I'll try a little cheese, Milly, please," he said; "my mother attempts cream-cheese sometimes, but the good lady is not a first-rate hand, though I consume her productions by steam, being passionately attached to anything connected with milk. Here's good health to both of you," he said, imitating very cleverly the duck of the head of sundry good folk who had drunk his health at the miner's dinner; "may it leave off raining as soon as it likes after I have robbed you of a supper, Milly."

"No robbery, Sir," Milly ventured to respond.

"What—what do you think of this—vintage?" asked Mr. Whiteshell, holding his wine-glass to the candle, and staring with one eye only at a very thick mixture.

"Very fair wine!" responded the mendacious Laurence.

" Shaken up a bit in transit," said Mr. Whiteshell, " but still a decent beverage."

" When the crust settles again it will be much better. If you'll take my advice you'll put it carefully on one side— chalk side uppermost—and not touch it any more till Sunday. It's almost a pity to drink it now."

" Well," said Mr. Whiteshell doubtfully, " perhaps it is— if you really won't, now ? "

And he held the bottle towards Laurence's glass.

" No, no, many thanks !" cried Laurence, repressing a shudder ; " it will be better and more clear if you leave it alone for a day or two. I have a fancy to try the spring water so famous in the Cleft."

" Milly's favourite drink, and always on tap here—something less than ' fourpence a pot in your own jugs,'" said Mr. Whiteshell, "and certainly more beneficial. I am almost a teetotaler myself, Milly."

" You by choice, uncle—and I by necessity."

" Oh ! Bung, the Tavvydale brewer, would not care to send a four-and-a-half gallon cask up the Cleft here—a worse job than carrying my carpet bag, Mr. Raxford."

" Yes, that's true. So," turning suddenly to Milly, " only a teetotaler by necessity ? "

Milly blushed again.

" Well, I scarcely know, Sir. I—I was alluding to a little jest of my uncle's that is not worth relating again."

" Being so sorry a jest," said Mr. Whiteshell drily, " like most of Uncle James's jokes. Now, if Uncle Oliver——"

" There, if you're going to be jealous of Uncle Oliver again, you'll make me cross and unhappy !" cried Milly energetically.

" He's not what I call——"

" Hush ! "

Milly glanced towards Laurence, and silenced Mr. Whiteshell for the nonce. Seeing that he looked a trifle discomfited beneath her reproof, she hastened to repeat her former words,

" Cross and unhappy, uncle," she said ; " and I have been counting on this visit—looking forward, as you know, so long ! "

" And you never are unhappy," said her uncle, brightening again, " not even in Wind-Whistle Cleft, Milly ? "

" I hope not—never," said Milly confidently.

"That's well ! " cried Mr. Whiteshell ; "I like to hear you speak out like that. I hope to always hear you answer just as bravely. They talk in books of the unattainableness of human felicity," he cried to Raxford, "and here, Sir, in a Devonshire gap, is a young woman confessing that she is as happy as the day is long ! "

" I never heard any one confess it before. Really happy, Milly ? " Laurence asked incredulously, " with nothing to regret in the past, and nothing to sigh for ? "

" No, no," she stammered, " not so happy as that, Sir ; for of course we all have regrets, and we all look forward— if it's even to heaven."

" Yes," said Laurence thoughtfully. It was a strange re- mark from the lips of one so young, and it embarrassed him by its earnestness for an instant.

" But I think—yes, I feel—that I am happy, uncle," she said, turning to Mr. Whiteshell, as if more able to make her exposition in that quarter. " I don't see why I should not be happy, for I have no one to please but myself in the Cleft, and I agree with my company very well indeed— though I don't let myself have my own way always."

" What do you mean by that ? " asked her uncle.

" And everybody's kind to me," she cried enthusiastically, taking no heed of the interruption, "and I meet with many friends, all anxious to do their best for me, and assist me, that I feel quite selfish at times. Why, even Uncle Oliver, with whom you don't agree always, Uncle James," she added archly, " is the truest and best of friends, and I am very—very—much his debtor."

" Hum," grumbled Mr. Whiteshell.

" Do you know what I have been making up my mind to do this summer ? " she cried, clapping her hands in her ex- ultation, and entirely forgetting Laurence Raxford ; " why, to make you and Uncle Oliver understand each other better, you keeping your sensitive nature down, and he showing more of the real kindness that is in him—for he is truly kind when he likes."

" Now if ever there was a representative of the nether millstone in our poor humanity it's that man," asserted Mr. Whiteshell ; " he gives offence at all turns, and to every- body—he's as proud as a peacock, and as rough as a bear. He don't regard feelings—he don't believe in them."

"Hush—hush—I say, you don't understand him yet. Presently you will. When you go away you will own to me how you have misjudged him."

"I shall be very happy, I'm sure. Perhaps he's better since his marriage—two years of that fun will take the impudence out of most men, and I should not be very much surprised if there was an improvement in that gentleman. God knows that there was room for it!"

"And I fight his battles for him in his absence, uncle," cried Milly, meaningly—"just as he fights mine, or I fight yours. So we'll have no more bad thoughts between us, for they do no good—they never did—they never will! Now," speaking very quickly, "tell me of yourself, and how you have been getting on in that dry and dusty London."

"Where the free air never comes, you told me once."

"I am still of that opinion," laughed Milly.

"Where the paths are not all manner of ways at once, and cumbered with roots and brambles, and that rubbish—slovenly picturesqueness, I call that. Why, they would not let such a place as the Cleft exist in London for any money. Am I not right, Mr. Raxford?"

"Quite right, so far as that goes," said Laurence, rising; "and just at the present time I am inclined to think that a gas lamp or two would be an improvement. I wonder if it rains now?"

Laurence opened the door and looked out, receding a step or two with a natural surprise, as a burly man, with a thick pilot coat turned up above his ears, almost thrust him back into the room.

"What are you doing here, man, and who are you?" roughly demanded Captain Athorpe, as he followed our hero into Milly's parlour.

"I'm waiting up for the rain, and my name's Raxford," answered Laurence; "is there any more information with which I can oblige you?"

"Oh! you, is it?—and *you*, too, Whiteshell?" he said, less harshly; "I didn't understand, and the *row* up here puzzled me. The Cleft has been a riddle to-night altogether, and I have been trying to solve it. *You're* not dead yet, then?" he asked Mr. Whiteshell.

5

"Not just at present, thank you all the same."

"Are you well?"

"Thank you again, yes."

"Then you don't look it. Milly," turning to his niece, "did you hear a gun fired some time since?"

"No," answered Milly.

"I fired it. Somebody was skulking round here after no good, for he wouldn't answer, and I swore that I would fire if he didn't."

"Great Heaven, Mr. Athorpe."

"Captain Athorpe, if you please," was the stern correction.

"It's not worth arguing about," said Mr. Whiteshell; "but no one has a right to assume the title of Captain without he holds that rank in the army, navy, volunteer service, or militia; but if it pleases you——"

"Captain's my title in these parts; I worked my way up to it hard, and I've a right to it."

"Oh! very well. It's a singular fancy—I don't object; it don't hurt me," said the ruffled little man.

"Well, what were you going to say?"

"I was going to observe, Captain Athorpe, of the mineral service," said Mr. Whiteshell, caustically, "that you might have shot *me*, if you were so handy with your gun as all that. *I* have been wandering about the Cleft all night."

"Why did you not answer, then? Have you danced yourself deaf by this time?"

"You never addressed me, and I am very happy to say that you never fired at me, and unless you have a particular fancy to be tried for manslaughter, I would not advise you to fire at anybody else. It's not what I call a nice amusement."

Captain Athorpe's brow lowered a little at this polite sarcasm of the smaller man, but he did not reply immediately.

"It was hasty," said he at last—"I—I suppose that I lost my temper; but we have had a host of tramps about here, and one vagabond made off with no end of linen, last week, from our hedge at the back."

"Ha! ha!—I beg pardon," cried Mr. Whiteshell—"did he, though, the rascal? After all Mrs. Athorpe's trouble of washing, too."

" Mrs. Athorpe never washes," said the mining captain ; "if you knew more of us you would know better than that. Will you make your stay at our place, Whiteshell ? "

" *Mr.* Whiteshell," corrected the little gentleman in his turn.

" Well, Mr. Whiteshell."

" Thank you," said he, trying to repress a grimace ; " I think I'll keep to the old quarters, if Milly don't mind."

" Why, it's a promise ! " cried Milly, "and you must not leave me, Uncle James."

" It's a great trouble to the girl," remarked Captain Athorpe ; " there's only this room and hers, and there's not much satisfaction in seeing you sprawling half the day on that sofa-bedstead, I take it. Besides, she can't afford it."

" Oh ! yes, I can," cried Milly.

" Sir, I'm not a sponge," said Mr. Whiteshell. "Milly Athorpe is not likely to lose a great deal by my intrusion here. And as for your kind invitation, why——"

" Uncle James cannot accept it," said Milly very readily, " for he has promised to spend a clear week with me— and I must make amends for want of room by warmth of heart."

" Which——" began the crotchety gentleman again.

" Which is common to all good friends in Devon—on this side of the Dartmoor Tors," interrupted Milly again before he could continue. "There, shake hands with Uncle Oliver, and tell him that you'll come another time, but now, even for him, it isn't fair to press you to break his word. Is it Sir ? " turning to Laurence again.

Laurence, lost in admiration at Milly Athorpe's tact, aroused himself to say,

" Certainly it is not. Captain Athorpe will not press his friend to break a promise, I am sure."

" I press no man against his inclination," said Athorpe, as he shook hands somewhat reluctantly with Mr. Whiteshel.. "There is my house by the Cleft if any one wishes to see me—I go out of my way to see no man. You are coming down the Cleft, Mr. Raxford ? "

" Yes—at once."

" The rain is over—we have it all of a lump in Devon," said Athorpe. "This way, Sir. Good-night, Milly—good-night, Whiteshell."

5—2

" Good-night, Athorpe," replied Mr. Whiteshell."

Milly bade her uncle good-night, dropped a second curtsey to the stranger ; and then Raxford, after bidding good-night also to Milly's uncle on the mother's side, followed Milly's uncle on the father's ditto, into Wind-Whistle Cleft.

" Now, Sir," said Captain Athorpe sternly, as they were proceeding down the slope together, " I must trouble you for an explanation."

CHAPTER VII.

THE UNCLE ON THE FATHER'S SIDE.

LAURENCE RAXFORD felt the blood rise to his cheeks, and his ears tingle unpleasantly at Captain Athorpe's question, crudely delivered as it was. He had not seen a great deal to admire in this brusque individual at any time, and though he was not the man to expect or wish that any obsequiousness should be paid him, even on the part of his servants, still he did expect, not unnaturally, to be regarded as a principal, and treated with a fair amount of deference.

Laurence answered, curtly enough :

" What do you mean ? "

" I ask you for an explanation, Mr. Raxford," repeated Captain Athorpe. " I don't see that you have any reason to make yourself at home in my niece's cottage—and I dispute your right to be there."

" Why ? "

" Why ! " almost shouted Athorpe—" why, because she is a girl as completely alone in the world as she is in Wind-Whistle Cleft, and if I didn't look after her, no one else would. Because she is young and pretty, and there are men who prowl after good girls' souls, just as if they held commissions from the devil. Because I know the world—I have knocked about in three-fourths of it—and I am sceptical of much good in it. And because I don't know *you*."

" If you knew me better you would trust me more."

" I don't believe that," contradicted Athorpe. " The more I know of a man the less I like him, as a rule. Showy and bright at first, occasionally, but on close inspection full of flaws. Now, you have no right to be in Milly's cottage, or seek Milly's society. She is a good girl—I don't think that there's a better anywhere—and I would not have her head turned by any flatteries from those above her in position. I promised her mother—though she was no friend of mine, mark you—that I would watch over the orphan whom she left behind in the Cleft, and I always keep my word."

Laurence bowed to the good intentions of Captain Athorpe; he respected them, and would assist them.

"You are right to demand an answer from me," said Laurence, "and if you had not been so hasty I would have given it you long ago. I made my first appearance at the Cleft to-night in the character of guide to Mr. Whiteshell, who had lost his way."

"Your first appearance?"

"Yes."

"And how many times have you spoken to Milly?"

Raxford coloured again at this cross-questioning, but the darkness in the Cleft spared his indignant blushes.

"I saw your niece for the first time this evening."

"For the first time in the Cleft, you mean."

"For the first time in my life, Sir," said Laurence, sharply; "and now, if you please, we will dismiss the subject."

"Very good. But as she works at the mine, and is superintendent of a batch of girls there, it don't seem very likely that you——"

"Good-night," said Laurence, suddenly striding on in advance of the doubter, and making off at a rapid pace along the narrow footpath. He thought that he had freed himself from this obnoxious being, and had asserted his own dignity at the same time, when Captain Athorpe came on after him, taking two strides to his one, and gaining on him rapidly, greatly to the annoyance of our hero, who had prided himself heretofore on being a rapid walker. He had a great mind to run for it, but his pride resisted an undignified retreat, and after a few more paces he allowed his persecutor to overtake him.

Captain Athorpe came swiftly upon Laurence, his heavy feet crushing down everything in his way, and a few minutes afterwards he laid a hand that fell like lead on the shoulder of the young man in advance of him.

"Wait a bit. I did not think that you were a bad-tempered man."

"You would try the patience of a saint, Athorpe."

"There, I believe all that you have told me. If I did not put my questions gracefully, why I am not a graceful man, and that must be my excuse. I am watchful and suspicious of most things."

"That must make you very miserable at times."

"It may—at times," he repeated; "and now you are a hot-headed fellow, like myself. That's singular."

"I am not hot-headed, Athorpe. It takes a great deal to aggravate me, and if you will consider the question at your leisure you will find that I have had to swallow a great deal to-night."

"There, we'll say no more about it. I don't dislike *you* at present. There's a something in you which perhaps I *might* like after a while," he added, thoughtfully.

"Thank you," was the dry response.

Captain Athorpe laughed not unpleasantly.

"Ah! you don't know what a compliment that is, Mr. Raxford," he said; "and now about your hot temper—take my advice, and don't give way to it any more."

"I tell you——"

"Yes, I know. No man is aware of his own imperfections—that is a strange truth, which puzzles me still, as well as other people. I used to be a very hasty man, but I've mastered myself with a strong hand."

Laurence thought of the shot that Captain Athorpe had fired in the Cleft that night, but held his peace to avoid further argument.

"You would not think to look at me—to judge by what you have heard of me at the mine, or from Mr. Fyvie, or old Waters at the office—that I had ever been a desperate character—a man whom nobody trusted, and whom everybody feared—a reckless, extravagant, half mad, drunken vagabond."

He stamped on the ground with every epithet that he bestowed upon himself, as though he would stamp the shame of his past life beneath the surface as he walked.

"No, I should not have thought that."

" What would you have thought ? "

" That you were a very steady, hard-working, honest, obstinate, conceited fellow," answered Laurence readily. That was his opinion of Captain Athorpe, and he very coolly expressed it.

" I don't consider myself obstinate, only firm now and then," said Athorpe quickly ; " and as for conceit, that's a lie. But I wish that you would hear me out—I think that I'm worth listening to."

" I am all attention," answered Laurence.

" I think that I make a decent sort of moral to young men like you. Most men in my place would have never *wrenched* themselves back to an honest temperate life. I was steady enough in your father's time, when Wheal Desperation was a bad speculation—but when I went abroad I went wrong, all at once, all manner of ways, possessed by unclean spirits. I don't know that I ever shirked my work—for I took no man's money under false pretences—but after the work, Mr. Raxford, I was a very brute—hated and feared as dangerous brutes are."

" And what saved you ? "

" Half a dozen things—a shock to my system, as I stood in peril of my life being dashed away from me with only a moment left to ask God to forgive me—the example of a man as good as I was bad, and one of my own set—the rescue from danger, and the sudden consciousness that came over me, showing me how truly bad I was. I took an oath —I kept it—even the oath against drink, which was the hardest to hold on to and live. So never be hasty, Mr. Raxford, it's the outpouring of evil."

" I shall remember your confession."

" It's a confession I'm proud of—*conceited* about," he said with emphasis. " I returned to England a quiet man, engaged to one of the best of women—my wife now, Sir ; and so I'm thankful and at peace. If you ask in Tavvy-dale the character of Captain Athorpe you'll get a good one."

Yours was a hard fight, and a successful one. I begin to understand you, just a little."

" I am glad of that. No man likes to be misunderstood," said Athorpe. " Here's the rain again. We shall have these heavy showers all night."

"I hope that they will keep off until I get back to the mine."

"My house is at the opening of the Cleft, and if you will accept of a bed it is at your service."

"Thank you; but——"

"But you do not like to be beholden to your servants. Well, it is a good feeling."

"It is not mine, at any rate."

"That's a silly old fellow—that Whiteshell," said Captain Athorpe, darting off at a tangent to a new subject; " no harm in the man, but precious little good—that is, good sense, at any rate," he added with a jerk.

"Milly's uncle, I understand."

"Yes, on the mother's side," he replied disparagingly. "Softshell would have been the best name for that family —they were all addled, Sir, everyone of them. How Milly grew up so shrewd and quick a girl has always puzzled me. For even my brother—one of the Athorpe stock—had not his natural change, and was terribly obstinate."

The darkness of the Cleft disguised Laurence Raxford's smile, or Athorpe might have found fresh cause for offence.

"As for this Whiteshell, poor, poverty-stricken old ape, with his jumpings and grimacings, I can't say I admire him. Milly likes him, and I dare say he's fond of Milly; but his company for a week or two must be a terrible nuisance."

" With that impression it was very kind of you to offer your hospitality to the gentleman."

Captain Athorpe laughed.

"I did that to aggravate him partly, for he had been sneering at me enough; you saw that. He's full of sneers at people; he always was fond of that kind of game. I knew that he would never come to my house."

"Then your concern for the inconvenience to which Milly would be exposed by his stay there was not genuine?" Raxford could not refrain from saying.

"Yes, it was," was the quick reply. "I'm always genuine, thank God! And if he had come, I would have done my best to make him feel at home with us. Though I did not expect him to say, 'Yes'—though it was one of my jokes, the invitation—still I should have been flattered a bit by his acceptance of the offer, and he would have been none the less welcome at my house. But he was too proud, you see

—though what he has to be proud of you'll *never* see, if you live till doomsday."

" He has been in a better position of life, I imagine ? "

" A trifle better," said Athorpe ; " somebody left him five hundred pounds, and he lost it in a fool's way, as might have been expected. He hired a theatre at the fag end of a season, when nobody was in town, and the weather was as hot as fury, and away went his money at once. He fancied that all the world was coming to see him dance in his new ballet."

" Dance ? " repeated Laurence.

" He has been a ballet master—ballet dancer at the royal houses, cutting all kinds of capers in his life. He's a dancing master now," said Athorpe, with bitter scorn ; " struggling on in some back street or other, Westminster way, living from hand to mouth, poor wretch ! He'll dance his shaky old legs into the grave, and there will be an end of him. What an occupation for a man with a soul in him ! "

" Every one must live," said Raxford, " lucky for the world that even out-of-the-way professions have their ad- mirers. What a state of affairs if there were no dancing masters, Athorpe ! "

" All the better," said Athorpe ; " what's the good of dancing ?—it's a snare and a delusion—it leads to no end of harm. I won't have him teach Milly his dodges ; we quar- relled upon that point the last time he was here. Whew ! here comes the rain in earnest, Mr. Raxford. Shall we run for it ? "

" Is it far to the end of the Cleft ? "

" Oh ! no distance. It's no use standing under these trees, they're wet through already."

As he spoke, a flash of lightning, blue and vivid, lit up the ravine, bringing suddenly into relief the bold masses of rock lowering on either side, the oddly-twisted trees growing therefrom, the rich luxuriance of foliage above, around, and under foot, the stream below beset with many difficulties in its progress down the Cleft, and struggling against them with low murmurings, that went " on for ever."

" No ; I do not care particularly for trees just now," said Raxford, breaking into a run along with Captain Athorpe.

" You'll have to put up at the miner's house, Sir," said Athorpe, with a short laugh.

"I'm afraid that I shall be troubling Mrs. Athorpe at this time of night ? "

"We are not people who mind trouble ; and we can't let you go by us in the storm, though we're not always *genuine*, Mr. Raxford."

"You brood on words hastily uttered, Captain," said Laurence ; "and that is a bad habit."

"Well, well ; I am not a saint ; I never set myself up for one," was the reply ; "take me as you find me, rough and ready, quick to resent an affront, but just as quick to return a kindness, and there's Captain Athorpe to the life. I know my own character ; if other people knew me as well I should not have an enemy in Tavvydale."

"You have no enemy, I am sure."

"One or two make me out morose, ill-tempered, unjust, anything ; well, let 'em. What should I care for their opinions ?—what *do* I care ? "

"Exactly," answered Laurence, for the want of a better reply at the instant; "have we much further to run ? I shall be wet through before I reach your house."

Ere he could resist the attention, a thick bearskin cape, which Athorpe had been wearing, was flung from the miner's shoulders to those of Laurence, and twisted in a suffocating fold about his neck.

"I forgot that I had it on," said Athorpe, as Laurence struggled and protested ; "and you're a man who can't stand change like me. I've been in all kinds of weather, and nothing hurts me—nothing can hurt me, for I'm made of iron and brass. I won't take it back, so it's no good your wriggling like that, Sir."

Laurence protested no further. Captain Athorpe had shot on in advance, and it was impossible for Laurence to overtake him. At the mouth of the Cleft he was standing coolly in the rain, waiting for our hero's appearance.

"Yon's our home," he said, pointing to a house a short distance in advance, and which the lightning illumined for an instant; "we'll make a run across the open to it, when you've got your breath."

"I'm all right," said Laurence, "when you're ready."

"Oh ! I'm always ready. Now, Sir."

The two men ran swiftly across the wild grass or

moorland that sloped upwards from the Cleft, the lightning flashing about them, and the thunder reverberating overhead. When they were close upon the house, proceeding along a gravel path towards it, Captain Athorpe let the leaden weight of his hand fall again on the shoulder of his companion.

"I welcome you to an honest home, Sir. You do me honour by your coming."

He hammered with the handle of the stick he carried on the door, taking no heed of the dainty brass knocker ready to his touch. A maid-servant, evidently scared by the storm, with her eyes distended, and her cap awry, opened the door, candle in hand.

"Once more welcome, Mr. Raxford. This way, Sir; Mrs. Athorpe will be very glad to see you."

CHAPTER VIII.

CAPTAIN ATHORPE AT HOME.

MRS. OLIVER ATHORPE, warned of the visitor's approach, was standing in the front room prepared for company.

"This is my wife," said Captain Athorpe, by way of introduction—"this is Mr. Raxford, Inez, the new partner at the mines."

"Mr. Raxford favours our poor home indeed," murmured Mrs. Athorpe, glancing at our hero for an instant, and then looking down upon the carpet.

"Not at all, Mrs. Athorpe," cried Laurence; "rather say that Mr. Raxford is a very selfish man to intrude himself upon your notice at so late an hour."

"All hours suit us, Mr. Raxford," said Athorpe; "we are not regular people here. Sit down, please. Inez, where's the wine and brandy and things—and the cigars? Sit down, Mr. Raxford. It's not so poor a home as my wife would have you believe, you know," he added, with a comprehensive sweep of his hand; "but poor or rich, you're welcome."

It was a well-furnished room; in the eyes of the Devon-

shire captains who visited here occasionally, a grandly
furnished apartment, indicative of much pomp and pride in
their comrade. The furniture was good, if heavy, and
solid enough for the board-room of a public company—
consisting of tables and chairs of Spanish mahogany, the
seats of the latter covered with maroon leather, evidently
with an eye to wear and tear. The floor was carpeted
with a florid Brussels, and the walls were adorned with
several oil paintings, some of them looking almost old and
undistinguishable enough to be valuable. Upon the tables,
the side-boards, in the recesses by the fire-place, even in
the fire-place itself, and on the mantelpiece, were scattered
many incongruous ornaments, relics of Captain Athorpe's
wanderings—tusks of ivory, shells of odd shapes, sizes,
and colour, lumps of copper, lead, gold and silver ore, fos-
sils, dried plants, stuffed birds, a dagger in a sheath, a
bilious-looking violin, with quaint carvings up its back, and
in one corner the identical gun which Captain Athorpe had
let off in the Cleft that evening, with a very fair chance of
reducing the number of Milly's relations.

Laurence Raxford noticed the furniture and adornments
by degrees and at a later time, Mrs. Athorpe sufficiently
arresting his attention at the period of which we treat. A
lady of five or six and twenty at the utmost, and young
enough to have been Captain Athorpe's daughter—possessing almost as slight a figure as Milly's, but with less
ethereality about it, having but the advantage of height,
Laurence thought, as he mentally compared the two women
whom he had met that evening. Mrs. Athorpe was pretty
also—had he not had Milly's face before him still, Laurence
would have been struck with her olive skin, her raven
hair and eyes, the contrast she presented to the pure white
and red of the Devonshire complexions. It was scarcely
an English face, Laurence would have felt assured, had not
the accents of her voice already struck him as peculiar,
if not foreign. Still she spoke English well and clearly,
and it might be the Devonshire burr after all. She was
certainly a wife for a man like Athorpe to prize and be
proud of; and Athorpe thought so still, though he had
been married two years. Two years ago this lady, of whom
we are treating, had suddenly taken her place at his side
in the miner's chapel at Tavvydale, and become his wife.

Where she had come from, Tavvydale folks did not know, and those who sought to inquire were informed, not too civilly, by Athorpe, that she was an old sweetheart for whom he had been waiting many years, and who had been waiting many years for him—where she had waited, and why she had waited, was simply the business of Captain Athorpe and his wife, and so they ventured to tell the few daring enough to press them close with questions.

Mrs. Athorpe opened the doors of her mahogany cellaret, and speedily produced the alcoholic fluids for which her liege lord had inquired.

"Really, I am ashamed to see you make all these preparations," said Laurence. "This is evidently a conspiracy to detain me till the next shower comes on."

"This one hasn't gone off yet," returned Athorpe; "do you hear the thunder?"

All three stopped to listen, and Mrs. Athorpe added, "It's a dreadful storm. Mr. Raxford will not surely think of venturing to the Wheal to-night?"

"I have told Mr. Raxford we have plenty of room, Inez," said Captain Athorpe; "and he will change his mind, doubtless, if the storm continues, which it will. Mix for yourself, Sir, if you feel inclined to patronise the grog. Or will you try the sherry, with my wife here? It's as good sherry as the stuff at the mine, with which they would have made me drunk, if I had let them. Now, Sir, what *will* you take?"

Captain Athorpe, as host, was at his best. Under his own fig-tree, he showed and evinced considerable geniality. His roughness sat well upon him even, and was not ungraciousness. He was nervous whilst Raxford remained dry-lipped in his establishment; and Laurence, seeing this, hastened at once to mix some whiskey and water for himself.

Captain Athorpe watched the operation attentively, and his wife, with one small hand—on which were half a dozen jewelled rings—beating a quiet little tattoo on the cloth, surveyed the operator furtively.

"Cigars," said Captain Athorpe; "though I don't smoke myself, I keep cigars for those that do. Try the cigars, Mr. Raxford, whilst we have half an hour's chat together, about the business, or something."

" I seldom smoke," answered Laurence, with a glance at Mrs. Athorpe.

" Oh ! I do not object to smoking, Mr. Raxford," said Mrs. Athorpe, quickly ; " or I would not allow—under any pretence—a cigar to be lighted in my presence. Would I, Noll ?—Am I not absolute here, dear ? "

Captain Athorpe's face beamed with smiles, as he looked at his wife laughing across at· him.

" She gives me my own way in everything, and thus spoils me for the world wherein there's no chance of getting it," cried Athorpe ; " that's why I'm so bad-tempered out of doors, Sir."

" His own way ! " cried his wife, with an affectation of pettishness that was slightly foreign, Laurence thought again ; " why, Mr. Raxford, after all, my husband is a very tyrant here, and for peace's sake, I am amiable and good."

" A tyrant !—what in ? " asked Athorpe.

" In your rules and regulations, to be sure—in the order and management of this fine house — in housekeeping matters, which men are *so* clever in—and in the colours of one's dress even. Oh! quite a Blue Beard ! "

Captain Athorpe struck that heavy hand of his smartly upon his knee.

" That's good—that's good," he cried, laughing ; " see how patiently I can sit here, and suffer myself to be con- demned. Half a glass of weak brandy and water only, Inez, for the tyrant—I have had one glass to-night, and this is in excess. I'm a mind," he said, suddenly and gravely, " not to touch any more."

Mrs. Athorpe thought that it would not hurt him after the rain that he had been in, and Captain Athorpe offering no further protest, the glass of brandy and water was shortly at his side.

" A single man has a right to show his politeness," said Athorpe ; " but we old married fogies must not humour the fair sex too much, or we get imposed upon. Then, of course, we're tyrants."

He looked at his wife, and laughed very heartily again. A man who could laugh like that, and look like that at his helpmate, was not an unhappy man. This brusque in- dividual would improve upon acquaintance.

" Ah ! but the fair sex humour the married fogies, at all events—or what would become of us poor women, Mr. Raxford ? "

" That's a good——Have you had any supper ? " he inquired, with a precipitancy that made Laurence start ; " I quite forgot to ask. Inez, Mr. Raxford has only had a wretched bit of bread and cheese at the most, and I *think*," he added, ironically, " we have something better to offer him in this house. Where's that cold lamb ?—where's that——"

" My dear Athorpe," entreated our hero, " I never take supper as a rule, and I have already fared well, and to my taste, at your niece's cottage in the Cleft."

Mrs. Athorpe's dark eyes were full of life and interest suddenly. The miner's wife was equally vigilant concerning Milly, it seemed.

" Our niece's cottage !—have you been there, Sir ? " she exclaimed in surprise.

" A nice young man this, you see, Inez ? " said Athorpe, indulging in an emphatic wink at Laurence, " I hope that you will give it him well, for I made no impression upon him, save to arouse his temper. I told him that it was not quite the thing to pay visits to young ladies living in lonely huts down the Cleft, and that we were sponsors here for Milly, but he objected to my interference."

" You are joking, Noll," said Mrs. Athorpe, but still with evident uneasiness ; " you would not have brought this gentleman home, or been in so pleasant a mood with every one to-night, if you had found him at Milly's cottage. Now, Noll, dear, what is it ? "

" I found him in Milly's cottage—more, having supper with Milly."

Mrs. Athorpe's lips compressed. Her hands interlaced themselves uneasily, and one or two joints more rigid than the rest cracked ominously. She sat there, looking very thoughtful for a while, no one offering to break the silence, and Laurence leaving the joke—the point of which he did not see very clearly—to the promoter of it, sitting with great complacency in his easy chair opposite.

" At supper with Milly at that time of night," said Mrs. Athorpe at last, " I did not think that Milly was so foolish and imprudent." Detecting a smile playing upon the

features of her husband, she said more eagerly, more
sharply, "Noll, surely it is not possible — you haven't
allowed—you cannot think it right that Milly and Mr.
—Mr. Raxford, I think you said—should form any en——"

"Hold hard, my dear!" shouted Captain Athorpe in
his alarm, "that's a wrong conclusion and a foolish one
—don't jump at it and hurt everybody's feelings. Ha! ha!
that's too good a joke—how quick you women are! Ha!
ha! that's something like a joke—what would Milly say
to that, I wonder?"

"It is a joke that we have carried far enough, Noll," said
Mrs. Athorpe very pettishly; "you should know better than
to tease me so."

"Well, I'm a brute—I always was a brute—ask the
good souls in Tavvydale what I deserve, and you'll guess
what an unutterable savage I am then," said Athorpe.
"I'll not tantalise you any further, Inez. My young friend
here, sitting so patiently under suspicion all this time, has
been acting as guide to a friend of ours to-night."

"What friend?"

"The old fellow of whom you've heard me speak more
than once—Milly's Uncle James."

"James—Whiteshell?"

"Yes."

"Milly's uncle," she said thoughtfully—"Mr. Whiteshell?"

"Yes, I said so."

"Indeed! And he is staying at the Cleft with Milly,
you say?"

"I didn't say so, wife, but he is, for all that. He'll have
a fortnight of it, and then go home with the horrors in
full blow. He's a queer old stick. He would not come
here at any price—I tried him, but it was no use. Mr.
Raxford says that I was not genuine in my invitation, but
I was. I meant what I said—if I don't admire the old boy,
I would have saved Milly the trouble of boarding and
lodging him; but he don't admire me either, and that's
awkward and humiliating. Mr. Raxford, do mix for yourself
again. Inez, see to Mr. Raxford's glass."

He pushed the whiskey bottle across to Laurence, who
shook his head and held up his glass half-full of the potent
fluid still. Mrs. Athorpe woke up suddenly as from a

dreamy unconsciousness of passing things, and assumed an animated manner on the instant, that puzzled Laurence, and even embarrassed him.

Yes, she was undoubtedly of foreign extraction, thought Laurence—sprightly, naïve, and interesting, betraying a trifle too much anxiety about the whiskey not being to Laurence's taste, an exaggerated fear that the water had not been hot enough, or that Mr. Raxford did not like whiskey, or was debarring himself the satisfaction of a cigar out of compliment to her, who liked cigar-smoke *so* much! She was not happy—it made her despair to see Mr. Raxford *so* abstemious—would he attempt a second glass of whiskey and water, if she mixed it for him, after a method of her own, of which she was a little vain— really?

"She mixes grog like an angel, Sir," affirmed Captain Athorpe, with becoming pride; "I should not have asked you to mix for yourself, with Inez—princess of all mixers —in the room. Clear away Mr. Raxford's luke-warm wash, girl, and take no denial. We may never have the honour again of a principal's company—and we'll tyrannise over him, now that he's in our power."

"The rain has abated, I think," murmured Laurence, by way of an excuse to withdraw.

"It's like the deluge outside," said Athorpe; "can't you hear it?"

There was a pause at this appeal, and the heavy rain without made itself heard on the instant, rushing and hissing furiously. The thunder rolled heavily along too, as they listened, and the lightning flickered behind the window blinds, and, like a spirit of unrest, was not still an instant.

"It's a terrible night, and Mr. Raxford is our prisoner. Say you surrender, Sir," she said.

She laughed, and shook her head at him, almost with a girlish sauciness. Yes, foreign decidedly, thought Laurence again—Frenchy, and inclined to overdo her style. She was very pretty, thus animated and evidently conscious of her prettiness; but the uncharitable impression seized Laurence on the instant, that all those little shrugs and attitudes and smiles were not so much impromptu as studies from the life, and before a dressing-glass. He did not like

6

her manner—take it altogether—and he was not quite cer tain that Captain Athorpe looked quite as amiable as he did a few minutes since.

"I think I had better borrow your bear-skin, and make a run for it, Captain," Laurence suggested.

Captain Athorpe shook his head.

"We wouldn't turn a dog out on such a night as this," he said. "Inez, when you have mixed that fresh whiskey, will you see that the best room is prepared for Mr. Raxford?"

Inez would see to it with great pleasure in a few minutes —but she must not be disturbed now—not for all the world —in this spirituous compound before her.

"There, Mr. Raxford!" she said at last, triumphantly; "when I come back, I anticipate all kinds of compli- ments."

"Oh! certainly," said Laurence; you may rely upon me."

Mrs. Athorpe departed with a musical laugh, and as the door closed behind her, Captain Athorpe turned immediately to our hero.

"What do you think of her?"

"Who?—Mrs. Athorpe?" asked Laurence, taken aback for an instant by this leading question.

"Yes. Is she not a bright, lively girl, of whom any man might be proud?"

Laurence felt compelled to respond in the affirmative.

"And she is always the same, Sir," said Athorpe, with a beaming face; "just the wife for me—just the wife I thought that I should take long ago, if I ever married and made myself a cheerful home. I come back from my work at the mine, half mad with rage at all the fools under me, who don't know their business; I come back full of a bitter gloom, that feels like a load upon me—and which isn't natural or to be accounted for, but there it is—and always here I feel the gloom go back, and the rage all melt away! It's then I feel it not so hard—for it is hard work sometimes—to be religious, for I'm chockfull of grati- tude! You understand me?"

"Perfectly."

"I dare say you think I'm an old fool—for I'm going on for fifty sharp—to talk like this. Well, I don't talk very often in this fashion, for I've a habit of keeping my thoughts to myself. I was an old fool, everybody hinted, to marry so young a wife—but I knew my own mind, and I knew Inez to be a good girl."

"Is Mrs. Athorpe an Englishwoman, may I ask?"

"Her mother was French—I knew her mother," replied the captain. "I was a long while making up my mind to marry, you see, for I thought it scarcely fair on my little housekeeper—a brave, bright, and good girl, that Milly!"

"She was your housekeeper, then?"

"Yes, till I married; then she went back to her father's old crib in the Cleft—a little place that Mr. Fyvie settled on her after my brother's death in his service. She's just as happy there as she was taking care of me—she's a girl that is happy anywhere."

"Who is that?" asked Mrs. Athorpe, entering.

"Our Milly," answered her husband.

"Oh! happy enough, I dare say," carelessly remarked Mrs. Athorpe.

Laurence fancied again that the red lips were compressed together, for an instant, and that a shade of seriousness settled upon the young wife's face.

"She is a happy-looking girl," commented Laurence.

"Do you think so?" was the quick answer of Mrs. Athorpe. "And pretty, of course? All men think Milly pretty."

"Yes, she is very pretty," asserted Laurence.

"I never saw it myself," she said, tapping the table again with her nervous fingers. "White and red, like a doll, certainly, but that's all."

"My wife was always inclined to be jealous of Milly, Mr. Raxford," laughed Athorpe. "You know what critics women are of each other, I dare say?"

"Jealous of Milly!" cried Mrs. Athorpe, indignantly; "not I, indeed. I only smile sometimes to hear her over-praised. It is this over-praise which has made the girl so vain—so far above her station. You know that!"

Athorpe scratched his head nervously.

"No—I don't," he ventured to assert. "She's independent, self-reliant, brave, but she isn't vain. And she keeps the louts at arm's length; and well she may, for a more

6—2

clumsy, or thicker-headed lot of clodpoles than we have at
Tavvydale, I never hope to meet."

"Mr. Raxford does not wish to sit here all night, Noll,
and listen to the praises of your favourite," said the wife.

"I dare say not! but I am an old bird with two chicks,
Mr. Raxford, and you will excuse my crowing over them
for once. Just try that whiskey, now. Hanged if you
won't let *that* get cold next, Sir."

Laurence drank the whiskey, and pronounced it admirable. Mrs. Athorpe smiled again, and said that he was
only flattering her, and that she was sure that Mr. Raxford
was a great flatterer—a terrible man.

Laurence went up to his room shortly afterwards, Captain
Athorpe leading the way, with a candle in each hand, like a
host of the old school.

"There, you'll sleep well, Sir, if the thunder will let
you," said Athorpe, placing the candles on the dressing-
table. "Good-night to you."

"Good-night."

When Captain Athorpe went into his own room, he
nearly fell over the skirts of his wife, outspread across the
carpet, on which she was kneeling, with her hands before
her face.

"Inez! why, what's the matter?"

Inez rose hurriedly, and with an agitated face.

"Nothing, Noll, dear, I was praying. Praying for you
and me to be always happy together. I don't think so—
oh! I don't believe so sometimes."

"Why, what has upset you—the storm, or the grand
company we have had, or that one glass of sherry at which
you sat sipping like a bird?"

"The company, perhaps. I don't like company—I am
always happy here alone, and strange faces upset me, Noll.
You know how sensitive and nervous I am."

"Well, yes."

"It's very kind of you to ask Mr. Raxford, and for him
to come. But we can't make a friend of him even if we
wished."

"We're as good as he is, if we're not so rich, girl. And
he's a man I think that I could take to. There's a straightforwardness in him that pleases me—it's something like
my own!"

"Yes, but we don't want his patronage—it's no use to us, and we're above it," she said ; "and you're so soon vexed and dissatisfied, that presently you and he would quarrel—I know that—and then *that* would damage your position at the mine."

"I'm not afraid of my position, wife. Noll Athorpe is considered worth his money anywhere."

"But you are quarrelsome. You don't deny that yourself. The less you see of a man, the better friends you are with him."

"That's true as a rule," said Athorpe thoughtfully, "and of course I don't think of asking Mr. Raxford here again."

"And—and this Mr. Whiteshell ? "

"Ah! what of him ? "

"I am so glad, so very glad, that you did not bring him home with you, dear Noll—you would have quarrelled with *him*, you know."

"Yes—that's probable, I must say. He'd vex a saint in no time."

"And then home would have been less happy, and you would have liked it less."

"No—I think not, whilst the woman I loved made it bright with her smiles, Inez. There, we'll keep no company, and ask nobody to see us—I think we are happier by ourselves, myself."

"I'm sure we are."

Captain Athorpe was in bed and fast asleep, a few minutes afterwards. He remembered being woke by a rattling peal of thunder an hour and a half later, and opening his eyes he discovered that his wife was sitting up in bed at his side, with her hands clutching her elbows, and her figure swaying slowly to and fro, as though its owner were in pain.

"Inez—Inez—what's the matter ? Aren't you well ? "

"I am afraid of the storm, Noll. I can't sleep to-night —and yet, I — I think I must have dozed off sitting here."

"And woke up in a fright with the thunder—that's it. There, lie down and shut your eyes again. Good-night."

"Good-night Noll," she repeated, lying down at his side thus adjured ; but when Captain Athorpe was sleeping heavily again, the restless woman silently struggled into a sitting position once more, and resumed that train of thought—whatever it might be—from which he had disturbed her.

CHAPTER IX.

MR. WHITESHELL IS LEFT TO HIS OWN RESOURCES.

LAURENCE was up early the next morning, but Captain Athorpe was before him, and ready with a breakfast which our hero had hoped to escape.

"You will excuse my wife," Athorpe said, "when I tell you that she slept badly last night. She's a nervous excitable woman, and the storm was a little too much for her."

"Pray make no apologies," said our hero. "I am afraid that I detained you both to a late hour last night."

"Not at all. We are not very early people at any time," said Athorpe; "sit down, Sir, and make yourself at home. You will not think anything of Inez's absence?"

"Certainly not."

"She knows well enough what is due to a guest—she is well-bred and well-born," said Captain Athorpe; "we both are *au fait* at all that, for we have mixed in society in our day—both having been travellers. What do you think of our place here?"

Laurence, taken aback by the question, thought, however, that it was a nice comfortable home.

"Ay, that's the phrase," said Athorpe, "a nice comfortable home! Well, I'm proud to say it is. I worked up for it and Inez, and there it is, and some money to back it in Tavvydale Bank. If I was to go suddenly out of the world —as my elder brother did, Milly's father—I shouldn't leave Inez so badly off."

"That must be a great satisfaction to your mind," said Laurence.

"It is," answered Athorpe; "and seven hundred and

fifty pounds isn't a bad sum to save for a man like me—
and all this grand furniture too, mind. You can see that
that cost money."

" Oh ! yes—I can see that."

" Very good, then."

Athorpe gulped down his coffee after this at a rapid rate,
and as five was striking by the eight-day clock on his stairs,
the mining captain and his principal sallied from the house
towards the mine.

All the way to business, Captain Athorpe was frank and
communicative ; he was a man who disguised nothing that
morning ; who, having made a certain way in life for himself was proud of it. He earned a hundred, or a hundred
and fifty pounds a year at Wheal Desperation, and that
contented him, and raised him above his fellows. He was
vain of his superiority, his position in the mining village
of Tavvydale, but there was a rough simplicity in his self-
conceit that was not disagreeable to witness, when once the
man was thoroughly appreciated. In Tavvydale, too, he
had done good in his day ; and if he were not admired or
always thanked for his good deeds, it was owing more to
the rough manner, or the ill-temper of the giver, than to
any want of effort on his part to deserve people's gratitude.
There were times when he was *almost* understood, and then
everything was marred by some harsh words or ungenerous
suspicion. He was only at his best within his cottage at
the opening to the Cleft ; but as he kept no company, and
as the few who knew him came only on business there three
or four times a year, Captain Athorpe had not been seen
at his best, save by his wife, his niece, and Laurence
Raxford.

The day was bright and fine, after the heavy rain, and
as they struck into the high road within three quarters of
a mile of Wheal Desperation, they came upon the miners,
and their wives and daughters, from Tavvydale, flocking
towards the several mines amongst the Dartmoor hills.
Those who were of Mr. Fyvie's community touched their
caps, or dropped their curtseys, to Laurence and Captain
Athorpe, wondering a little at the propinquity of master
and man.

One man of six feet three in height at least, loose-
limbed and awkward, sandy-haired, and with a face so full

of freckles that it looked as though he had dipped his
head into a pailful of them, touched his cap with the rest,
though Laurence felt assured that the young giant did not
belong to Fyvie's mine.

"Marning, Captain," he said to Athorpe; "she be on
yander."

He grinned from ear to ear, and jerked his thumb in the
direction they were going.

"Morning, Churdock," answered Athorpe; "and who is
she?"

Churdock blushed like a girl, but he laughed like a
horse at this question.

"Why, you know—o' course. There she go."

"Who—Milly?"

"Es—es."

"Then why the deuce didn't you say so?"

"I did. She's as spry as a lapwing this marning. She
got company at the Cleft."

"Oh! you know that, too. You didn't get a shot in
you last night, did you—humbugging about there in the
dark?"

"Who?—Oi? I warn't there."

"When were you in the Cleft, then?"

"This marning."

"What's the good of *you* being there?—it isn't your
way home, or near your home, unless you climb the
rocks."

"Noa," answered Churdock, beginning to grin again, and
then becoming suddenly very serious, "it isn't."

"And as nobody wants you there, you must be a bit of
a nuisance."

"That's true, Captain, I'm afeard," said Churdock, looking fiercely at the ground — "I don't say that ain't
true."

"Ah! you're a poor mite," said Athorpe, striding past
him.

"And that ain't true neither," shouted Churdock after
the Captain; "and you know better."

"So I do," said Athorpe to Laurence, as they walked on
at a good pace towards the mine; "but it's as well to
freshen him up a bit."

"Who is he?"

" One of Mill'ys admirers—a fellow at Clifford's mine—
—Bully Churdock we call him in the village. Milly could
lead him anywhere by holding up her little finger; but
the devil himself couldn't drive him, if he was of a different
opinion. He's our representative man in Tavvydale—we
pick him out to do the wrestling in the Cornish matches;
he's so clever at the kicking."

" Ah! I remember. You kick in Devonshire?"

" When we're hurt, especially," was the dry response.

" Are you a Devonshire man, Captain?"

" Yes—born in Tavvydale too; and though I have
wandered many thousands of miles away from it, here I am
once more, and settled down for good. I've made up my
mind not to go five miles from it again."

" A rash resolution, which may be altered by circumstances, Athorpe."

" Not that," said Athorpe, confidently; " I never found
much comfort out of Devon; I should feel going wrong—
going back to all the harm from which I have escaped—if
I left Tavvydale. So I stop, Sir, for ever!"

He stamped his foot upon the ground, to give force to
his assertion; and judging by the hard expression of his
face, it seemed possible that nothing could take him from
his birthplace, or was likely to shake for an instant the
resolution he had formed. And yet he spoke rashly and
untruly, as men confident in a future that is hidden from
them always speak.

" And here's Milly," he added, coming up with our
heroine, who, in her cotton dress, stout shoes, and flapping
bonnet, was well disguised enough, until she turned her
smiling and blushing face towards them at her uncle's
salutation. She curtseyed again to Laurence—an act of
deference on her part that made Laurence blush in his turn,
although he had almost grown accustomed to the reverence
of the peasantry by this time.

Milly had been walking very rapidly towards the mine,
and with a brighter colour on her cheeks, looked prettier
than ever.

" You did not take a holiday to-day, Milly," said her
uncle; " that's a good girl, who knows her duty too well to
shirk it. What's that old frog going to do all day to amuse
himself?"

Laurence noticed that the colour deepened still more on Milly's checks.

"Uncle James, you mean," said Milly; "oh! he will amuse himself very well till I return this evening—a little contents him and makes him happy."

"I suppose he'll fish in the stream there. It's a fine day for it."

"I don't think that he likes fishing—he gets low-spirited over it, he says."

"He's not always in the best of spirits. A fortnight in the Cleft, Mr. Raxford, generally floors him—he left here three years ago more of an idiot than he came."

"It's a great change from town—and he's so much alone here. I—I thought of asking to-day for a week's leave, Mr. Raxford," she said, looking at Laurence for the first time.

"No—I won't have that," interposed Athorpe; "you must not spend a whole week in idleness — losing money, too, at your age, with health and strength to work for it."

"He's getting old, and needs companionship," said Milly; "and he has been always like yourself—a good friend, and very dear to me. I don't see much of him, and I—I know that he's happy enough when I am with him. Why, I make him happy"

"He should know how to amuse himself without taking up your time," grumbled Athorpe; "I don't see the use of it —it's sheer waste, Milly."

"I shall make up for lost time—I always do that," cried Milly; "and I haven't had a holiday this year. But if you really think it kind to let him stay there by himself—just as lonely as you were before Aunt Inez came home and I had gone back to the Cleft—why, I'll—I'll not ask for leave."

"Your uncle can't think that, Milly," said Laurence; "that's not like him, and so the holiday is granted."

"She must ask Captain Peters, who's the surface captain, and he'll lay it before Waters, who'll knock off twelve shillings for it—that's the rules. You must not interfere over people's heads, young man, for it isn't a partner's business, and makes enemies."

"Very well," laughed Laurence; "but they shan't knock the twelve shillings off, at any rate."

"Yes, they shall," jerked forth the uncle; "if we don't

do our work, we can't take any money. I think, Milly,"
he added, with a short laugh, "we are independent enough
for that."

"Yes, Sir, to be sure," cried Milly, flushing again; "it's
very kind of you, Mr. Raxford, but I—I don't want twelve
shillings. No—it's only the holiday—a week's sunshine in
the Cleft for Uncle James."

"Milly *is* independent, you see. Well she may be, with
money in the bank like her uncle. So much money, that
all the young fellows are running after her, Mr. Raxford,
and pretending that it is for her good looks. Why, she has
saved ——"

"Ah! what with my little savings and the money which
my uncle banked in my name on his marriage-day, I'm quite
an heiress!" cried Milly.

"If she didn't waste so much money on books—though I
don't mind her reading books—if she didn't set up for a
geni—*us*, Mr. Raxford."

"Ah! now you are going to speak ill of me, and I am
only fond of your praises, like a selfish niece as I am. I'll
not hear any more—I'll run and coax Captain Peters before
the rest begin to tease him."

Milly darted away, and Captain Athorpe turned with a
grim smile upon his world-beaten face.

"Spoilt a little—fond of her own way more than a little—
but really a good girl."

"Doubtless," asserted Laurence.

"And a clever girl, too; though I sneer at her outlandish
ways, just to keep her down a bit. You would never guess
what a lot that girl has taught herself, or how she works
night after night at all kinds of studies that can't be any
good to *her*. She's proud, you know; and though its
objectionable at times — and aggravating," he added, his
brow furrowing as though a disagreeable reminiscence had
shot across it, "still it's right to have a good opinion of
oneself, and it keeps *her* right. Why, here she is again."

"Oh! uncle, I have forgotten to ask a favour of you!"
cried Milly, returning as quickly as she had departed.

"What favour?"

"That you will not be angry with me for lending your
violin to Uncle James—I told him that he might call for it
if he was dull to-day without me."

"That's cool at any rate," said Athorpe; "how do I know whether he can play it, or whether he won't break it? You might have told him to call to-morrow, and not have taken French leave with *my* property."

"Ah! you'll not be cross about that, Uncle Noll," cried Milly; "you never play now, and he must practise, poor gentleman! Aunt Inez will let him have it when he tells her who he is, and why he has come."

"If she believes him," said Athorpe. "Well, mind, if he breaks the thing, he must pay for it. I never liked lending anything."

"Especially an ornament like that, uncle," said Milly archly; "a saffron fiddle, with a wreath of buttercups carved on it."

"There, be off, you hussy. You have some of old Whiteshell's impudence this morning as well as your own, or you're trying to show off a little before the master here."

"Oh! uncle," and Milly hurried away now in real earnest, and was seen no more by Captain Athorpe that morning.

Meanwhile Mr. Whiteshell was already thinking of Captain Athorpe's violin as a means of distraction until Milly's return. After his niece's departure, he had closed the door of the cottage behind him, and skipped down the green slope to the path along which he had forced his way with Laurence Raxford yesternight. Turning from the direction of Captain Athorpe's cottage, he had sauntered, with his hands behind him, still further up the Cleft, following the turnings, windings, ascents, and declines in the path before him, and not paying a great deal of attention to the beauty around him, the wondrous wealth of picturesqueness which at every step revealed a new feature of light and shade, and colour. A wild and striking loveliness about this Wind-Whistle Cleft—a loveliness all its own, distinct in features from a Devonshire valley, a Welsh glen, or a Cumberland mountain pass, and yet possessing the attributes of all three allied to its own originality. Narrow, confined, and tortuous this Cleft in most parts; a place where the wind found considerable difficulty in escaping, and moaned strangely in its efforts at times, thereby accounting for the appellation which had clung to it for more generations than we wot of. Shut in by hills on either side—hills clothed with every form of verdure—hills, rugged, bare, and frowning, from which the verdure had slipped below the path, and formed an under-cliff ending with the stream; and hills from which shot a very forest of trees, all gnarled and twisted in their efforts to catch the light, or to evade the wind. On a dull day the place was dark enough, but on so bright a morning as this, following last night's storm, it seemed like an entrance into Paradise. The sun's rays were struggling through the foliage to gild the stream below; there was a gentle fluttering of every leaf with the soft breeze astir there; and every bird of song in Devon seemed to have fluttered to the Cleft that morning, intoxicated with joy and harmony.

All this did not suggest itself to Mr. Whiteshell; he was a man who regarded the Cleft lugubriously, and had not a love for the country in his heart. The sudden change from his own home had not had that beneficial effect common to total changes; he evidently breathed no freer for the contrast everything presented to Milk Street—a close and dirty locality, abutting upon Tothill Street, Westminster—he was a man who loved town, and clung to its associations.

"I *never* saw such a place as this is," he groaned to himself. "It makes one very miserable."

He stood deliberating with himself as to the expediency of proceeding further up the Cleft, shook his head, relieved himself by a heavy sigh, and retraced his steps to the cottage, taking the key from his pocket and unlocking the door cautiously.

"The simplest thing in the world to have got in here during my absence and robbed the house; and then have waited till I came back to finish the job by cutting my throat. It's all very well for Milly to say that nothing of the kind happens in Devon—strange things happen everywhere."

Mr. Whiteshell looked round him, assured himself that the place was as he had left it, sat down and tried to find a book that would suit him from Milly's store in the recess, gave up the attempt, and emerged into the Cleft again, locking up as before.

"To think that a man fond of society should ever come here for a change!" he muttered, by way of self-reproach, as he set off again, this time in the direction that Laurence and Captain Athorpe had taken last night. He had Captain Athorpe's violin on his mind now; he was partial to the violin, and somewhat clever with the instrument, and his objections to the mining captain were not so strong as his anxiety for a little musical distraction on his own account.

But after two or three hundred yards' progression, he brought himself to a full stop again, and stood in his favourite and Napoleonic attitude, with his hand behind him, looking on the ground.

"I don't see," he said, throwing his head back suddenly, and drawing himself up as we novelists have it, to his full height—which thus drawn up was exactly five feet two, "I don't see why I should ask a favour in that quarter, and perhaps have it refused me. If the wife is anything like the husband, I shall only find myself insulted. No, I don't see it."

Not seeing it after this grave deliberation, Mr. Whiteshell changed his tactics, and slid with considerable celerity, like a fawn in a shabby suit of black, from the path to the very edge of the stream—a stream fretting, murmuring, and foaming against the many obstacles in its way. It had been at war with the hills that hemmed it in from times remote to all men. It had fought its way like truth, and found its way like it to the broad haven; but it had fought hard and well, and had still to fight occasionally. In the winter months the hills dislodged yet huge pieces of rock, and hurled them at the stream, which for awhile, half blocked in its career, and disturbed by opposition, paused to gather force, to swell with its restraint, and then to glide round them, making a new way for itself, but for ever afterwards murmuring a reproach at these intrusions on its quiet life. There were rocks and islets, with the trees growing on them still; here and there, with the trees broken down, and falling across the water, where they whitened, and became moss-stained and lichen-covered — altogether as disturbed and blocked a mountain stream as ever gave beauty to an English valley. Mr. Whiteshell picked out a boulder of a few tons weight that had missed a watery grave by an inch or two, and after spreading a silk handkerchief thereon, gave a spring, took a seat, drew his knees up to a level with his chin, and clasped a pair of thin bony hands around them.

"Perhaps some one will come to fish presently, and then I can talk to him—or a maniacal artist, or a tourist, or a something."

Mr. Whiteshell waited almost patiently for these objects of interest, looking at the water and its rock-strewn bed meanwhile, wondering if the fish found it inconvenient to turn so many corners, and then suddenly doubting if there were any fish at all there.

"I never saw a fish, not even a stickleback," he said, disparagingly. "I expect it's not lively enough here, even for fish."

Mr. Whiteshell seemed inclined that morning to burst into little soliloquies, or it was an invariable habit of his to think aloud. Still nursing his knees, and presenting a grotesque appearance in the landscape, he said, his thoughts evidently reverting to Milly—

"I hope she'll obtain her holiday. That will make it more amusing for me—and she promised, whenever I came again, that I shouldn't be low-spirited. She's very good—and I'm very selfish—but I hope she'll get her leave. That Mr. Raxford won't like to say no, after eating so much of Milly's bread and cheese."

Then he must have continued to think of Mr. Raxford, for presently he said, nodding his head at the water, which was his only confidant—

"I don't know that I ever met with a man I liked so much. He put himself a good deal out of the way to oblige James Whiteshell, and so James likes that man."

That being fully accounted for to the satisfaction of the speaker, he thought very naturally of Captain Athorpe, who had looked in to inquire the reason of the noise at Milly's cottage ; and then finally he came round again to Captain Athorpe's violin.

"I think I'll just call and put the question delicately," he said ; "I'd rather ask Mrs. Athorpe—I'd rather ask the devil," he added irreverently, "than that crab-apple of a man —that ill-mannered incongruity. A more uncivilised, unpolished, disrespectful, objectionable, three-cornered wretch, than Captain Athorpe—Captain, indeed !—I never met in all my life. I don't say, Milly," he went on, as though Milly was by his side, and had entered a protest against his verdict, "that your Uncle Athorpe hasn't a good trait of character ; but as it is no business of mine, as I don't want to see it, and should have to put up with all his bad traits before I got to it, or understood it, why let him keep it to himself."

It relieved Mr. Whiteshell, this imaginary dialogue. Milly never cared to hear Uncle James's opinion of Uncle Oliver, but always checked it, and endeavoured to turn the conversation; therefore it was pleasant to speak out for once all that was in his thoughts, though he had no listeners but the rustling trees which shadowed him and the water rushing and rippling round the boulder on which he was heaped.

"Aren't you dead yet?" he quoted from Captain Athorpe's last night's address to him. "What a greeting to put to a man whom he had not seen for three years, come next July. I'll not borrow a violin from such a man as that."

Mr. Whiteshell grew very red in the face, whilst brooding over the indignity that had been offered him—he was a man who stood upon his dignity, and plumed himself upon the courtesy of his address to others. There was an odd old-fashioned gentility about the man, born of his profession, that elicited amongst his London neighbours a certain amount of respect towards him, and rendered the incivility of Captain Athorpe more apparent.

"I've come a long way, and spent a good deal, to be insulted like this," he said, "just because he's saved a little money, too. I won't have his fiddle. Where's my handkerchief, I wonder."

The old gentleman, depressed in spirits by his late indignities, or the solitariness of the Cleft, found tears in his eyes, and desired to wipe them away. But the handkerchief was not in any of his pockets, and was not discovered till he rose to go away, when he found that he had been sitting on it all the time.

"I have got the horrors stopping here," he said; "I'll try another walk. I knew that I should get them in this place—I said so last night—I always catch them. It's a miserable locality—not a living creature within a mile, I'd wager a sixpence."

He climbed up to the path, examined his boots, which were muddy now by reason of his excursion to lower ground where the last night's rain had settled, tried one sole by touching it with his hand, evidently possessed by the grave doubt that he had been reckless with his shoe-leather, and then went on in the direction of Uncle Oliver's cottage. Half way from home, Mr. Whiteshell was relieved by the sight of a living and reasoning being, sauntering in his direction, and swinging a roll of paper in his hand.

"Here's a gentleman out for pleasure, poor thing," said Whiteshell, "I'll take the liberty of bidding him good-morning. It may be a relief to him to hear a fellow-creature's voice."

Mr. Whiteshell brightened up at the prospect of society, and as the gentleman approached, raised his hat in that formal and stiff-backed way, which had already astonished Laurence Raxford. The gentleman raised his in return, responded to Mr. Whiteshell's good-morning, looked somewhat hard at him, and then gave vent to the extremely English interjection of "Hollo!"

Mr. Whiteshell stooped at this sign of recognition, but failed to call to mind the features of the gentleman confronting him.

"Really—I have not the pleasure," he said politely. "I don't think that it is possible in such a hole—place, to be recognised by anybody, simply for the reason that nobody thinks of coming here."

"I never forget faces. Your name is Whitesmell, and you used to live in Milk Street, Westminster. I was in Westminster five or six years ago, making inquiries about a new Ragged School there. You were good enough to assist me with a great deal of information."

"Whiteshell—not 'smell,'" corrected the gentleman addressed, before replying to the latter part of the preceding remark. "Quite right, Sir—I have had the pleasure of a fleeting acquaintanceship with you. I was struck—very much struck with your energy and arguments—so young a man interesting himself in so good a cause. But," was the dry rejoinder, "we never got the schools, Sir."

Mr. Engleton took off his hat, and ran his gloved hand through his wiry hair.

"No, not yet, you haven't," he said, a trifle disturbed by Mr. Whiteshell's peroration. "A parcel of fellows, parsons, and those sort of men, wanted to form a committee, and shut me out of the management — to object to half my ideas as unnecessary, profane, revolutionary, and all that bosh. And I worked very hard too, to bring the thing about."

"I think, Sir, that that idea of yours concerning dancing

7

—teaching our poor, ragged bits of humanity a little of the
graces of life, as well as its sternest lessons, an idea border-
ing upon genius."

"Dancing? Ah! yes, it was a good idea," said Mr.
Engleton, complacently : "but of course everybody objected
—everybody always does. But upon my honour, now I
come to think of it, I'm very sorry if, in any way, I raised
hopes of a situation for yourself. I was premature in my
ideas—my own enthusiasm carried me away, in fact, and
possibly embarrassed others with myself."

"Well, I *was* a little hopeful," confessed Mr. Whiteshell,
"for you spoke as though it was all settled. But when you
never favoured Milk Street with your presence again, I, being
a bit of a philosopher, and used to disappointments, did not
grieve much."

"That's right, old man," said Engleton, cheerfully—
"that's true philosophy. I intended to have written an
apology to you, but it slipped my memory."

"Pray don't mention it," said Mr. Whiteshell, raising his
hat at the intended compliment. "An apology was neither
required or expected, Sir."

"If in any way you were—anything out of pocket," suggested Mr. Engleton.

"Which I was not—which complaint has not been my
misfortune hitherto," said Mr. Whiteshell with becoming
dignity. "I am a man in a humble walk of life, Sir, but I
pay my way, and can afford now and then to take my tour
in Devonshire, you see."

"Indeed. I'm glad to hear that. I should like all the
poor in London to have their tour once a year," said Engleton enthusiastically—" to get up monster excursion trains,
and float themselves for a day or too into the pure air, and
sunshine. I have had this idea some time. If we could
obtain a few thousands of generous contributors, now, it
might be carried out to some extent."

"I should be happy to add my subscription," remarked
Mr. Whiteshell, rather pained to think that his appearance
had suggested the idea of poverty taking its holiday, and
desirous of disabusing Mr. Engleton's mind of that impression as speedily as possible.

"Oh, thank you," said Mr. Engleton, surprised by this
reply. "We must consider the project presently."

" An artist, I presume, Sir ? " said Mr. Whiteshell, with a glance at the roll of paper in Mr. Engleton's hand.

"Not at all," was the reply. "I'm sketching out a little ground-plan for a row or two of cottages in this Cleft. I'm looking for an eligible site."

"A row or two of cottages," cried Mr. Whiteshell. "Ah ! that would be a blessing here. Some chance of society then."

" If I could only find an eligible site. How far does this Cleft extend, Mr. Whiteshell ? "

" The Lord knows ! I've never been to the end of it. The further you go the more awful it is—that's all that I can say."

"Awful ! I never met with a more beautiful spot."

" Spots depend upon taste," said Mr. Whiteshell ; "if you're fond of damp grass, it's a splendid place."

" You know that girl's cottage, half a mile further on, I suppose," said Engleton, leaning his back against a tree springing out from the rock, an action imitated by Mr. Whiteshell, whose heart leaped at these signs of a long stay in the vicinity.

" That girl being my niece," replied Mr. Whiteshell, "and that cottage being my resting-place for the next fortnight, I should think I did."

" Oh ! indeed," said Mr. Engleton ; "well, there's a site in that quarter, if I can persuade Mr. Fyvie to allow it to be built upon. Are you at all handy at plans ? "

" Not what may be called a first-rate hand," evasively answered Mr. Whiteshell, who had never had a plan before him in his life.

" You know what small-roomed houses are, and how poor people swarm in them, irrespective of health, decency, or anything else ? " said Mr. Engleton warmly. " Now look here, Mr. Whiteshell. This, I take it, is an improvement."

Mr. Engleton unrolled his ground-plan—an outline sketch or diagram, with little dabs of pink and blue in divers places, which caught the eye of Mr. Whiteshell at once, who asked what they meant.

" I'll tell you, if you'll be quiet a moment," said Engleton ; and then the two went into the subject, Mr. Whiteshell not at all interested, but clinging to the expounder for company's

7—2

sake.　A spice of selfishness in the old gentleman's character has already been remarked ; here it appeared again after its odd fashion.

Mr. Engleton, a shrewd young man in his way, very quickly perceived Mr. Whiteshell's lack of interest, or knowledge, and rolled up his sketch again.　He was going further along the Cleft to make a few measurements, and Mr. Whiteshell did not volunteer his services—in fact, was thinking of the Athorpe violin again, and whether it would not be better company than this reformer.

"May I ask you, Sir, before you resume your highly important studies, whether you are acquainted with Captain Athorpe—or have taken any notice of Captain Athorpe's cottage at the opening of the Cleft ? " asked Whiteshell.

"The cottage I know—Captain Athorpe I do not."

" May I trouble you again ?—may I venture to ask if you have observed the lady at that cottage ? "

" Yes, I have—what of her ? "

" Does it strike you, speaking more confidentially, "that she is a bad temper—irascible—a woman who would—who would snap a man up with hard words, for instance ? "

Engleton laughed.

"Why—have you a favour to ask, Mr. Whiteshell ? "

" It may be considered a favour, certainly," answered the other.　" I ask it in my niece's name, not in mine, of course."

" Well, I don't think that you need fear," said Engleton. " She is young and foreign-looking.　I think I remember knocking at the house you mention for the loan of a pencil, to replace one which I had lost on my way, and it was proffered me very gracefully by Mrs. Athorpe."

" That's a good sign—you were a stranger, I suppose ? "

" Quite a stranger."

" That looks very well," asserted Mr. Whiteshell, taking in another button of his coat, and pulling his hat firmly over his brows.　" I thank you," he said, taking his hat off the instant afterwards in salutation ; " you relieve my mind, for I cannot face discourtesy in any shape.　It upsets me."

" Good-morning," said Engleton, feeling compelled to raise his hat in return, and rather annoyed by this elaborate formality.

" A moment, Sir," cried his companion.　" Will you allow

me to hazard one more inquiry ?   That pencil—was it returned ? "

Engleton gave a fillip to his ear with his rolled up
plan.

"N—no, it wasn't.   I quite forgot it.   I am afraid I have
a bad habit of forgetting things."

Mr. Whiteshell remembered the Westminster Ragged
School, with the dancing accompaniment, and inwardly coin-
cided with Mr. Engleton.

"If you have a spare pencil in stock, it might be a little
introduction," suggested Mr. Whiteshell.

"Upon my word, you are as frightened of the ladies as I
am," cried Engleton, "but—unfortunately, I have but one
pencil with me."

"No matter," said Mr. Whiteshell coolly ; "I'll take your
apologies for the omission, if you have no objection.   Sir, I
have the honour to wish you a good-morning."

Hats elevated again, and then the gentlemen proceeded
their separate ways—the elder one tripping along with considerable agility until within sight of Captain Athorpe's
cottage, when he came to a full stop, and reconsidered the
question.

"I don't think I'll ask for the violin after all," he said
aloud ; "it's an old thing, and very much out of order I know.
Why should I expose myself to the humiliation of a refusal
from an Athorpe ? "

He appeared to decide the question by turning his back
upon the cottage, then it was once more reconsidered—bringing Mr. Whiteshell to another full stop.

"Still I don't see it, if I require relaxation in the place—
and it would be a pleasure to Milly to hear me play, and I
might teach her a fashionable dance or two before I left the
Cleft.   Because these Athorpes have saved up a paltry
hundred pounds or two, are they so much better than I, or
has it made their blood equal in purity to mine ?   Here
goes ! "

Mr. Whiteshell wheeled round and went off at a rapid
pace, straight ahead this time, waiting for no man, and no
man's resolution ; proceeding onwards with a very red face,
and looking fiercely behind his bushy white moustache.   The
click of the latch of the garden-gate did not deter him,
neither did a vigorous application of the little brass knocker

make his heart sink. He was prepared for the worst, but he hoped for the fiddle.

The door was opened, not by the servant on this occasion, but by Mrs. Athorpe herself.

Mr. Whiteshell raised his hat.

"Madam, my name is Whiteshell. I have taken the liberty to ——Inez !—Good God—is it Inez Bouquié ? "

"Hush ! " cried Mrs. Athorpe. "I did not think to see you—I had hoped——Come in, Sir, and let me ask you to be merciful and silent, for an old friend's sake."

"Merciful ! " repeated the dancing-master, vaguely, as he followed her into the sitting-room — the best room — of Captain Athorpe's grand house.

CHAPTER X.

OLD FRIENDS.

MRS. ATHORPE dropped into a corner of the substantial couch, and wringing her hands silently together, looked down at the carpet; Mr. Whiteshell, with his own hands clasped together also, took a seat facing her, and looked intently—almost pathetically—into the face averted from him.

"To think that I should find you—you of all women—in this house—of all houses in the world."

"Yes, it is strange," she murmured ; "but I have been waiting for this discovery, expecting it, and praying against it. You will not be hard with me ? "

"It is no business of mine—it is not my nature to be hard with anybody," replied the dancing-master.

"I have settled down here for good—for very good, I hope, old friend," she said, almost coaxingly, "and am doing my best to make everybody happy. Mr. Whiteshell, I have succeeded—I have learned to understand myself better since I saw you last."

"Ah ! the last time that we met you came to me, a wretched girl, for advice ; you were greatly troubled, and I did my best to talk to you as to a daughter whom I loved, to warn you of the folly and danger of a new companionship. But Inez, you were wilful, and had your own way; and I prayed that you might see your error before it was too late."

"I did," cried Inez, quickly, "and I was saved. I did not forget your warning—the warning of the dear old master who had been ever kind to his little Inez, his favourite pupil, his daughter—and salvation came, just as you prayed it would. There was no harm—oh! Mr. Whiteshell, there was never any harm from the beginning to the end. My pride stood my friend as well as you, and there really was no harm!"

With every reiteration of this statement, she looked eagerly into the face of her companion, and at every protestation held her hands towards him, imploring, as it were, that he should trust her. As he still looked at her with that strange, perplexed, and pitying look, which altered not at her appeal, she became more agitated and solicitous.

"I was very young and vain, but my heart was strong, old friend," she cried. "Fond of admiration, and of the applause that came to me night after night, and made me giddy, but always on my guard, remembering the fate of many like me, and seeing many sink away from right without an effort of their own. If the temptation came to me in my turn, why, I was stronger, and knew better, and however the envious might rail against me, I was still strong in self-defence. There was no harm from beginning to end —no harm, James Whiteshell, so help me God! There, you will believe me now"

"Yes, I believe you. I am very glad. But the man——"

"When it came to the parting with him, and he faced me with his duplicity and craft, I flung him off and never spoke to him again."

"Where is he now, poor girl?"

"Abroad—some people say dead. I don't care which myself."

"I should think not, now," said Whiteshell; "you are the wife of Captain Athorpe, of Wheal Desperation. I always thought that you would make a good and cheerful little wife, but I never dreamed that, sobering down, and setting aside all girlish vanities, you would have chosen a man so opposite to yourself in everything. Are you happy?"

"Very!"

"He is kind to you, then?" asked Whiteshell, doubtfully.

"He is very kind—for he has every confidence in me."

"I am glad to hear that—if I am surprised," he added, his old dislike to Captain Athorpe peering out here despite him, "I rejoice none the less at your assertion. And he knows all?"

"He knows nothing," she answered, sinking her voice to a whisper. "I met with him in France, where I had flown from temptation, and he took pity on my loneliness; and full of trust in him, my mother's friend, I promised to become his wife."

"But your stage life, have you told him anything of that?"

"No. He would not have married me if I had. He had a horror of plays and players, engendered by a past acquaintance with them; he had seen much of the world's evil; he was almost sceptical of any good when I first knew him. But he became very generous and noble—we did not marry in haste—and I thought that it was worth a struggle to win him, and do my best to make his home and life happy. Until to-day, thank God, I have succeeded—now you come, and I can't see my way."

"Do you think that I would betray you?" asked Whiteshell, reproachfully. "I would only advise you again, Inez, to your own good."

"Well?" she said inquiringly.

"I would tell him all, I think."

"You do not know what a hard, suspicious man he is," she said, "how uncharitable to every one but me, how different from every man whom I have met, how unforgiving of a wrong or a deceit, however innocent the deception may be. We are both happy now; let us keep so to the end."

"He is certainly eccentric," mused Mr. Whiteshell. "You are right, perhaps, though I don't advise you, understand, to secrecy. I never liked secrets; they explode at the wrong time, and cover everybody with ignominy."

"You will not tell him anything—you will not come here, or, coming here, profess to have known me before to-day? That is all I ask of you, my old master, friend, and father."

She leaned towards him, and took his withered hands in hers. The dark eyes were full of tears, but the face was expressive of more hope now.

"I promise that," he murmured.

"And you will not tell that girl?" she cried eagerly.

"What girl?" asked Mr. Whiteshell.

"That Milly. She is very quick, and a chance word would give her the clue to my humiliation. She does not love me in her heart, and might be glad of——"

"Hush! hush! Mrs. Athorpe. This is the old jealousy, which you have not got rid of with the new life—which has been always in the way You don't like Milly?"

"Yes, I do," she answered, petulantly. "I like her for herself—I like her because *he* likes her, because she is earnest and true; but she is not kind and loving to me, her uncle's wife. She is not what I expected."

"In all my life," asserted Mr. Whiteshell, "I never met with a girl so good, pure, and unselfish!"

"You think so now?—you thought so once of me, when I was your favourite."

"But Milly——"

"Oh! Milly is very good in her way," said Mrs. Athorpe, carelessly; "I know nothing against her, except her odd pride in herself, and in that uncomfortable home of hers. And we agree together pretty well, and after all *I* love her. When do you leave the Cleft?"

"In a fortnight."

Mrs. Athorpe sighed. It was a long holiday—a long time to wait before she could breathe freely. Mr. Whiteshell noticed the look, and was quick to reply thereto.

"You are sorry that I leave no earlier—you don't trust me, Inez."

"Don't say 'Inez' again—it may become a habit with you, and appear strange to others. No, I am not sorry— the change will do you good, and I can trust you."

"Yes, you can."

"I heard that you were at the Cleft last night," she said; "and have been fearful of this meeting. Now my heart is at rest, and I am glad."

"That's well. And I'm glad, too, girl," he replied; "for

I find you mistress of a comfortable home, and anxious to remain so. All the old caprice, the flightiness, shall we call it, and the little vanities subdued—or gone?"

"Gone," said Mrs. Athorpe; "I have settled down!"

"That's well," he said again; "that's very well."

"Hush! now. Here is my servant coming back from Tavvydale, and I am Captain Athorpe's wife, who is in doubt still as to the reasons for your coming here."

"I called with Milly's love, to borrow your husband's violin," explained Mr. Whiteshell; "Milly thought that it would amuse me whilst she was away. Do you think that an objection would be urged in *any* quarter, now?"

"Not any," said Mrs. Athorpe, taking the violin down from the wall; "it is an old-fashioned instrument enough; and my husband never plays it—it is in good hands at last."

With a grace that was evidently inborn, Inez Athorpe placed it in the hands of the old dancing-master, whose face brightened up at her praise.

"Ah! if it hadn't been for so many years of jig-tunes, I might have been a professor, and earned my ten guineas a night at solos," he said, with a sigh, as he turned the violin over in his hands; "but I was content with quadrilles and galops, and was never particularly ambitious. You remember——"

"No, no—I remember nothing, Mr. Whiteshell!" she cried; "and you—have you forgotten?"

"True. I am corrected. Who was that came into the house just now?"

"My servant."

"Keeping a real servant, too!—well, I congratulate you —and happy with Captain Athorpe—why, I shall think better of *him* after this. What an excessively ugly violin this is, to be sure!"

Mrs. Athorpe laughed very merrily at this. Her spirits had risen again, and she was like herself—like the Inez whom Captain Athorpe had ever known.

"You must not say that, for my husband prizes it for its ugliness, or its antiquity, or something."

"Not choosing his violins on the same principle that he has chosen his wife," said Mr. Whiteshell, quite gallantly; "there, you see that I am still a courtier, In——"

"Yes, yes. And you will go now, Mr. Whiteshell. God bless you for your confidence in me—for believing all that I have told you," she said, in a lower tone; "above all, for your promise to respect the motives for my silence. Now there is nothing in the world to sigh for."

"Glad to hear that, for it assures me how content you are—you, the wild, restless being that you were! Good-bye."

"Good-bye. Think of me in London now and then."

It was a hint to come no more to Captain Athorpe's cottage, and he accepted it as a hint that was worth respecting, for the sake of her future relations with a man whom she had more or less deceived.

He took his departure somewhat thoughtfully, with the violin under his arm, and the bow swinging between his finger and thumb. Truth was stranger than fiction; and it was very strange that the girl in whom he had been deeply interested years ago—who had vanished away from his life like a dream figure—should start up amongst the Devon-shire hills, the wife of the man whom he disliked and who seemed, to his imagining, the man the most unsuited for her, of all creation. He, stern and hard and unpolished, and she fretful, capricious, vain, and childlike; and yet happy together, those two. It *was* strange!

She was capricious certainly; he would have thought so still, could he have seen her after his departure. The ordeal had been passed successfully, and she was safe, and luxuriating in her safety. Sufficient for the day had been the evil thereof; the weight off her mind, she felt free as the air again, and happy as the birds that dart through it. She opened the piano in one corner of the room, and dashed off into a light waltz tune, singing the while; she closed the piano, but continued to sing as she moved about the room; she was humming softly the same tune when she stood on tiptoe on the hearth-rug smiling at herself in the glass above the mantelshelf, and congratulating herself on her good looks, as well as her good fortune.

Half an hour afterwards, the April nature of the woman had changed again; and she was lying on the couch, face downwards, with her hands before her face, weeping silently and bitterly.

CHAPTER XI.

CROSS-QUESTIONING.

MR. WHITESHELL, still in a ruminative mood, proceeded towards the house in the Cleft. Within the last hour had arisen a distraction from the thoughts engendered by his solitude, and he gave way to it as he wandered homewards with a step less light than usual. He had .the day before him—the day all to himself in the Cleft—and there was no occasion for haste. When he reached the tree against which he had set his back to talk with Mr. Engleton, he assumed the old position, raised the violin absently to his shoulder, and gave two or three dismal scrapes across the strings with the bow.

"Poor girl—or lucky girl, it's very doubtful which," he said. "I have always called her poor girl, until to-day— little thinking of the escape which she had had. Lucky girl to be Oliver Athorpe's wife—hum!—it's not a nice berth, take it all together, but still lucky for her. So we let the past between us float away with less noise than that suicidal stream below there—and of all the wretched instruments of music that have ever been in my hands, this is the worst and harshest. I'd back a sixpenny fiddle from a toy-shop to possess more harmony than this thing. It's like its master, every inch of it," he grumbled ungratefully; "and to carve all this rubbish on its wainscot back, too."

Another scrape or two, and then a burst of musical laughter in his ears, followed by a clapping of hands.

"There, now he is happy," cried Milly; "quite at home, even in Wind-Whistle Cleft."

"What, you here, too, Milly!" cried Mr. Whiteshell, brightening up. "How did you manage it?"

"Why, I asked for my holiday, and it was granted at once," said Milly. "This day into the bargain, somehow."

"Somehow!" repeated her uncle.

"Yes. I think Mr. Raxford arranged it, though I did not ask him, or expect a favour from him. That is the **worst** of gentlefolk, uncle."

" What is the worst ? "

" They don't like to be indebted to us even for shelter from the rain, without making a return. Captain Peters told me at twelve o'clock that I need not wait any longer, and I am almost sure Mr. Raxford spoke to Captain Peters."

" Very kind of Mr. R. He's the only good tempered native I have seen yet in Devonshire. Everybody's cross here—I suppose it's the cider."

" Why, did you ever see me cross ? "

" Ah ! you're the exception to the general rule, sauce-box," said Mr. Whiteshell ; " who was thinking of you, do you think ? "

" What else have you had to think of except your spoilt Milly ? " asked our heroine.

" One or two things ; it has not been an uneventful day," said Mr. Whiteshell, thoughtfully.

" And you had the courage after all to secure the violin ? " she said, as they wended their way back to the cottage ; " well, my aunt did not frighten you very much, I hope ? "

" Not much," responded he.

" Was she kind to you—really ? "

" Is she not always kind, then ? " asked Mr. Whiteshell quickly.

" A little variable at times," said Milly, " but soon turned by a word to be kind — that's the best of Aunt Inez. But," looking down grave and thoughtful, " I wish she liked me with all her heart, just as other people do."

" Conceited minx to fancy so," cried Mr Whiteshell ; " who are the other people, Milly ? "

" Oh ! everybody," she said, laughing ; " I don't know why—I don't ask them why—I don't deserve it. I'm a vain, conceited, stuck-up, ignorant, pert young woman."

" Mercy on us, what a criticism ! " exclaimed her uncle, " and you look as grave as if you believed it yourself."

" So I do," she replied ; " and that is why I don't deserve so much affection from my friends. I'm above my station, and full of grand ideas—such funny ones at times, turning my poor head round and round anyhow ! Some of them down in Tavvydale see that well enough, and yet they have the courage to love me all the same. Isn't that wonderful ? "

Mr. Whiteshell chuckled at the look of surprise, the round eyes and pursed up mouth of Milly Athorpe.

"Truly surprising," he said, however ; "and you believe in everybody's love for you except in your aunt's, then ? "

"Oh ! I did not say that aunt disliked me," cried Milly ; "I don't believe that. I have fancied more than once that I have not judged her fairly and honestly, but still I have thought—now and then—that she has not been exactly kind to me."

"What made you think so ? "

"I don't know—I can't say—I'm a poor little girl without a reason to offer. I try to make her like me, and Uncle Oliver long ago made me promise to like her, which I do."

"With all *your* heart ? " asked Mr. Whiteshell.

"Yes, with all my heart," she answered confidently.

"She agrees with your Uncle Oliver ? " said her companion, as they went up the slope towards the cottage.

"Yes, and makes uncle's life bright. She's a merry little thing, and can play the piano and dance like a real lady. I wish I could dance—I feel as if I ought to dance in the very gladness of my independence in this dear old home to-day."

"It *is* a home to dance for," said Mr. Whiteshell ironically as he passed into the cottage, removed his hat, and sat down heavily in the first chair by the door, "but you shall dance in it for all that before I leave the Cleft, Milly."

"We will have rare fun whilst you are here, uncle, for this is my holiday as well as yours," she said ; "we'll be as happy and as busy as my bees outside."

"Ah ! those beastly bees," said Mr. Whiteshell, "I can't go near them by twenty yards but what they fly at me. You have actually got another hive, too, I see."

"To be sure—each hive's a little fortune to your Milly. They buy all my honey at the great house, uncle."

"Very kind of them—I wish they would buy the bees," he said.

"Something has put you out this morning, Sir," said Milly, pausing to regard her uncle more attentively ; "you are always sharp and hard when anything has disturbed you. What has happened ? "

"Bless the girl—nothing," cried the alarmed relative ; "I'm not sharp to-day—I've spent a charming morning ; seen all the scenery, been down by the stream there, sitting on a damp rock building up my castles and my rheumatism, bit by bit, my dear. But there, lay the dinner cloth while I tune up your uncle's violin, and give you an idea of the music fashionable in town, and on all the barrel organs."

Mr. Whiteshell began fiddling away at once—darting into all kinds of street melodies—operatic selections of old times, when he had musical ambitions—snatches of extempore madness, quaint and dreamy, with which he became absorbed himself, forgetting time and place and listener, until the latter roused him at last by her warm commendations.

"Oh, it's very beautiful," said Milly; "how can you do it? What a lucky idea it was of mine to think of the violin!—how the holiday will pass now! Why, that's a nice instrument, after all."

"It improves upon acquaintance."

"Yes—it's like its master," said Milly archly.

"Why, you heard me in the Cleft, then?" said Mr. Whiteshell, surprised. "Now, that was too bad, to listen to my mutterings! What else did you hear?" he asked uneasily.

"Nothing else, except your harsh and wicked verdict on my Uncle Noll. Now, for that, Sir, you shall learn to love my uncle before he goes away. I have warned you already of the task that I have set myself."

"We'll say that he improves upon acquaintance, too," said Mr. Whiteshell. "I'll not be hard upon the man. I don't know him, and he don't know me. There, granted that, Milly, for I can't bear malice or hatred in my heart."

"I'm sure of that."

Mr. Whiteshell set aside his violin, tucked up his coat sleeves, rubbed one hand against the other, drew a chair towards the table, and sat down, beaming with smiles. The possession of the violin, and Milly's return home, had brightened his thoughts, and he was a very amiable relative after that, full of affection and anecdote, and presenting the best side of his character to the light. It was a cheerful little dinner-party, for Milly was delighted with her holiday, and pleased with the presence of her Uncle James, for whom she had still the child's affection. It pleased her to see him at his ease, nodding and smiling across the table at her, and assuring her that he had never felt more happy;

that he was very glad he had come to the Cleft—regard-less of expense, and the complaints of a few pupils, who had begrudged him any change—to see his sister's child again. It was a duty, and, in the fulfilment of it, he was delighted. He insisted upon the port wine being produced, and drink-ing Milly's health in it, and Milly drinking his; and after two glasses of port wine he was happier than ever.

"I really think the country is looking up a bit," he affirmed.

"Would you like to see the Cleft cascade this afternoon? After last night's rain it will be beautiful."

"Thank you. I'm not so anxious for cascades as all that," he said with a shudder. "I'll rest here till the evening, at all events—and give you your first dancing lesson, Milly."

"Oh, that was only my jest. I don't think Uncle Noll would like me to learn dancing; it displeased him when Aunt Inez showed me the waltz step—and he warned me of you three years since. He thinks dancing a frivolous amusement."

"Very likely. I don't suppose that he's much of a dancer himself. But you, Milly, have a right to seize every accom-plishment that turns up. You are a girl with your way to make in the world. Why, how old are you?"

"Eighteen, uncle,"

"Eighteen!" said Mr. Whiteshell. "Dear me, how the time flies! And I thought that I was coming down here to look after a little, lonely child, left moping in a valley. Eighteen years of age!"

Milly had cleared the dinner-table by this time, and could devote her whole attention to her uncle. She curled herself at his feet, clasped her two hands on his knees, and looked up into his furrowed face.

"Isn't it dreadful," she said, "to think that I am getting old!"

"Why you'll be thinking of a husband, next."

Milly shook her head, and laughed. Oh! no—that was not very likely, she said.

"I don't know that," said her uncle gravely. "I have known girls younger than you get such thoughts into their heads. But then they were very forward, audacious young things, you know—brought up with no true sense of decorum. What are you laughing at now?"

"Why, Uncle James, I'm afraid that I'm one of those audacious young things myself."

"Come, come; we won't have that! You don't mean to tell me——"

"Yes, I do. For they made me think of being married, and of sweethearts, and of all those sorts of things—oh! nearly two years and a half ago."

"Eh?—who did—when was it?"

"Somebody wanted to marry me, when I wasn't sixteen —just after your last holiday in the Cleft, when you went away low-spirited. I was quite frightened at the offer at first, but I've got used to being courted since, Sir."

"I dare say you have," said Mr. Whiteshell, pathetically. "Poor girl, so your troubles have commenced; and people actually come all this way, and down this miserable gully, to make love to you? Tell me about it, and rely upon a man of the world for the best advice, my niece."

"Well," said Milly, in a business-like way, beginning to check off her lovers on her fingers, and looking very pretty during the enumeration, "there was Bully Churdock began it, and——"

"Who's Bully Churdock?"

"A big goose, that minds his old mother's house on the great hill at the back here; he works at another mine amongst the Dartmoors, and, oh!" with a merry, ringing laugh, "he is awkward, and bashful, and very fierce to any-body who comes this way! I dare say it was he at whom Uncle Noll shot last night, for he will play at hide-and-seek in the Cleft; and he is so good-tempered in his clumsy way to me, that I do pity him—there!"

And to Uncle James's amazement, the tears came suddenly to Milly's eyes, and were brushed away by an impatient hand.

"Why, Milly, dear, surely you—you have been seriously thinking of Mr. Churdock?"

"No, I haven't—not seriously," said Milly, quickly; "but I feel sorry for that big giant of a man getting me in his head and confusing his brains. He had no right to think of me, and *bother* me," she added, pettishly; "and he should have been satisfied with my 'No;' and gone away after other girls more suited to him, and that would have liked him in time—for he's not a very great stupid when you

8

know him thoroughly, uncle. But, oh! dear, he won't go away, and although he never teases me, and seldom speaks to me now, yet I know he's watching me, and that makes me as wretched as himself."

"He must be a nuisance," mused Mr. Whiteshell. "I— I think that I should speak to the police—this may become serious."

Milly laughed at this.

"Why, we have only one policeman in the village, and Bully Churdock told him once that if he looked his way he'd crack him like a nut."

"What a savage!"

"But then Bully had been drinking, and it was feast-time," said Milly, "and poor Bully always takes too much at that time, and I'm afraid at others now. And that makes me cry a little, to think that perhaps I drove him to it, for I couldn't marry him!"

"I should think not," said Mr. Whiteshell; "you deserve a better fate than to become a Mrs. Bully."

"I wonder, now," said Milly, looking up again, "what *is* to become of me!"

"Ah! how many of us wonder like that!" said the old man, suddenly verging on the pathetic. "If we could only look ahead and know—and be all the more miserable for knowing, most of us."

"I shouldn't," was the quick reply.

"Why not?"

"I should prepare for it, if it were misfortune—teach myself with all my strength to bide the day when it would come. And if it was good fortune, why, I should be more satisfied than I am."

"But I thought you *were* satisfied."

"Why, so I am in my way," said Milly, cheerily. "I have nothing to fret about, and it is nice to be liked by every-one, after all."

"And who else has liked you, Milly—I mean in the Bully Churdock style?" asked her uncle.

Milly recommenced her calculations.

"There was the young man at the chapel next—you'll see him next Sunday, when he stands up and gives out the hymns, opening his mouth like a young blackbird, uncle. It's very wicked of me to say so, but I always think of the little birds that I feed in the spring—orphan birds, left alone in the Cleft like me."

It was remarkable how Milly darted from one subject to another—how one thought suggested another, and carried her away from the first topic of conversation, bearing her in a sentence from grave to gay, and the reverse. Probably her lonely life in the Cleft, with but few opportunities of conversation, was partly the reason for this. The old man watching her, thought of Mrs. Athorpe at this juncture, of her variable and impulsive nature in the old days, and fancied that perhaps it was best for Milly to live alone in the Cleft. And yet Inez had never been like Milly; she had been more watchful of the world in which she had been cast, more womanly and old at the age of this girl, kneeling there before him, as loving, innocent, and almost as child-like, as when he had seen her three years since. Mr. Whiteshell had his faults, but a want of affection for his niece was not amongst them. He stooped and kissed her, saying :

"Not alone, with old Whiteshell living, Milly. No more alone than he is, with you to think of in his front parlour in Milk Street. But Mr. Blackbird—what of him ? "

"I did not say his name was Blackbird, uncle," said Milly, all sunshine again; "how oddly you bring things round. His name's Hawkins, and he has property of his own."

"And you don't like him or his property ? "

"Not at all—though he leads the singing at the chapel."

"Very good—any more of them ? "

"One or two," said Milly, pouting ; "who had nothing but their impudence to back them—mining people, that were good enough to think of me, but whom I could never like. Why, uncle, I feel myself too high for all of them at times, and it makes me wicked and proud. It's the books, I know—but I cannot give them up, for they are dear old friends of mine."

"Nothing like a good opinion of yourself, Milly," said Mr. Whiteshell ; "I like a proud woman, not so proud of herself as of her good name, and her position in the world, wherever it is—even in the Cleft, for the matter of that."

"And Milly Athorpe has a good name, and is proud of it, and will strive all her life to keep it," cried his niece,

8—2

enthusiastically; " but still," sinking her voice, and looking dreamily before her, " she wonders now and then what will become of her!"

" I hope," said Mr. Whiteshell, very gravely, " that you haven't one idea in your head?"

" What is that?"

" That you are pretty enough, almost scholar enough, to marry a gentleman. That is the most dangerous thought —the most delusive snare—that can trouble a girl in your position, Milly. I have seen so many—so very many— build this folly up in their weak brains, until it made them fit for nothing good."

Milly coloured very much, but her eyes were not lowered from her uncle's gaze.

" I may have had a kind of dream that I knew would never come true—a dream of a HERO," Milly confessed; " but I have laughed at it myself in waking."

" There is no gentleman about here—no man calling him- self a gentleman—who dares to speak to you, or to hint in any way that you are very, very pretty, Milly? No one anywhere above you in position whom you feel that you could love?"

" No one whom I could love amongst the real gentlefolk," cried Milly, lightly; " upon my honour, uncle, no. The real young gentlefolk that I have met once or twice in life," said Milly, with her red lips quivering with scorn, " have told me to my face what gentlemen they are, and how poor girls like me should flutter at their compliments, and thank Heaven for the good looks which have lured such graudees to jest with us. No, no, amongst all of *them*, not one for Milly Athorpe—I think, Uncle James, she is too proud for that."

" Bravo!" cried her uncle; " I think so too. Books haven't done you any harm, if they have taught you to respect yourself, and be chary of great men's compliments; they are the best of books that warn without ensnaring—I'll look them over presently."

" It is not the books now," said Milly. " For we have gentlemen about here sometimes—at least they call them- selves gentlemen, and wear black coats—and we have some foolish and vain girls, and then comes scandal in Tavvydale —undeserved sometimes."

"Which picks out the purest for its shaft now and then —well, you are better in the Cleft than in the village, if the last is a mischief-making place."

"Oh! but I go down in the village to fight the battles of the falsely-accused," said Milly; "and I have a school-class on Sundays—and we are very busy down there always."

"A lively place occasionally," said Mr. Whiteshell, drily; "villages are regular nests for fretful gossips, and I dare say you have enough to do, if you interfere with other people's business. Give me the violin, my child, and let us change the subject."

"I don't think that I'll learn to dance," said Milly, thoughtfully; "I feel too serious to-day. Dancing in my position of life, after all, is not an accomplishment that I shall want."

"Perhaps it's as well," mused Mr. Whiteshell, taking the violin from Milly's hands. "I won't press the point; it's not worth thinking about, and you're not naturally awkward, my dear. There's a lightness and gracefulness about you that reminds me of my early days, when I was a ballet master, and earned fair wages."

He dashed into some lively dance music which the reminiscence conjured up, and Milly sat and listened to him, gathering together her usual good spirits in the hearing, and finally seizing the tune and humming it along with him.

"That was very popular thirty years ago, Milly," he said, looking across at her.

"Any one could dance to that, if the heart was light enough," cried his niece.

"I begin to think that this is a splendid instrument," remarked Mr. Whiteshell, quite enthusiastically, and still in the heart of his tune.

"How bright it makes the place—oh! why shouldn't I dance? I'm happy enough now, uncle, and all the gloomy thoughts have flown away for good. Can any one waltz to that tune?"

"I can make a waltz tune of it," said her uncle, suiting the action to the word; "but what do you know of waltzing?"

"Did not I tell you that Aunt Inez showed me the waltz step?—and have I not seen them dance at Tavvydale House, when Miss Hester has let me peep into the ball-room, where they've been **very** gay ? To be sure I can waltz—look here ! "

Milly, full of life and light, now spun round the room gracefully and rapidly, whilst her uncle played the violin, stamped his foot to keep time, and shouted forth his surprise and his applause.

Uncle and niece were in the midst of their revelry—the heyday of their holiday—when a stream of fine people flowed suddenly into the room, and took the place by storm.

" Well, in all my life—I never ! " exclaimed Mrs. Llewellyn.

~~~~~~~~~~~~

CHAPTER XII.

MRS. LLEWELLYN.

THE fine folk who had thus taken by surprise uncle and niece consisted of Mr., Mrs., and Miss Llewellyn, Hester Fyvie, and her cousin, Mr. Llewellyn, junior—to whom we drew attention in our second chapter as a young man taking a gloomy view of things in general, and oppressed by the idea of Laurence Raxford having cut him out of the partnership—and one or two more visitors at whom the reader has glanced in the third chapter of this history.

They streamed into the house "just as if it belonged to them," Mr. Whiteshell remarked afterwards, and took possession *en masse*, with Mrs. Llewellyn as central figure in the picture.

"Well, in all my life—I never ! " Mrs. Llewellyn exclaimed then.

Milly stopped dancing, turned very red, and looked in a bewildered manner from one to another of that select circle by which she was enclosed. One face of the assembly was only a friend's face, and that Milly, in her confusion, failed to take comfort from, notwithstanding its comical, even its consoling expression. Mrs. Llewellyn, very erect and stiff in the back, was a clincher to all comfort at that particular period. Mrs. Llewellyn, with an opportunity to improve the occasion, stood with her gloved hands outspread, amazed at the profanity upon which she had intruded. Mr. White-shell, submerged in the shadow of her voluminous skirts, sat hugging his fiddle to his breast, and waiting somewhat nervously for the opportunity to assert his independence.

"To think that a girl with her bread to earn, and a home to keep, should be engaged in this unprofitable and frivolous occupation! To think that here, in the heart of a mining district, a poor creature's vanity should lead her to practise dancing in this wretched hovel. Hester, surely this is not the girl whose praises you have been singing all the week—your protegée?"

"Yes, this is my protegée," said Hester, with her usual alacrity.

"You form your favourites out of very odd material," said Mrs. Llewellyn; "and you must see, Hester, that this is not a proper way for a person of this description to spend her time?"

"Certainly not—most decidedly and indisputably not," affirmed Mr. Llewellyn, jerking his head forward with every adverb; "as Mrs. Llewellyn very justly observed, 'In all my life I never!'"

"And as for you, Sir—an old man with one foot in the grave," said Mrs. Llewellyn, wheeling round, and facing Mr. Whiteshell, "I am astonished at you, offering encourage-ment to a young woman to forget her sphere, and launch herself into the pomps and vanities of a wicked world. Sir, you know as well as I do, that you are instilling into this poor girl's mind a love of society and amusement that may be, from this day, her bane through life—her *bane*, I feel it my duty to remark again."

Mrs. Llewellyn was evidently improving the occasion. At Tavvydale House she had not had a fair opportunity, albeit it was her special *forte* to utter protests, and render people uncomfortable. Here had come to her a splendid chance to condemn the manners and morals of the lower classes; and as when a chance occurred, Mrs. Llewellyn dashed at it, regardless of time, or place, or human feelings, in a rampant, bull in a china shop kind of fashion, so there was nothing unnatural in her behaviour that particular afternoon.

"You, Sir," still addressing Mr. Whiteshell, "sitting there, with one foot in the grave," she repeated by way of fixing that impression upon the sinner before her, "ought to be ashamed of yourself."

"Madam," commenced Mr. Whiteshell, after swallowing some unwieldy substance that had been sticking in his throat, "I've nothing to be ashamed of, that I am aware—I have never been ashamed of anything that I have done in life, or considered myself answerable to anybody save myself for my actions or opinions. I don't know," he continued, tucking the violin under his arm, with emphasis, "whom I have the pleasure to address, or what your business may be, but it strikes me very forcibly, that if ever there was a cool and unwarrantable intrusion upon the privacy of——"

"Uncle," cried Milly, at this juncture, "these are visitors from Tavvydale House, and very welcome here."

She dropped a curtsey with her usual quickness, and then stood demurely waiting the pleasure of her guests.

Mr. Whiteshell was astonished at his niece's humility, and continued to writhe uncomfortably on his chair. "That's no reason——" he began.

"Don't bandy words—don't bandy words—don't bandy any impudence with your betters, Sir—we don't want any more bandy anything," said Mr. Llewellyn, pompously.

"It's absurd," said Mrs. Llewellyn.

"It's extremely absurd," added her husband, "to take any notice of these people. They're never grateful for advice, and always give it back in impudence—I have remarked that," he said, turning to one of the party, "from a child."

"Mr. Llewellyn," said his wife, "you will allow me to be the best judge of· when it is time to take notice of an error. When I see wrong in any shape or under any circumstances, I have the courage to protest against it."

"I don't deny that," said Mr. Llewellyn, "and indisputably you are right, so far as that goes. But I don't see, my dear, much occasion to remain longer in this deplorable building. You've spoken your mind, you know," he added, confidentially.

"I can't go any further just at present," said Mrs. Llewellyn; "I don't care about the cascade, and I'll rest here till you all come back, please."

Mr. Whiteshell's instinctive politeness could not keep him

in his seat after this admission. He rose and placed his chair at the disposal of the lady, with one of his best bows. Mrs. Llewellyn dropped heavily into it, and without an acknowledgment of the gentleman's courtesy, proceeded to open a large fan, and make vigorous efforts to obtain coolness therefrom.

"I think that I would rest a little while, aunt," suggested Hester; "the path down the Cleft is very fatiguing, and the one to the cascade still more so. Milly, will you show these ladies and gentlemen the way to the cascade? I did not expect to find you at home, and had volunteered as guide myself, though I should have led them all wrong, I have no doubt. Can you spare the time, do you think?"

"Oh! yes, Miss Fyvie."

"Let that old fiddler show the way," said Mrs. Llewellyn; and the old fiddler aforesaid stood upon tiptoe at once, and looked very red behind his white moustache; "I should like to talk to this girl quietly."

Milly looked scared, and turned almost an appealing glance towards Miss Fyvie. Hester was ready to respond, but on this occasion Mrs. Llewellyn was too quick for her.

"You know very well that you are acquainted with every step of the way, for the matter of that, Hester," said Mrs. Llewellyn; "and that I can't be left here with no one to attend to me—if I had one of my fits, for instance."

Mr. Whiteshell registered an inward wish that this objectionable woman had had one of them—a nice long one —before starting for the Cleft that afternoon.

"I intend to stay with you, of course, aunt."

"And spoil the party, or compel me to drag all that wretched way down to the dribble, because of your obstinacy. Why can't the girl wait here?"

"I will wait if you wish it, Miss Fyvie," Milly hastened to say.

"Very well," replied Hester; "there's a good girl," she whispered; "I shall not be long, and you need not mind a word she says, Milly—it's only Mrs. Llewellyn, and she has been put out to-day about something, and is just a little cross with everybody. Let her have her own way, and say nothing.'"

The party prepared to move again—Miss Llewellyn, who

had remained stiff and stony all this time, now carefully tucking up the silk skirt of her dress.

"If Mr. Raxford should pass this way, aunt, you can tell him that we take the lower path, striking to the right, where the Cleft divides—he will not be long coming up in the carriage we have sent for him."

"I'll tell him if I see him," said Mrs. Llewellyn.

"And Mr. Engleton?" suggested Miss Llewellyn, suddenly and spasmodically.

"Oh! I had quite forgotten Mr. Engleton; and here's Cousin Jane anxious about him, aunt," cried Hester, laughing; "why, where can he be? Milly, have you seen a young man with black hair, with his hat on the back of his head, and his hands full of papers, wandering about here to-day?"

"The gentleman who sketches?" asked Milly. "No, he hasn't been this way to-day."

"Pardon me, Milly, but he has," corrected her uncle; "Mr. Engleton and I have been conferring about a little matter we once had in our heads together. He was in the Cleft this morning."

"Which way did he go?" asked Mrs. Llewellyn, sharply.

"Further up the Cleft, Madam."

"Then why don't you go and find him? You seem to have nothing to do, but play profane music all day," she said; "I think it would be better for you to find Mr. Engleton, and tell him that he's wanted."

Mr. Whiteshell, bursting with anger, endeavoured to reflect upon this new proposition calmly, and failed.

"Hester," said Mrs. Llewellyn, "ask this man to go, and give him something for his trouble. I can't manage these people—they're very rude and obstinate about this part of Devonshire. I suppose it's the mines."

"In my case, Madam, it's *not* the mines," said Mr. Whiteshell; "I don't happen to have the pleasure of being a resident in Devonshire. On the contrary—I beg your pardon."

This to Miss Fyvie, who had suddenly arrested his attention.

"You are Milly's uncle, I imagine?"

Mr. Whiteshell bowed.

"May I ask the favour of your doing your best to find

Mr. Engleton for us ? " she said ; " we all wish to return in the carriages that are waiting in the high road, near Captain Athorpe's cottage. Possibly if you find Mr. Engleton, you will tell him that, please—it will be better than joining us at the cascade."

"Very good, Madam," said Mr. Whiteshell, with a low bow ; "I will go with pleasure."

He set down his violin, seized his hat, and departed on his mission, flitting with agility before the company, now strolling leisurely along the path. When fairly out of sight of all intruders on the solitude of the Cleft, he gave a thump to his hat and burst into soliloquy, after his customary way of giving vent to his feelings.

"To oblige a lady, anything that lies in James Whiteshell's power—always, for ever and ever. But to be browbeaten by that bony woman, who can't be a lady, anyhow, I'm certain, it's almost too much to be borne, even for Milly's sake. What a woman !" he ejaculated again; " why, it's Captain Athorpe over again in petticoats."

Meanwhile, the lady on whom he had bestowed this adverse criticism was left alone with Milly Athorpe. She had planned this, and schemed for this with no small amount of tact, and here she sat at last triumphant in the sitting-room of the house in the Cleft. It had all come round just as she could have wished, and the arch-conspirator had been so far successful. Milly, as ignorant of the plans that had been woven round her as the company that had filed out of her cottage, stood by the open door, watching for Mr. Raxford, and glancing askance at Mrs. Llewellyn now and then.

A real lady this, thought Milly—unlike Uncle James, she granted that, for only real ladies were connected with Tavvydale House, in Milly's opinion. Nevertheless an odd specimen, with the ways, to a certain extent, of one or two old women in the village, and looking not unlike Bully Churdock's mother, she thought, who was tall, stout, and straight, and presented to observers a pair of cheek-bones as high and hard and repellent. And yet Mrs. Churdock had not that harsh, grating voice, or was in any way intensely disagreeable, as Mrs. Llewellyn was. Never mind, thought Milly, something has put her out, and great people as well as little ones are put out at times ; she would make every allowance for Mrs. Llewellyn, as she had done already, for Hester Fyvie's sake.

"You can shut the door and sit down," said Mrs. Llewellyn, loftily ; "there's no occasion to keep me in the draught."

Milly closed the door, but did not respond to the latter portion of Mrs. Llewellyn's demands. She bustled about the room, took up her uncle's violin and bow, and carried them away into her inner room, returning in a few minutes to set a chair or two straight, and wheel her little table into the centre of the room, whence it had been pushed aside for the convenience of Milly's "steps" at an earlier period.

"I asked you to sit down, young woman," said Mrs. Llewellyn, still more loftily, "it fidgets me to see people moving about."

Milly sat down at this second appeal, and wondered if the colour had died out of her face yet, and feared that it had not, she felt so hot and nervous.

Mrs. Llewellyn, after a deal of preparation, fixed on her nose a pair of gold-mounted glasses, from which trailed a long and massive chain, and got Milly sternly and carefully within range. Milly glanced up for an instant, looked down at her crossed hands in her lap, looked up again, and found herself still under the influence of that calm, steely stare ; lowered her large hazel eyes again, felt warmer than ever, and shook hands with herself rather more firmly.

"You're not a bit pretty, after all," said the lady, lowering her glasses, and closing them with an angry snap. "You've a good complexion, and not bad eyes, and that's all you have to be proud of, let them say what they like, and turn your head as they may. You think you're pretty, I suppose ? "

Milly looked up frankly.

"Oh ! yes, I'm pretty."

This outspoken and confident statement took Mrs. Llewellyn's breath away for an instant. When she had recovered from the effects of Milly's assurance, she informed herself at once that she never did—never !

"That is, everybody says so," said Milly, noting Mrs. Llewellyn's dismay ; "and I don't think that everybody would tell stories. But I'm not more fond of myself for that, Madam. I wish sometimes that I was a little different ;

but as I can't be, I put up with it, and all the trouble that it brings to me."

"Trouble. What do you mean?"

"Nothing," said Milly, not so frankly this time; "but it *is* a trouble, and one is, as you say, likely to have her head turned by what all her friends say."

"You're—you're an extremely vain young person," commented Mrs. Llewellyn.

"No, I am not—not yet awhile, at least," cried Milly.

"And bold in your way—with a bad habit of contradicting your superiors," added the lady. "Well, anything to the contrary is not to be expected. What are you going to the door again for?"

"I was afraid that Mr. Raxford might pass."

"Let him. It's no business of yours."

"Miss Fyvie said——"

"And *I* say 'Let him!' He will find Miss Fyvie without your interference, you may depend. You know this Mr. Raxford, it appears?"

"Yes, Ma'am."

"Oh! indeed! How's that?"

"He came here last night. He was kind enough to show my uncle the way down the Cleft."

"Ah, I suppose so," added Mrs. Llewellyn; "just as I thought, and just like all the rest of the men. And what do you think of Mr. Raxford?"

"That he is a very kind, good-hearted gentleman—a true gentleman, Madam, I am sure."

"You need not be sure of anything in this world—it's not becoming," reproved Mrs. Llewellyn, putting on her glasses again, and focussing poor Milly. "And so the true gentleman was here last night. How long did he stay?"

Milly met Mrs. Llewellyn's cold stare this time unflinchingly.

"Till the storm abated."

"Ah! yes; there was a little rain, I remember," she said; "and may I ask how often Mr. Raxford comes here, and waits up for the storm?"

"He has never been here before," was the calm answer—an answer too calm, a woman of more perception than Mrs. Llewellyn might have perceived.

"You know Mr. Engleton?"

"By sight—yes."

"How often has he been here *sketching?*" she asked ironically.

"I don't know—his sketching is no business of mine, Madam. I——"

Milly paused, and left her sentence incomplete. She was going to add, "I mind my own business," and then the thought of Hester Fyvie—the daughter of the patron to whom she felt she never could be grateful enough—arrested the retort uncourteous.

"He speaks to you here?—don't deny it," Mrs. Llewllyn said, with more asperity.

"He bade me good-morning once."

"You know Mr. Jonathan Fyvie?"

"My master?—why, of course I do. Know him—ay, and love him, Madam, with all my heart, which is ever ready to do him service. He gave me this dear home of mine, because my poor father died in his employ—he has been always kind to me, more than kind, for the sake of my orphanage, and I—I hope—am grateful!"

This enthusiastic outburst had no effect on Mrs. Llewellyn, whose hard face had set in shadow more.

"I was speaking of young Mr. Fyvie—you know that."

Had the flame ever left Milly's cheeks since this inquisitor's appearance, it would have come back then, as it deepened then, and added to the suspicions of the questioner.

"I did not know that."

"Will not the answer do for him—just as it stands?"

"No," murmured Milly, in a lower tone.

"You know him, too, of course?"

Milly again replied in the affirmative.

"And you encourage him, too—don't deny that! You are either very foolish, or very ambitious, and build too much on your looks."

"Don't say any more, please."

Mrs. Llewellyn paid no heed to this hastily-uttered remonstrance. She was full of her subject, and went on.

"I warn you, girl, of your danger—I have come to warn you. Your doll's face," she said, vindictively, as though Milly's good looks aggravated her in spite of herself, "will bring you to ruin, if you dream of captivating a man of the world like my nephew. Take a woman's advice, and give up your designs in that quarter—beware of such a man, as of a fox. You hear me?"

"Madam," cried Milly, "what do you mean?"

Milly had risen, and was standing very erect, and at a little distance from her tormentor. Her voice had lost its clearness of articulation, and was husky with emotion.

"A man, young and romantic, like Mr. Raxford, might succumb to the designs of a pretty woman, but my nephew —never. So I warn you for your own good; and I warn you in secret to hold yourself aloof from our family. Milly Athorpe, I know you better than you know yourself. I have been on the watch here."

Mrs. Llewellyn had become heated by her warning; with her tall ungainly figure swaying to and fro as she spoke, with the hard face, reddened by excitement, and the big gloved hands gesticulating with vehemence, she looked less like "the real lady" than ever.

"You hear me, you young fool," she said, coarsely, "or haven't I spoken plain enough? If not, I tell you—one woman to woman—that——"

Milly flung open the door of her cottage with an impatient hand.

"Leave my house, Madam!—you insult me, and I will not have it."

"What—what—is that the way you receive an act of kindness from me?"

"I dispute such kindness—I won't have it. You should blush to offer it—you *are* blushing!"

"Do you know who I am?" cried Mrs. Llewellyn.

"Do you know to whom *you* are speaking?" rejoined Milly, forgetful of all respect to rank and station now. "To a girl who has a good name of her own, and will keep it— one who is respected here, and has never heard a word against her till you came with your slanders this afternoon. Madam, I have borne enough—you will please to leave my house!"

"I shall not go till I choose," said Mrs. Llewellyn, stoutly; "and I don't think," with an ironical laugh, "that you are strong enough to put me out. You can leave off these stagey manners, and shut the door, as soon as you please."

"You dare to remain!"

"You dare to tell me to go!" almost shrieked the lady, "when I have come here for your own good. You dare to tell me that you have not allowed young Jonathan Fyvie to make love to you. Why, last summer—as far back as last summer—I saw you and him together talking in the Cleft— you know it!"

Milly turned as though she could annihilate Mrs. Llewellyn at this new charge, and even that good lady felt uncomfortable for an instant beneath the girl's indignant glances.

"You don't deny it—there."

"Madam, I do deny it. I have been taught to speak the truth."

"You never spoke of this."

"And I have been taught to respect my employers—and —I have tried!"

"Respect!"

"I—I might have explained, had you treated me fairly," said Milly, "might even have broken my word, for the sake of my name, had you been more kind and charitable—now, I only ask you to go, believing whatever pleases you best."

"Milly Athorpe, I wish to speak to you in earnest," said Mrs. Llewellyn, eagerly—"I wish to trust in you. I have not told you all that I came to this place for. I have been hasty, and spoken too abruptly—it is my way—I have never studied refinement. Now we are alone, and have had this foolish quarrel out, let me—why, she's gone!"

The door was open, and Milly had disappeared, leaving her house to the possession of the enemy. Mrs. Llewellyn rose in her amazement, walked to the door, and looked down the slope, and along the Cleft path right and left, but there was no sign of Milly.

"The girl must have flown," muttered Mrs. Llewellyn; "and all because I have found her out in her artfulness. If she had only stopped, it would have been so much better for her and me. I begin to fancy that I have acted rashly."

She returned to the chair she had quitted, took her square chin in her hand, and stared hard at the empty fire-place. Milly's impetuosity had evidently baffled her, and she sat there with the look of a disappointed woman.

Presently she altered her position suddenly, and looked towards the open doorway, darkened by a shadow.

" Ah ! you have thought better——what, Jonathan ! "

" Heard that you had come on to the Cleft, and spun along after you," said Mr. Fyvie, junior, entering the house. " Where have they all gone ? "

" Down the Cleft. Where *you* been these last four-and-twenty hours, and what is the matter with your arm ? "

Jonathan looked at his right arm, which was supported by a sling, and laughed very pleasantly.

" Oh! a bit of a sprain, aunt," he said. " That confounded horse of mine made a bolt of it last night and threw me. I think that I shall shoot the brute. Where's Milly ? "

" How should I know ? " answered his amiable relative.

CHAPTER XIII.

MILLY IS CONSOLED, AND HER UNCLE ONCE MORE ASTONISHED.

MRS. LLEWELLYN was right. Milly had flown down the slope, and along the Cleft ; she never knew how she got out of sight of the cottage, and scarcely understood the motive which impelled her on so rapidly afterwards. There was a vague sense of seeking Captain Athorpe's protection, of telling him all, and trusting in his strength and pride to stand her friend ; but that motive grew less powerful as she proceeded, and finally brought her to a full stop for reconsideration.

Her uncle was a hasty man—worse still, a suspicious one. What would he say when she told him that Jonathan Fyvie had met her in the Cleft, and that she had never spoken of the meeting to him ? Would he believe her statement ?— surely he would do so, after the first outburst of passion was over, and shelter with his strong arm and his stout heart the child of his dead brother.

Then Milly began to consider if it were worth all the words, the suspicions, and the quarrels which would follow her revelation. She had been taunted, reproved, suspected by an ill-tempered woman, whom she might never see again, and who, at least, had made no mischief with her name at the great house. A woman who might have spoken

9

without due consideration, and would repent of her rashness in cooler moments—just as most people repented. But oh! she was a terrible woman—coarse, distrustful, and uncharitable, and the thought that her good name was in the power of that woman—above all, that her own explanation after this would not avail her much—brought back, suddenly and fiercely, all the past emotions which had hurled Milly, as it were, from the house.

She had felt strong till then—strong to resist, and to hold her ground firmly and honestly, as she had held it in the Cleft. Now she gave way, covered her face with her hands, and began crying very bitterly with the reminiscences of the insults that had been heaped upon her, until a voice startled her by its proximity.

"Why, Milly, what's the matter?"

"Oh! Mr. Raxford," she said, looking up, and fighting desperately to clear away her tears with both hands, "it's nothing—nothing at all."

"Crying fit to break your heart, and rousing all the echoes of the Cleft with your sobs. Why, I thought that you were the happiest girl in Devonshire!"

"I was happy until this morning," said Milly.

"And now you're only the happiest girl in Wind-Whistle Cleft," he said, "the female sex therein being limited to one. *I* could have sworn that you were breaking your heart, and, by Jove! you turned me all goose-flesh to hear you. I don't like to hear a woman cry, Milly."

Milly looked at him. He had evidently been startled by her grief, and was more pale than she had seen him yester-night.

"There, I shan't cry any more," she said; "please go on to the cottage, Mr. Raxford—you'll find Mrs. Llewellyn there. The rest are at the cascade."

Laurence was very quick in leaping to conclusions—leaping the right way, and on to the very debatable ground sometimes, as he did in this instance. Mrs. Llewellyn at the cottage, his experience of that estimable lady, Milly in tears, and ostensibly turned out of her own house—he saw the hitch in the machinery at once, and very frankly expressed his opinions.

"I see now," he said, laughing—"it's Mother Llewellyn who has been stirring up the household gods. Ah! and she can stir, too; she has been taking pity on your poor birth and your bad blood, perhaps?"

"She has not been bestowing any pity upon me!" cried Milly, indignantly.

"I'm right, I see. There's a prophet for you, Milly!" he said—"come to me to sift out a mystery. It *was* Mrs. Llewellyn, then?"

"Yes, it was."

"Oh! never mind her," was the easy advice proffered here, as he sat on the stump of a tree, swinging his legs backwards and forwards as he spoke. "I'm sure that anything that that old lady has said there's no occasion to cry for. She means very well in her way, but it's not a nice way; and she's a trifle uppish, but you soon get used to it; and half she says and does is mere playfulness—a kind of playfulness that takes a long time to understand, but she intends no harm. Here, let us go back together, and I'll induce her to offer an apology—quite a handsome apology for her."

"I shall go back presently, Mr. Raxford—please leave me now, and don't say that I have met you, or told you that she made me cry. Why, what would she say to that, too!" was the indignant exclamation here.

"Oh! she would have her little joke about that, I dare say," said Laurence, drily; "I'll not say anything, as you wish to let the matter drop. Have you seen young Mr. Fyvie?"

"No, Sir."

"The coachman told me that he came this way a little while ago," said Laurence; "I suppose he's somewhere in the neighbourhood."

"Did the coachman tell you that he saw him here?"

"Yes."

"How long ago?" was the eager question; "if I could only—perhaps he came by the river's bed, a favourite walk of his, Sir, and thus you missed him."

"And thus I missed him," repeated Laurence, looking over the bank at the river's bed aforesaid; "it's not a walk that I should have fancied Jonathan taking—too rough and scrambly for him. Well, are you better, Milly?"

"Yes, Sir—all my bad tempers have cried themselves away."

9—2

"And you are the happy Milly again ? "

"I shall feel happy soon, I hope."

Laurence thought how pretty she looked standing a few paces from him, with her nervous little fingers pleating up her dress unconsciously; certainly the prettiest girl whom he had ever seen—and he had had an eye for beauty all his life, too, an innocent eye, purely artistic, and with no vulgar habit of winking. And Milly, in trouble, had awakened his interest as well as his passive admiration—and Milly's embarrassment puzzled him, and seemed a something different to last night's bashfulness. Still he *was* a true gentleman, and deserving of Milly's past encomiums; he saw that she was getting more confused the longer he stayed there, and he hastened to withdraw.

"One moment, Sir," Milly said, to his astonishment; "it's a rude question of mine, perhaps, but do you really think that no one pays much heed to what Mrs. Llewellyn says ? "

Laurence reflected for an instant.

" I don't think anybody pays a great deal of attention—I don't," said Laurence, "and I never met with anybody who did. I'm sure, Milly, that you need not be alarmed."

" Then I will not," said Milly with alacrity; " she—she has not said anything that I care about—that can do me any harm—or that is true. I'll shake her off my mind, Sir."

She gave an impetuous toss to her head, as though by that gesture she shook her off at once, and Laurence cried—

"That's well, Milly."

" Only my pride after all, standing in the way of my own happiness," she said. "To think that I should let the Athorpe pride get the better of me too ! "

" Ah ! pride's a bore in its way," remarked Laurence, " and yet my mother has always told me that I never had pride enough or high notions enough—and I fear that my low ideas have even worried her at times."

" You have a mother ? "

" Yes—the best-tempered, largest-hearted woman in the world, Milly."

" If I had one—if I could call mine back to take my part ! " cried Milly earnestly, " or to sit down by my side, and keep me from utter loneliness."

"There, you're going to begin again — and upon my honour," he said with affected lightness, that, however, had its effect, "you're old enough to know better."

"Yes—you're right, Sir."

Milly smiled at her companion's comical gravity; and Laurence left her smiling, and congratulated himself *en route* on the extraordinary tact which he had displayed in soothing the ruffled feelings of the maiden.

At Milly's cottage he found Mrs. Llewellyn sitting in state, with Jonathan Fyvie leaning against the mantelpiece engaged in the ungentlemanlike occupation of aggravating her. These two had been sparring politely from the moment of their meeting, and Mrs. Llewellyn had evidently, from her heightened colour, and the disturbed condition of her bonnet strings—which she had a habit of tightening in moments of excitement—had the worst of the conflict.

Not that Jonathan had fought his battles without receiving several hard hits, but then hard hits never affected him; he took things easily and deliberately, not letting his own feelings be wounded much, and caring very little for other people's. Possessing a temper that was difficult to disturb, he made not the slightest allowances for folk less graciously endowed than he.

"Ah! Laurence, just in time," he said as our hero entered; "here is Mrs. Llewellyn fretting about you—wondering what can keep you so long from pleasant company? The horses did not upset you as my brute did last night, I hope?"

He touched his wounded arm lightly as he spoke, and Laurence said,

"Thrown, Jonathan?"

"Lightly tilted off—that's all. Nothing to speak of."

"Glad to hear it," said Laurence, "and glad to see you, Jonathan, though I wish the meeting had occurred one mile further on."

"At the mines, you mean? Why the mines are where I left them last!"

"Yes," answered Laurence.

"And I can't play the working partner—the hard-working partner like you, Laurence. Are you not tired already of the excessive application?"

"On the contrary, I like the application vastly."

"Ah ! you are the industrious and I the idle boy. Wait till you are my age, young fellow," he said with mock solemnity, "When the world has palled upon you, and 'Nil Admirari' is the one true motto to swear by. You got my cigars all right?"

"Thank you, Jonathan—yes. I should have written to thank you for your attention."

"Oh ! I hate letters," replied his partner, "I'm glad you did not. Are you going down to the cascade?"

"Certainly I am."

"Mr. Raxford is in no hurry, at all events," said Mrs. Llewellyn ; "upon my word, if I were Miss Fyvie, I should not compliment him on his lover's haste."

"If you were Miss Fyvie—ah ! what a sister I should have to counsel and guide me," said Jonathan.

"And you require counsel, Heaven knows!" said Mrs. Llewellyn.

"But, then, what an aunt I should lose," he said, making a wry face at Laurence.

"That'll do, Jonathan—you are never more of a black-guard than when you think you're satirical," the good lady said bluntly ; "what are you going to do now?"

"I'm going to smoke, if I am fortunate enough to obtain your permission."

"Not in this house, at all events. Not whilst I am here," she said, rising with becoming dignity ; "Mr. Raxford, will you see me to the cascade?"

Mr. Raxford could but bow and express his willingness to escort her in that direction.

"You will join us, Jonathan?" he said.

Jonathan, who had immediately dropped into the chair vacated by Mrs. Llewellyn, turned his handsome head languidly round.

"I'm not fond of cascades, Laurence — they're very monotonous and damp," he replied ; "besides, I'm tired, and almost an invalid, with all an invalid's caprices. If you see Milly——"

Both Mrs. Llewellyn and Laurence halted and looked more intently at the speaker, who did not appear, however, to be struck by their new interest.

"If you see Milly, tell her it is rather dull work here alone, and that I have no objection to company."

"You'll never stop," began Laurence, when he felt Mrs. Llewellyn's firm grip upon his arm.

"This way, Mr. Raxford," she said. "I think that I can find the cascade for you, and we must let Mr. Jonathan have his way. An obstinate man, for all his easy manners, Sir."

And with this Parthian dart at her nephew, she convoyed our hero from the house—our hero still far from satisfied.

"I'm sure that he will distress Milly very much by retaining possession of her house like that," said Laurence; "upon my word, it's scarcely fair."

"Milly is used to visitors at all times and seasons," was the pointed reply; "hers is a pretty face, that draws 'the fellows' to it! You are not afraid of your partner paying too much attention in that direction, Mr. Raxford?"

"Afraid!—why no!"

"Not even of Milly being impressed by so great a gentleman as *he* is," nodding her head in the direction of the house they were quitting.

"Milly can take care of herself, I have no doubt."

"Milly knows Jonathan Fyvie by this time, and how far she can trust him. If I was she, I would keep clear of that place until——"

"Why, Madam, you don't think that he would be brute enough to say one word to render a defenceless girl afraid of him! I don't know my partner well—I scarcely understand him; but if you think that, is it fair to——"

"I think that Milly is safe enough—you need not be alarmed, Sir," she interrupted; "here comes her natural protector, to stand between her and all harm, if she is not strong enough to protect herself."

Laurence might have wondered more at the bitterness—even the coarseness—of this masculine woman's words, had he not felt grateful—for a reason that he did not attempt to explain to himself—at the sudden appearance of Mr. Whiteshell advancing up the slope, talking to himself, and shaking his head energetically to and fro. The little gentleman was bent double in the ascent, and, tired with his search for Mr. Engleton, was toiling upwards evidently with difficulty. At the sight of the lady and gentleman above him, he made an effort to appear less fatigued, as though his character for lightness and agility was at stake, and made the rest of his way more buoyantly towards them.

"Oh! here's that wretched old man," muttered Mrs. Llewellyn.

Whether Laurence was also inclined, out of the perversity of human nature, to annoy Mrs. Llewellyn, or was really genuine in his warmth of greeting, was a doubtful point; but he extended his hand frankly to Mr. Whiteshell, as they approached each other.

"Good-afternoon, Mr. Whiteshell," he said; "I hope that you are well to-day, and have shaken off all the ill-effects of last night's journey?"

Mr. Whiteshell stood upright, and took his hat off with his left hand, as he seized Laurence's right. He was grateful—intensely grateful—for Laurence's notice of him in the presence of a woman who had treated him ungenerously.

"Thank you, I am very well, Mr. Raxford. A charming day, is it not?"

"A beautiful day. You will find a gentleman in sole possession of your cottage, Mr. Whiteshell; but he will not give you any trouble."

"Oh! another of them," said Mr. Whiteshell, with a blank expression of countenance; "very well, then—we must make the best of him. And Milly?"

"Is in the Cleft—coming home, I believe."

"What did she go out for?" he asked, with a suspicious glance at Mrs. Llewellyn.

"Well, I can't answer that question myself," said Laurence.

"But I can," said Mrs. Llewellyn; "because she was rude, and not disposed to listen to well-meant advice. I would have talked to that child like a mother, if she had only had a little patience."

"Hasty at times — like *her* mother," explained Mr. Whiteshell; "a girl imbued with a certain amount of impulsiveness, which, however, always leads her right. A quick instinct, I call it."

"Never mind what you call it," said Mrs. Llewellyn; "where's Mr. Engleton?—you found him?"

"I found him," repeated the dancing-master.

"Alone?" was the sharp inquiry.

"Well, he was in company with—with a thirty yard circular measure, and a long stick," replied Mr. Whiteshell, prolonging the lady's evident anxiety as far as possible ; "and I delivered your kind message. Good-afternoon."

"That's a hateful old scamp," observed Mrs. Llewellyn, before he was out of hearing; "presumptuous, officious, garrulous, everything that is objectionable in elderly persons of that class of life."

"Pardon me," said Laurence, frankly ; "but I don't think so."

Mr. Whiteshell heard Laurence's remark also, and went towards his niece's cottage with a lighter heart in consequence. He broke into a soliloquy after his usual fashion, and went upwards muttering aloud,

"He don't think so," he said. "Bravo, Mr. Raxford ! That's one in my favour, and one I owe you, my young champion. A good and honest fellow, who is not afraid of speaking out — a gentleman, with all the true gentility that respects old age, its crotchets, feelings, and position ; upon my honour, I like that young man very much indeed ! Why, there's something in his smile that warms one's heart like wine ; and—good gracious, talking about wine, there are three glasses yet in the bottle, and a man alone in the house with them ! "

There was no forced agility in Mr. Whiteshell's remaining steps ; he bounded with airiness up the slope, paused for an instant to snatch a new breath from the fresh air in the Cleft that day, skipped through the open door into the house, and then skipped backwards once more to the threshold, reaching out both hands to clasp the sides of the doorway, and save himself from falling.

Jonathan Fyvie, who had been sitting with his face towards the empty fire-place, staring intently before him, and puffing away at his cigar, turned at the entrance of Mr. Whiteshell, and looked at him dreamily.

"All in one day—rising from the dead, and bringing back to life the troubles which I hoped had died with them," he exclaimed. "I see it now. God forgive me if I am wrong, but I think I see it all ! "

"Come in, old gentleman—and excuse the smoke," said Jonathan.

"I am com—coming in," answered Whiteshell, advancing

slowly forwards at this invitation—"coming to unmask you!"

"Eh?—who are you—a madman?"

"An old man, who knew you six years since in London, and knew nothing to your credit. A man who thought you bad then, and believes you worse now. From beginning to end, I'm sure I see it all, and it is a dreadful story."

"I don't know you."

"You were always a liar; and you have taught her to lie. She lied to me this morning, God forgive her; and I know now why there was a doubt in my heart, despite all her protestations."

"You are speaking of—Milly?"

"Of Inez Athorpe—you can't deceive me any longer. You can't lead me wrong again," cried the old man indignantly; "or teach me in any way to swerve from that which is my duty. I must tell all."

"No, don't do that! You are wrong in your judgment still—I swear to God you are," said Jonathan Fyvie, waking up to an excitement and an animation that were new to his character, or to us, witnesses of it hitherto. "Shut that door—turn the key in the lock for a moment. Sit down, Whiteshell. It is all easily explained."

Whiteshell hesitated.

"It might be worth your while to murder me," he said. "I can't tell how far your laxity of principle extends."

To Mr. Whiteshell's astonishment, Jonathan Fyvie produced a pistol from his pocket and flung it towards him. The old man caught the weapon adroitly enough, and looked from it to the man who had hurled it towards him.

"There—that is loaded. I carry desperate weapons, you see. It is necessary in this place! I am in your hands now, and you can shoot me if you have a doubt of me. Man, you must listen, or your folly will be the ruin of us. Lock that door!"

Whiteshell locked the door at this second adjuration, and then approached the last speaker, who had crossed his arms on the back of the chair, and had turned round somewhat to bury his face in them.

"I am ready, Sir," said the old man, taking the seat Milly had recently occupied.

"Thank you," murmured Jonathan; "this is kind of you."

"For her sake—not for yours, Sir."

"Yes, yes; and for her sake, I thank you."

~~~~~~~~~~~~~~~~~~~~~~~~~~~~~~~~

CHAPTER XIV

THE CASCADE.

MRS. LLEWELLYN and our hero proceeded in the direction of the cascade, both silent for awhile after Laurence's quiet but firm defence of Mr. Whiteshell. Mrs. Llewellyn was not disposed to quarrel with Laurence that day, to resent as an affront every remark that was opposed to her views. Though a little irritated her, still there were times when she could bear a great deal, if not disguise it—and she was inclined, for a definite period, to put up with the mild opposition which Laurence might feel inclined to offer. If she were clumsy in her scheming, still she was a great schemer all the same.

The path to the cascade was narrow as well as circuitous, and necessitated Mrs. Llewellyn proceeding on in advance; this assisted her views, and concealed a face that was in the habit of betraying her—that had already betrayed her that day to Milly Athorpe. She trudged on, taking long strides like a life-guardsman, and evincing none of that fatigue of which she had previously complained to Hester. Laurence in the rear was left to admire the upright carriage of the lady, the breadth across the shoulders, the elevation of the head, which sent the lace bonnet down her back—to admire also the courage of Mr. Llewellyn, who had at an anterior period taken such a wife—however fine and portly—to himself. When she looked round once or twice at him, and her hard, grey eyes, high cheek-bones, and Roman nose confronted him for a fleeting moment, he admired the courage of the Treasury clerk more than ever.

Mrs. Llewellyn resumed the conversation when she had led the way by the lower path, that seemed to dip into the Cleft itself, and then to alter its mind at the last moment, and wind gracefully close to the bed of the stream, under a canopy of foliage that shut in everything, and would have rendered everything as still as beautiful, but for the babbling of the water at their feet.

"You met this Milly as you came down the Cleft to-day, Mr. Raxford?" she asked.

"Yes," answered he.

"And last night she tells me that you had supper at her house—and very proud and vain she appears to be of the honour."

"Indeed!" said Laurence, "it takes a very little to make Milly proud, then."

"A girl's head is easily turned," said Mrs. Llewellyn. "The more's the pity. Did she tell you that I gave her quite a scolding?"

Then she looked round for the first time, and Laurence admired Mr. Llewellyn's courage, as aforesaid.

"Well, she seemed as if she were a little put out. She's not used to scoldings, I dare say, poor girl!" said Laurence.

"Why poor girl?"

Laurence was taken aback at this, though Mrs. Llewellyn was trudging on now, a grim Mentor to this Telemachus.

"I don't know why. Because she seems to me very much alone in the world—a girl without a friend or confidant. Possibly it's her peculiar position in the Cleft which suggests the fancy, rather than proves the fact."

"She has two uncles—one's an idiot, and the other is a madman, but still she's not without friends!" remarked the lady.

"And all the mining people are her friends too, I hear—so my pity is out of place."

"Take care, Mr. Laurence, pity is always akin to love, especially that pity which founds its interest on a pretty girl."

She looked round again—this time with an expression intended to be arch and playful, but which succeeded only in making Laurence Raxford shiver. If ever there was a man deserving of a statue of gold, that man was Mr. Llewellyn, thought our hero!

"Forewarned is forearmed, Mrs. Llewellyn," he said, laughing. "I thank you for your caution."

"It is freely given, Sir," she answered; "and I am glad

for once to find you grateful. *You* think Milly pretty, of course ?"

"Yes, she is pretty," was the frank reply.

"*Very* pretty ?"

"Yes—I think that she is very pretty."

"I am of the same opinion," confessed the lady, with a happy forgetfulness of her previous criticism. "It is a dangerous gift for a girl like her—such girls are always vain, eager for admiration, and romantic. You have made good use of your time and liberty here, for you seem to have turned her head. She can talk of nothing but what a gentleman you are."

Laurence certainly gasped for breath at this; Mrs. Llewellyn was not a woman fond of quoting praises second-hand to him or her on whom they had been bestowed. She quoted them harshly now, as though they displeased her in the utterance; and Laurence did not feel inclined to disbelieve the speaker—on the contrary, felt a thrill of delight pass through him, which was perfectly unaccountable. It was pleasant to think that Milly had let this avowal escape her ; he liked to be thought all that was honourable and good, and though Milly had had but little opportunity of judging, still her criticism was none the less acceptable.

He laughed, however, as though the matter was a very good joke, so far as it went. Of such hypocritical stuff are the men of the present day made, fair readers.

"Very kind of her, I'm sure," he said ; "the result of my extra exertions to obtain her a fortnight's holiday. All bribery and corruption on my part, Mrs. Llewellyn."

Mrs. Llewellyn, suddenly hearing voices in advance, came to a full stop, and faced our hero. She had an instinctive perception that she was succeeding in this quarter, and the final *coup* had yet to be made. Probably it would have been better to allow the subject to drop at this juncture, but then Mrs. Llewellyn was not graceful in her strategy, and exposed her hand very often in her eagerness. Laurence Raxford, shallow enough on this particular afternoon, was seized then with a certain amount of suspicion at the lady's anxiety. He had long ago set her down as dogmatic, eccentric and vulgar—opposed to him from their first acquaintance together, and seeing in him but a rival to her son's advancement—and he began to feel astonished at this sudden interest in him. It might be all very genuine—all very natural; but he did not exactly understand it, and from that moment he stood upon his guard.

"Mr. Raxford, I am a woman of the world," she said—"a plain speaker enough, calling things by their right names, and seeing most things in a clear light. I don't suppose that there's anything in Milly's head but a silly admiration for a man above her sphere—these country girls are silly in that way, the whole of them—and I'm sure that you would not encourage the fancy for one instant after you had been warned of it. It might give you a bad name in these parts, and set my high-spirited, but jealous niece against you. So it will be better, if you're a man of discretion, not to throw yourself in Milly Athorpe's way—not to see her again, if you can help it."

"Madam, I saw this Milly Athorpe last night for the first time."

"Oh! I don't believe that. It is not likely."

Laurence's face changed colour at this flat denial.

"Just as you please, Mrs. Llewellyn," he said quietly.

"If it is true, why, then, it is the more remarkable," she added; "you need not take offence at my surprise."

"I trust, Mrs. Llewellyn, that this ridiculous story will go no further," said Laurence.

"Oh! you may rely upon my secrecy."

"It isn't a secret exactly," said Laurence, annoyed at the turn which the dialogue had taken; "but people—all sorts of people—are quick with their suspicions about here, it seems; and the whole matter is very foolish, and might lead to mischief."

"Just what I say," said Mrs. Llewellyn, innocently. "Why, there was that hare-brained nephew of mine, people said, inclined to make love to Milly, when there was no ground for it, save a few of those compliments with which you men are prolific, and which Milly took with a very ill grace indeed; for I must say Milly is a proud girl, and dislikes attentions *generally*."

If he was king of England to-morrow, he would present Mr. Llewellyn with the Victoria Cross, thought Laurence, amidst the confusion of his brain, engendered by the remarks of his companion and tormentor.

"But you may rely upon my secrecy," she said again, this

time in a loud tone; "I am not a woman to make mischief."

"What are you talking about so intently?" cried Hester Fyvie, suddenly appearing upon the scene. "I shall be eaves-dropping next out of sheer curiosity."

After Laurence had exchanged greetings with his betrothed, he could not fail to notice that there was a spot of red on either cheek, as though something had arisen to vex or embarrass Hester—a girl generally pale as a statue. Still she was very glad to see Laurence again, and there was a timid pressure of his hand, by way of return to his lover's greeting. And it was not the mysterious words of Mrs. Llewellyn that had helped to flush Hester's cheeks, thought Laurence, or his welcome would have been less warm and friendly.

"What a time you have been, Laurence," she said half-reproachfully; "I have been actually preaching sermons here to keep my audience together. Why, I thought that you would be glad of a holiday."

"So I am," answered Laurence, "but I was at the bottom of the mine when the carriage came, and a miner's dress, with a candle in my cap, was scarcely appropriate to the Cleft."

"Is Mr. Engleton here?" asked Mrs. Llewellyn; "the old man said that he had found him."

"Yes. He and Jane are quite confidential, aunt. Don't interrupt them."

"Oh! Hester, what a frivolous girl you are!" said Mrs. Llewellyn, as she proceeded along the path, to judge for herself of the accuracy of her niece's statement.

Hester and Laurence went on slowly together, as well as the narrowness of the path would admit.

"You are coming back to dinner with us, Laurence?" inquired Hester.

"Why of course I am. It was very kind of you to meet me half way."

"I had a letter from your mother yesterday."

"Ah! she writes to you now as to a dear daughter. Well, and cheerful, and busy, I hope—sending no end of love to me, although I received it first hand two days ago."

"Yes—she sends her love to her dear boy. And now," she said, with that Fyvie quickness, which Laurence had noticed more than once before, and which, in its pleasant crispness, had helped to win Laurence, "why does the dear boy keep a secret from me, and trust in—Aunt Llewellyn ? "

Laurence was perplexed by this interrogative, conveyed, as it was, half-jestingly. The whole matter, though not worthy of an explanation, was exceedingly difficult to explain. He did not respond very readily to Miss Fyvie's inquiry, and the red spot on either cheek certainly increased in circumference, and spread itself for an instant in a roseate flush over her whole face. For the first time it struck him that Hester could be angry.

"If it really *is* a secret," she said, with a great deal of the pleasantness quenched from her voice, " I'll say no more about it."

" It is not worth a moment's consideration, Hester," he replied.

"Is it worth an apology, Laurence, for treating as a jest that which was a matter for earnest conversation between you and my aunt ? "

" For Heaven's sake, Hester, don't talk of making me an apology ! " cried Laurence ; " there's no secret in the case, I tell you. The whole affair is absurd and nonsensical."

" Oh ! very well."

Hester was too proud a girl to press the question further, but she was possessed with a natural curiosiy to know what it all meant, and in her heart angry with Laurence for not offering that explanation which it was his right to make to her. A lover, in her eyes, had always been one possessed of no secrets in which his betrothed could not share ; and here, at the very commencement of an engagement, had arisen a something or other which he had enjoined Mrs. Llewellyn to keep from her. Evidently he had done that, or what could her aunt have meant by those last words which she had just caught. Her aunt had promised secrecy, and added—and these were the galling words which Hester could not get rid of, and which stuck like a burr on her thoughts—"*I am not a woman to make mischief.*" To make mischief !—whatever could Aunt Llewellyn mean by that? — what mischief, and with whom? The more she considered these minor points, the more Hester thought that she had been slighted ; and as she was a girl who had been petted and spoiled all her life, the greater seemed the indignity, coming, too, from the man who had spoken of love to her.

Laurence considered the subject concluded for good. He was glad that it had passed away without an explanation, for he could not gracefully tell Hester that Mrs. Llewellyn fancied that Milly Athorpe was in love with him ; it *was* all nonsense, and so dismissed as nonsense for ever ! Hester was a sensible girl, not to press for a solution to the absurd mystery which Mrs. Llewellyn had erected. He was admiring her common sense just as Hester had made up her mind, like a vexed and positive girl of twenty years as she was, that she *would* find out what it all meant. It was unkind of Laurence to put her off like that, she thought, as the tears rose to her eyes, despite her—it was very unkind indeed.

Hester Fyvie was no heroine, simply a woman—one of those young women whom we meet very often in life. Capricious in many things, earnest in few ; quick-witted, but a little suspicious, as quick-witted girls always are ; vain of herself and her surroundings, in a small degree ; romantic, warm-hearted, and having strong likes and dislikes ; ready to make any sacrifice, or to make herself a vixen, just as circumstances turned up, in fact, an impressionable, inconsistent girl of twenty. She was very fond of Laurence, the first man for whom she had taken more than a fancy, and of whose love she was proud ; but for all that she was resolved to punish him for his easy indifference to her curiosity.

A curve of the narrow path, a dip suddenly downwards to a lower depth, where half a dozen huge rocks served as stepping-stones for the adventurers, and then Laurence and Hester crossed the stream to a mossy bank on the other side, where were congregated the guests from Tavvydale House, and where to the right of them, falling from the rocks some fifty feet above, swept a thin sheet of silver, that dashed its spray at their feet, and then swept on amongst the boulders, to swell for ever the waters of the Cleft.

" Oh ! this is the cascade, Hester, is it ? " asked Laurence ; " well, it has a pretty effect, if it is not absolutely grand and imposing."

"It will do for Devonshire," said Hester pertly. She had been nursing her indignation for some time now—she

10

had been very grave and silent, without his appearing in any way troubled by her new demeanour. It was quite time to show that she was offended with him—just a little!

"Yes—Devonshire must be thankful for what it can get in the way of waterfalls," he answered, after a furtive glance at Hester.

"I don't see anything in it myself," said Mr. Llewellyn, standing on one of the stones in the centre of the stream, surveying the fall, with his hands in his pockets, and his head on one side ; " it seems a kind of fuss about nothing to me."

"We make a fuss about nothing occasionally," said Laurence.

Hester quite jumped at this—jumped very unnecessarily, and hugged the reproof to her breast, taking it all to herself, and smarting under the words which Laurence had uttered quite innocently, and without intending a double meaning. Mr. Llewellyn had appeared to wait for a reply, and Laurence had given one without a moment's consideration, not seeing how a wrong interpretation might be put upon it, until Hester's sudden start suggested the idea. Then he turned very quickly to her, who turned very quickly away from him, and escaped his words altogether, resolving to have war to the knife for that day at least.

Hester went at once to the side of Mr. Engleton, who *had* been conversing with Miss Llewellyn, but had found means to change his position to the edge of the stream, where he stood in a critical attitude, not unlike that of the Treasury clerk's.

"What do you think of our poor despised fall, Mr. Engleton ?" Hester asked almost coquettishly. "May I ask you to be my champion against all these insidious attacks upon the beauties of Tavvydale ?"

"Don't they like it, Miss Fyvie ?" asked Mr. Engleton.

"I have not heard a word in its favour yet," she replied.

"It's very poor," cried Mrs. Llewellyn; "I always said that it was very poor."

"It's very pretty, I think," Mr. Engleton affirmed, in the face of all these disparaging remarks ; "but it's a pity that it can't be turned to some use. I don't like to see waste."

"Waste," said Mr. Llewellyn; "where's the waste, Sir ?

It goes into the Tavvydale stream, and is of some use, I suppose."

"Or it wouldn't have been put there," said Miss Fyvie, suddenly bursting forth in a pious direction.

"And after it has joined the other streams we find it very handy at our mine," added Laurence; "it does all the work there."

"Our mine!" growled Mr. Llewellyn junior to another young gentleman, looking almost as sulky as himself; "he has soon got into the tall talk, Bowers."

"He just has!" affirmed the inelegant Bowers; "it's like the lot."

"Handy for the mine—exactly," said Engleton, "and rewarded for its handiness by arsenical deposits. Now, I should like to see this rush of pure clear spring water falling for ever down Holborn Hill, for instance."

"Bless my soul, what a remarkable idea!" ejaculated Mr. Llewellyn, still poised upon his stone in the stream; "what for, Sir? And what's to be done with it when it gets to Farringdon Street?"

"It might flow on into the Thames, just as this flows into the Tavvy—and in the heart of London, Sir, it would be the best drinking fountain for the masses that could possibly exist. Fancy, for an instant, that cascade, with its —with its——"

"Trimmings," suggested Mr. Bowers.

"With its natural features, just as they are developed in this instance," continued Mr. Engleton, without paying any heed to the last suggestion made him, "standing in the streets of London to gladden the souls of the poor. Fancy that water a fountain, at which the thirsty wayfarer, and the tired workman might drink—where a man, turning suddenly from the stir and turmoil of the City, might find a picture of Arcadia. Fancy, from your point of view, Mr. Llewellyn—excuse me one instant——"

"Good Gord, Sir!—mind what you are about. I'm going!"

Before the words had escaped Mr. Llewellyn's lips, the speaker had gone!—or at least one leg had gone up to the knee in the stream. Mr. Engleton had sprung lightly and suddenly on to the stone, coming into collision with Mr. Llewellyn, who had turned upon him with the clutch of

10—2

despair, upon discovering his basis of support slipping from under him.

"My dear Sir—I beg your pardon," cried the shocked Mr. Engleton, dragging at the gentleman who had betrayed so great an interest in his poetic idea, "I'm afraid—I'm afraid you're wet."

"I should think I was, Sir," bawled Mr. Llewellyn, losing his respect for Mr. Engleton along with his temper, as he drew one limb, wet and dripping, from the stream; "I dare say I've caught my death by your infernal clumsiness. Yes, I said my *death*, ladies and gentlemen," he added with a hyena-like smile at the company, "and that appears to amuse you very much, though I don't see anything to giggle at myself. Mrs. Llewellyn, I'm going home!"

"Really, I'm very sorry," murmured the distressed Mr. Engleton, as his late companion leaped from stone to stone till he reached the path by which they had come to the Cleft.

"You had better keep in motion," cried Mrs. Llewellyn. "Mr. Raxford, tell him, please, that he had better keep in motion."

Mr. Raxford, thus adjured, crossed the stream to give that valuable advice to the gentleman with the damp limb, standing now on the opposite bank, stamping, and, we regret to say, swearing his hardest.

"Keep in motion!" cried the disgusted Mr. Llewellyn, "I'm going—ain't I?"

"I mean, I would not get into the carriage," cried his wife from the other side.

"What does she say?" growled Mr. L., who was a trifle deaf occasionally.

"That you ought *not* to get into the carriage, Sir," explained Laurence.

"How the devil, Sir, am I to walk all the way home!" yelled Mr. Llewellyn, beating a retreat nevertheless, and last seen on the upper ground trotting gracefully down the Cleft, with both hands clenched.

Mr. Engleton remained very much distressed at the dismay he had created. He was near-sighted, he confessed, and had not calculated his distance in the interest of his subject. It was very foolish of him, and he regretted exceedingly the annoyance that he had evidently caused Mr. Llewellyn.

Mrs. Llewellyn and her daughter hastened to comfort the crest-fallen theorist, and Hester, Laurence thought, was equally solicitous. Another fuss about nothing, at all events, he considered, as he walked back with the rest of the party in the direction of the carriage. Along in Indian file till the path widened, and then Laurence found it impracticable to reach Hester's side, or attract Hester's attention, so engrossed was she with Mr. Engleton's remarks, and so shut out was he by the ladies and gentlemen in his way.

He felt, after a while, a little annoyed at remaining so long in the background—not jealous of Mr. Engleton absorbing Hester's sole attention by his dreamy speculativeness, not feeling inclined to be jealous even, but vexed with the general position of affairs, and with Hester's indifference to his whereabouts.

The party sauntered on till they reached the slope whereon was Milly Athorpe's cottage, and where Jonathan Fyvie waited for them, handsome and smiling, like a fair hope they had met by the way.

"Now, ladies and gentlemen, I think that we have had enough of Wind-Whistle Cleft for one while," he said in his usual shy way, and without looking at those whom he addressed; "Uncle Llewellyn ran by here ten minutes ago as fleet as a race-horse. I could not overtake him myself. Is it a match against time?—and what are the odds? Shall we proceed?"

No reply being offered in the negative, the party swept onwards, whilst Mr. Whiteshell and Milly watched them from the higher ground.

"There's that girl again!" muttered Mrs. Llewellyn.

CHAPTER XV.

NOT QUITE SATISFIED.

LAURENCE, though driven in no very pleasurable frame of mind towards Tavvydale House, was still of opinion that all would be well, and everything different in the evening. Chance had separated him from Hester, and thrown him into contiguity with those two jackanapeses, young Llewellyn and Bowers, who talked all the way in the carriage about the dogs they had had, and the horses which they had backed for forthcoming races.

"What an uncomfortable kind of afternoon it has been," he thought when he was in his dressing-room, arraying himself in that full-dress suit which he kept now like one of the family at Tavvydale House; "and what a horrid old woman that Mrs. Llewellyn is! Hanged if she hasn't almost made mischief about nothing."

He did not wait in his room until the dinner-bell rang, but went down stairs into the drawing-room, and thence through the open window on to the lawn, with the hope of finding Hester—just as he had found her once or twice before in the courting-days that were only a little while ago, and yet, for an unaccountable reason, seemed further off than he knew them to be. But though he wandered about the grounds until the bell rang, he was not rewarded with a glimpse of Hester Fyvie, and he returned into the drawing-room just in time to see Mr. Engleton escorting his *fiancée* across the hall, followed by the regular stream of guests assembled there. He was in time, however, to offer his arm to Miss Llewellyn, who was polite enough to say "Thank you" for his attention. A meek woman this Miss Llewellyn, with no energy of her race in her — taking everything placidly, and saying but little to any one, if it could be possibly avoided; receiving the snubs of her mother even graciously. Laurence had admired her placidity, just as he had her father's courage, in an off-hand, desultory way; and possibly of all the "stuck-ups," as he termed them, who had been eating and drinking lately at Mr. Fyvie's expense, he liked this apathetic girl the best.

He was glad that she was his companion at the table; she did not expect a brilliant talker—brilliant talk, in fact, always embarrassed her—and as it was not in his line any more than hers, the position probably suited them both. Both could look round them and ahead of them between the courses; and it was strange that both looked more than once in the same direction, namely, towards the positions occupied by Hester and Mr. Engleton.

This was the dullest dinner-party to which he had ever received an invitation, he thought; if the dinner itself had been as flat, stale, and unprofitable as the conversation of the guests assembled to do justice to it, what a position Mr. Fyvie would have lost in the county! It was one of those stupid overgrown dinner-parties, too, where strange faces glowered at every corner, and people intruded upon one's path, whom one hoped never to meet again, under any possible circumstances. We have all had these ghastly nights at our friend's table, and set the result down to bad taste in selection, instead of to our dark hours when good people with wings at their backs would have been even voted bores.

He had never seen such a hideous conglomeration of people, thought Laurence—all the objectionable company that had held possession of Tavvydale House for the last month, added to a round dozen of specimens of polite society in the neighbourhood—fellows who could talk of nothing but horses and hounds; fellows with white neck-cloths, who had brought their divinity with them, and fellows who could not talk at all, and had had evidently no other purpose in coming, save to make an onslaught on the meats and drinks provided for the occasion. Then there was Mrs. Llewellyn, to crown all, towering above everybody, and overshadowing everything, talking at one end of the table in a loud voice that was heard at the other, sitting with her elbows squared and partaking of every dish that came round to her, in quantities that even startled the footmen.

"When does Mrs. Llewellyn think of going home?" asked Laurence suddenly, and not too graciously of his companion.

"Papa returns to the office next week, and we shall accompany him, I dare say."

"You have had a long holiday," he remarked thoughtfully; and then brightening up suddenly, lest his tone of voice should have suggested his wish to see the family out of the house, and so have pained "the best of the lot of them," he added, "I hope that you have enjoyed yourself at Tavvydale?"

"Oh, vastly."

"It is a pretty place."

"Yes, and one meets with nice company here."

"Yes—very," was the dry response; and that was the substance of the conversation which Laurence Raxford supported at the dinner-table whilst the ladies were present.

When the ladies had withdrawn—and he noticed that Mrs. Llewellyn put her arm round her niece's waist affectionately as they passed out of the room—he was compelled to launch forth a little more, to respond to a few remarks of his host and senior partner, smiling like a father at him from the head of the table, even to discuss the rules and regulations of a charity school in the vicinity with an enthusiastic young curate next to him, until Mr. Engleton, scenting a subject, dashed in with *his* views of charity schools, which had been, he asserted, the one study of his life. Then some one proposed the health of the partners, Fyvie, Fyvie and Raxford, and the senior member of the firm, smiling in his friendly way towards Laurence again, insisted upon Laurence returning thanks as the youngest member of that flourishing undertaking amongst the Dartmoor hills. The senior had responded for his health as host, and was not going to have all the talking to himself, and Jonathan Fyvie never spoke if he could help it—he was always too nervous, he said, to face a general community. Laurence returned thanks briefly, and dropped into his seat again in a more morbid condition of mind than he had risen therefrom. He was glad when a grand move was made at last for the drawing-room, and when it was in his power, being near the door, to beat the first retreat, and pass across the hall into the large drawing-room, and seat himself at Hester's side, without any preliminaries. Hester was talking to Aunt Llewellyn as he crossed the room, and he noted that the conversation suddenly ceased as he came within ear-shot. If that old woman had not already begun to make mischief, it was odd to him !

"Not intruding upon any gunpowder treason, I hope, ladies ? " he said, with an affected lightness of demeanour that was far from well done.

"Oh, no," said Hester shortly.

Hester was still inclined to resent the afternoon's want of confidence ; she had not half "served out" this young man yet. Time enough presently for a general amnesty, a few tears shed upon his shoulder perhaps, and a delightful reconciliation. Hester was already looking forward to that picture in the future, and it was becoming uphill work to keep him at a distance ; but poor Hester thought that she had a duty to perform to herself, and if she did not assert her supremacy—her rights—in the early days, what would be her position in the latter ones, when their engagement was an affair of long standing ? He must know her better, and have no secrets from her—live no life apart from her— and *this*, in the fair beginning of their hopes together, would be a lesson to him !

So Hester said, "Oh ! no," with the Fyvie sharpness, that was *not* pleasant to the ears of him whom she addressed.

"Then I shall not be considered an intruder," said Laurence, taking his seat on the couch where no room was made for him by the drawing closer into its folds the voluminous silk skirt of the maiden.

"Young gentlemen are never considered to intrude upon young ladies' society," said Mrs. Llewellyn, looking round at Hester in quite an affectionate manner.

"She's up to something," Laurence thought, at once, for he had never been regarded in this playful way before.

Our hero strove to be gay and at his ease, and failed in obedience to the rule governing all vain efforts. His manner was soon dashed by the quiet, lady-like, unsympathising way in which all his communications were received. The reason was very apparent to him—she had not forgotten that little discussion in the Cleft ; well, he must take an early opportunity of resuming the subject, and explaining all the folly connected with it, if it were necessary. That did not trouble him so much as Hester Fyvie's manner of resenting it, and that told him that in his ideal picture of his lady-love there was at least a flaw of which he had had no cognisance. If Mrs. Llewellyn would only leave them for a little while together, all might be explained now, he thought; and whether that thought gave expression to his face, and was seen by a sympathising friend in the distance or not, certain it was that Mr. Fyvie suddenly came up and offered his arm to his sister-in-law.

"My dear Mrs. Llewellyn, I want to introduce you to a most charming person."

"Who is she?" asked Mrs. Llewellyn, without rising from the couch.

"Well, *she's* a *he*," said Mr. Fyvie jocularly; "and though we need not tell Mr. Llewellyn, he has been struck with your manner, and is exceedingly anxious to have the honour of an introduction."

"Then why didn't you bring him to me?"

"Well—there's a reason," said he very mysteriously.

Mrs. Llewellyn, astonished at the sudden impression that she had created, rose, and sailed away across the room with Mr. Fyvie, who bestowed a parting wink on his junior partner—evidence of the inborn vulgarity of the man, his fair freight would have thought, had she seen that *œillade.*

Laurence watched Mr. Fyvie escort his relative to a whist table, where three innocent looking old folk were waiting a fourth to join them in a rubber, then he turned to Hester with his usual frankness.

"Hester, *is* anything the matter?" he asked.

"No—no," answered Hester slowly; "what should be the matter?"

"Then if nothing's the matter, there remains no occasion for any remarks upon nothingness," said Laurence; "but I had a faint idea that——"

"That what?" said Hester quickly, as he paused.

"That you were offended with me."

"Oh! no," said Hester, tossing her head this time.

Laurence objected to these negatives; they encumbered his way to the explanation that was necessary, and he thought Hester did not shine in this false light at all.

"That Mrs. Llewellyn may have said——"

"Excuse me, Laurence, but Mrs. Llewellyn has said nothing," interrupted Hester; "and however much **you** may dislike or fear Mrs. Llewellyn, I hope that you will not mention her name in that disrespectful way to her niece."

Laurence was taken aback at the reproof, and gave vent to his astonishment in a very unrefined way.

"Well, *that* is a good one," he said emphatically.

"May I ask what you mean by *that* expression?" said Hester, emphasising her demonstrative pronoun also.

"If I haven't heard you speak in the most *un-niece-like* manner of that estimable lady, Hester."

"I did wrong, then, and you have done worse by imitating me. I love Aunt Llewellyn very much indeed."

"Well, that's very kind of you, and I wish that I could follow your example."

"Don't insult me, Laurence. I can bear want of condence better than a mock—mocking satire!"

"Hester, I'm going to put every confidence in you, if you'll only listen patiently."

"I don't want to listen."

"I thought that you were more patient, upon my honour —not so childish, pettish, irritable—what is it?"

Hester turned round at this reproof; he was indeed beginning early to school her into submission; he was not likely to gain a patient hearing, or be readily pardoned, after that last expression.

"Very well, Sir," she said between her closed lips— "very well, Sir!"

"But if you will look like the Hester of a week ago— —just for one minute—I will——"

"Mr. Raxford, you may favour me with an explanation of your eccentricities, when I ask for it," cried Hester, more pettish and childish than ever now; "and if you'll take the trouble to pay a little more attention to my mamma, instead of making yourself and me ridiculous before a room full of people, it will be all the better. Mr. Engleton, will you attempt this duet with me that we practised last night?"

"I—yes—certainly," cried Mr. Engleton, who was advancing at this juncture; "but I'm out of voice—very— to-night."

Laurence gave a hasty rub to his curly hair with both hands, and made no effort to supplant Mr. Engleton in his escort of Hester to the piano. All this was very new and very puzzling, but it did not irritate him, so much as it surprised him. He had believed Hester Fyvie to be one of the most amiable girls whom he had ever encountered, a good-tempered, light-hearted, merry girl, with whom a man might naturally fall in love,—not a girl ready to take offence at every trifling misconception, and to revenge herself, in her own way, upon him for his share in it. He was surprised, then—nay more, he was sorry; and had Hester turned at that juncture, she would have been startled at the sorrowful, wondering face which was bent in her direction.

A keen-eyed old gentleman, who seemed ever on the watch, noticed it, instead of his daughter.

"Why, what ever are you looking so dismally at, Laurence?" asked Mr. Fyvie in his partner's ear; "is Hester in one of her teasing moods, or have you and she been teasing one another?—nothing wrong—eh?"

"Wrong, Sir!—I hope not," said Laurence, shaking off his dull impressions at once; "not even a lover's quarrel yet awhile. I don't like quarrelling—it's not in my way."

"Neither does my girl—God bless her!" said the old gentleman, rubbing one hand briskly over the other; "so you will be a very happy couple. She's full of spirits, and fond of teasing people at times; but if ever there was a good, sound-hearted girl, it's Hester—she's the flood of sunshine in the house of Fyvie!"

The father slapped Laurence on the back, as though he congratulated him on that sunshine which would gladden the younger man's house in good time; and Laurence felt it steal to his heart again whilst Mr. Fyvie spoke.

"Yes," he said, "I saw how she brightened home when I first came here, innocent of all your good intentions."

"And fell in love accordingly—falling into the snare, too, which I, like a crafty old huntsman, had set for you. Well, it all comes round like a pleasant story-book, and I have nothing to perplex me;—a good partner to take care of Jonathan, and a good son to take care of her. Laurence, I'm as happy an old dog as ever lived!"

"I wish sometimes that you had not this high opinion of me," said Laurence restlessly.

"That's an odd wish," said Fyvie; "why, if I had not

the highest opinion, do you think that I would have set my heart on you, boy, all these long years? You are just the man that I prophesied your mother would make of you, if left to herself. There's all the frankness and good-temper of that mother, and the humility of your father, allied to a perseverance that is all your own; and so you are Jonathan Fyvie's friend, too. Gad, Sir, these are something like compliments from old Jonathan, too! Let us go and talk to Mrs. Fyvie now."

Laurence was surprised at this second intimation of Mrs. Fyvie's presence, and it struck him then that both father and daughter were anxious that the mother should be as interested in him as they were. And possibly Mrs. Fyvie had not received a fair share of his attention, and he had taken her languid ways, her listlessness concerning all mundane matters, too much as a matter of course, and she had, despite all this, expressed a word or two concerning his inattention. He made amends at once; he rather liked Mrs. Fyvie, despite her stateliness. She was a lady who had suffered too much in life to smile readily at the life around her; but for all that she was a true lady, suggesting no thought of her Brobdingnagian sister.

Laurence and she got on very well together for the remainder of the evening. Laurence devoted himself exclusively to the mother, and by the story of his week's experience at Wheal Desperation, the mistakes he had committed by relying too much on his book knowledge, and the scoldings in consequence that one or two captains, who were his teachers—Captain Athorpe amongst the number—had scrupled not to bestow upon him, brought the smiles to Mrs. Fyvie's worn face.

Laurence was not afraid of putting himself in a ludicrous light at times for the better effect of his anecdotes, and he had a graceful as well as straightforward way of relating his incidents of actual experience, which told in his favour with all listeners. He pleased always when he was anxious to please, as we have already remarked.

Mrs. Fyvie reclined in her easy-chair, and thought, too, that Hester was a lucky girl to have become engaged to this young man—that it was a good thing for everybody, after all, though there was no money on his side. Her sister had not thought so; her sister had said more than once that it was a mésalliance, arising out of an unnatural partiality on the part of Mr. Fyvie for Laurence; and she had had a dreamy idea once or twice that though Mr. Fyvie must have his own way, still Hester might have done better, until Laurence did good service for himself that evening by paying his respects to "dear mamma." Still Laurence watched Hester from the distance; he had a faint hope that she would veer round in his direction presently, making the *amende honorable* by that course of action, just as he was making amends for any pain he had given her by submission to her last orders. And Hester was pleased —very pleased—to see him at her mother's side, and in a day or two she would accord her free forgiveness, she thought. But on that evening, not at any price, even the price of his reverent submission! The dear fellow must fully understand that she was not to be treated like a child —although he *had* called her very childish—and that there were plenty of people in the world ready to fall down and worship her as well as Laurence Raxford. He must be proud and jealous of the love which he had won—which, she thought, with the Fyvie pride predominant just then, she had let him win too easily.

So she coquetted faintly enough, and in all good faith, with Mr. Engleton, who certainly liked it after his first surprise, and seconded her little scheme for making her lover miserable; whilst the lover, not miserable at all—and that was the most annoying part of it!—chatted away by her mother's side, laughed heartily once or twice, and almost made the mother laugh. Once she fancied that he was looking anxiously, even reprovingly, in her direction, but that might have been fancy! He certainly was not half so angry with her as she was with him—*ergo*, said this young lady, with a leap forwards to an objectionable conclusion, he did not care half so much about her.

"What a desperate flirt that Hester is," said Mrs. Llewellyn, confidentially, in her sister's ear, tilting her chair backwards from the card-table, the better to convey that verdict to Mrs. Fyvie—"why don't you ask Mr. Raxford to stop it?"

Laurence started at this intrusion on Mrs. Llewellyn's part, but he was on his guard now, and answered readily enough for himself:

" Mr. Engleton will not try to cut me out ; he is too good a friend of mine," said Laurence ; " he is only detailing to her, after all, one of his pet schemes. I can tell that by his animation."

" And you're not a bit jealous ? " asked Mrs. Llewellyn, with evident interest.

" Upon my honour—not a bit."

" Every confidence, Laurence," murmured Mrs. Fyvie ; "that's well—for she deserves it."

" Yes—but there was a something once," croaked this Roman-nosed bird of evil omen, "between Mr. Engleton and Hester—you told me so yourself, Charlotte."

" I fancied so," said Mrs. Fyvie, quite scared by her sister-in-law's charge, "and told you so. But neither Mr. Fyvie nor Hester would believe anything of the kind."

" Now, Ma'am," testily cried a gentleman at the card-table—the very gentleman who had expressed his anxiety to be introduced to Mrs. Llewellyn, "will you have the goodness to lead ? We're all waiting."

Laurence felt a shade more annoyance after this, though its evidence rose not to the surface. If the poor design lurked in the mind of any one present to annoy him, he would be more likely to die, than to show any sign of dissatisfaction. He felt, after Mrs. Llewellyn's avowal, that he had a harder part to play, but he played it admirably, and deceived all lookers-on.

" I suppose that you will come more frequently, when you are better acquainted with mining operations, Laurence ? " asked Mrs. Fyvie after this.

" Being sure that everybody will be glad to see me more frequently," answered Laurence ; " to be sure I will."

" Everybody will be glad of that," she said, "and you haven't found us really at home yet, Laurence. That is without all these good people, who are excellent company, but try one's health very much. You cannot conceive," she said languidly, "what an effort it is for me."

Laurence had not witnessed any vigorous effort on the part of Mrs. Fyvie to set her guests at their ease, but that good lady always believed that she had exerted herself considerably, and at any rate, showed as complete signs of exhaustion at the end of the evening as though she had done so. After a while she dozed off, and Laurence, anxious not to disturb her, rose gently, and joined Miss Llewellyn for the few minutes that remained before the party broke up for good.

When the outsiders had gone home, and the insiders were bidding each other good-night, Laurence offered his adieux with the rest—coming round at last to Hester's side.

"Shall I see you again before I leave to-morrow?"

"To-morrow," said Hester, surprised for an instant, and then vexed at having exhibited her surprise, "you do not stop till Sunday, then?"

"I shall not begin holiday-making yet awhile, Hester," he said; "at ten o'clock to morrow-morning, I shall be at Wheal Desperation."

"If you're in so great a hurry, nothing that I can say will induce you to remain longer, of course. Good-night."

"Shall I see you to-morrow before I go?"

"No — you will not," was the rapid answer to his question.

"Very good," said Laurence; "will you wait here for a few minutes, then?"

"Thank you, but I'm in as great a hurry to get to my room to-night as you are to run away to-morrow."

But she waited all the same, although Laurence, taking her at her word, and not believing for an instant that she would alter her mind, went up to his room, and locked himself in for the night.

Jonathan tried the handle of his door, half an hour afterwards.

"What !—the key turned on all intruders, Laurence," he cried; "I was coming to smoke one of my cigars with you, old fellow. Not asleep yet?"

"Trying, Jonathan."

"Ah! then I'll not disturb you. Good-night."

"Good-night."

Laurence Raxford, if he were trying to sleep, was adopting a very extraordinary method of doing so. He was sitting in his shirt-sleeves on the edge of his bed, studying the pattern of his carpet. His face had lost all its pleasant expression, and had become very grave and earnest; he had looked far less thoughtfully at the moon the last time we accompanied him to this chamber.

At the table, on which a light was burning, were writing

materials, and an unfinished letter. As Laurence had not caught in any violent degree Mr. Whiteshell's habit of soliloquising, probably the letter may afford a clue to this young man's ruminations.

There is a suspicious paragraph, that may stand for his thoughts—and it, at least, tells us of what he has been thinking.

"Everything bright around me, dear mother, and no future for you to be anxious about any more. All the romance gone out of me, too—you who said that I was too romantic for every-day life! Here am I, who had a dreamy idea of marrying a sylph, or something of that kind, engaged to be married to Hester Fyvie, a fair sample of that every-day stock against which I have more than once energetically protested. Hester sends her love."

When Laurence had done thinking, he re-read his letter, and then tore it quietly into fragments. He was evidently resolved not to do anything in a hurry ever again.

CHAPTER XVI.

MR. WHITESHELL BIDS EVERYBODY GOOD-BYE.

LAURENCE went away early the next morning without catching a glimpse of Hester. He went away before any one was astir in the house save the servants, having resolved on a brisk walk to business after his early breakfast. He felt that he wanted a walk which would do him good, and dissipate all the thoughts born of last night's brooding. A week hence he should be himself again,—he felt very much like somebody else at present,—and a week hence there would steal back to him, at Tavvydale House, the fair woman who had accepted the offer of his hand, and told him frankly that she loved him. Again that odd, unaccountable thought that it was a long time back—years back almost—when they were boy and girl, and acted hastily, like boy and girl, in settling matters after a few weeks' acquaintance with each other. He had seen no one in the

11

world whom he liked so well, and therefore he was sure that
he was in love : he had met a benefactor of an uncommon
stamp, and he had seen where the wishes lay of that benefactor. His heart had been full of gratitude, and he had
been anxious to show it; but still he loved Hester Fyvie—
loved her very much indeed, and was bound by honour to
make her happy ever afterwards. If he had thought her
faultless once, and now found her, as he had phrased it in
his letter to his mother, "a fair sample of the every-day
stock"—in three words, an every-day woman—why, so
much the better for him probably. Out-of-the-way wives
have out-of-the-way hobbies, which lead to confusion, and he
was still the lucky fellow whom everybody envied.

He walked to Wheal Desperation, and in less than two
hours was underground in his miner's dress, studying things
practically, and forgetting the strange young woman who
had perplexed him yesternight—who was not *his* Hester,
any more than she was herself on that occasion.

Next week he received a letter from Hester, informing
him that she was about to spend a few days in town
with her relatives, the Llewellyns, and that if he *wished*
to see her before she went away he must take a very
early opportunity of calling at Tavvydale House. Laurence
frowned over this epistle, held it at arm's length, tossed
it at last almost contemptuously away. He did not relish
the curt satire of the note, though he would have shown
himself satire-proof in her presence ; he was vexed to see
that she still bore in remembrance the little difference
that had arisen at their last meeting, and could coolly
underline the word "wished," as though she doubted
what his wishes were.

He went to Tavvydale House that evening—which
was another stupid evening, with a crowd of people
about the drawing-room, killing time with music and
whist—such an evening as had already stamped itself upon
his mind as a highly objectionable one for a sensible man to
spend, especially as there was a difficulty in speaking to
Hester for five minutes together. He found the opportunity
at length, for she was not too anxious to avoid it, and then
came the explanation which both had wished for, and, which
attaining, did not set things right.

Laurence related that absurd suspicion of Mrs. Llewellyn

concerning Milly, and Hester laughed at it, too, and confessed that it *was* absurd, and all would have passed off after the fashion which both had anticipated, had not Laurence mentioned Hester's manner on their last evening together, and dropped the most delicate hint in the world that it did not become her. This, instead of asking pardon for his misconduct, and expressing a resolution founded on a rock never to do so again! This, after evincing a want of confidence in her! Hester "showed off"—not in a great degree, for they had kissed and made it up—but just a little, having expected more humility from her lover, and having been taught to expect it from all the novels that she had ever read. Hester could not see that she had been in the wrong in the least, and as Laurence could not perceive that *he* had been in the wrong, each parted with the idea that it was a pity that the other was so obstinate. Another cool and quiet meeting would have been all the better for this young couple, but it was denied them at the time, and the chance never came again in all their after lives.

The next day Laurence was at business again, and Hester was rattling away to London in a first-class compartment along with the Llewellyns—people in whom Laurence was not particularly interested.

Another week, and then a gentleman called at the mines, and asked if he could see Mr. Raxford. Mr. Raxford was studying the accounts that day in the inner office, sacred to partners.

"Did he send in his card, or state his business?"

"He regretted that he had left his card-case in London—and he said his name was Whiteshell."

"Oh! show him in."

Mr. Whiteshell, bearing in one hand the carpet-bag which Laurence a fortnight since had assisted him in carrying, and in the other a something in green baize, made his appearance shortly afterwards.

"You will excuse me entering with my hat on, Mr. Raxford," he said, "but I am loaded, you see—borne down with the weight of my luggage and my spoils. I thought, Sir, that I would take the liberty of calling to pay you my farewell respects."

"It was very kind of you, Mr. Whiteshell," said Laurence; "will you take a seat?"

11—2

" Thank you."

Mr. Whiteshell carefully put down his carpet-bag, set his green baize mystery on the top, took off his hat, let drop therefrom a huge pocket-handkerchief, which he picked up, shook out, and wiped his face and forehead with. When he was seated on the chair facing Laurence, our hero fancied that he was not looking so bright and well as a fortnight's absence from business should have made him. He was paler and more lined, unless Laurence's earlier glimpses of him had deceived him.

" My visit is a liberty, Sir, that I am sure you will excuse," he said after a pause, during which he seemed to glance anxiously around him, " and it's only poor old Whiteshell's way of expressing the gratitude he owes you."

" My dear Sir, I don't see that there is anything to be grateful for," said our hero ; " you were benighted, and I helped you on your way to the Cleft."

" Knowing that I was a poor man, and that you were a rich one. It was an honour, Mr. Raxford."

" A very queer one," said Laurence, " and we'll say no more about it. You have enjoyed yourself in Devonshire, I hope ? "

" For one week better than I expected. I should have enjoyed myself more, if I could have kept my mind at ease. That, Sir, seemed giving way at times."

He spoke with a sudden excitement that startled Laurence, who waited for the further explanation, which was not offered him.

" You will excuse me," said Whiteshell, " I am not speaking by the card ; I am scarcely myself to-day. Leaving old friends in Devonshire always upsets me, and I talk at random."

" The walk up the Cleft this hot day has been too much for you, Mr. Whiteshell."

" Perhaps it has ; and with nobody to help me with my luggage either," he said drily, " no generous fellow with youth, health and strength on his side ; upon my word, Mr. Raxford, I admire your character very much," he cried.

" Oh ! you're very good," laughed Laurence ; " and now, before you start afresh, I must pay back that glass of wine I owe you."

He touched the bell, and the old housekeeper from the

outer regions responded, received her orders, and shortly afterwards placed on the table a decanter of sherry and two glasses.

"I'm giving you a great deal of trouble," said Mr. Whiteshell.

"Not at all."

"I'm in the way this morning ; you're very busy ? "

"On the contrary, not in a business humour, and glad of an excuse to turn my back upon the books."

"Ah ! ha ! " cried Whiteshell, brightening up a bit, " just as glad as I am to turn my back upon Devonshire, if it wasn't for poor Milly—a girl that I love very much, Sir, and look upon as my own flesh and blood."

"A good girl ; there's no doubt of that."

"Thank God !—no doubt of that," repeated Whiteshell. " Mr. Raxford, I drink wine with you."

Both men raised their glasses, and bowed over them, Mr. Whiteshell most elaborately.

"You do not walk to Tavistock ? " asked our hero.

"What, eight miles ! " cried the old man. " Oh, no. My friend Captain Athorpe," added he with a chuckle, "has been kind enough to say that he will drive me to the station, if I meet him here at twelve. I came here a little before time to say good-bye to you, Sir, feeling somehow that I should not be snubbed in this quarter."

"But how are you going ? "

"Captain Athorpe has managed all that," said the old man. " I think that the landlady at the inn has promised to send a small cart up here at twelve; and I am not too proud for carts in the country, though in London they *are* a little derogatory."

"Captain Athorpe and you are good friends at last, then ? "

"At last," said Mr. Whiteshell. " Milly did her best to make us so, and, despite of opposing elements, she succeeded. Why, we had quite a party at Captain Athorpe's house, and I am sure that we all enjoyed ourselves very much."

His face assumed a depth of shadow that was in contrast to his words, which faltered on his lips as he concluded.

"Very much," he repeated, however, and this time more decisively, as though distrustful of the impression he had himself conveyed to his listener, "for one only requires to know the man to feel at home with him. A blunt but honest fellow, with his heart in the right place. A man who has roughed it half his life, and over half the world—been a trifle wild in his day, too !—but a man who means well, and deserves that everybody should mean well by him. I think they do,—I hope they do ! "

He clasped his hands together and nearly dropped his empty glass. Then he rose, set his glass on the table with an air of alacrity that was assumed to hide his nervousness, and went back to his seat.

"Pray tell me when you are tired of me, Mr. Raxford," he said. "I believe that I have a quarter of an hour to wait before Captain Athorpe is ready, and I can spend that in the outer office."

"You were not in a hurry to get rid of me at the Cleft, Mr. Whiteshell."

"No, but I may be in the way here," said Whiteshell, "or your partner may come in."

"That is not likely."

"The younger of the two, the son, is not often here, then ? " he asked anxiously.

"Very seldom."

"Not often in Devonshire, he tells me."

"Well, he wanders about England a great deal, and takes a great deal of pleasure, as he has a right to do, with a fortune at his fingers' ends. You have seen him ? "

"Yes. He spoke to me at the Cleft that day the company came. He bears a good name in these parts ? "

"Why should he not ? "

"Exactly; why should he not ? I am glad to hear that he does," stammered the other ; for a good name is soon lost, and people in high positions are shafts for the envious and malicious. If they speak no harm of him here, he must be a pretty—good—sort of a man."

"I hope you think so ? " asked Laurence.

"Who—I ? Oh, I have no right to say anything to the contrary against a man who says 'good-day' to me, and simply asks what has become of all his friends. How many minutes have I left now, Sir ? "

"Ten."

"Only ten, and," he added, with a rapidity of utterance

that again elicited the surprise of Laurence at his eccentricity, "I have so much to say—so great a favour to ask of you!"

"Of me?—what is it?"

"That you would take down my address, No. 22, Milk Street, Westminster, and keep it where you will be able to find it—on any emergency, that is."

"I don't understand."

"Neither do I; but if you will kindly take a note of it, and oblige a man getting weak and nervous with advancing years."

Laurence made a note of it at once. When he had finished he found that Mr. Whiteshell had risen, and was looking anxiously over his shoulder at the memorandum.

"I am never happy, knowing that that girl is living in the Cleft alone," he hastened to explain, with one hand on Laurence's shoulder; "it is a false position, strong as she is in her innocence. You don't know how I love that child, Sir; how I feel sometimes as if there will come a great danger to her, living in that solitary place, with never a friend, never a true friend in whom to trust.

"There is her Uncle Athorpe—the man of whom you have spoken so warmly."

"Harsh and crude, with no knowledge of women, and most unfit to be a woman's counsellor."

"And Captain Athorpe's wife."

"Yes—yes, there is Captain Athorpe's wife. But then she is not exactly English, and she dislikes to hear any woman praised too much by others—a small weakness, and very womanly; and—and she is, though a good woman, I believe, sensible, and far-seeing, and accomplished; yet she is not a woman to give the best advice to *my* girl. I hoped she was," said he, "before I came here to look about me for myself; but in all confidence—mind, in all confidence, I don't think so now! There is a something that I don't exactly understand in In—Mrs. Athorpe; and perhaps it is as well that there is not a very great affection between her and my niece. So you see, Mr. Raxford, that Milly is very much alone."

"Well—yes."

"It is extremely strange, but there is only one person I should like to see interested in Milly—sufficiently interested to watch over her from a distance, and at odd times—making sure that she was well, and confident, and happy. Only one—and that's *you*."

"My dear Sir !" exclaimed Laurence, in astonishment, at this cool proposal.

"Of course it cannot be," he hastened to add, "for you're one of the masters here, and she's a girl in your service, though quite a little lady in her way. I am merely speaking," he added, with a low bow, "of my confidence in you, and of what, under other circumstances, might have happened. I don't know that in all my life," here another bow was made, "I ever met so true a gentleman, and—and my heart is rather full to-day."

He passed his hands over his eyes, coughed, stamped with one foot, then the other ; paced the room twice, and finally sat down again. Laurence did not press him to accept another glass of sherry ; he fancied that Mr. Whiteshell must have been saving his port wine till the last day, and then have taken it all at once before starting homewards.

He was glad that Captain Athorpe's loud voice was heard asking in the outer office if any one had called for him that morning.

"Here is the captain," said Laurence. "Step this way, Athorpe," he cried through a little open window that communicated with the next room.

"Company and all, Sir ?" inquired the captain.

"Yes—to be sure."

Captain Athorpe came into the room, followed by Milly, who would not venture further than the open door.

"Here's another holiday, or half-holiday taken, Mr. Raxford," said Athorpe; "I told Peters that he was far too easily talked over by the girls."

"I thought that I must see you into the train, Uncle James," said Milly. "I couldn't make up my mind to that last good-bye of yours."

"God bless you, my child ; you are very kind," said Whiteshell.

"Kind ! And I came away without carrying the violin for you, as I promised."

"It was no weight. This, Mr. Raxford," taking up the green baize bag, "is a present kindly made me by my friend here."

" Oh ! it was no good to me," said Athorpe, with his customary inelegant way of putting himself in the worst light. I've got something better to do than play that thing now—and it is in your line."

" Yes. But it's a good violin ; and it was a good and kind offer, Athorpe."

" I don't see it. But you're welcome to it, with all my heart, Whiteshell," said he, " though my wife was at the bottom of the idea. She thought you had taken a fancy to the thing, she told me."

" She was always generous," muttered Whiteshell.

" So, Milly, you kept your promise, and made these two friends ? " said Laurence.

Milly forgot her embarrassment at this direct appeal, and she answered quickly enough,

" Yes, Sir ; I am pleased to say that they are very good friends, and will always keep so for their Milly's sake, I hope. The two in the world who wish me well should not remain any longer apart, I thought, and I tried hard—very hard—to make them understand one another."

" I believe that Milly's going with us to make sure that we shan't quarrel by the way," cried Athorpe, with a hearty laugh.

" Oh ! you don't think that ? " said Milly.

" Captain Athorpe, in good faith, and to show that we intend nothing of the sort—that we understand and esteem each other from this day forth—I shake hands with you again," said Mr. Whiteshell.

" All right," returned Athorpe, taking James Whiteshell's hand ; " there, my lass, are you any happier for that ? "

" Yes, I am," cried Milly—" that's as it should be ! "

" We'll drink each other's health at parting, too," cried Whiteshell, with an easy flourish of his hand towards the sherry, as though it was his especial property—" Mr. Raxford will not object to two more glasses being rung for ? "

" Certainly not," said Raxford, smiling more at the astonishment of Captain Athorpe and his niece than at this modest appeal from Mr. Whiteshell.

The glasses were brought in, but Milly escaped into the mining-ground ; she had not the courage to drink wine in the office of the master.

" Why, there's that Milly——"

"There, let her be," interrupted Athorpe ; "the girl knows her place, and it's as well that she should keep it. We're all in the wrong place, perhaps, just now," he added, with a glance towards Laurence.

"Not at all."

"Not at all," said Mr. Whiteshell, "for Mr. Raxford is not a proud man, and looks not disparagingly at his inferiors. I have been telling Mr. Raxford——"

"We haven't much time to spare," muttered Athorpe— "the trap's waiting in the yard."

"Then we'll drink—you and I, Athorpe—Mr. Raxford's health, as well as our own. Your health, Sir, and good fortune be with you."

"Thank you. *Your* health," said Laurence, "and a safe and pleasant journey back to London."

Mr. Whiteshell offered his thanks in return, and then faced Captain Athorpe, who was nodding towards him over the wine in his hand.

"And your health, Captain Athorpe," he said ; "I hope that you, too, will know contentment all your life—you and your wife—peace, love, and trust ever between you !"

"We're sure of that," cried Athorpe—"never man or woman understood each other better."

"You don't know how glad I am to hear you say that."

"It's not much business of yours to feel glad about it," said Athorpe—"but it's kind, and so thank'ee. Why, Whiteshell, if the love and trust were gone, the devil himself had better be your friend than I."

"No, don't say that. That's not manlike," cried Whiteshell.

"If you please," the housekeeper screamed in at the open door, "Milly says as how you'll lose the train, Captain."

"I'll cut the horse in half first," said Athorpe ; "here, give me the bag, and you catch hold of the fiddle."

"I am ready. Good-bye, Mr. Raxford."

"Good-bye, Mr. Whiteshell."

"When we meet again—if ever we meet again, Sir—I hope that all of us will have as good opinions of one another and be as deserving of them," he said ; "if we don't change as the world goes round, and see no change in others to regret, we may consider ourselves well served."

In the after-time Laurence Raxford thought often of this old man's words.

" If we don't change as the world goes round, and see no change in others to regret ! "

He was repeating the sentence to himself a minute or two after Mr. Whiteshell's withdrawal, when Milly suddenly came back into the room, her manner more nervous and shy than ordinary.

" When I return, Sir, will you—will you be kind enough to allow me to speak to you in confidence ? It is important."

" Certainly, Milly. I shall be here all day."

" Thank you," she murmured, and hastened from the room again, leaving Laurence very much perplexed.

CHAPTER XVII.

THE BEGINNING OF DIFFICULTIES.

LAURENCE waited patiently for Milly's return from Tavistock, puzzled still by the reminiscence of Milly's excited demeanour, and yet trying to forget it in the account books over which he bent. Still hers was a face not easy to forget when it had come suddenly between him and his business thoughts ; when around it and its possessor hovered—or seemed to hover—a mystery beyond his fathoming. A face that was very beautiful—he owned that—and which touched him by its expression of distress. He was to meet it ; it was to cross him despite his quiet life ; despite the commonplaces which were round him, and of which it and him were parts.

Laurence felt a little uneasy, though he regarded matters soberly enough. He thought that it was as well that Mrs. Llewellyn had gone to London, and could not possibly be aware that Milly desired an interview with him—was to have an interview, even if it were only for the purpose of giving him a week's warning first hand. It was strange to seek an interview alone with him—scarcely discreet in a girl who was looked upon with a little envy by her contemporaries. She had spoken very hastily—probably it was a hasty idea of hers, and she would repent of it in due course, or bring her uncle with her. After all, there was certainly something of a mystery here.

Three hours afterwards Captain Athorpe and his niece returned, and both went to their respective duties. Laurence waited and worked all day without seeing either of them.

In the evening the copper gnomes rose from below ground, and went their way; the surface workers, women, children, and old men followed them, and Laurence believed that Milly had gone with the rest, thinking better of past intentions upon second consideration. Laurence was inclined to the opinion that he was glad of this, when he had had his tea— a steady-going six o'clock tea, provided for him by the housekeeper—and was sallying forth to wander round the deserted works, after a habit that he had already acquired.

The huge water-wheels were motionless, and all the machinery they moved was silent with them when he went out of the office and strolled leisurely towards the sheds where the copper washing and smashing and sorting went on. Under the first shed, leaning with one arm against the trough, and looking thoughtfully down at it, stood Milly Athorpe, her flapping head-gear thrust back from her face —a fair picture, with the sun's rays long and shaft-like darting in through the open shed upon her.

" What ! not gone home, Milly ? " said Laurence.

" No, Sir, I was trying to find courage to speak to you," she said, " to come in and trouble you with all the nonsense that is not your business. And then I was thinking that perhaps I had better tell my Uncle Oliver."

" Ah ! why not ? "

" Because he is firm and quick, and might do harm instead of good. Because it is not necessary—and my Uncle James asked me, if ever I wanted a friend, *you*," looking up fearlessly at this, " he was sure, might be trusted."

" Your Uncle James has an excellent opinion of me— entirely through helping him with that heavy bag to the Cleft. I am a bad adviser."

" Oh ! Sir, I don't want your advice," said Milly readily ; "I have been taught too long to rely upon myself. But I think that I may trust you to do me justice. I think that it is part of a master's duty to protect his servants."

" Surely it is," responded Laurence, struck by the girl's

new and proud manner, "and the master will do his best, rely upon him."

" I know it."

Milly was silent for a short while after this, and Laurence waited patiently, until she recovered from that evident embarrassment which she felt in stating her case, despite all her confidence in him.

"Uncle Oliver is too abrupt, and would make enemies, I fear. Mr. Fyvie is a good man, and his daughter is a good lady, but somehow—I can scarcely tell how—I can't speak to them, and I might set the father against him. So with nobody else to help me, Sir—no father, mother, elder sister, I come to you, the master."

" Well, what can I do, Milly ? You are like all the ladies —a long while arriving at the subject."

"Because I wanted to explain why I select you, Sir. I—I hope you understand the reason. It is a bold one, perhaps, that keeps me here—but he said that I could trust you."

Milly collected her scattered forces, and then dashed into the subject.

" They have been speaking of me in Tavvydale," she said, hurriedly; "somebody has said in Tavvydale that young Mr. Fyvie came courting me in the Cleft last summer, and that I encouraged him. No one knew that he ever stopped me in the Cleft, except Mrs. Llewellyn—and she has set this story going."

"What of it ? No one will believe it."

" For all that, Sir, it is an ugly charge against me, and I am a girl easy to attack, and with no friends to defend me. I am told—I believe it is false—that Jonathan Fyvie is often in the Cleft again. Now, this Jonathan Fyvie is *your* friend—and I want you to ask him to do me justice. He knows the truth—and can stop the slander if he likes. And he *must*," cried Milly warmly.

" In what way ? "

" By telling that strange lady how it came to pass, that he thought me defenceless and weak, and how I stood my ground, and shamed him."

"He has dared to insult you ? "

" Sir, he was gentleman enough—there, I own that," said Milly—" to go away at the first rebuff, and come not again to wound my pride by his attentions. He went

away, confessing that he had not acted well by me—and
I think that he will confess as much to any one in Tavvydale, who believes that I was weak enough to lead him
on. Will you ask him ?"

" Yes—I will ask him," said Laurence slowly.

" He must tell Mrs. Llewellyn all the truth. She would
not believe me—and she," with a shudder, " will come back
again."

" Is Mr. Whiteshell aware of this ? "

" No, Sir ; young Mr. Fyvie would not listen to Mr. Whiteshell, and it would have added to my uncle's distress, rendering him more miserable in London. I don't want anybody miserable about me."

" Well, Milly—I will take an early opportunity of seeing
Mr. Jonathan. He has not acted well—and he must do his
best to rectify the error."

" I think he will. He *is* not a bad man—only weak as
a child, and vain as a woman. If I could see him—if I
could go to the great house without adding to the suspicions
against me, I would not have come to you like this."

" I am an odd fellow to take for your confidant, Milly,"
said Laurence, " but at all events, I will do your bidding,
as gracefully and delicately as I can."

" Ask him, when he hears what is false against himself
and me, to state the truth—he will do that."

" He will do that," echoed Laurence.

" The truth first of all to his aunt, who disbelieves me—
and I will thank him. There, that's all ! "

Milly gave an impetuous tug to her sun-bonnet, and
prepared to depart. Suddenly she turned again to
Laurence.

" I thank you, Mr. Raxford, for undertaking this commission for me," she said ; " you will not think me presumptuous in asking for your influence. You, I hope at least,
understand my motives, even if I have acted hastily in this
—acted wrongly."

" No—not wrongly, Milly."

" You have a mother living, I think you said once ? " she
asked, looking wistfully at Laurence.

" Yes—the dearest, and the best of mothers, bless her
heart ! " cried Laurence enthusiastically.

" A friend, and a guide in everything—one to trust in, Sir,

and to be sure of comfort from. Well, Mr. Raxford, I was motherless at eleven years of age ! "

Laurence felt the tears rise suddenly to his eyes, at this strange girl's earnestness ; he saw her lips quiver, despite her effort to be firm ; he was touched by her isolation.

" But not friendless, Milly," he hastened to remind her ; " I believe that you have a host of friends at Tavvydale."

" A host of friends in my books, and they are always welcome to me," she said, smiling, " and one or two living beings whom I call my friends, but who don't understand me. And that's natural," she said after a pause, " for I don't understand myself."

" How's that ? "

" Oh ! it's a long story," she said, becoming suddenly shy, " and not worth your hearing, Sir. Good-night, and thank you."

She dropped a curtsey suddenly, and made Laurence blush at her naïve simplicity. It seemed strange to receive this act of deference from her—from a girl who had taught herself to speak almost like a lady " to the manner born." And yet she was but an overlooker to a gang of mining women, and had she not been pointed out to him as very good and beautiful, had she not crossed his path so strangely, he would have known her simply as one of the many who toiled from sunrise to sunset in the service of Wheal Desperation.

Now he did not know what to think of her, though he thought a great deal about her for the next hour and a half.

He thought, too, what a shame it was that Jonathan Fyvie should have marked that innocent girl out for his attentions, and again her cry, her appeal to him, as it were, in that one word, " Motherless," rang in his ears, and made strange vibrations at his heart.

Young, beautiful, and yet so friendless—living alone in a gap between the hills, and trusting in God for her protection ; it was a defenceless life, he thought, and one to which she had rashly exposed herself.

He would go over to Tavvydale House to-morrow, and see his partner, Jonathan ; and whilst making up his mind to that, and deliberating in the twilight where Milly had left him long since, that partner, like a ghost conjured by his own thoughts, advanced towards him across the mining ground.

"I thought that I would give you a look up, and bring a few more cigars with me, Laurence," he said, as he advanced, and offered his hand—no longer in a sling—to shake; "it's deuced dull work at Tavvydale House just now. I'm off to London to-morrow, and I thought that it was but common civility to call and bid you good-bye, and ask if I can do anything for you in town."

"Thank you, Jonathan—you can. Shall we go into the house?"

"Not just yet. I never liked that poky, wooden edifice; and you and I can enjoy our cigars out here. Any news?"

"Yes—a little."

Jonathan sat down on the edge of the trough, and produced his cigar-case.

"Wait till I light up, then, Laurence. Will you join me?"

"Presently."

"Very good, old fellow. Now I'm all attention. What's the news?—and what can I do for you?"

~~~~~~~~~~

CHAPTER XVIII.

THE PARTNERS.

LAURENCE regarded the handsome man before him with a certain amount of pity, as he sat there carelessly on the edge of the trough, swinging one leg to and fro, and fumigating the summer air with his favourite "brand." A man with all the advantages of wealth and position before him, and who had misused both; a man indolent and selfish, and to whom he was allied for good—whom he should have to regard as a brother presently, and whom he already felt that he distrusted.

"The news I have for you, Jonathan, and the favour that you can do for me in London, are very closely allied."

"Anything wrong with Hester?" he asked. "Oh! we'll soon make that right. Though how people can fall out with one another for life everlasting, puzzles me. I never quarrelled in my life—not even with a woman, who is the devil at times."

"I wish to speak to you about Milly Athorpe."

"Eh ? "

Jonathan took his cigar from his mouth, and was evidently surprised in the extreme.

"Why, what on earth have you to do with Milly Athorpe ? or I either ? "

"Not much. It's not a long story, Jonathan. It appears that the poor girl is likely to be talked about in the village."

"Ah, a canting lot of dissenting sneaks are sure to have something to talk about ; and I suppose they will tell that infernal fire-eater, Athorpe, and then a grand combustion will be the consequence. But what is it to do with me ? "

"It is said by Mrs. Llewellyn that Milly and you were seen together in the Cleft last summer. They talk of Milly Athorpe and you at Tavvydale."

"Let them."

"These rumours do not affect the man much—in some sets enhance his reputation, perhaps ; but they are a life-long torture, or a moral death, to the poor girl connected with them."

"Last summer, my dear Laurence," exclaimed Jonathan. "Why there have been a hundred reputations slain since then, and the peasant girl is still blooming in the Cleft."

"She asks you to tell the truth to Mrs. Llewellyn, who believes her to blame. She asks you to speak in her defence whenever it may be necessary—that's all."

"She has chosen a queer ambassador, Laurence," replied Jonathan. "I should like to know the reason for the choice ? "

"Well, it was a flattering one to me. She believed that she could trust me."

"You are a lucky fellow to have won Milly's confidence, Laurence. How is that you have been more successful than I ? "

"Jonathan, I do not think that we need treat this matter quite so lightly," said Laurence, with great seriousness. "Here is a young girl unable to defend herself, assailed—or on the point of being assailed—by the weightiest slander that can fall on woman. You, I take it, are the cause—

12

you will surely be man enough to bear all the blame yourself ? "

"Just as you please," said Jonathan. "I don't mind bearing all the blame to oblige you two—I shall survive the burden. It is of no consequence to me what people say ; people say anything, according to their fancies, nowadays —and I am at your service."

If he had said this with more earnestness, Laurence would have thought him more likely to fulfil his promise ; but Jonathan maintained his easy flippancy of discourse, and continued smoking with extreme placidity. The whole affair was trifling to him, and he regarded it as a trifle.

"Tavvydale folk, Jonathan, assert that you are still to be seen frequently in the Cleft."

"Does the Cleft belong to the Tavvydale folk, or to the Fyvies ? " said Jonathan. "A curse upon their impudence," he cried, with the first exhibition of anger showing itself, despite his effort to be cool. "Who are the fellows that report progress of my movements, and lie concerning them like this ? Though I deny these frequent visits, as they call them, yet I deny still more strongly the right of anybody to question me concerning them. Does Milly say that she has seen me there ? "

"No."

"And as, according to the gospel of Tavvydale, Milly would be the first to hear of it—for Milly is the prettiest girl in Devon—it must be a lie from beginning to end. Why, I am almost inclined to lose my temper—let the scandal float away with the smoke of this cigar."

"It is a scandal, then ? "

Jonathan regarded Laurence attentively for some seconds without replying ; on his lip, Laurence was sure that there hovered a defiance of him, or a sharp reproof for his intermeddling. But the answer came at length, humble enough for the senior partner.

"Purely a scandal. I am not Milly's champion—I know very little about her. She may be as chaste as snow, or as artful as the fiend, for what I know, or care. I was half drunk when I made love to her one evening in the Cleft last year, and I dare say that I was rude to her, until she scorched me with her indignation, and swore that she would go that night to the governor for protection. By all that's holy, Laurence, it was as fine a piece of rustic virtue, as was ever seen in an Adelphi drama. Genuine or sham, it mattered little to me ; it had its effect, and I apologised. I have not seen the girl since, and it's deuced hard, therefore, to begin apologising again, and in every unaccountable direction that turns up. These affairs die out of their own weakness, if let alone, I think ; but to rake over the embers is to raise the flame. It seems to me," he said thoughtfully, " that Milly is anxious to play the heroine here."

" She has a good name to preserve."

" She must be very fond of notoriety," said Jonathan ; " or living in solitary confinement has turned her head a little. Has she told this to Athorpe ? "

" No."

" That saves a row, at least, for the man is not to be trusted ; he would come with his blood up to demand an explanation of me, and strangle me, if he could, before the explanation was given. Milly has acted wisely there—I don't like Athorpe—I never did. I never met in all my life with a man or woman who liked that brute."

" I think that he is an honest and straightforward man."

" Ah ! you have an excellent opinion of everybody—but me," said Jonathan, moodily.

" I do not form my opinions in a hurry, Jonathan—and you I do not profess to understand yet. I hope——"

" Well—what do you hope ? "

He spoke with more of the Fyvie sharpness than Laurence had witnessed in him before—spoke eagerly almost, and waited as eagerly for the answer.

" I hope," concluded Laurence, " that beneath this seeming indifference to the world's opinion—this affectation of selfishness and laxity of principle—this utter carelessness so alien to your race, there is much good waiting its time. I believe that there is—for a name will descend to you that it will be your pride and honour to keep as spotless before the world as your father kept it before you. There, that's a long speech, Jonathan."

Jonathan flung his cigar away, and appeared to consider its purport.

" Ah ! don't be mistaken, Laurence," he said at last, and without looking at our hero again ; " the good that there is in me, you see before you, and that grows weaker every day.

12—2

I'm not a bad man—I'm not worse than ninety of every hundred men whom I meet, and it's only when one comes across a fellow like you—though you may be a better actor than most of us, that's all—that I feel desperately small. You understand me?"

"Partly," answered Laurence.

"But I don't consider myself a bad man," reiterated Jonathan Fyvie; "I would go out of my way to do another a service, and that's not a bad trait of character. I don't profess to be able to resist temptation when it asssils me at the right or the wrong time. I have met, God help me, with more temptation than most men, and so have given way more. When I was a younger man, I was led wrong by a lot of fellows older than myself, Laurence—and I never got over that fall—never."

"Your father and mother——"

"My father treated me too much as an equal, and my mother was always an invalid. I had my own way at twenty years of age, my purse full of money, and my head full of folly, and there was not a soul to tell me that I was drifting the wrong way."

"But you knew that it was the wrong way?"

"I had been told so at church; but out in the world everybody seemed on the same road, and if I saw any harm, why, I shut my eyes to it. Laurence, I was nearly saved and—by a woman."

Jonathan's face flushed—Laurence could see it yet, though the twilight was deepening rapidly, and they sat in shadow there.

"I did my best to deceive an honest girl, Laurence, and she, loving me with all her heart, a poor, vain, weak child, nothing more, became suddenly strong at the eleventh hour. At that last moment she did her best to save me; she did not know how close she was to success before she fled the danger that was round us both—or how I tried to become all that she had wished to make me after I had lost her. Well, I failed, but no one can say that I didn't try hard. Pooh! how hot it is to-night—not a breath of air stirring in the place."

He took off his hat and held it listlessly by his side, until it dropped from his hand to the ground, where he let it remain. He had become pale now, and there was a strange painful expression on the face.

" And the woman ? "

"She forgot me," he said, with an intensity of bitterness that Laurence was not prepared for. "She went away, believing that I was not worth remembering — and she married."

"Have you seen her since ? " asked Laurence.

"Yes, and told her what she might have made of me had she feared me less, and upbraided her, and made quite a heroic scene of it—more after your style than mine. All this, the romance of the thing now—the French romance, perhaps—but still a lift from the dead level of monotony."

"Jonathan, you have never been wicked enough to seek to win that woman's affection from her husband ? "

"She never had much affection for him," he said, fiercely ; "it was mine by right."

"But you have not——"

"I have not led her away from her duty," he concluded, with a sneer. "No. She is still the heroine after a fashion, and after a less high standard. But she sees now that she did not quite save me—and she is sorry for her lack of courage. I sit upon her heart a lasting reproach, making her miserable in her turn. But there is no harm. God strike me dead when harm shall come of it."

He dashed his clenched hand upon the trough, and then winced with the pain that the action had caused him. He rose, picked up his hat, and walked up and down the shed three or four times, stopping as suddenly in his perambulations as he had commenced them, taking his cigar-case from his pocket again, and seeking refuge from his excitement in the old habit.

"I wish you would join me, Laurence, and be sociable."

Laurence took a cigar at his request, and the two strolled on together about the grounds.

"You go to London in search of her again ? "

" In search of her—or to avoid her, and forget her in the excitement which London provides. There, we'll drop the subject. I hope that I have proved to you that I'm not a bad fellow—not wholly a bad fellow—although you know the worst of me. I lost my chance of salvation, and a woman is to blame for it—as a woman is to blame for all the ills that happen upon earth."

"Would she have saved you, or been lost herself, Jonathan ? " said Laurence. "It is a difficult problem to solve."

" She knew her own strength," said the other ; "and she ought to have known me. It's all her fault, whatever happens."

" I would not think that. It is not——"

"It is not worth thinking about any more," interrupted Jonathan. " We set it on the top shelf for ever, and I retire within myself, and make myself a fool no longer. Why, I have been acting all this time."

He laughed, and slapped Laurence on the shoulder ; but the laugh was forced, and the acting altogether of the poorest quality.

" I am content enough. One of the lucky fellows, with a fortune made for me, to win the respect of men, and a face that women seem to like ; the world is fair and bright enough, and I am not the man to see the darkness in it, and complain. I enjoy life, and I go on with the stream ; he is a saint or a hypocrite who finds fault with my career."

" I find fault, Jonathan ; but I am neither one nor the other."

"You are a very young man, and have not met with your temptations yet," said he, lightly. " Preach to me of my vanities, and of your own uprightness, when you are eight years an older man."

" Are you going ? "

" Yes, I am going now. I have left my horse in Tavvydale village, and have a mile's walk before me. Good-night —nothing *more* that I can do for you in town ? "

"Nothing more, thank you. You have the courage to defend this girl—it is your promise ? "

" I will defend her against all the old women in the universe," he replied. "Good-night."

He went out of the great gates, which were still open, and sauntered leisurely along the high-road, with Laurence looking sadly after him, as after a rudderless ship left to drift its purposeless way.

When he was out of sight of his partner, Jonathan threw his second cigar away, and walked rapidly onwards, as though a host of second thoughts gave impulse to his pace just as it altered again the face to that stern but better expression which Laurence had noticed at an earlier period. Finally, he was idling along once more, with his hands behind him, regardless of time or the distance between himself and home.

When the Cleft lay on his right, dark and indistinct, and the distant light in Captain Athorpe's cottage was the only sign of life about there, he came to a full stop, and remained silent and motionless until a hand was laid upon his arm, when he started back and trembled somewhat.

"Oh! I was in doubts if you was alive or a stattoo," said a deep voice; "I see now—it's young Mr. Fyvie a-watching here."

"Watching, fellow!" said Jonathan indignantly. "I'm not watching."

"Resting, mayhap?" replied the questioner, his voice becoming more deep and harsh, "as you do rest sometimes about this place."

"How do you know?"

"I rest too—rest or watch, that no harm's meant to them who be better than yourself. When meant in arnest, reckon up how much your life be worth, Sir, for it's risky business."

"Who *are* you?" asked Jonathan, peering hard into the face of a man who seemed to tower above him like a Colossus.

"No servant of your'n, but a man who can take his own part, and other people's, directly they ax help o' him. I'm Churdock."

"I don't know you."

"Bully Churdock—straight, and fair, and honest—meaning well—allus."

"Glad to hear it—it's a credit to you," said Jonathan, coolly. "Good-night, my man."

"Ah! it's time to say good-night, though no thanks for it. I shan't sleep no better for such good-nights as your'n. Oo!"

And with this disparaging interjection, Bully Churdock turned away.

Jonathan went on leisurely towards the Tavvydale Inn, round which were many of the men who worked at Wheal Desperation. Here he mounted the horse that had been waiting for him. He met with plenty of deference in the village, to make up for Bully Churdock's incivility, but it did not please him, and he rode away from it as speedily as possible.

He rode home like a madman, lashing his horse all the way, and went at once to his room, locking himself in for the night, along with the thoughts to which that strange night had given birth, and wherein he had never felt more strong or—more weak.

CHAPTER XIX.

THE TAVVYDALE FEAST.—ACT THE FIRST.

LAURENCE RAXFORD received a letter from Jonathan Fyvie two days after their strange dialogue at Wheal Desperation —a flying epistle, written in great haste, containing but a few lines, and almost undecipherable.

"Dear Laurence," it ran, "penance done, and the angry virtues appeased. I have satisfied Aunt Llewellyn that no one was to blame in the Milly-detraction case, save your heroic friend, J. Fyvie."

Then followed a postscript, not pleasant for Laurence to read :

"The ladies here are puzzled at your interest and championship. Be ready with your defence—*your turn !* "

Laurence frowned at this. His turn !—it was a phrase to be protested against, although there was only that ill-blurred epistle before him. His turn !—who was to reproach him, and why was it necessary that he should do penance ? Surely Hester—for the letter somehow implied that Hester was not pleased with his interference—would not again revive the subject of this mining girl, or see an officiousness in his conduct respecting her ? He had not sought the office of mediator, but had it thrust upon him.

Laurence had written to Hester three days since—a rambling, lover-like epistle, with a little news and a great deal of nonsense therein, and had been already surprised in a mild degree at receiving no prompt reply thereto. "Letters timely written *were* rivets to the chain of affection," with Laurence, just as "untimely delayed," they were " rust to the solder." He had his crotchets, and one of them was a punctiliousness with regard to answering letters, and to receiving the answers of others. It was a business-like habit that stood him in good stead in hours of business—out of them it was a matter that disturbed him unnecessarily. He set down every man a snob who was too dignified, or too busy, or too indifferent to answer a letter written in good faith, and though he was correct enough in the main, yet he allowed no exceptions to the rule anywhere, or under any circumstances, and after Jonathan Fyvie's "hurrygraph," he began to think that he was very badly treated by his *fiancée.*

When a week had passed, he was sure that he had been badly treated, and he went to dine with Mr. Fyvie, senior, at Tavvydale House, inclined to assert as much, and fortunately more than inclined to hold his tongue and keep his "slights" and "snubbings" to himself. Hester was coming back in three or four days, Mr. Fyvie told him at dinner, and though he considered that he should have been the first to receive that news, he swallowed the affront along with his boiled chicken, and betrayed not by a glance his annoyance. He was going to marry into a great family, and great families were eccentric; let him appreciate the honour, and keep the silver lining of the cloud for ever turned towards him—it was his own fault if the shadows engulphed him.

A very quiet dinner this, after all the fuss that there had been at Tavvydale House—quiet enough, and dull enough, with Mr. Fyvie rather disposed to sit in state till the cloth and Mrs. Fyvie were removed, the latter suffering from sick headache, against which she had been languidly protesting all day.

Left to themselves, Mr. Fyvie expressed it as his opinion that he should be glad when Hester came back—her absence took the brightness out of the place, he thought.

Laurence thought so too, but refrained from committing himself by an opinion, out of respect for the feelings of his companion, who launched after that into a business channel, and bore his junior partner with him.

"You have had time to study mining matters to the full lately, Laurence," he said, "are you tired of work yet?"

"Not I, Sir."

"And Wheal Desperation suits you?"

"Very well, indeed."

"I thought that it would; and your fresh blood and new euergy will suit Wheal Desperation," said Mr. Fyvie; "but

I would not keep too long to the practical part. Familiarity with your men will lead to the usual result."

"They are a quiet, hard-working, painstaking set of men, Mr. Fyvie," said Laurence, "and we already understand one another."

"How long do you give yourself below ground ? "

"Three months more, Sir."

"Very good; and then to look after the general welfare, and my son Jonathan into the bargain. You must not grow tired of *him;* but lead him, by degrees, and by example, to the beaten track. Now, about the Tavvydale feast ? "

Mr. Fyvie was not disposed to linger upon the merits or demerits of his son ; he dropped a hint, almost a sigh, at the same time, and then seized another topic of discussion.

"The Tavvydale feast—what is that ? " asked our hero.

"It's a kind of saturnalia—half-holiday and half horse-fair," explained Mr. Fyvie, "peculiar to Tavvydale ; and affords a capital excuse to waste time and spend money. There'll be a wrestling match or two, no doubt, and some broken shins by way of a wind-up. It's a general holiday at our mines, and one of the partners is always expected to run down to Tavvydale, and take an interest in everything that's going on. You do not object to mixing with the masses, as Engleton calls them, for one day ? "

"Not at all."

"You need not stop long—only to show yourself for a while, and let the good people understand that you are not too proud to make one of them. They will be grateful to your patronage for ever."

"They are very welcome to it."

"I believe that boy of mine has gone to London expressly to get out of the way. He's shy of these things."

"Yes—he's rather shy," said Laurence thoughtfully.

"When I was a younger man, I used to like a day's holiday at Tavvydale—a day's drop to a lower level, where there was less show, and more natural gaiety. It did me good, and I believe all the popularity I enjoy dates from the Tavvydale feasts. I hope Hester will be in time to walk through the village with you."

Laurence hoped so likewise.

"Everyone of condition, or position, gives a kind of feast to his neighbours on that day—open house and plenty of cyder. Farmer Hughes will take the lead with agricultural friends, and Athorpe, as head captain, with the mining folk. You will take care, like a good general, to appear at both houses; at Athorpe's rather longer than the others. If you're not a proud man, and I do not think that you are, you will find plenty of amusement. A holiday will do you good, Laurence—you're looking pale."

" The hot weather, Sir."

" Oh, or else you're in love," said Mr. Fyvie, with a quiet chuckle of satisfaction; " and after that shrewd guess, we'll drink the lady's health, and then go and see after Mrs. Fyvie's headache."

The rest of the evening in the drawing-room, both gentlemen doing their best to dispel the megrims of the lady occupant, and both failing on this occasion.

" I believe you miss Hester more than you care to acknowledge," said Mr. Fyvie. " Shall I send for her to-morrow ? Shall Laurence go to town and fetch her, Charlotte ? "

" Never mind me," sighed Mrs. Fyvie; " don't stop the poor girl's holiday on my account. Oh, dear ! "

Yes, it was dull there without Hester—dull with a vengeance ! Laurence was glad to get to his room, although it was only to indulge in those thoughts which sank all his spirits to zero. No one ever knew but himself how long he sat at that open window, staring moodily before him, and wondering at his own dulness, and his own unthankfulness at all the good things of this life—a fair future, and a wife as fair to match it—which had fallen to his share, just as he was girding up his loins to fight for them. It was almost like a disappointment to have them meet him like this ; he felt that he was happiest at his labour, and when he worked hard with his men it seemed like working for a living then —not otherwise. Industry checked by good fortune, undeserved and unlooked for, had not certainly conduced to much happiness, or else his looks belied him.

Mr. Fyvie had expressed it as his opinion that Laurence was looking pale ; and when Laurence went to the Tavvydale feast, the few who knew him—mining proprietors, farmers, &c., in the vicinity—asked him if he was *quite* well— notwithstanding that he had determined to be in good spirits that day, and prove himself a worthy successor to his senior partner.

The village of Tavvydale was, like its villagers, in full dress for the occasion; there were flags—most of them extempore productions—streaming from first-floor windows, and over beer-shop fronts; all Tavvydale was in the streets, the agricultural portion buying and selling the oddest specimens of horseflesh—for it was more an exchange for " screws " than anything approximate to a horse-fair—the mining portion interested in the booths that had been erected in an adjacent field, or laying their various bets on the wrestling to come off later in the day, or drinking beer and cyder in quantities that rendered seeing anything after twelve A.M. a matter of uncertainty. The miners were in their Sunday best, and the mining girls in something more than that—in bright new ribbons, and smart new gloves, in the gayest of hats, with feathers, and plumes, and wreaths, odd copies of " the fashion," minus the extravagances of colour and style, which charmed these humble folk, and made them, for the day, distraught with finery.

There were no ungainly bows, and rapid curtsies for Laurence Raxford *en route* that day; mining people in their very best, keeping high holiday, were proud to say good-day, and to look pleased at the young master's advent, but they were independent fellows off duty, and every man and woman was on an equality on feast days.

" A good-day to you, Mr. Raxford. I'm glad to see you fall in with our old ways, instead of keeping at arm's length of us," cried a voice close to him, in the High Street, and Laurence turned to greet Captain Athorpe, dressed in black, as for a funeral of importance.

" Ah! good-day, Athorpe."

Athorpe wore his holiday look with the rest, too, and had almost smoothed out the furrows in his brow with the self-satisfied air which he had adopted for the nonce. For it was natural, whether ill or well pleased, to allow his shaggy eyebrows to droop over his eyes, and to keep his face, earnest and rugged as it was, in a chronic state of frown.

" I don't suppose you expected to find me dressed in this style ? " he said, " but I like old customs, and I follow them, even at a sacrifice. I'm Tavvydale born."

" And a credit to Tavvydale," said Laurence, smiling.

" Yes, I hope so," said the other, receiving the compliment

quite gravely; "to be sure, just as you say, Mr. Raxford. You'll see the wrestling?"

"Yes."

"And dine with one of us? Farmer Hughes's feast will take the shine out of mine, and be more genteel in its way, possibly, and you'll please yourself, Sir."

Captain Athorpe spoke half anxiously, and half sullenly. He desired the presence of the new partner in Wheal Desperation; he believed that it was his right to secure so illustrious a personage, just as he had always secured a Fyvie since his return to Tavvydale; but he did not convey the hint delicately.

"You don't want to pass me over to Farmer Hughes, I hope, Athorpe?" said Laurence, who understood his man now. "I'm not in the agricultural line, and can't talk of crops, and cattle, and grass lands. I shall be more at home at your cottage, if you'll not think me in the way."

"Not exactly," said Athorpe, visibly brightening. "An honour, Sir, which will make us hold our heads a trifle higher. I didn't press you, because I never press anybody," he jerked forth, "because it isn't my way. But I'm glad, of course, and—thank'ee."

"Mrs. Athorpe is well, I hope, captain?"

"Well, and busy, bless her heart!" he answered; "it's not much of a holiday for her, she has to work like a nigger to get things ready by one. We dine at one, and I dare say there'll be twenty of us; all the captains will look in, and their wives, and the clerks. They ought, you know," he added, testily, "and if they don't, they can stop away."

"The miners——"

"Oh! our men! They'll look in at odd times in the afternoon, for drink; and there's the Desperation tent up over yonder, at Mr. Fyvie's expense, Sir. Ha! ha! he's a good fellow!—for *I* say it, and I don't deal in compliments very often. Have you seen Milly?"

"Your niece? Not this morning."

"Come and see her in holiday trim, then, at the head of her feast in the Sunday-school—you won't know her hardly. I don't make *her* vain by saying anything about it, but it's a sight worth seeing, if you're so minded."

"I place myself in your hands," said Laurence; "and expect to see all the wonders of this little village."

" This way, then."

Captain Athorpe led the way along the main street, strutting with no small degree of importance by the side of his partner, exchanging salutes with most of the passers-by, not particular about cutting at the horses with his stick, if they came in his way, or bullying their proprietors if they raised any objections to the liberty

" A parcel of horse-copers and vagabonds," he said disparagingly ; " I don't see what they want here, or what good they do. They're out of place, and a disgrace to us. Up here, Mr. Raxford."

Captain Athorpe turned out of the High Street, made a cross-cut with our hero across a triangular bit of grass, whereon were gingerbread stalls and a few caravans, crossed a little stream by means of a " tumble-down " arch of old red brick, went down a lane, cool and shady between two high hedgerows, and halted suddenly before a building of fair exterior, with a faint pretension to Gothic.

" These are our miners' schools, where most of the children come on Sundays, and take their learning like lambs. A heap of learning they get hold of this way, too—why, I was brought up in one of these places myself!—the old school, which Mr. Fyvie pulled down, to make room for this new one. He might have had it plainer, and more like our chapel, but he came out handsomely—he always does. God save the Fyvies ! "

" Amen."

" They've done good, so I say that heartily," cried Athorpe ; " otherwise, rich as they are, I shouldn't care a button for them. Not my way, indeed."

" Good-morning, Captain Athorpe," said a little wiry man in black, who came out of the schools at this moment.

" Ah ! good-morning, Mr. Wells," answered Athorpe ; " I have brought Mr. Raxford—the new partner at Desperation—to see the schools and the school feast—and the school teachers, he being a young man, you know," he concluded, quite jocularly.

The dissenting minister and our hero raised their hats at the same moment—the former not disposed to smile at Captain Athorpe's joke.

" Not much amusement for a young man here," said Mr. Wells ; " but a good study, and a fair moral, if he is a

Christian. You are interested in the education of youth, perhaps, Sir ? "

"Oh! yes—very," was Laurence's easy answer.

He feared that it was scarcely a true reply to the minister's inquiry, but Mr. Wells appeared to expect it, and he gave it him. Now he reflected upon the matter, Laurence was sure that the education of the miners' children had been close to his heart for a long time past. At all events, it should be, for here were the broad impressive footsteps of the senior partner, and it was his duty to follow in them.

"We had a gentleman here a month ago, one of Mr. Fyvie's visitors, and he went very deeply and earnestly into the mode of education here, and suggested one or two—I may say one or two hundred—alterations that he considered necessary. He was coming again, with Mr. Fyvie, he said, to go into the whole matter afresh with me ; but he has not honoured me yet awhile."

"You are alluding to Mr. Engleton, I think ? "

"Engleton was the name."

"He has gone to London."

"Bless my soul—gone!" ejaculated Mr. Wells ; "why, he has a great many papers of mine in his possession, the whole system—my system—of school teaching, with which he was evidently struck. When is it likely he will return ? "

"I cannot say," answered Laurence ; "you will hear from him shortly, no doubt."

"Is Milly within ? " asked Athorpe ; "I don't think my friend, Mr. Raxford, cares to wait here any longer—and we're keeping you."

"Not at all. I shall be happy to act as cicerone."

"We're only going to look in a moment, and there's no occasion to trouble you," said Athorpe, less civilly ; "Milly can explain as well as you, Sir."

"Very good—very good," said Mr. Wells ; "certainly she can. The Lord's blessing on her, Mr. Athorpe, for a better, truer girl never lived, I think."

"That's kind and hearty—and Milly should be proud of your opinion."

"I wouldn't make her proud by any praise of mine," said Mr. Wells, with a glance towards the open school windows.

"You can't make her proud," replied Athorpe.

"No—with all her cleverness, not proud. A girl fit for

any sphere of life, Sir," he said, turning to Laurence again. "and calculated to adorn it. We are proud of Milly Athorpe, in Tavvydale."

He went away after this encomium, and Athorpe nudged our hero suddenly with his elbow, as the minister trotted off.

"Now, my wife says it's all nonsense, but I say it ain't—parson as he is, and old enough to be Milly's father, too."

"What is all nonsense?" asked Laurence.

"His liking Milly, and half inclined to ask Milly to marry him, and take care of a family of eleven by his first wife. But I don't think Milly would like it, for all her duty to the black-coats, and I know that I shouldn't."

"Why not?" asked Laurence, carelessly.

"Well," said Athorpe, reflectively, "Milly's young, and pretty, and merry, and he's a miserable old *cove*, and I never took very kindly to parsons, owing to early training, I suppose, and early ways of mine, which weren't square. A little preaching," he said with a grimace, "goes a great way with me—and though Milly's fond of sermons, she isn't fond enough of him to marry him; even if it wasn't all nonsense, as Mrs. A. says. I've picked the man out for Milly, and I shall wait patiently till he turns up, and takes her from the Cleft."

"And your *beau-ideal* of Milly's husband?" asked Laurence.

Captain Athorpe gave a fillip to his ear, and nearly knocked his hat off.

"A frank, straightforward man like *me*, for instance, with no nonsense about him. Some one with a bit of money put by—some one in trade. Milly's quite good enough for trade, and too good—much—for the lazy beggars about here. I don't want to turn her head with foolery," he said, dropping his voice, "and I wouldn't have her marry a gentleman, for all the world; but she's too good, and clever, for the class she mixes in. I don't like her working at the mine at all; it's beneath her—it lowers me—but she says her mother did, and she's not proud in that way. I think she's a little proud of herself, at times—but why shouldn't she be?"

"Ah!—why shouldn't she be?"

"I'm proud of her," said Athorpe, "though I keep my

feelings to myself. I can say this—that I never, in all my life abroad or here, saw such a face as hers—not even in a picture, where they cut it fine enough. Well, Sir," laying his hand on Laurence's arm, "it's a something to say that we Athorpes own the prettiest girl in Devon, and I say it when she's not in hearing."

Athorpe walked to the first open window, which was but breast-high, and Laurence imitated his example. The two men looked in at the school-room, where the feast had already begun, and where Milly sat as high priestess, in the holiday trim to which her uncle had recently alluded.

In the noise and excitement of a hundred and fifty children let loose in that school, upon counters of cakes and lemonade ; in the efforts of the teachers, almost as excited as the children, to preserve a fragment of order, by keeping a hundred and fifty pairs of new boots—everybody in new boots—from jumping all at once, the heads of the watchers there were not observed at first.

Yes, Captain Athorpe might be as right as Mr. Fyvie, and Milly be the prettiest girl in Devon—famous county for bright faces as it is. Laurence, leaning on the window-sill, thought that *he* had never seen so beautiful a girl in all his life ; but then he had been a boy tied to his mother's apron-strings, until a few months back. And this was a new Milly —not the girl he had supped with, or the aggrieved one who had met him in the Cleft, or the indignant mining forewoman, claiming from the master protection for a servant in his employ, against a slander that had reached her ears. In all phases a beauty that had troubled him—shadowed his memory, as it were—but on that feast day, a fairy in grey silk, looking as true a lady as any whom he had met at Tavvydale House ; graceful, womanly, and unlike anything or anybody that was ever likely to cross his path again.

"I give her a silk dress once a year, a birthday gift," said Athorpe in his ear, as Laurence looked thoughtfully into the school-room, and wondered why his heart sank as he looked. "It's my wish that she would wear silk on Sundays and holidays ; and though Mrs. A. don't exactly like the idea, she can't say that it don't become the girl. That's a tidy row in there, I must say."

13

" Silence—silence there!" cried one of the teachers; "there, I declare Milly shan't sing, if there is not less noise. Milly shall go home and leave you all."

" Noa, she woan't!" chorussed a hundred and fifty voices; and then there was a grand rush of about a hundred and ten towards the favourite teacher, the remaining forty preferring the refreshment counter, and holding on to the dishes of cake till the last.

Milly was laughing and trying to keep at a respectful distance the boldest of the school, who would have climbed into her lap, when she caught sight of the intruders on the school feast; she rose, and came at once towards them, blushing a little as she advanced. She did not curtsey to Mr. Raxford on this occasion—she was on her own domain, and queen there.

" Good-morning, Sir—good-morning, uncle. Would you like to see the school, Mr. Raxford? All the visitors have been here long ago, and my little ones are almost too rude for company after visiting hours."

" They'll spoil that dress," said Athorpe in a low growl; "you should not have put it on until you came to dinner with us."

" I'm afraid it was rash," said Milly, looking down at her crumpled skirt ruefully, " but they told me that I was to dress very smart to-day, uncle. Will you come in?" she repeated.

" Just for a minute," answered her uncle; " it's part of the ceremonies of the day."

They left the window and went round to the door, where Milly was waiting for them.

" A school teacher also, Milly!" said Laurence as he entered; "why, I do not know half your accomplishments yet!"

" I come here on Sundays to teach the little ones all I know—which is not a great deal, Sir."

" It must be hard work."

" Oh! they are glad to see me here—and Mr. Wells and his friends are anxious that I should come—and it's not hard work to be of help anywhere."

" You are more at home teaching here than teaching and watching the bigger children at the mines, I see."

" They are more disobedient at Wheal Desperation," said

Milly laughing; "but I don't know that they like me less —the big ones. I hope they don't."

"It appears to me that you have two lives, Milly."

"Half a dozen, Sir, I fancy sometimes."

They entered the school, where the advent of strangers caused a hush amongst the children for a few minutes, followed by stifled laughter, gurglings, and gaspings behind pocket handkerchiefs, sudden pushes forward into the middle of the room, and sharp pinches from spiteful boys in the rear, on all the available portions presented to them by boys in advance. Finally, as much noise as had preceded their entrance, and a grand rush and struggle for cake again.

"We don't try for the best behaviour on days like these," said Milly, half apologetically.

"And if you did, you wouldn't get it," said Athorpe; "it's a regular bear-garden of a place just now. There's a little beggar lifting himself off the ground by your skirt, Milly— here, young fellow, drop that, will you?"

"Oh, this is curly-headed Johnny Churdock," said Milly, roughing his hair the wrong way with both her hands, and eliciting much choking laughter in consequence; "the best of little boys when he has his slate and pencil, and somebody's looking at him."

"It's a whole holiday," said Johnny, a sturdy youth of eight; "and brother Bill's going to fling the Cornish man and break his shins, and I'm to have front place to see Bill give it him."

"Bully never said that, I know," said Athorpe.

"Yes, he did—because I wasn't to worry Milly of a Sunday by being idle no more—and no more I have been!"

"Good Johnny," said Laurence, taking him in his arms, and turning him upside down; "and Milly will bring him up to something better than kicking people's shins, if he never worries her any more, I'm sure."

"Milly hasn't sung yet!" cried Johnny from his inverted position, "and she always sings something new—something out of her own head, about us—every Tavvydale feast. And don't we laugh—the lot of us! Oooh! don't tickle, Sir!"

Laurence was always at home with children; brought up alone, an only boy, it was strange that he should have a love for them, and feel an interest in their joys and sorrows

13—2

whenever brought in contact with them. Naturally, then, he was a man to whom children took, with that rare facility which is an instinct true and unfailing to lead them where they shall find open arms, and kind words. This was a man whom children understood, and when Johnny Churdock was turned upside down, the children of the Tavvydale miners knew their man at once, flung off all restraint, and went pell-mell at the new arrival.

The teachers were scared at first—prim young women, and shopkeepers' daughters from the village outside—and when Johnny Churdock made a clutch at Mr. Raxford's neck-tie, it was almost time to interfere, and Milly's voice was heard in mild reproof.

"It's all right," cried Laurence, "I give myself up to their tender mercies, and he who is too bold I'll punish after my own fashion. Johnny, as you have misbehaved yourself, and nearly spoilt the set of my collar for the day—out you go."

And to Johnny's amazement, and doubts as to whether the affair was to be considered in a serious light or not, he was picked up by Laurence, and dropped through the open window on to the grass without, amidst a roar of laughter from the rest of the school.

"Now, Captain Athorpe," said Laurence, "you have brought me into this place—support me by following my example."

"No—it's not in my line," said Athorpe, sitting down on a form in the corner, and shaking his head to and fro. "I haven't spirit enough and youth enough for that fun. I dare say I should lose my temper over it—but I can sit here and try to laugh a bit at the young ones. Milly, are you going to sing?"

"Presently," said Milly shily.

"Something new—you've been at that verse-making nonsense again, I know."

"Yes—it is nonsense, uncle—children's nonsense, and only fit for children."

"Which is a hint to go," said Athorpe, "for we shall never get Milly to sing in polite society."

Laurence hoped that he might be allowed to remain an auditor, but Milly shook her head, and laughed at his request, and then was scared with affright at the idea of masculine visitors and critics on her "nonsense verses," and turned quite pale as Laurence sat down by Athorpe's side.

"I think we'll go, Sir," said Athorpe, "we're spoiling the thing now—we're overdoing it."

"By all means, let us be off, then," answered Raxford, rising; and the two, after a few more words, went out of the school-room into the bright sunshine, where Johnny Churdock was found with his pinafore to his eyes sobbing violently.

"Hollo! what are you making that row for?" inquired Athorpe.

"I—I—I—did—didn't mean to hurt—the gen—genelman's collar," said Johnny, "and I—I don't want to be out —out here no longer!"

"Johnny, you little wooden-head, can't you tell fun from earnest?" said Laurence, stooping over him, and quite concerned at being misunderstood even by this miner's boy; "why, you're not half a man! Here's a penny to spend not to be so soft again."

"I'm not saft, Sir, on—only I thought it was—arnest," he said with a smile struggling through his tears.

"There, be off with you."

And Laurence tilted Johnny on to the grass, who was up with a bound again, grinning this time from ear to ear.

"Maybe, Sur, ye'll—ye'll shove me in agin?" he suggested.

And Laurence picked him up, and passed him through the window at once, eliciting another shout of laughter at the reappearance of the obstreperous pupil.

"I must go home now," said Athorpe, "and see how things are getting on, and if Inez is ready for the company. You'll not forget, Sir—at one precisely."

"A hungry man never forgets his invitation to dinner," said Laurence.

"It's not an invitation—nor for the like of us to ask you, Sir," said Athorpe, "but it's open house to-day, and the best of company makes us rather proud. That's it."

Athorpe strode away in a temper befitting his holiday suit, and left Laurence standing on the grass, unconscious that Milly had stolen to the door, to make sure that all listeners were gone before she began her song. Turning suddenly, however, he startled himself and her.

" I beg pardon," said Laurence, " you wish me gone, I see. No eaves-dropping allowed, Milly ? "

" I am ashamed of my own nonsense," said Milly ; " but, it pleases them, and makes them happy. And it's looked for now."

" Good-day, then. Oh! before I go," he said, stopping again, " is it worth speaking any more of a commission with which you charged me ? "

" Yes, it is," she said, eagerly ; " what does he say ? "

" That he was to blame, of course, and that he has informed Mrs. Llewellyn so."

" He might have done that more generously and quickly," said Milly, scornfully ; " but still I am happy now. Thank you, Sir, very much," she added, with the tears rising to her eyes; " it was a great liberty on my part to ask your help—you have been very kind."

" You took Uncle Whiteshell's advice, and Uncle W. is a very sensible man," he said, trying to turn the matter into a jest, " and knows the best advisers."

Then he sauntered away towards the green, on which all Tavvydale had congregated now, meeting Bully Churdock on his way, who frowned at him, and " made faces " at him after he had passed, although he was not aware of that latter indignity.

<hr>

CHAPTER XX.

THE SECOND ACT OF THE TAVVYDALE FEAST.

Laurence looked in at Farmer Hughes's, and then wandered about the village, in his character of proxy for the Fyvies, and representative of Wheal Desperation, thinking that he should be glad when it was one o'clock, and he could gracefully effect his escape.

They were very noisy in Tavvydale now, and exceedingly argumentative with their noise. The Fyvie tent was open, and had evidently been liberally patronised. Some of the miners of Wheal Desperation tried to set up a cheer as Laurence passed, forgetful of their equality, or full of past gratitude for little kindnesses, and offended other miners not in the Fyvie service, who wanted to know " Who be *he* that he should be hoorayed at on feast-day ? " A question that led to quarrelling here and there, and kept the one policeman peculiar to Tavvydale, with two coadjutors borrowed from Tavistock, busy and remonstrative. But taken altogether, there was as much happiness as noise in the village, and the village girls kept the place ringing with their laughter. A fair-day, a feast-day, and a holiday—a day to be remembered in Tavvydale, and marked with a white stone till feast-day came again.

At five minutes to one he was in sight of Captain Athorpe's cottage, with its proprietor standing at the gate looking out for him, and half a dozen mining captains walking about the front garden in their best clothes, and with huge stick-up collars, looking and feeling uncomfortable under the pressure of the coming hospitality, and the tightness pervading their Sunday suits in general.

" Why, this *is* punctuality," cried Athorpe, after consulting his large silver watch ; " one to the minute. I mind the time when young Mr. Fyvie dined here—that was the second year I kept house and home here—and came in for cold joints instead of hot ones. For "—with a shake of the head—" I wait for nobody."

" Good-morning, gentlemen," said Laurence, returning the salute of the officers, who ducked their heads solemnly towards him ; " this reminds me of the dinner at the Wheal two months ago."

" Only we're more at home here, in our way," said Athorpe.

The captains looked askance from one to the other, and Laurence could see that they doubted that assertion. It was hard and up-hill work for these men to feel at home in Captain Athorpe's house. They did not agree with Athorpe very well for the remainder of the year, and it was more for form's sake than for friendship that they were assembled there that day. Athorpe was "a bit of a bounce," they thought, and too full of his fine house, and his fine wife ; but he had got the lead somehow ; he was liberal and hospitable on feast-days, and it saved other people trouble and expense, and—there they were in consequence.

Mrs. Athorpe, in black silk, with a gold brooch, and gold

ear-rings, was ready to welcome Laurence to the house. She was looking paler, he thought, than on the occasion of his being rain-bound on his homeward journey; but she was very pretty, with a pretty consciousness that she was looking pretty, that again suggested the foreigner to Laurence.

Charmed to welcome Mr. Raxford to her humble home—full of wishes that it was more worthy of the honour that he had done them—anxious to please in every way, to look her best, and to let those best looks impress and startle—restless under the responsibilities of a colossal dinner and of twenty guests—for the captains had brought their wives, and there they were all of a row on one side of the dinner-table, dumb with awe at Mr. Raxford's presence—flushed and nervous and excitable.

Laurence felt that if he did not make an effort to suit himself to his company, the feast would be a failure; and he dashed at once into general subjects—talked about everything that he had seen or heard in the village, and gradually thawed the tongues of the rest of the community, with the exception of an old lady, who turned out to be the wife of Captain Peters, and who curdled his blood by pausing constantly, with her knife in her mouth, to listen to every remark that escaped him.

"You're not getting on, Mrs. Peters," Athorpe shouted out, and frightened her; "you're not enjoying yourself, Mr. Raxford. I hope you'll all eat heartily, and all enjoy yourselves. Whatever you see, help yourselves to, ladies and gentlemen, if nobody won't help you. Mr. Raxford, I hope Mrs. Athorpe is attending to you, there—pooh! it's hot enough," he cried, pausing to pass his broad hard hand over his forehead. "Open the window, wench," to the servant, "and save us from being stewed alive. You *are* all enjoying yourselves, I hope—and I hope that there's enough to eat."

This was a joke duly appreciated, as there were three or four joints smoking on the table, flanked by innumerable vegetable dishes.

"I wish Milly would come," said Mrs. Athorpe to Laurence, in a lower tone; "we can't get on without her at these feasts, Sir. She knows all these good people better than I do, and understands their ways—what their crotchets are, and what pleases them best. Or else they like her ways better than mine, and regard *me* as an interloper here."

"You have not been in Devonshire all your life, Mrs. Athorpe ? "

"Oh, no."

"But you like Devonshire ? "

"Yes. I am used to it now. I try to like everything and everybody—try, oh, very hard at times ! "

Laurence fancied that a new expression—one of pain almost—crossed the features of Mrs. Athorpe whilst she spoke, but her manner was very variable, and he could make nothing of her, except that she was like a woman who had been spoiled and petted by her husband, and was at times less womanly than childlike. Probably the best wife that a hard, unmalleable man like Athorpe could have chosen, he thought; but certainly the last woman that would ever have taken his fancy, pretty as she was. If he had been a man in a lower sphere of life, a clerk at the mines, for instance, like the young men in the Desperation office, he would have known no greater ambition—no greater happiness—than to have fallen in love with Milly, and settled down in a house at Tavvydale, luxuriating for ever in that happiness which so clever, good, and beautiful a wife would infallibly have brought him.

"What do you think of Milly ? " Mrs. Athorpe inquired at this juncture ; and the question came so close upon his thoughts as to startle him.

"Of your—niece ? " he said.

"Yes—is she very pretty, after all ? "

"Very pretty," answered Laurence—"why, yes, there can be *no* question about that."

"But the prettiest woman in all Devonshire!—that is an exaggeration, and nobody can know that," she said almost pettishly ; "if Milly thinks so, why that accounts for the poor chance her sweethearts are offered of securing her."

"Why ? "

"She may be vain enough—I tell her that she is—to expect a real gentleman to fall in love with her some day. That is," she said suddenly and vehemently, "the worst of thoughts for any woman like her."

Did she agree with Mr. Whiteshell in this ?

"I don't believe she has it."

Mrs. Athorpe did not appear to notice this denial.

"The worst of thoughts, unsettling a woman from chances less ambitious—ending in the disappointment which is no less cruel for being natural—driving the weak fool mad at times—I—I have told Milly so, but she only laughs at me," Mrs. Athorpe concluded, more hastily, after encountering Laurence's wondering stare.

"Now, I hope you are enjoying yourself, Mr. Raxford," chimed in Captain Athorpe again; "I don't believe," with a rap of the handle of his knife upon the table, "that anybody's eating as if he enjoyed it. Peters, take some more beef, man."

"Thank you—no more—quite a hearty dinner," murmured Peters.

"I don't believe it," answered Athorpe; "Inez, do see to Mr. Raxford. He'll go away and say we were stingy next, and tried to starve him."

"Tried to diet him for a week at one effort," cried Laurence.

"Ha! ha!" said Athorpe; "that's a good one. That's—oh! here you are, Miss, at last," he cried, as Milly entered the house; "too late for anything but cold meat, and serve you right, too. Where have you been?—that old Wells didn't get courting you after the children were gone?"

The captains laughed at this; some of the captains' wives looked shocked, for they pinned their faith to Mr. Wells, and believed him above all sublunary thoughts; Milly smiled and shook her head; Mrs. Athorpe bridled up more than was necessary, considering the extempore nature of the joke.

"Don't you think any man can look at Milly without asking her to marry him, Athorpe?" she said, with an impudent toss to her head; "how can you be so foolish, dear?"

"What a terrible thing it would be, too," said Milly, laughing; "and what would become of me?—and whom should I choose out of them all?"

"I dare say you know well enough about *that*," said Captain Peters, drily; "trust a girl for having the right man in her head, though she is as dumb as a mouse till her dying day."

"Oh! you're always full of nonsense, captain," said

Milly, lightly, although the colour came to her face in spite of her.

"Would you go out of Tavvydale in search of the favoured one, Milly?" asked Mrs. Athorpe.

"I don't know that I should," answered Milly, in the same saucy tones, and a hearty peal of laughter followed her answer. She was in high spirits that feast-day—all was well with her—even the shadow of the old accusation had been removed by Laurence Raxford's agency, and Milly was at her best, and looked so.

"Well, sit down, lass," said Athorpe; "find a seat somewhere, and begin your dinner. We shall have the wrestling over—and Inez won't get out to-day."

Milly looked round for a vacant place, but the guests were thickly packed, and there was only one slight gap between Mrs. Athorpe and our hero, and that she studiously avoided. Was it treason to Hester Fyvie, far away in London, recking not of faithless swains, or the natural desire of a young man to have the prettiest and best at his elbow, or a fancy born of nothing, and to fade away after that day into the nothingness to which it belonged, that filled the mind of the principal guest with the intense wish to have Milly at his side? He did not know, he did not seek to know, but he watched her round the room, looking in every direction but his own; and had not Mrs. Athorpe engaged him in conversation, and thus fixed him with her eyes, he would have edged his chair still nearer to the masculine neighbour on his right.

"Sit down, Milly," cried Athorpe; "don't wander about the room like a fly, girl. There's room by Mr. Raxford—if he don't mind."

Milly, thus reminded of a vacant place, hesitated for a fleeting instant, that was unperceived by any one save Laurence, and then came round with the self-possession that a drawing-room life might have warranted. Laurence felt that she had not wished to sit by him, that it was an embarrassment to her, and placed her between the hostess and the "right-hand man;" and though he disliked the hesitation, he could but admire the tact with which she made the best of it at last. He was in dreamland, he thought, altogether; this girl appeared to possess a dozen characters in one, and in all phases to arouse a marvellous interest. She was a study, and he was fond of studying character, therefore the interest was natural enough !

Mrs. Athorpe drew her chair a little aside, making room for her niece-in-law, between Laurence and herself, and it was evident that for a while there was a shade of displeasure upon the brow of the hostess. A little put Mrs. Athorpe out, thought Laurence, studying character less forcibly in that direction also, and Mrs. Athorpe *was* put out a little. She liked attention from the principal guest, and that her friends should see that that attention was offered to her as her right; she did not like Milly in company, so close to herself, for it suggested an odious comparison between them ; and she was vain of her good looks, and her manners, and jealous of all those qualities in others. The reader has seen this already for himself, and Laurence, though apt to judge the best of everybody, almost fancied that he saw it, too.

Did Milly see it ? She devoted herself entirely to her uncle's wife, paid her attention in the room of Laurence, told her the incidents of the day, assuaged that restlessness of manner which seemed natural to Aunt Inez, softening and brightening the foreign woman, who turned, at last, like a spoiled child that had been petted and humoured, to an amiable, even a lovable mood.

Milly ate but a little dinner, for her heart was full of her holiday, or the many tasks which she had imposed upon herself had robbed her of her appetite. Her uncle noticed this, as he appeared to notice everything from under his shaggy eyebrows. If he had but contented himself with silent observation, he would have spared his niece more that day But he had a horrid habit of speaking out all that was in his mind.

"Can't you eat, either ? " he blurted forth ; "why, if all the meats were poisoned, we could not have had less justice done them."

"I have made an excellent dinner, uncle," said Milly.

"Yes—for a sparrow. You weren't hungry ? "

"Not very hungry, perhaps.".

"Or you did not like Mr. Raxford to think you had an appetite," he said roughly. "Well, there's nothing like being fine, when you've got fine clothes on to match."

"Oh ! uncle—you're too hard on me to-day," said Milly, half reproachfully, and half jestingly.

"If Mr. Wells has been courting her," said Captain Peters, taking up the old joke of his host, "that accounts for it."

A little more laughing, a rebuke from Mrs. Peters, Mrs. Athorpe laying her hand upon Milly's.

"Milly, what do they mean by this jest ? There's nothing in it, surely ? " she asked, in a low tone, but which Laurence could not escape.

"Of course, Mr. Wells has said nothing to me," said Milly, in the same low voice, "and it's all nonsense."

"But now I come to think of it——"

"He would not think of so great a folly, aunt."

"Nor you ? "

"I ! " exclaimed Milly. "Not I indeed."

"Not even for position—to be a minister's wife, child ? " was the question asked, almost eagerly.

"Not even for position."

"I felt sure of that," said Inez ; "you would marry for love, then ? "

"Or not at all," was the answer, lightly made still, as though still treating the subject lightly, but to Laurence's ears, which would not close themselves in spite of him, possessing an under-current of earnestness and meaning. Was he getting romantic, and building a foolish story out of nothing ?—he could fancy that the boy's thoughts, wild and improbable, were coming closer to him.

"Keep to that—however low your love may be, Milly," whispered Inez, excitedly, "and you will be happy."

"Yes," said Milly sadly.

"Was she thinking of Bully Churdock ? " wondered Laurence.

Captain Athorpe's servant, with a "help" in the shape of an old woman, who had had no interest in keeping holiday with the rest of the aborigines, were clearing away the fragments of the feast now, and replacing them by four decanters of wine—several plates of fruit, and a handful of long clay pipes. This was the dessert of Captain Athorpe, who was fond of doing everything in style.

"Wine before the ladies put their bonnets on, and smoke when their backs are turned, gentlemen," said Athorpe. "Mr.

Raxford, try that sherry—it's quite up to the Wheal Desperation mark, I fancy."

The sherry was drunk, and a favourable verdict pronounced
upon it; the ladies retired in due course; the pipes were
lighted; the gentlemen took more room unto themselves, and
talked of former feasts and horse fairs, or strolled into the
garden, pipe in mouth, and preferred fresh air with their
tobacco. Laurence preferred the fresh air without the pipe,
and was in the garden looking towards the Cleft in the hills,
with Athorpe by his side, pipeless also.

" Upon my word, a pretty spot to pitch a tent, captain,"
said Laurence enthusiastically; " here a man might rest,
and be happy as well as thankful ! "

" Sir—I am happy," said Athorpe proudly.

" I am very glad to hear you say that."

" I haven't a nice way of showing it—I'm rough and ready,
and plain-spoken—but I'm happy, and I hope I'm not ungrateful in my way," he said thoughtfully, looking up the
moment afterwards to ask if Mr. Raxford was sure that he
had enjoyed himself.

" Very much indeed."

" I thought you would—you're not a stuck-up fellow,"
said Athorpe; " that's why I feel at home with you. For,"
laying his heavy hand on our hero's arm, " the man who
shows that he's above you—by ever so little a bit—is an
ass."

" And the worst of asses, Athorpe."

" *And* the most disagreeable."

Laurence was about to add that he did not consider
himself above present company, so could not take any credit
for his humble manners ; that he was a junior partner, a
little more than a clerk at present, taking but a small share
of the profits—all this an explanation that would have been
unnecessary and out of place, he thought a moment afterwards—when the ladies came into the garden one by one,
and a few led the way towards the village, quickly followed
by the company *en masse*.

It seemed a general separation without thanks for the
hospitality that had been proffered by Captain Athorpe, who
did not allow much opportunity for thanks, having been the
first to move towards the village, with Mrs. Athorpe on his
arm. Milly was left behind, evidently to superintend home

matters for a while, and Laurence strolled leisurely back, wishing that it had not been an unceremonious break-up.

He saw but little more of the festivities appropriate to the occasion ; and it struck him suddenly that playing the patron here was a bit of a bore, and that it was hard work to evince an interest in the sports which were going on around him. He could not account for the sudden change in his feelings ; it was not pride, for his mother had often accused him of not having notions "high enough" for his sphere, we have said—she who had known better than he in what sphere he was destined to move. It was sheer indifference to wrestling matches, foot races, and gingerbread nuts ; and he believed now that he had shown himself quite enough to please the Tavvydale folk, and Mr. Fyvie. Then Milly came upon the scene again, meeting friends at every step, and having a word to say with people of all degrees, like the universal friend to all that she appeared to be.

Laurence and she met more than once in the crowd, but she looked down as he passed, with a smile of consciousness at his presence that was pleasant to witness, although it embarrassed Laurence, who had become confused as to her position in society, and was more inclined to address her as a friend than as a servant of the property amongst the Dartmoors. He forgot his intention of going back to his quiet roosting-place on the mining estate, and he was absorbed in the problem above mentioned, when old Mr. Fyvie, with his daughter on his arm, suddenly appeared before him, like ghosts of the old time—a far-off time that, in his new bewilderment, seemed scarcely to belong to this day.

"Hester ! " he exclaimed, "this is indeed a surprise."

"An agreeable one, I hope," said Hester, almost hesitating before she placed her hand in his. "You look startled at my appearance, Laurence. Frightened, I may say."

"No, not frightened, at any rate," said Laurence ; "startled to find you here, imagining that you intended a longer stay at Mrs. Llewellyn's and not having been favoured with any information to the contrary."

"Oh ! didn't I answer your letter ? " she said, carelessly. "Well, I am here to answer it in *propria personâ*. How long have you been here ? "

"All day."

Hester elevated her eyebrows, but said no more to him—
on the contrary, turned quickly to her father.

"Are we going home now, papa ? Have we had enough
of this rude gathering ? "

"I think we have done all that is necessary—showed
ourselves off to the best advantage, and proved that we
weren't a bit too proud to mix with our humble friends.
I didn't want to come at all," he added ; "Laurence was
representative here, but you would come to make sure that
our village beauties were not setting their new caps at
him."

"Laurence knows that I am not so ridiculous a being as
that," said Hester, taking the insinuation in a more serious
manner than it was conveyed ; " at least, I hope so."

"Laurence is aware that you are perfect, my love ! " said
Mr. Fyvie, drily ; "and——Ah ! Milly, and what have you
been doing all day—breaking the hearts of all the young
fellows, I suppose ? "

"I think not, Sir," said Milly, dropping her old curtsey,
in spite of her silk dress, before this star of the first magnitude.

"At a hundred tasks to make everybody at home, at any
rate," said Fyvie, senior. "Hester, you have not forgotten
Milly Athorpe ? "

"Oh ! no, I have not forgotten her," said Hester, coldly.
"Are you well ? "

"Yes, thank you, Miss Fyvie," stammered Milly, changing
colour on the instant, and not prepared for any coldness of
demeanour on the part of the old friend.

Hester turned to Laurence.

"Are you coming back with us now, or do you intend
finishing the evening here ? " she said, in an aside.

"I am coming back with you."

"I thought——"

Hester paused, and struck her skirt three or four times
impatiently with her closed parasol.

"Well ? " asked Laurence.

"I thought that—that you might wish to stay here.
That there were attractions more to your taste in the neighbourhood."

"Hester ! " he said, as they turned away.

Milly had seen the whispered conversation, but had not

heard a word of it. She saw that Miss Fyvie was not in a pleasant mood, that she was even inclined to snap Mr. Raxford—which was a consolation to her, and rendered her own snubbing of little importance, though it was the first that she had received from that quarter.

She was looking after Laurence and Hester, with Mr. Fyvie a few paces in the background, nodding and smiling to those faces which were familiar to him, when some one shook her mantle suddenly.

" William—oh ! is that you ? Have you been lucky in the match ? "

William Churdock, vulgarly called Bully Churdock, otherwise Big Billy, and by pert young mining hussies, Big Silly, stood towering at her side, with a half-sleepy, half-sullen, downcast look. Bully Churdock was very red and very dirty about the face, and wore a heavy flannel coat, buttoned to the chin.

" It don't matter whether I be lucky or not, I ain't *he !* " nodding his head in the direction that Milly had been gazing. " I ain't the likes of he—and that's it ! "

" Churdock, don't talk nonsense ! " said Milly, indignantly, and possibly glad of a chance of snubbing some one in her turn. " Who has won the match ? "

" Well, it bean't me," answered Churdock ; " and you'll think wus of me than never. He licked me, the cus ! "

" I'm sorry to hear that, William."

" He didn't lick me fair, mind you—the Cornish wagabond ! I'll smash him yet—by gor, I will, Milly ! You won't think the wus o' me for being licked ? "

" Not I."

" I thought you'd think better o' me if I won and I tried my hardest for you and Devon. But he wor a sneak ! "

" How was it, Bully ? " asked Milly.

" Why, lookee a-here. He looked at my boots, and he said they warn't fair, and I got horn inside—so I had—so he might—noboby said he mightn't ! Wull, he wouldn't wrustle if there was any kicking, he said, and then, by gor, when not laying by for kicks, I wasn't, he came one, two, across my shins, and floored me. But I'll have the rights o' him, see if I doant, before he's older much. I'll go and get drunk ! "

14

" No—don't do that, Bully. How will you be able to see your mother and little Johnny home, up the hills ? "

" There's lots about to see 'em home. I've been larfed at, and I can't bide larfing. But I won't drink if it'll tease ye."

" That it will, then."

" And ye'll think the same o' me ?—no wus ? "

" No worse, certainly."

" Never no better—it ain't likely never no betterer—I doant expect that now, lass. I understand it all—you can't be liked so well by any one else, but I bean't fit for you— odds, my life—no ! It can't be ever—eh ? " he asked, gloomily.

" Why never, William Churdock ? "

" You'll go and marry——"

" I shall never marry," interrupted Milly, " so hold your foolish tongue."

" Never ?—oo ! that's foin ! "

" Never in all my life ; I've made up my mind, so rest easy, Bully, and go away now, and don't drink—there's a good friend."

" I'll be strang as a hoose—I'm all right now ! "

He went away, limping very much, but less crest-fallen, and Milly looked after him sadly and dreamily.

" Never to marry ! " she said—" never to marry any one *now !*—poor old Bully Churdock ! It's all plain before me like a book, and," letting her hands fall to her side almost despairingly, " there's no help for it, Miss Milly."

~~~~~~~~~~~~~~~~~

CHAPTER XXI.

A LOVERS' QUARREL.

IT was a very quiet ride to Tavvydale House—a dead level of calmness presaging a storm. The three occupants of the carriage, that had been waiting in the outskirts of the village, found but little to discourse upon during the homeward drive. Mr. Fyvie glanced from his daughter to Laurence, and back again, divining the situation, but at a loss for a reason. He attempted once or twice to lead the conversation, and start a topic on which all three might grow eloquent ; but finding that he was rewarded with nothing but monosyllables for his pains, he crossed his arms on his chest, curled himself into a corner of the carriage, and made preparations for his usual afternoon's nap.

There had been a lovers' quarrel—a little tiff, or something, he thought, philosophically, and all would be well when he was out of the way. Laurence had not been punctual in his letter-writing, or Hester had found something to be jealous about—women were always exacting, and Hester, though the best girl under the sun, was of a jealous disposition. He had known her jealous of his kindness to Jonathan, but she was a child then, and she should have outgrown that complaint by this time. Memorandum—to leave these two odd beings to themselves as early as convenient after dinner.

Laurence sat facing Hester, looking thoughtfully at her, as at a new specimen of womankind that had crossed his path, and had been hitherto unknown to him. And this was a new Hester ; he had never seen her before, and he gazed at her very earnestly, studying her as she sat there pale, passive—almost statuesque. She would not look towards him.; she kept her eyes fixed upon the parasol in her lap, or upon her gloved hands, holding each other with a clasp that was evidently hard and firm. After Hester's petulant remark and Laurence's reply, recorded in the last chapter, not a word had been spoken between them; and Laurence was in doubt whether Hester was sorry for that little impatient outburst, or felt that he deserved it. He, too, should be glad of the opportunity for explanation that a *tête-à-tête* would afford them both ; latterly, they had misunderstood one another, or missed a few roses from the path which they had been pursuing together. She had changed, he thought, or her character was developing itself to him. He had not understood her before their engagement, and her best manner—her most gracious moods—had possibly deceived him. He hoped not, but he felt aggrieved at her suspicions, and he took no blame unto himself, for he did not—would not—know himself at that time.

Neither a proud nor a vain man, he was still confident of

14—2

his own virtues—his honour, firmness, everything that makes man manlike. He felt that a word pledged or a promise given was a pledge or a promise for ever, and he was sure that he would have died rather than break one or the other. He would have marched to his own misery, but he would have kept his faith, he felt convinced ; and thus assured of his own steadfastness, it vexed him—terribly vexed him—to see this evidence of distrust shown by one who should have been the last to doubt him. He hoped that she had spoken hastily ; he believed, or he tried to believe that she had ; he believed also, now, that they had never understood each other, and that that better understanding would result from a calm, dispassionate consideration of their foibles. He would say their foibles for the sake of argument, for she believed that he was either weak or deceitful—but he would convince her how honourable a man he was. It did not suggest itself to him that he had only to convince her of his love—and it was strange that, amidst all this brooding, that idea came not uppermost in their ride back to Mr. Fyvie's house.

Laurence did not take his place at the dinner table that day. He stated that he had dined at Captain Athorpe's and could not face another array of comestibles ; he would dress and go into the drawing-room, if his friends would kindly excuse him.

"I excuse and sympathise with you," said Mr. Fyvie ; "I remember the Tavvydale feasts, and the strong stomachs that were required to keep up against them. Lie down for half an hour, or have some soda water, Laurence."

"No, thank you, Sir."

"You're looking as sick as a dog—I'll swear you feel so."

"I have a headache—that's all."

"Ah ! you have been drinking too much."

Laurence looked indignantly towards his partner at this insinuation, until he noticed the smile with which the comment had been accompanied, then he laughed and shook his head in dissent before he went away to his own room. Verily he was becoming tenacious, he thought now. Quick at taking offence, and seeing covert insinuations where not one was intended ; he must be more watchful of himself ; doubtless he had misunderstood Hester after all, and a few words would dissipate the "difference" between them.

When he descended to the drawing-room, he found that Mr. Fyvie was the sole occupant.

"Oh ! Laurence," he said, half-opening his eyes, the ladies are in the garden, I believe. What a time you have been dressing, to be sure ! "

"Have I ? " asked Laurence absently.

"For a young man not supposed to be very slow in his movements," said Mr. Fyvie; "well, you'll find the ladies in the garden."

Laurence was making his way to the French window, when his partner called him back.

"Oh ! by the way, Laurence," he said carelessly, "don't keep Hester too long in the night air, and—try to be as agreeable as you can. The girl's not exactly herself after her long journey. Girls are not always alike, you know! "

"No, Sir," said our hero, regarding Mr. Fyvie dubiously.

"They require humouring rather than thwarting. In my courting days I let the lady have her own way. It saved discussion and promoted harmony. You'll shut that window after you, Laurence—thank you."

Laurence went into the garden, not very well pleased to receive his cue from his intended father-in-law—not understanding thoroughly why a hint as to his course of conduct should have been offered by Mr. Fyvie. Laurence was sure that he was not a quarrelsome man ; on the contrary, a good-tempered, warm-hearted fellow, to be influenced by a word at times, and his partner's hint was not acceptable. He knew the right method of conducting himself as well as any man, and to be schooled as to his deportment was not pleasant, even from a friend so interested in his well-being as the gentleman whom he had left dozing in the drawing-room.

He had expected to find Hester alone, and he was not disappointed. He went straight to the place where he had imagined he should find her—and in this supposition he was correct also. Everything was as he had anticipated, and if there were a cloud in the way, why, a breath would dispel it. Hester, regretting her peevishness, was waiting for him to say how sorry she was, he thought, until Hester rose as he approached her, with the evident intention of returning at once to the house.

"One moment, Hester," said Laurence, intercepting her;

"you know that I am anxious to speak to you—to ask you for an explanation? Pray sit down again."

He pointed to the garden-seat round the great elm-tree on the lawn—a favourite spot of hers before she had ever seen him—dear to her now, out of that very love for him which he had made her confess there a little while ago.

She wavered for an instant, then looked very steadily into his face.

"I am going back to the house," she said.

"Presently we will go together," said Laurence, returning Hester's gaze as steadily; "but you will sit down now? I ask this of you as a favour."

"I cannot see the necessity of remaining here."

"But I can."

"Very well, then," and Hester, with lips compressed—they were thinner lips than he had imagined, he thought—sat down reluctantly on the garden-seat, and let him take his place beside her.

Then there ensued a pause, which was embarrassing to them both—which was broken at last with some degree of haste by Laurence.

"Hester, all this is childishness," he said; "I thought that you and I understood each other better."

"I never professed to understand you," said Hester; "I thought——"

"Well," said Laurence, seeing that she ceased abruptly to express her thoughts, "I am waiting patiently for an explanation—I hope that I deserve one."

"Explanation!" said Hester, almost contemptuously; "I think that an explanation is due to me, Laurence."

"I shall be happy to explain anything that may appear to you mysterious, or wrong in my conduct," said Laurence, more gravely; "you have only to state your charge against me."

"I have no charge to make," said Hester, peevishly; "I am going into the house. Don't stop me, Sir, for I *will* go in."

But Laurence placed his hand on her wrist, despite her assertion, and she did not struggle very much to keep her word, albeit her face shadowed still more. Yes, this was a new Hester Fyvie, and he did not understand her yet.

"There, Hester, let us look at the matter less seriously,

whatever it may be," he said, kindly; "something has disturbed you to-day, and it is hard that I should suffer for it."

"If all this is childishness," she said, quoting a word which had grated upon her five minutes since, "don't talk to me like a child—I can't bear that."

Laurence was looking down at the grass with his hands clasped together, and missed the impatient gesture with which her words were accompanied—the hasty dashing away of the tears from her eyes.

"We will begin at the beginning, Hester," he said gently; "where you left off, for instance. 'You never professed to understand me—you thought——?'"

"I thought that you were different from any man whom I had seen before, and I find that you are like all the rest."

"I don't wish to be exceptional," said Laurence; "I don't suppose that I am better or worse than the majority of men at my age—but *you* should think me better, considering the position in which I stand to you."

"Ah!—I can't now," said Hester, sadly.

"You think less of me than you did—you tell *me* this!" said Laurence, very quickly. "Hester, you suspect my honour?"

"I do not understand you," said Hester; "your motives may be very good and pure, but they are open to suspicion, and I have not been the only one to suspect."

"Well," said Laurence, gloomily, "I should have been above suspicion from you—and you should have been above listening to the malevolence of others."

"Laurence," said Hester, paler now than her wont, "I will not be reproved like this. You are clever at turning the tables upon me, but it would be more straightforward to prove that I have thought unjustly of you—more like you!"

"I am ready," answered Laurence.

Then there ensued another pause, during which Laurence sat as rigid and hard as the trunk of the tree against which he leaned; and Hester beat one little foot impatiently upon the grass, anxious for the whole truth, doubtful how to elicit it gracefully, and conscious that it was not a generous task which circumstances had imposed upon her.

She would have been glad now to have dropped the discussion, and let him take her to his heart, and forget everything that had marred their bliss; but it was too late, and she must prove, at least, that she had not been fretful, capricious, or childish. She was vexed more with herself than with him—for she felt, now, that it lowered her to speak of all that had led to her distrust.

"You know," she said at last, in a low tone, "what has disturbed me?"

"No."

"You can guess?"

"Pardon me, Hester, but I will not try to guess. I have a faint idea of one cause for your suspicious, but still I cannot think it possible."

Hester bit her lip; he would not assist her in their mutual explanations, and she must prosecute this task herself. It was better to do it quickly, and end the foolish story.

"I said that you were like other men—for all men whom I have met are prone to vanity, and are to be influenced, more or less, by the face of a pretty woman—no matter the woman's position in life, so that she is very pretty. You are interested in Milly Athorpe!"

Laurence felt a twinge at his heart—a spasm, as it were—though he had prepared for the accusation. Hester was jealous, and he was bound to her for ever, and it was all very foolish; but still the twinge came, and he could not have kept it back to save his life.

"Yes, I am interested in her," he answered, frankly.

Hester was not prepared for this response; she had expected an indignant denial, a scene perhaps, ending in a shower of tears, and a grand reconciliation, and his reply checked the better feelings that had been rapidly gaining ground with her.

"Why?" she asked, with her old abruptness predominant.

"Not because she is pretty," answered Laurence, "but because she is original, and seems to me very lonely and friendless—and because she is, in mind, education and manners, different from her class. Because a girl, self-taught, as she is, must have been possessed of an uncommon energy to attain to her anomalous position. Lastly

because her good name—which is her greatest pride—
has been in peril lately."

" And you have been her champion ? "

" Yes."

" You had no right. " It was officious, intermeddling,
wrong."

" I did not seek the office of her champion; I was sorry
that she came to ask my mediation."

" But flattered by her confidence in you—and taking up
this girl's cause with all your heart."

" You are jealous of this poor mining girl, then ? "

" I am too proud to be jealous of *her !* " cried Hester,
scornfully, if somewhat irrelevantly; " but I know that she
is a beautiful girl, vain of her absurd studies—romantic,
ambitious, perhaps designing. And that girl places confidence in you before her relations, and you are ready to
accept her confidence, caring nothing for the good name
she risks with you."

" Her Uncle Whiteshell was foolish enough to tell her to
put her trust in me—her master—rather than her Uncle
Athorpe—and she was afraid that Athorpe's anger might
affect your family."

" She said so ! Do you think Jonathan would have been
afraid of one of his own men ? "

" I cannot tell. Jonathan has told you all, I perceive."

" Jonathan came to Aunt Llewellyn's and took all the
blame upon himself—just as you and Milly wished."

" Just as every honest man and woman should have
wished also, Hester."

" If there had been any reason for it all. But Milly's
enemies were all in her imagination, which disturbs her
reason sometimes."

" Mrs. Llewellyn was not——"

" I will not hear about Mrs. Llewellyn," cried Hester.
" I will not hear that mining girl defended by you in this
manner. It is an insult to me, and I cannot endure it ! "

" You mistrust me still, then ? " said Laurence, rising
with her; " mistrust the motives which led me to be her
friend, and lower yourself with me by your suspicions.
Hester, I am sorry for this—I deserved more confidence, I
am sure. Engaged to you as I am, I would rather cut my
tongue out than address a word of affection to another

woman. And you think that I have been making love to Milly ? "

"She may have been making love to you instead," said Hester, in reply. "I have said that she is ambitious and romantic, and she is as eccentric as her Uncle Athorpe. I don't blame her."

"Don't blame her ! " echoed Laurence.

"I don't blame any girl for fighting her hardest to improve her position. She knows the power and the value of her face, and she may have seen that you are impressionable. Is she aware that we are engaged to each other ? " asked Hester sharply.

"I have not considered it her business to know that fact, or mine to convey it, Hester," was the answer.

"I will excuse a village girl's ambition, then," said she petulantly ; "but she is a fool, for all that—and her poetry books have made her foolish."

"Surely your thoughts are more weak than hers, Hester," said Laurence ; "for that girl has never had one thought of me, and it is not natural for you to think so. You have been made the dupe of others."

"No ! " cried Hester vehemently.

"I believe that Mrs. Llewellyn has set you on to make this charge against me—to lower you by its assertion, and me by the ridiculous defence I am compelled to make."

"You have been to her house in the Cleft—she has come to you after mining hours, asking you to be her friend, and defender—you have been to her school this morning—you dined with her at her uncle's house—you sing her praises to my very face ! "

"Will you consider that my position——"

"Do you tell me that a man studies position when he is attracted by a pretty girl ?—or am I wholly ignorant of the world ? Laurence, I know the world too well for that."

"Pardon me, but you are very distrustful and weak—that is all."

"You are weaker than I," said Hester. "I don't think that you would play me false intentionally ; but you are— yes, you *are* like the rest of men, easily influenced and flattered, led on, thinking no evil in your heart, but letting evil overtake you in the end. I am not likely to put up with your flirtations in any direction. I will reign absolutely, or not at all."

"You surprise me," murmured Laurence, as they walked on slowly towards the house—"you humiliate and confound me."

"If you are sorry——"

"No," was the interruption here, "I am only disappointed."

"In yourself, or in me ? "

"I am disappointed in you, Hester," said Laurence; "I had believed that you were a woman of great faith, who would have rather been the first to take my part against all comers, than the first to charge me with dishonour. This knowledge of mankind of which you boast has been confined to a few specimens, and you judge me by them. I judged you as a perfect woman, loving me with all her heart, and above suspicion of me; I find you irritable, jealous, paving the way by your distrust to the misery of both. So, Hester, I am disappointed."

"The girl you courted is not the girl by your side now ? "

"Scarcely."

"Then seek your ideal somewhere else ! " cried Hester passionately. "You never loved me, only out of gratitude to my papa; and I will not have your charity bestowed upon me any more. Both acted hastily—both were deceived—and it is well for both that we can pause before more harm is done. Mr. Raxford, you are free ! "

Laurence stopped, thunderstruck at his dismissal; for an instant he could not realise it; then he plunged after her as she swept onwards towards the house, and arrested her before she reached it.

"Hester, is it possible that you wish to sever this engagement ? "

"It was hasty and ill-considered. Let it end."

"Not now, Miss Fyvie," said Laurence, very white and firm; "you are excited, and speak without consideration. I will wait seven days for your verdict. In that period—should I not hear from you meanwhile—I must accept your determination as final. Meanwhile, I beg you to believe that it is no wish of mine that we should part—that I do not consider this an end to our engagement—that you have treated me ungenerously, and that I love you."

He believed so in the excitement of that moment—he had tried always to believe so from the first day of his engagement to her—but he was not the master of his own thoughts then, and he was more heroic than human.

<hr />

CHAPTER XXII.

SEVEN DAYS TO CONSIDER.

LAURENCE RAXFORD went away to the mines the next morning, and Hester was left to ponder on her quarrel with him, and on the result which had followed it. She was not satisfied with the events of the preceding night; scarcely conscious of all that she had said in her impetuosity. She had been vexed with her lover, and had let him see that she had a fine womanly temper of her own. His words had stung her more than her accusations had troubled him, and she had told him that he was free to love another woman, if it pleased him.

Hester brooded upon all this; in her anger she had cancelled this engagement; in her cooler moments she tried to believe that it was better for them both—that it was what both desired now. He had never loved her, and was glad of the opportunity to break with her; let it be so, if he wished it, for she was a girl whose pride would not accept gratitude for affection. Then she wished—for she was but a girl of twenty years of age, and this was the first man with whom she felt her life's happiness might be trusted—that she had dismissed him with greater calmness, and less passion; his last reminiscence of her had been a woman with the airs of a virago—a something like the Aunt Llewellyn, whom Laurence disliked. Why could she not have waited till the morning, and dismissed him for ever—ah! for ever —in a cool and lady-like manner, befitting the heiress that she was?

She treasured up his parting words, but they only irritated her more, for they were barriers in his way towards her. He had not accepted her resignation of him, for he had seen that she was not like herself—but he had given her seven days to think upon her hasty words, and silence after that period was to convince him that she had spoken from the heart. Silence !—as if she could write to him, and tell him that she had been in the wrong—that she loved him very much still, and could not afford to part with him ! That was humbling herself in the dust before him, and praying him to take her back again. If he really loved her—if he considered that he *was* bound in honour to her—he would not insist upon this condition. He would come to her again, and ask if her determination to set him free was final, and so part with her in cool blood ! She believed that he would come ; and she would not write to him. He had no right, after all that she had said, to expect an acknowledgment that she was hasty in her verdict ; he would come and seek his answer, and beg her, perhaps, not to cast him off.

But when five days out of the seven had passed and no sign was made, Hester grew very anxious, despite her firm demeanour, her every day face set to father, mother, and friends. She had said nothing of the quarrel to any one, for if it were made up again, there would be no necessity for the story ; and as he went away—perhaps for good !—he had told her that he loved her. Surely he would come back to tell her so again, unless he was glad of the accident that had stepped between them—unless he had never loved her, after all !

But he had said that he loved her !—and he had always been frank, and earnest, and truthful, fearing nothing in his way, caring for nothing that opposed his honourable progress. He *had* been so different to other men—so devoid of pride and affectation—so capable of winning the affections of all with whom he was brought in contact, by a charm of manner, which was wholly his, and which had won her before his lips had thrilled her with a confession of his passion. He was not a proud man, and he would not go back to the mine to treasure up every word that she had uttered in her haste ; that was unlike him. He would make every consideration for her petulance—for he had seen that she *was* childish in her manner, and had told her so—and he would come back to ask if her resolution was final ; and then— why then, they would understand each other better ! He would leave it till the last day but one—not till the last day, that would be too cruel !—and she dressed herself for dinner with more than usual care, full of belief in her own prophecy.

"I have an idea that Laurence will run over this evening," her father said also; "it's a fine day, and he's fond of a long walk."

But Laurence came not, and Hester ate but little dinner, and was thoughtful—intensely thoughtful, during the progress of the meal.

"Is anything the matter?" her mother ventured to ask —even her placid, unobservant mother, when they were together in the drawing-room.

"Nothing, mamma—that is, nothing more than usual."

"I fancied that there was—you look so scared, my dear," she answered.

Hester went early to her room, and opened her writing-desk with trembling hands. She placed the paper before her, pushed her hair back from her forehead, and then stared hard at the unwritten sheet. Yes, she would write—not to ask him to come back to her, to take pity on a woman who had not said what she intended, but to upbraid him for not asking if her determination to part with him was really irrevocable. She might write that without suspicion — in all fairness—ay, in all despairing love, if it were necessary!

Hester seized the pen and dashed off her missive—paused to read it over—tore it into a hundred pieces, and began again, to again enter upon her work of destruction after the completion of her task. Verily a proud young woman this, with the blood of her mother's family running through her veins—a young woman who preferred her own unhappiness to a confession of her faults. The desk was clanged to, and Hester rose, firm as a sea-cliff—as hard, angular, and white.

"Let him go, then!" she cried. "I will not write to him, if he values me at so little!"

She did not sleep till the daylight stole into her room—the light of the last day that was left her. She was asleep when her maid—her favourite maid, who had been transferred from Mrs. Llewellyn's service to her own—who had travelled with her from London, and who had been more kind and respectful lately, as though she guessed her young mistress's love troubles by intuition—tapped lightly on the panels of the door.

" Come in—what is it ? " Hester asked, starting up in bed eagerly, full of the one thought that possessed her.

" A letter, Miss."

" From—from the mines ? "

" Yes—one of the men has brought it over, and is waiting an answer."

" Give it me, please—and tell the man to wait. I will ring for you, Mary, presently."

" Very well, Miss Fyvie."

The maid withdrew, and Hester tore open the letter. Yes, it was from Laurence—containing a few words hastily written, but proof, strong as Holy Writ, that he was not anxious to take her at her word. He reminded her that it was the last day left for consideration of her wishes ; he waited for the truth, and if there was no answer, he would understand her too well, and accept his dismissal in all humility. If she thought it for the best that their engagement should be cancelled, he would think so too. She had her future happiness to consider, not his.

Hester shed a few tears—not of mortification—over this letter, put on her dressing-gown, and opened her desk with the same haste as on the preceding night. She was less hard to please in her choice of words now, and the pen skimmed rapidly over the paper.

" He will understand this—he cannot expect more than this till we meet," she said, with flushed cheek and panting breath ; " I am sure that he will understand me ! "

The letter asked him to come that evening, expressed a faint regret that he had held back till the last day, and reminded him that on that night he should have her final answer.

" And when he comes, I will ask him to forgive my suspicions, and we shall have nothing to quarrel about ever again—poor Laurence ! " murmured Hester.

She rang the bell for the maid, who responded quickly to the summons.

" Give that to the man at once."

" Yes, Miss."

Exit maid, swiftly along the passages of the great house, pausing at the top of the grand staircase to look behind her, around her, on all sides of her, before she opened the letter in her hands, and read carefully every line of its contents. Then the letter thrust to the bottom of her pocket, and the spy tripping as lightly down stairs, as though Heaven had blessed her for her curiosity.

"Oh! Passmore," she said to the heavy-browed man wating in the hall, "I've kept you waiting, perhaps, but my young lady was asleep, and wouldn't wake up to read the note at once. There's no answer—Miss Fyvie don't see any necessity for an answer."

"Very well."

"You understand this?"

"Oh, yes!"

"Because you don't seem to understand everything, Passmore. When you go to London, you'll brighten up a bit, I dare say. I'm going back to London myself, to my old place, too. I can't bide Devonshire. And you *are* really off to London?"

"I guv warning last Saturday—I goes next Sunday. Scurshun."

"For good?"

"For good, Mum."

"I hope you'll get on in London, Passmore. No answer —good-day!"

*   *   *   *   *   *   *   *   *

Hester waited in vain for Laurence that night—just as she had rehearsed in vain that day a hundred pretty speeches that should win him to her arms again, whence he should never more have the chance of an escape. She waited, but the hours stole on—dinner, dessert, tea, till all chance was over, and she was like the ghost of yester-night again—only a ghost with a greater load at her heart.

"He misunderstands my letter—he wilfully misunder-stands it," thought Hester, "and he will not come near me again!"

Still she sat up late for him, hoping that something had detained him on the road; and when she had bidden her father and mother good-night, and they had gone to their room, she stole down stairs once more to wait in that grandly furnished drawing-room for the lover who was never to enter there again.

He might come very late, to tease her till the eleventh hour, she thought. But even the twelfth hour struck, and then she knew that every hope of him went away with the last chime. She glided from the couch to the carpet and buried her head in her hands, and cried long and silently to herself—shedding those bitter tears of disappointment, remorse, and baffled love, which I pray every one of my readers has escaped. The trial is for the few, but there are a few who suffer keenly, even in the life apart from novels.

"Oh, dear!" she sighed wearily at last, "he will never —never know how I have loved him!"

END OF BOOK THE FIRST.

15

BOOK II.

TRAGEDY IN TAVVYDALE

CHAPTER I.

FREE !

LAURENCE RAXFORD was really free, then ! The engagement was at an end, and all the love-dreams connected
therewith had gone the way of many dreams before them.
It had been a passing fancy of Mr. Fyvie's daughter ; a
little romantic episode crossing the monotony of every-day
life, lasting a few months, and pleasant whilst it lasted.
But it had been a match made up in a hurry, with no sober
forethought to consolidate it, and at the first shock the frail
links had been shivered, and suitor and maiden stood apart
once more.

Was he sorry ? Was this hero of ours truly and intensely sorry for the disruption of the engagement ?—for
the firmness which had put an end, once and for ever, to
the hopes of a wife from the great house ? It is a difficult
question to answer; Laurence was not inclined to sift to
the depths himself, and his own thoughts were terribly
perplexing.

He was not a selfish man, therefore the position that he
had lost, and the heiress that had escaped him, was not so
much a matter for grave speculation, as the way in which
he had lost her. He was mortified at his banishment, at
the jealousy, the sternness, the implacability, which, after
seven days' consideration, could thus contemptuously dismiss him. He was sure now that Hester had never loved
him, and though it was a mercy that he had not taken so
stern a woman for his wife, still the blow to his pride was

none the less acute. He had been vain enough to believe that this rich man's daughter had loved him with her whole heart, and would have made any sacrifice for him. He had fancied that he had detected her love before he had avowed his own, and that discovery had rendered him grateful, eager to make her happy, and a little thoughtless as regarded his own feelings, and, after all, it was but a passing fancy, and so had ended like one.

How the result would influence his future, disappoint Mr. Fyvie and his mother, reduce him to that sphere to which he properly belonged, he saw at once, and was more than resigned to. He felt the stronger for that ; more like his old self, when his way to greatness was not clearly defined, and he thought that he had his own fortune to make ; in every way he should be a freer man, and, the first mortification passed away, a happier one. He had begun to settle down to ease and affluence at two and twenty years of age, and he was young and Quixotic enough to feel that there was something nobler and higher in letting his chances go by him, and seeking others for himself. In the lower estate he should meet with friends more suited to his tastes, and that would recompense him for the wealth that he was to lose with Hester Fyvie.

To analyse more deeply Laurence's thoughts, to set him apart from that self-depreciation, that inner vexation born of the lover's quarrel, it is not saying too much to add that he was not sorry for his freedom. There was an intense satisfaction, however well disguised, in feeling free to follow his own happiness, wherever he believed it likely to be waiting for him—in knowing that there was no one in the world who could balk him of anything on which his heart was set—or who had a right to step between him and his wishes. This engagement had never satisfied him, had been at times a reproach to him, as though he had been the willing tool of his father's friend and his mother, and bargained with them for a wife in exchange for a share in a copper mine. Though he had fought himself into the conviction of his love for Hester—though he was certain that he should have made her the best of husbands, and been ever true to her—though he would have suffered a martyrdom rather than have moved one step himself to sever the engagement formed between them—it *was* satis-

15—2

factory to think that he was his own master again, even at the price of her disdain, and of his conviction that he had never been fairly understood. But he did not blame her very severely—nay, more, he took his share of blame with her, for he had acted on impulse also, in the whirl of the new world into which he had been thrust. Soberly now he could review the past, and thank God that two lives had not been cast away in the waters into which they had plunged. Whatever happened in the future, all was well!

Laurence took a week to mature his plans, and then he buttoned his coat firmly to the chin, like a man setting forth on a journey that required coolness and firmness, and walked all the way to Tavvydale House. There he learned for the first time that Mr. and Mrs. Fyvie, with their daughter Hester, had left for London last night, and he returned to write a long letter to Mr. Fyvie, in lieu of that interview for which he had prepared himself.

Laurence sat up half the night writing — tearing up many sheets of paper before he had struck off the epistle that seemed appropriate to the occasion. When finished, it was an odd letter—as odd as he was, though he considered himself the most prosaic, matter-of-fact fellow with whom he had ever been acquainted. He alluded very briefly to the termination of the engagement, and referred the father to his daughter for the explanations most befitting; then he dashed into the one subject uppermost with him—the partnership which he had obtained under false pretences. He spoke of his resolve to surrender all claim upon the property, and to become independent of foreign aid for his success in life. He expressed his gratitude for the confidence that had been placed in him, and for the offer which had been generously made him, and which he too thoughtlessly or too selfishly had accepted; but he repeated his resolution more than once, and with all the firmness that words could convey, to remain no longer a partner in Wheal Desperation. For a few months he would maintain his position as clerk, overlooker, anything that might be of service to Mr. Fyvie; but he surrendered from that day all claim upon the estate; and he prayed his father's old friend not to think the worse of him for his independence, or for the cause that had brought about his resignation.

Mr. Fyvie did not answer this letter, and Laurence was

aggrieved at his silence. Laurence was sure that he had
not been to blame in this matter—that it was not his fault
that the engagement had been broken off, and that he had
acted honourably in withdrawing his name from the firm
immediately that Hester had given him up, and, at all
events, and under every circumstance, he was entitled to a
reply. However, Mr. Fyvie would presently return to
Tavvydale, and then he would face him with his determination, and end this comedy of errors. Meanwhile, let him
work as honestly and persistently in the service, as though
he were still the junior partner, whose interests were identical
with the Fyvie's.

There was one letter which Laurence did *not* write, and
which, if he had written, would have altered, for better or
worse, the sequel to this story. That was a letter to his
mother. He had begun one or two, but had changed his
mind. His mother was very happy now — happy in
London, thinking her son's position for ever secured—let
her keep so for awhile, without any interference on his
part. She would only distress herself unnecessarily about
his future again, and in her impulsiveness and regret dash
off in search of Hester, or Hester's father, and render the
whole affair more embarrassing for everybody. It would
be better, he thought, to know more about his own future
—to be a little more certain of success in it—before he
told his mother everything that had happened since she
had left Devonshire. She was satisfied, and he would not
distract her thoughts from the peace by which she was
surrounded, until he could assure her that his truer happiness—his better life—lay in another direction to that which
she had indicated.

Two or three weeks after this, he was thinking of his
mother again, and half inclined on this occasion to take a
journey up to London, and break the news to her before it
reached her from another direction, and spoilt the idea
which had kept him silent so long, when Captain Athorpe
sent in word that he should like to see him for a moment.
This was on the Saturday night, when Athorpe had emerged
from below-ground, and was ready to go home.

" Show him in at once," said Laurence to the messenger,
and Athorpe and his niece Milly entered the room at his
command.

It was a strange instinct, but Laurence was prepared for her advent, although no notice had been given him that she would accompany her uncle. He was not surprised at her appearance before him, although his heart sank at the old curtsey, which was associated with her mining habits, and which told of her immeasurable distance from him as a friend. Far away from him, and unapproachable in her humility— and yet the girl of all others in the world of whom an heiress was jealous—the girl who had been the innocent cause of altering two lives for good. He could but regard her with interest after that, a something approximate to his fate that crossed and recrossed his path, casting a strange shadow thereon, or mingling with its brightness—which ?

"There, you'll be as glad as I am, Mr. Raxford," said Athorpe, in his usual loud tones—"it's done at last, and my pride's satisfied."

"What is done ?" asked Laurence, in a bewildered manner.

"Milly gives up all this," he explained, with a comprehensive sweep of his hand, as though Laurence and the counting-house were included in the category, "as beneath her, just as it is. They've been scheming to make more of a lady of her in Tavvydale, and I've given her a good talking to, and so she comes, as in duty bound for that matter, to say good-bye to the masters, and to thank them for all past kindness."

Laurence looked at Milly, blushing and shy as ever in her mining dress, and wondered what it meant. He only understood that she was going away for a reason satisfactory to her uncle, and he said,

"You are going to leave us, then, Milly ?"

"Yes, Sir. He didn't like to see me on the works, and perhaps I have lately got too proud for them. I don't know why—it suits me—it was my mother's work before me, and I have been happy here."

"You'll be happy anywhere, Milly, for you're not a grumbler," said her uncle; "and if in teaching yourself to be above the louts around you, you've learned the trick of holding your head higher, why, that's but natural, and I'm glad to see it. Why, if I didn't think myself better than all the thick heads in Tavvydale, I'd cut my throat to-morrow, and make one fool the less here."

"Ah ! we can't spare you, Athorpe," said Laurence, " and so it is lucky for us that you haven't a very bad opinion of yourself. As for your niece, why, if it's for her advancement in life, we must spare her with all our hearts, I suppose."

"She'll be more of a lady, at all events," said Athorpe, " my wife's delighted, for she never cared to see Milly slaving here."

"Are you—are you going away from Devon ? " asked Laurence, with an evident interest in the question.

" Who ?—I, Sir ? " exclaimed Milly, almost indignantly ; "oh ! I would not give up my dear little home in the Cleft to be a lady in earnest. I don't feel that ever I should be happy out of it."

" Milly will take her husband home there when her time comes, I think," laughed Athorpe.

" *When* her time comes, she will," said Milly, meaningly.

Laurence did not understand this any more than her uncle, who, after considering that reply for an instant, and staring at his niece with eyes very much distended, said,

"I hope he'll like the crib already furnished for him, then. You know old Wells, Sir ? " to Laurence.

" Oh ! uncle," said Milly in mild reproof.

" That hop-o'-my-thumb parson, who, I told you, was uncommonly kind to Milly," said Athorpe with a wink ; " well, he has been so pleased with Milly's Sunday teachings, and he thinks so much of Milly altogether—almost as much as Milly thinks of herself, mind you !—that she's to be schoolmistress altogether to the little varmints. A tough job, but it's a rise in life, and comes all of her own cleverness, and that's what makes me proud of her."

And Captain Athorpe was proud, and showed his pride on that day.

"You will like the change, Milly," said Laurence, "it will suit you better than the custody of fifty unruly young women."

" They were not often unruly—they were generally very kind and obedient, Sir, and liked me," said she, looking down at the ground ; "and it has been hard to say goodbye to them all, and leave half of them jealous of me."

" Jealous ? " repeated Laurence.

" Well, you see, they are only women," broke in Athorpe

at this juncture, to Laurence's dissatisfaction, "and the poor things can't help it. Milly has been one of them, and they don't care for her being anything else. They can't read or write, and they don't like Milly being a scholar—especially as she had the impudence to teach herself. And Milly can sing—like a bird—and leads all the little girls' howlings at chapel, and they never fancied that much—and just a few of them look infernally ugly and platter-faced by the side of her, and *that's* a nuisance—and now, to crown all, Milly's to do lady's work and turn governess. Why, women can't stand all this at once, and so she loses a few friends—poor thing !" he added ironically.

"Friends whom she can afford to lose," said Laurence. "Well, Milly, I congratulate you on assuming a post more suitable to you—and for that reason I am glad to think your term of service ends here."

"Thank you, and you will tell old Mr. Fyvie that I did not go away rejoicing—glad to leave the mine, which has become a part of home almost. I might have had," she said very thoughtfully, "one or two wicked pangs of dis-satisfaction, the result of my own schooling, but they were few and far between, and all things taken together, Sir, I have been—really !—very happy. Away from here, I hope I may be as content."

"Why, hang it !—what's to make you discontented ? " cried Athorpe.

"Nothing, uncle," was the reply, "but——"

"But what ? "

"But we can't be at rest when we like—and a rise in the world does not always lead to happiness, I have read."

"Ah ! you *have* read, until you've become addlepated. Well, bid Mr. Raxford good-bye—I don't suppose that you and he are likely to see each other any more, or that it matters to anybody if you don't."

"I hope we shall see each other, though," said Laurence, so hastily and warmly that Milly stole almost a frightened look towards him.

Laurence stammered forth, "The few friends in Tavvydale that I have made I am not willing to forget during my short stay here."

Two parts of this brief speech were taken up and re-echoed by his listeners.

" Friends ! " said Athorpe.

" Short stay ! " repeated Milly.

" Ay, friends, if you will allow me to call you both so," said Laurence, " for I am a stranger in this place, and with you I have been only at home. I don't care to feel entirely alone in Tavvydale," he added almost impatiently.

Captain Athorpe looked thoughtful.

" Upon my soul, I don't understand ! " he blurted forth, at last; " you can't call us friends—proud as we are to hear you say it—it would do no end of harm to you, and us. Though I'm not a humble-minded man myself, I like to meet with one at times—it does me good, and keeps me in my place. But, Sir, I know my place, for all my bounce."

" I wish I knew what mine was," said Laurence, doubtfully.

" A place that any one might envy," answered Athorpe. " The partner in a great undertaking, that you deserve a share in."

" Not a partner," corrected Laurence; " it is all a mistake that will be shortly corrected here. A partner under certain conditions, which cannot be fulfilled now, and which reduces me to *my* place, Athorpe—a clerk at the desk."

" No, Sir, I hope not ! " cried Athorpe, in astonishment. " Why, what has happened ? "

" It's a long story, that I will explain some day," said Laurence. " There is no mystery about it, and you may tell everybody upon the works, Athorpe."

" Not I. I'm not a goose, to go cackling all this to everybody—even if I quite believed it. Mr. Raxford, I should be very sorry to believe this."

" I hope not. It is for the best that I should work for my living, like—like Milly here," said Laurence. " I have taught myself to believe lately that it is the best and most honourable course lying open for me."

" Well, I'm confounded at present," said Athorpe, giving a vigorous scratch to his head.

" And, for the present, the subject is not worth discussion," said Laurence; " we'll talk of this some other time. Meanwhile, if I call upon you at Tavvydale, don't overwhelm me with thanks for my patronage," he added, smiling at the bewilderment still visible on Captain Athorpe's countenance.

"We shall be honoured, Sir, of course," said Athorpe.

"Not honoured, but pleased, I hope. And Milly, with time on my hands here, and no one at the great house glad to see me——"

"You have quarrelled with Mr. Fyvie," said Milly, quickly.

Laurence shook his head, and smiled again. His disappointments did not weigh heavily upon him or he would not have jested at them so lightly.

"And no one at the great house glad to see me," he repeated. "I may turn Dissenter, and come to chapel one fine morning or evening, to hear how the little ones improve in their singing."

Was it the spell of this girl's wondrous beauty that made him say this—a spell that he need not resist any longer, and which had rendered every sacrifice devoid of bitterness? Was he heart-sick at the coldness, the shallowness, the hypocrisies of the higher life to which he had belonged, and glad to descend to the lower ground, where the air was less keen and frosty, and true friends might welcome him? He looked at Milly as he had never dared to look at her before, and he understood, perhaps, then, why Hester's separation from him had not cast him down —why he had lived two lives, and been of two worlds lately, daring not to understand either till that day.

"Well, you've dazed us!" muttered Athorpe; and then he and his niece went away very thoughtfully down the road to Tavvydale.

Would they have been "dazed" still further to see Laurence close his account-books, after they had left him, and take two or three turns up and down the room, looking prouder and stronger than they had ever seen him; to hear him cry, almost exultingly, in the face of the Fate which he courted rather than defied, "Free of them all— and my own master?"

CHAPTER II.

HIS OWN MASTER.

LAURENCE RAXFORD never knew—or professed not to know—when his dissatisfied time set in; when he became no longer the staid, methodical, business-like being, who had stood at the head of affairs, and won the respect of his subordinates. The change that had come over his love dream had affected his fortunes, likewise—and he lost more than Hester Fyvie when he quarrelled with her in the grounds of Tavvydale House. That loss he believed had affected him—nay, worked a wondrous change in him. He was not the same man; he had not the same thoughts—he was restless, excitable, and eccentric.

He was sure that he did not grieve at the possible change in his position; he was more than prepared for that, although at a loss to account for the thrill of pleasure which accompanied at times his calm survey of his prospects. He had made up his mind to descend the ladder, and it would have been a disappointment to know that there were kind friends ready to balk his self-sacrifice. He had sketched forth his future career without helping hands to assist, and he was young enough, we have already said, to feel proud of achieving his own independence. Regarding matters soberly now—when his brain was less cool than it had ever been, this was !—he felt almost ashamed of his past decision — to revel in the wealth which a friend more earnest and industrious than he had accumulated. He had stolen into the partnership, like a thief—accepted a wild story about his father as gospel, and founded his claim to the mine upon nothing; he should be glad when Mr. Fyvie returned, and agreed with him that it would be better for all parties that he should gracefully withdraw. Mr. Fyvie saw that it was better, doubtless; his silence after Laurence's letter to him might be taken as consent, and their first meeting would settle everything. Upon that meeting would depend Laurence's future course. He was unresolved whether to leave

Tavvydale for good, or remain a clerk, or general manager upon the estate. That depended a great deal upon the wishes of his old partner and friend; but he thought that he should like to remain in Devonshire, and that he would be content—more than content—with any post that might be offered him. He knew that he was of service to the estate now—and that he should do justice to any position in which he might be placed.

But partner he would *not* remain; and he had begun to pave the way for his descent from greatness, by apprising Captain Athorpe and his niece of the changes that were shortly to ensue. He told Mr. Waters, the old clerk, also, and then left the news to circulate for itself, which, contrary to the principle of news, remained for a marvel at a stand-still; Captain Athorpe and Mr. Waters being endowed with the rare faculty of minding their own business, and Milly, less taciturn, having other matters just then to occupy her mind. So Laurence Raxford was dissatisfied and restless, although content with the future, wherein he would be a poor man. Restless, he believed, because every-thing was in a state of abeyance, and nothing was settled; because his was a mind that would put things at once into shape, and suit itself at once to the change.

It was hard work beneath the surface now; it was harder to be shut up in that counting-house, with the books before him; it was most hard to be left to himself, after work was over, and to feel, for the first time in life, how lonely he was. He had had a conviction that he could feel at home under every circumstance, and take even the ills of life with philosophy; but he was wrong after all, for the isolation amongst the Dartmoors had already become a trial to him.

It could not be, he thought, that he missed society at Tavvydale House, or had lost confidence in himself since a young woman had capriciously dismissed him from a place in her regard; he could not—or even yet he would not—fairly confess why life, after office hours, seemed void and purposeless to him.

On the Sunday—the second Sunday after Milly had left the service of the Fyvies—he thought that he would walk across to Tavvydale to chapel. He had heard a great deal of the Dissenters at Tavvydale, and though his mother had made a Churchman of him, he thought that it was but fair to study all sects, and judge for himself as to which was the simpler and more earnest worship. But when he was in Tavvydale his courage—much to his own amazement—suddenly deserted him, and he felt half inclined, even on a Sabbath morning, to anathematise his own pride, which kept him out of the barn-like edifice, after walking a considerable distance with the express purpose of hearing service therein.

He held back from the troops of miners and miners' wives who walked into the chapel, and after watching at a distance until the eleven o'clock bell had ceased ringing, he crossed to the little church in the fields, and sat out the service there—very grave, but very absent—along with a scanty congregation of Tavvydale shopkeepers. Coming out of church, he hesitated for awhile as to the expediency of returning to the village; then he faced about, and went homewards at a rapid pace, and, for the first time in his life, snapped up the old housekeeper about his dinner being done too much.

But in the middle of the week he was in Tavvydale again; there was a watchmaker in the place, and his watch wanted cleaning, regulating, and general tinkering of some kind, and in the cool of the evening he walked over to the village. His watch left in trust, he found himself strolling round the school-room, where the children had had their feast a few weeks since, and he affected to remember—for he was deceiving himself still, after a transparent fashion of his own—that Thursday night was a practising night with the little ones, and that Milly always did her best on that occasion to hammer the airs of the next Sunday's hymns into their thick little heads. Here he waited patiently—or impatiently, it was doubtful which—until the rehearsal of this congregational singing was over, and he could bless every youngster for the haste with which he or she tumbled out of the doorway, and ran along the path to the village. After that a middle-aged lady, in a capacious bonnet, and wearing worsted mittens, issued from the school-room, and said " Good-evening " to Laurence, as though to an old friend, and Laurence raised his hat, and repeated her words, and wondered where on earth he had seen her before. Finally,

Milly Athorpe, locking the school-room door behind her,
and then advancing towards him with the key in her
hand—swinging the key carelessy to and fro on her finger,
and looking down thoughtfully at the garden-path—the
prettiest of girls, in the brownest of studies.

The reader is aware that Laurence Raxford had always
been proud of his self-possession in difficult circumstances,
of the ease with which he could shape himself to any
society that confronted him, confident in his own powers
to carry him off with flying colours. He did not understand how it was that he felt very much confused as she
approached him; at a loss even to account for his presence
there, supposing that she should be curious enough to inquire the reason for it. All this was out of the common
way, he knew, or he should not have felt so uncommonly
strange. "This is romance!" he whispered to himself, as
she advanced.

It had been a spell upon him longer than he knew, or he
cared to confess, and he need resist no longer. He was his
own master, he repeated, and here lay his happiness, or
after misery, he knew not which—it rested with this girl,
who was so different from all women whom he had ever
met, and whose position had first attracted, then bewildered
him. Not her great gift of beauty, he was certain, in the
first instance, but her loneliness, her courage, her goodness,
her faith, and, after that, her angel's face, perhaps. Yes, it
was romance—the romance of his first love, coming as late
in life as two and twenty years of age, and coming all the
fiercer for the long delay. He knew then that it had been
only gratitude—common gratitude for a great kindness—
that had led him to anticipate Mr. Fyvie's wishes, and propose in haste to Mr. Fyvie's daughter. For that act he
was verily ashamed, and he blushed at his own cowardice,
like an honest man, led astray for a moment, and detected
in his weakness. He had been humiliated for *his* weakness, his foolish way of evincing his thanks for great
favours, and he accepted the shame as part of the punish-
ment which he naturally deserved. He was glad that it
had all ended in the right and true way, and he rejoiced
at the coming change in his position—at his coming full
in life—as men less romantic than he might have exulted at
their rise. Yes, very unworldly, very romantic, even very

foolish, we may set down young Raxford at this juncture; but then he was thoroughly in love, and after that, as Dekker says, "a man's gon!"

"Mr. Raxford!" exclaimed Milly, becoming aware of our hero's propinquity at last.

"Yes, it is Mr. Raxford," said Laurence; "I hope that he has not frightened you very much, Miss Athorpe?"

She was no longer his servant; she had risen in life, and he dared not call her Milly any more.

"Only a very little fright," answered Milly, "for I did not expect to find the master in Tavvydale this evening."

"The master's watch was out of order," he said lightly, "and repairs are neatly executed in Tavvydale. From the watchmaker's to the high-road is a short cut across the green here, and hence my sudden appearance and your alarm, Miss Milly."

There could be no objection to "Miss Milly," he thought, and "Miss Athorpe" had grated very much on his ears, and thrust him to an objectionable distance. He was a man who detested formality.

Milly did not see her way to a reply to this; she was always at a loss for words in Mr. Raxford's presence, and she walked on silently, with the old master by her side.

"I was curious to know, also, how the change of life agreed with you, and have taken the liberty of waiting to make my inquiries."

"You are very kind, Sir," murmured Milly.

"No—only very curious," answered Laurence, persevering in that forced lightness of demeanour, which was not natural to him at that time, and which Milly was quick enough to see, and had already begun to wonder at.

"I think my progenitors must have been very inquisitive, meddlesome mortals in their day, and the old weakness has cropped forth in the last of the Raxfords. I want to know —I am very anxious to know, Miss Milly—if this change of life is all that you conjectured?"

"I don't see that it——" began Milly, then paused.

"That it is any business of mine," concluded Laurence quickly; "exactly so, but then my ancestors are answerable for that. And yet it is business of mine, now I consider the question more closely."

Milly looked up at him suddenly, then looked down again.

She did not understand his new way ; she saw that he was different in his manner towards her, that he was neither natural nor unembarrassed. If he had not walked uprightly by her side—with so martial a tread, in fact—she might have fancied that he had called in at the " Swan," or the " Fyvie Arms " in Tavvydale, as well as at the watchmaker's. When Bully Churdock was " out of sorts," he went straight to the " Swan," if there was no friend to stop him *en route.*

" Why is it your business ? " asked Milly, with the faintest exhibition of preciseness, as one putting herself on guard against future compliments.

Laurence detected the change in her too, and was not pleased at it. He began to fancy that all the world mistrusted him, and was ready to feel an aversion for him, now, without due cause. He felt also that he was not in a good temper that evening—that a something had put him out, and rendered him in an aggravating mood. He would continue his light and airy demeanour for the present ; it masked his real feelings, and it enabled him to see his way more clearly along that path upon which he had entered, and along which Milly trod. He would pursue his way, if confident that his happiness lay in that direction, or he would turn back with the mask to his face—to his heart !—and no one the wiser for the reasons that had lured him there. He was a philosopher, calculating on his future now—and for ever resolved to be wise and wary—making no rash plunges, and dragging down nobody with him to the depths !

" Why is it my business ? " he reiterated ; " because I believe that sudden changes are not good for any of us—and as my life is on the verge of a transformation too, I should like to profit by example."

" I don't understand," answered Milly.

" You have risen in life—how has the change affected you ? "

" I cannot say, Sir."

" It unsettled you, surely ? "

" No," answered Milly. " I had expected the change, and it did not come with a shock to me. Perhaps I am a little prouder, now the chance has come for holding my head higher than the rest of my acquaintances—but no one has noticed that yet."

" Are you any the happier ? "

Milly paused to consider this question.

"Yes," she said at last, "I think that I am."

"I am very glad to hear it," replied Laurence, with more earnestness, "for a rise in life does not always tend to that. I rose in life a few months ago, Miss Milly, and have been since that time so unsettled, so unlike my true self, so unhappy, in fact, that I am looking forward, with all my heart, to the time when I shall return to my past life."

"You should have been more grateful for your good fortune, Mr. Raxford," said Milly, thoughtfully.

"Yes—but it was not good fortune, for it turned my head, and made a fool of me. I shall be glad to belong to the working-classes once more—really and truly glad!"

"The working-classes," said Milly, with a wondering stare from her great eyes in his direction—"you!"

Laurence nodded his head emphatically.

"Yes, the working-classes," he repeated.

"I don't know why you jest in this manner—and to me," said Milly slowly, and with her brow contracted in the faintest degree as she looked down at the ground; "you are a gentleman—and have always been one."

"Thank you for so good an opinion of me," said Laurence. "But—where are you going?"

"I will bid you good-night here," said Milly, pausing in the main street of the village upon which they had entered.

"You are not going home to the Cleft to-night, then?"

"Presently. I have to leave the key at Mr. Wells's."

"Ah! that is the minister's," said Laurence; "well, after calling there, you will return to the Cleft?"

"Yes," said she, disturbed a little by Laurence's eager questioning.

"If—if you would allow me to wait here for you. It is a late hour for you to be alone on a country road."

"No one will hurt me," said Milly confidently.

"May I ask to wait here, as a favour?"

"No, Sir," said Milly, very firmly and quickly; "if you please—Mr. Raxford—you will go home."

"If you wish it, then—I will go."

And Laurence Raxford marched away homewards at once, leaving Milly surprised, perplexed, and almost angry with him. She went to the minister's house and left the key there—wasting a little time with the housekeeper in general

16

conversation ; talking of the weather, the grass lands, the school children, the last news in Tavvydale, the housekeeper's rheumatics, which were "worse and worse," and scarcely conscious of the topics she started or took part in—thinking all the while of the eccentric young man who had stopped her at the school-house door, and walked with her to the village. She was on her way home at last, fearful that he would be waiting for her somewhere on the road, and hoping that he would not, because she had expressed a wish to him, and it would be kinder of him not to cross her path again. And he did not appear, which *was* generous, and saved her from the embarrassment of a false position, and at which she should have rejoiced rather than sighed as she turned into the dark Cleft. Well, perhaps she was rejoicing for all that—for he had respected her wish, and taken his departure, when he was certain that he was not wanted, sacrificing all his wishes to hers. And that Mr. Raxford had wished to be her companion along the high-road was evident enough, and that was pleasant to think upon, although she tried to frown and beat the thought away.

At home in the Cleft—with the door barred against the outer world—this fair hermit lighted her candle, and sat down to her books. She kept late hours at the cottage, for she had studied all her life therein—struggled hard to know more than the rest of her little circle, with a wild craving for book learning, that was like the instinct of genius struggling amidst difficulties to rise. She had risen, and she *was* clever—more clever than any one knew but herself, for Milly Athorpe was no boaster ; she took a delight in concealing her discoveries, her conquests over the incongruous materials into which she delved, and at which she worked none the less hard for being conscious that her attainments were profitless and scarcely satisfied herself. Her mother had brought as her dowry to her father the oddest collection of books in the world, and Milly had waded through the whole of them, mixing them up together, after a fashion of her own, and when puzzled at a mystery, trying hard to solve it. Well for her, perhaps, that there were a few old novels in their midst—to relieve the drudgery of dry treatises, and that Milly read them, and tried to understand them in their turn, or Milly's idiosyncrasy might have disordered her ideas more than it had done—for Milly was afraid at times that she was not quite right in her head. The Athorpes had always been eccentric—her uncle was eccentric now—and why should she be exempt any more than the rest of them? She knew that she understood her books better than she understood herself, and that aggravated her occasionally. But then, Milly never studied herself—never sat down soberly to consider her character, in all its manifold inconsistencies; she had a suspicion that she was ambitious at heart, and tried hard every day to keep that feeling undermost, taking credit to herself lately in having succeeded.

Taking credit till that night, when the pride came back in spite of her, she was assured; but a new, wild, bewildering pride, which puzzled her, for it almost verged on happiness. She would have sunk it in the oldest and dustiest of her volumes—a collection of Featley's sermons, written when a Charles was on the throne; but her thoughts were too powerful that night for sermons, and she pushed her brown hair from her temples, clutched her head with both her hands, and went off into dream-land, where figures born of her new pride hovered so near the foreground that they seemed parts of waking life.

In her room, long afterwards, she seemed, like Narcissus, to have fallen in love with her own face, she looked so long and steadily—and yet so sorrowfully—at it in her little dressing-glass; and later still it was a Niobe—weeping and distraught—on which the moonlight shimmered, as she knelt by her maiden couch, and tried to convince herself of the wickedness and futility of such thoughts as hers.

The next day she was the Milly Athorpe that she had ever been, she believed; strong to resist, to conceal, to bear —forgetting herself, and trying in her own circle to be, by others, remembered. When Sunday came she was startled —terribly startled, for the blood flew from her face to her heart on the instant—by the appearance of Laurence Rexford in the chapel, sitting quietly there throughout the service, and only once gravely looking in her direction.

She went homewards very nervously, believing that she should meet him again, and hoping that she should not, until the Cleft was reached, when she was sorry that she had not seen him, just for a moment, and heard his deep voice express a hope that she was well. It was wrong of

16—2

her to think of him at all ; she knew that, and she tried
hard to shut him out of her mind ! and, failing that, to set
him out of her reach. Yes, let him be high above her as
the heavens ; he was a gehtleman, kinder, more courteous,
and altogether very different to the few gentlemen whom
she had ever seen—treating her, and those about her, as
an equal, and speaking with a grace and tenderness that
was almost womanly in its refinement ; but for ever
removed out of her sphere, and one whom it was wicked
to think about. A wild fancy of hers, such as women had
had before, and suffered from—simply the hero of her
own visions, and a man that she would have put in print,
could she have written a book—a man whom she would have
been proud to love, had she been a lady born, and was too
proud to dream of in her low estate. No one understood
more keenly the difference of position between them than
Milly Athorpe, though she had studied human life in Wind-
Whistle Cleft.

Milly hoped, at last, that she should never see him again
—that in all her life he would keep away from her, and
teach her, by his absence, to be as happy and content as
she was before she knew him. He, of course, had never
given one thought to her—that was not likely ! His kindness of manner was natural to him, and he did not consider
how different he was to everybody else, and how possible it
was for women humble as herself to love him in their hearts,
and wish that fate had placed them nearer to his sphere.
If he would only go away now—if he had not even aroused
her curiosity as to the fall in life which was before him, and
to which he seemed more than resigned !

On the Thursday, Milly Athorpe went to her evening
school again, remembering that it was just a week since he
had been curious enough to wait for her, and wondering,
more than ever that night why he had waited, and whether
in all his life he would ever wait again. She believed that he
would, although she did not confess as much to herself, until
coming out of the school that summer evening, she found
him there once more, waiting patiently for her, with his
back against the gate, and his steadfast eyes bent full upon
her, as she came with faltering steps towards him.

"You must not scold me," he said when she was near
him, "it is very wrong of me to dog you like this ; but I

said a little while ago that we were friends, and friends generally say good-bye to each other before they go away."

"You are—going away, then, Mr. Raxford !"

"Yes—I think," he added, with a short laugh, "that there is little doubt of that."

They went silently together along the cross path towards the village for awhile—each unwilling, or at a loss in what manner, to break the silence. Suddenly and abruptly Laurence said,

"May I resume the conversation which we began last Thursday here ? "

"Is it necessary ? " hesitated Milly, in a low voice.

"Yes—for my—purpose, I think it is," said Laurence ; "and you will not run away from me till I have finished ? "

"I am going to Mr. Wells."

"Yes, I know—with that confounded key," added Laurence, almost savagely ; "but I shall wait for you this time."

"Mr. Raxford—I——"

"Miss Athorpe, you distrust me ! "

"Oh ! Sir—I do not."

"Thank you for that avowal—I will wait, then."

He did not resume the conversation of a week ago at that time ; he walked with her, speaking of the schools, and her interest therein, until the main street was reached, when he repeated, "I will wait," very earnestly ; and Milly, with her heart beating painfully fast, did not set an interdict upon his resolution. There was something new and strange about him, but she felt that he *was* to be trusted, and that there was no harm in walking with him for a little way. She was bewildered at his manner, at her own confusion, at everything that night. All was unreal, and apart from the every-day track ; he had sought her out again ; he had looked at her very earnestly ; he had asked her to let him wait there, to say good-bye to her ; he had come all the way from the mine rather than leave Tavvydale without seeing her again ! Could he really, *really* be thinking of her above all the women in the world ? And had she a right to let him think of her like that ?

When she came back to him, Milly was trembling and pale, and it was well for her, she thought, that he dashed into his subject and became too absorbed to notice her.

"Miss Athorpe—Miss Milly," he corrected, "I hinted to you last week that when Mr. Fyvie offered me a partnership in the mine, he raised me to a post that I was not fitted to occupy, and placed me in a false position. I became unhappy. I felt that I had no claim to be there after a while —I knew that it was part of a compact to which, for another's sake, I have no right to allude, farther than to say that that compact must now be for ever unfulfilled on my part. So I am going to-morrow to London, in search of Mr. Fyvie, to tell him that I would prefer my own independence to a share in his possessions—I am going to find, if possible, the happiness I lost in coming here."

"Are you not acting very hastily?" said Milly.

"I am compelled to give up my partnership—I feel it a greater clog upon my honesty every day; and I am quite anxious to be poor."

He laughed a little irrelevantly at this, and Milly looked up at him with more confidence.

"You are acting very rashly, I can only say again," she replied; "there has been a quarrel, and you are seeking out of bitterness to do that of which afterwards you will repent."

"There has been no quarrel between me and my partners —that is a mistake," said Laurence; "and I would not act hastily for the world. Miss Milly, you *must* believe that."

"I think you told me once that you had a mother living —what will she say?"

"Well, when she hears the whole story, she will applaud me very much for my resolution—for she is an unselfish woman, whose happiness lies in her son's."

"I don't believe that you will be any happier for being poorer," said Milly; "that is beyond my comprehension."

"I am compelled to give up the post. I am filling it under false pretences," said Laurence, warmly; "it is not honourable for me to remain."

"Oh! then you will be happier, of course. But you don't know what it is to be poor—very poor, like some of us in Tavvydale. And if you offend the Fyvies, what will become of you, Sir?"

Laurence laughed more naturally at this.

"I shall be able to earn my own living as a clerk somewhere, even if my old friends turn their backs upon me. I am a very conceited man, with faith in my ability to keep

my head above water. So I shall go away to-morrow full
of confidence in my own resources, and whether I come back
again or not depends upon—*you*."

His voice became very harsh and low, and to a less quick
ear than Milly's there might have seemed anger in its tones.
Had there been anger—the fiercest and most intense—it
could not have taken the maiden so rapidly from him in her
first surprise.

"Oh! Sir—oh! Mr. Raxford," she cried, hurrying away
as for her life.

"Well, Milly, that's the plain truth," he said, keeping
pace with her, and speaking very rapidly and earnestly;
"for I love you very, very much. God knows when I loved
you first—before I had a right, perhaps—but there was no
escaping it, and now, without a chance of you, there will
come no happiness, whether I be poor or rich, from this day.
Oh! Milly, you are so different from all the world to me,
and if I might only hope to work for you as well as for myself, I should have a giant's strength to make my way in
life. Don't—don't say that this love of mine is all in vain,
dear Milly—save me from that bitterness if you can, for you
are my one hope, and I must give up without you."

"Sir, you are a gentleman—I was your servant, almost
your slave; you are jesting with me, perhaps—you are not
conscious of all that you are saying to a poor village girl."

"I am only conscious that I love you as I shall never
love another woman," cried Laurence—"that this is not a
rash impulse of mine, but the well-considered act of a man
judging for his own felicity. Are you afraid of my poverty?"

"No, Sir. Oh! if—if you were only of my class!"

"*Then* you would love me," cried Laurence, seizing his
advantage. "You are a schoolmistress, and I a man out of
work at present—the advantage is with you, and you must
look down on me and pity me. Milly, may I love you?
—will you share your fortunes with me, and love me in
return?—you and I together all our lives, finding true joy in
our affection, and caring nothing for misfortune if we are
together. Milly, will you let me teach you how to love me?"

He passed his strong arm around her, and drew her,
trembling, but almost unresisting now, to his side, where
she let him tell her once more of his love, pouring his soul
forth in words that were full of fire, and truth, and eloquence,

to her—changing her life and life's tasks for ever after that, and bringing upon all a heavy shower of happy tears.

Have we a right to follow Laurence Raxford further in his escort ?—is the description of this lovers' walk necessary to us or to our plot ? Are not lovers walking together every day, and talking this nonsense, or this sublimity, just as Laurence and Milly talked? All, as the penny-a-liners say when they are at a loss for ideas, more easily imagined than described ; for such happiness as fell to the lot of this couple can be estimated by all of us who have trodden in the early days the path of roses.

They were very happy, for their hearts were young, and full of love for each other. This was an idyl to Laurence —a realisation of a far-away dream to Milly—and each had faith, and was not hardened by society.

" Oh ! Laurence," Milly whispered at last, " if it should not be true ! if this should be a wild fancy of yours, to die out, and for me to die with ! "

" Is it likely ? "

" I will not believe it too intently until you come back from London," she said—" come back with your mother's consent to ask my uncle's. Till then, I am silent about this."

" Until I come back and relate to you all those details, which I am not inclined for now, Milly—which are in the way now."

This was said at the entrance to the Cleft, where Milly wished to part with him, and where he caught her in his arms, and kissed her as his betrothed, whispering once more of his love for her before he tore himself away.

Thus poor Bully Churdock, ever on guard at the Cleft's mouth, saw the lovers from his post of observation, and understood at last that there was no more chance for him, and gave up, walking away with his knuckles in his eyes, like an overgrown baby as he was.

CHAPTER III.

THE PARTNERS.

L<small>AURENCE</small> R<small>AXFORD</small> was spared the necessity of a long journey to London in search of his senior partner. This was a new stroke of luck in his way, he considered, and parted him not from Milly, in the first flush of his conquest.

A note, that had been delivered by hand at Wheal Desperation, awaited Laurence on his return. It ran—

"M<small>Y</small> <small>DEAR</small> L<small>AURENCE</small>,

"Expect me in the morning, to talk over the affairs of state with you.

"Yours ever sincerely,

"J<small>ONATHAN</small> F<small>YVIE</small>."

A brief letter, but neither reserved nor unfriendly, which Laurence was glad to see, for he would not have parted in cold blood with one who had evinced so great an interest in him as Mr. Fyvie had. He would have waited more nervously for the coming interview, twenty-four hours ago, and rehearsed more intently those speeches which he considered necessary ; but now there occupied his business ideas, and came between him and all calm reflection on his resolutions, the one bright thought of Milly.

He could think of little else save that girl ; the avowal that he had made to her, and the love that he had won from her. Every word that she had said to him before their parting, every little confession of her first liking for him, her first interest, he dwelt upon with the doting fondness of a youth five years his junior. This had been her romance, and he the hero of it ! He knew then—for the first time, —what a cold, passionless affection he had had for Hester Fyvie, and how for Milly he could sacrifice every hope in life, but the hope of making her his wife. Poor Hester !— he contrasted his two loves together, and the "born lady" suffered terribly by the comparison. The one was artificial, proud, even jealous and unforgiving ; and the other bright, amiable, clever, and original—a self-taught woman, who had taught everybody to love her, and who loved him first of all the world. It was pleasant to be loved like that ; he understood Milly's character now, and he knew that she would put her whole faith in him, and have no secrets from him. She was touched by his descent to her, for she had looked at him as far above her dreams. But she had loved him for all that—he understood that fact, and revelled in it. She had regarded him with loving eyes from the distance, wishing that she was only a real lady, for him to take a fancy to. If Milly had been a different being to any girl who had ever crossed his path, so had he been to Milly Athorpe—a something new and strange, that had bewildered her knowledge of character, from the day he had carried her uncle's bag down Wind-Whistle Cleft. He had shown more interest in the people round him, mixed with them more, and seized every opportunity of gaining their good words ; and he had been to her ever a kind friend. From the glowing imagination of the girl she had created a hero, and worshipped it afar off, with all her heart and soul. Laurence was her *beau-ideal* of what a man should be ; and set apart from her by the stern laws of society, she had thought that she should never marry, but keep true to her hidden faith in him. There was a wild, but intense satisfaction in nursing this secret in her bosom, until there fell upon her path in life a flood of sunshine. He had told her that he loved her ; and it was this confession which had altered both man and maiden for the better. Here was a real love story—a love story out of the common, and both were less commonplace, and more like those poor simpletons we meet in books sometimes. The only fear of these two beings was that Laurence might not be poor enough to render all things satisfactory. If he were but cast on the world without a shilling, thought Milly, that she might prove it was only for his dear self that she had loved him! Without that, he would always have a faint suspicion that it was his place in the world, rather than his place in her heart, that had lured her into his arms.

Laurence was thinking of Milly to the last moment. Not till the tall figure of Mr. Fyvie inclined a little forwards, to come in at the doorway, did he turn from love to business, and face the man whom he had disappointed. Very sorry for the man, as he looked into his lined face as he approached ;

but he could not mourn for the disappointment, for it had saved him from a life's mistake.

He was astonished at the cheerful greeting with which Mr. Fyvie met him in the first place, at the heartiness with which the old man wrung long and silently his hand.

"You must not be angry with me for not answering your letter," said Mr. Fyvie ; "it was a foolish letter, and did not deserve an answer. You wrote in haste, and if I had answered in haste—which I never do—it would have been a folly, for which no after repentance would have been sufficient atonement. I like to face my opposition, and look or talk it down, Laurence."

He took the seat facing our hero, waited for Laurence to resume his place, with his back to his desk again, crossed his hands over his gold-headed cane, and then paused for anything that Laurence had to communicate.

Laurence felt that an up-hill task was before him, in the face of this friendliness of manner, and deliberated what to say—deliberated too long, for Mr. Fyvie's crisp voice said suddenly, "It's all nonsense, you know. Confess as much, like a man, Laurence ! "

"I acted very rashly, very foolishly; I did not consider, Sir, how unworthy I was of the position to which you had raised me—how unfair it was to you and your son."

"You heard my story of Wheal Desperation—you understood my reasons—it was *un fait accompli*, this partnership."

"I—I thought then that your daughter would be my wife, Sir, and that I might work for her share in the property. But that thought is over for good, and I am an usurper here. Mr. Fyvie, I cannot remain your partner."

"You and Hester have had a silly quarrel, I know that ; but if you two are as sensible as I fancy you are, you will kiss and be friends again."

"Friends I trust we may be some day, but to assume our old positions together is utterly impossible."

"No, don't say that," said Mr. Fyvie, very anxiously ; " she and you should not so readily seize upon the first excuse to balk an old man of the wish that lies nearest his heart. Why, Laurence, I was prouder of you than of my own son— and my soul was full of rejoicing when you asked Hester to have you."

"I know it, Sir—I know it," murmured Laurence.

He had seen that wish, and responded to it out of gratitude, and hence all the cruel mistakes that had arisen.

"Well, then, there is not a formidable obstacle to leap over," said the old man; "a little of Hester's pride—the Llewellyn peacockism, I call it—to surmount, and I am wrong in my estimate of women, if she will not thank you for the opportunity of extending her forgiveness. Come, you are not a hard man—and you have the courage to make a woman's heart light by a little humility. There, it's no good beating about the bush—Hester is very miserable, I'm sure."

"Not on my account, Sir," replied Laurence. "I am very, very glad to think that it was not a hasty parting between us, but the result of mature deliberation. She saw that we were not fitted for each other, and our parting was for the lasting peace of both of us."

"You think that?" said Mr. Fyvie, looking up again.

"Sir, I am sure of it."

"And you are sure, too, that she is convinced of this rhodomontade. Well, you are wrong there, I am certain, although I do not profess to understand either of you. And had I been Laurence Raxford," said Mr. Fyvie, pointing suddenly with his stick at the subject of his remarks, "I would have had a fairer and clearer explanation before resigning so readily the woman whom I had once professed to love."

"Miss Fyvie had seven days to consider whether she had dismissed me in haste—I did not accept her resignation of me at the time that she made it—on the last day I sent——"

"Damn it, Laurence, why didn't you come yourself, instead of irritating people with your confounded messages?"

"I felt assured that I should not have been welcome, and I was right."

"I'm inclined to think that you were in the wrong, unless —unless you never loved my child. Then, I can understand it all."

Laurence did not answer. All was ended; why should he pain this old man further, or add a deeper sting to the pride of the woman who had quarrelled with him? He knew now that he had never loved Hester, but he could not humiliate his best friend, and his best friend's daughter, by that cruel confession. Let them think that he had loved her very dearly until the breaking off of their engagement; but do

not let him openly avow that it was simply gratitude that
had led him to make Hester Fyvie an offer of his hand. Let
him resign his partnership, with his chance of a rich wife,
and let these new grand folk forget him, and tell their " set "
how Hester cast him off. That was his penance for his rashness, and he accepted it.

"Think the best of me, Sir," said Laurence; "the best
you can in the future which separates us."

"I shall not think the worst of you yet," said Mr. Fyvie,
with an effort to smile ; "I believe that you and Hester will
make it up, for all your desperate obstinacy—I don't consider the engagement at an end between you—*there.*"

"Mr. Fyvie, you must do that," said Laurence, alarmed
at this assertion ; "it is ended between us—it was your
daughter's wish—I beg that you will never couple our names
together—for her sake as well as mine. Sir, it can't be."

"Oh ! yes—it can. We shall bring it all round in good
time, and you will tell me some day what a fair prophet I
was."

"Sir, we are not talking seriously—this is a jest—it is
impossible that I can ever be your daughter's husband now."

"You are not married already—are you ? "

"No, Sir."

"By Jupiter ! you haven't been fool enough to get engaged to another woman !" cried the sharp old gentleman.

The story must escape sooner or later, Laurence felt
assured. For Milly's sake he had better speak out at once
—that was simply doing Milly Athorpe justice. He would
have spared his old friend and benefactor—the friend of his
dead father—could he have done so ; but he knew now that
it was beyond his power.

"I have proposed to one more my equal in position, Sir,"
said Laurence.

Mr. Fyvie drew a deep breath, and looked very hard at
Laurence. The last hope that he had had died out of his
face as he surveyed the young man before him.

"And the lady ? "

"Is Captain Athorpe's niece."

"Milly ? "

"Yes, Sir," replied our hero.

"Good God ! Laurence, you have never been so rash as
this !" gasped forth Mr. Fyvie ; "this is either a mad re-

venge, or a wild infatuation—this is cruel to the girl, and anguish to yourself."

"Pardon me, Sir, but I shall make her my wife—make her as happy, with God's blessing, as I am sure that she will make me."

"But the difference of position."

The old cry—the shriek of that amazed world of fashion and gentility which Laurence despised—irritated him, despite his effort not to pain the old man more than he could help.

"Love will make amends for the outraged feelings of society," he said ; "and the difference of position exists only in imagination. I am not a rich man, Mr. Fyvie—I have no chance of becoming rich."

"Mr. Raxford," said the other, very firmly, "suppose we drop this babble of a difference of position, and let me tell you of a difference existing between you and me. You are weak and changeable—and I never swerve from a determination that I have formed. *You* should know that."

"Well, Sir?" asked Laurence.

"You became my partner, and accepted the responsibilities of this business, seeing that I was but fulfilling my duty— my promise—to your father. Pray, make no mistake in this—*I* do not resign you!"

It was a bitter taunt in one sense, and it struck home. Laurence winced for an instant, then replied,

"I cannot have a fortune that I do not deserve thrust upon me, Mr. Fyvie."

"You would break your word with *me*, too, then."

"I would beg you to allow me to withdraw, and let some one in whom you will feel presently a greater interest, assume my place here."

"You would break your mother's heart."

"My mother will be content with her son."

"You are my partner—and I hold you to your bond, Laurence," he said, softening again ; "with all your rashness, your want of common-sense, and your eagerness to sacrifice name and power—your haste to get rid of Hester, even—still I hold you to your promise. It was not for Hester's sake, but for my own, that I took you into partnership."

"Sir, I think that you are wrong. And if you are not——"

"Excuse me interrupting, but I am right. Laurence, I need the services of one true friend at my side—and my son will need one more than himself when I am dead, for he is very reckless. Will you cast us both off in this ungrateful fashion?"

"I am not ungrateful, Mr. Fyvie—I will work for you, if you wish it, with all my heart here—but I cannot be your partner."

"As an overlooker here, or manager, you would have no influence with Jonathan; as his friend and equal, he will esteem you and let you reason with him. I ask you, Laurence, for the sake of my wife and daughter, to see after their future when I am gone. I—I have heard enough to-day to break down my faith in any human being. I don't," shaking his head wearily, "think so well of you as I did, but if you are really grateful, unselfish, generous, you will remain a master here."

"Impossible," muttered Laurence.

"If," said Mr. Fyvie, sinking his voice to a whisper, "if Jonathan has been indiscreet—lost much money—and imperilled our position, would you stand by us till the storm was over? *There!*"

"Mr. Fyvie, you cannot mean——"

"Hush! hush! Laurence, there are disappointments that come all of a rush to the self-satisfied—don't let your going away be one more of them to me," said the old man; "there is wealth enough underground to pay a dozen debts like Jonathan's, and we will work together for him, and this shall be the last crop of his wild oats."

"But——"

"But we will say no more just now. There are clerks with long ears in the counting-house, and I only want one true friend at my side, to keep me from giving way altogether. Stay—I beg of you."

"For a short while, Sir—at your wish—if you *can* have confidence in me."

"I have every confidence. And now, about this foolish love affair with Milly Athorpe—has it gone so far that it cannot be——"

"Mr. Fyvie, I must beg you to be silent," implored

Laurence ; "I am unsettled—irritable—half mad ! I seem to have been dreaming this last hour. May I ask you to leave me, and let me think of all that you have said ? "

" Yes, I will go at once, Laurence."

Mr. Fyvie rose, and walked very thoughtfully to the door, coming back to lay his hand on Laurence's shoulder.

" I trust in you," he said.

" I will deserve your trust, Sir," answered Laurence ; "and believe this, that, however much my feelings have changed towards Hester, it is NOT my fault that we are separated. Do not misunderstand me, Sir," he added, very quickly, " it was better for us both that the engagement should end between us, I am convinced of that. But I did not break off the match ! "

" What does Milly say to this story ? You have told her of the quarrel between Hester and you, and it enhances her triumph, and makes her doubly proud of her conquest. You might have spared our pride that, Laurence."

" I have said nothing of the past engagement between your daughter and me," said Laurence.

" And you will not ? "

Laurence hesitated. He had kept silent out of consideration for the old love, but he had already doubted the policy of the measure, and afar off in the darkness, glimmered a lurid spark that might indicate danger.

" There should be no secrets," he began, when Mr. Fyvie stopped him petulantly.

" This is a secret that belongs to our house ;—surely you will spare us the gossip and scandal of a country place ? You will not humiliate Hester so completely ? "

" By saying that it was she who dismissed me—who grew tired of me, and full of distrust—does that humiliate Miss Fyvie ? "

" She was jealous, and for a good reason, *they* will say in Tavvydale," said the other, " if you blurt this story forth."

Laurence coloured.

" Well, Sir, I will not blurt it forth. The story is ended —it is a sealed book between us, and only at a future time, when I am on defence, perhaps—when there may be a reason for me to speak—will I mention my past connection with your daughter."

"Thank you," said Mr. Fyvie, gratefully; "thank you for myself and Hester."

He moved towards the door again.

"We will say no more about it now—it is all over! You have not acted like a worldly man, and we'll place that to your credit. Good-day—I shall come here next week again, unless you—ah! you will not do that."

"I must remain here, Mr. Fyvie."

"Yes, I see. And now, where is Jonathan?"

He paused in his progress towards the door to put that question to our hero, who looked back in an amazed manner at him.

"Jonathan, Sir?"

"Haven't you seen him? He has been at home all the week."

"No—I have not seen him."

"I thought that he was coming here last night."

"He must have called in my absence, Mr. Fyvie," said Laurence; "I was in Tavvydale yesterday evening."

"He may have done so. He has not been at home since yesterday morning," said Mr. Fyvie, as he went out of the room, looking older and more feeble than he had entered it —as was natural, for he went away disappointed in his hope of bringing Laurence back to Hester's feet.

CHAPTER IV

GOING WRONG.

LAURENCE RAXFORD sat and considered this new position of affairs, after the door had closed upon the senior partner. How could all this affect him in a worldly sense?—how would it affect that course of true love which would have run so smoothly had life been mapped out according to his own ideas?

He was sorry—intensely sorry—for the news that the estate was in difficulties, and he felt then, as he had felt in Mr. Fyvie's presence, that he could not desert the good ship in distress. His duty lay in keeping to the old post,

17

and neither by a word nor sign betraying to the outside world that there were difficulties at Wheal Desperation.

He would have been glad to have sunk the partner at once, and become the clerk and working man, that he had told Milly he was. He felt like an impostor now— a man who had won Milly's love by false pretences. He was still one of the heads of the firm—above Milly in position, and unable, in justice to his partners, to explain why he had not kept his word, and dropped from great-ness to the lower ground. He could not tell her all— and half confidences, he knew, were as bad as no con-fidence at all. Still, reflected this unworldly, super-heroic young man, he *was* comfortably poor, and Milly would believe him when he told her that he was not likely to be rich. There would come a time, after the storm was over—when the new lode for which they were seeking had proved a success perhaps—when he could withdraw with pride and honour from the partnership, and pass to the clerk's desk, proving to all that he was a man of his word, and that it was not greed of gain which had brought him to Wheal Desperation, or kept him there a principal so long.

What he could honourably explain, he would at least attempt at once. There must not be any misjudging his conduct, or setting a false interpretation on his actions, from that day forth. Milly must be told more of his life —all the secrets of his life with which business had nothing to do. Captain Athorpe must know at once that he had asked his niece to love him; the whole world at Tavvydale must know it, ere it began to forge a story for itself.

When he had first told his love to Milly, he had said nothing of his past engagement to Hester Fyvie—how it had begun, and in what a foolish yet lucky manner it had been broken off; he had considered that it was more kind and honourable to Hester to say nothing of that match—that it would spare the feelings of a proud girl, who might in the future be grateful for his silence—that least said, in fact, was soonest mended.

Once he had hesitated, and stood on the brink of his confession—and then turned back for Hester Fyvie's sake

—for the sake of the pride of a family that he respected. But he thought, for all this, that it was not a wise promise that he had made the old gentleman who had recently left him ; he could see that there were elements of discord to be aroused by foreign tongues, hissing forth this story ; he could scarcely believe now that it was fair to Milly Athorpe.

He was vexed that he had promised Mr. Fyvie to be silent—although it was only a half promise, which any one less scrupulous than he would have easily broken. Then he thought, or tried to think, that it was more honourable, more manly, to hold his peace—and that after all, at any time in the future, when it might be necessary—which was not likely either !—Milly at least would believe his explanation, and have faith in every word of his statement. Under all circumstances of life, with her at his side, he should not have one regret. Yes, this young man was very much in love, and it was lucky for Hester Fyvie, as well as for himself, that she had let him slip so easily through her fingers. For though he was an honourable man, and would have walked uprightly, and been a dutiful and good husband all his life, still there would have been one thing lacking ; in the harmony prevailing there would have been one note out of tune, and it would have jarred eternally upon the peace of home. Laurence was resolved that morning to dispel a little of the clouds that seemed enwrapping him, despite his abhorrence of mystery. If he could say nothing of his past love, of the coming trouble to the business, of future struggles for himself and partners—and for Milly, perhaps when the crash came, which he feared only for the Fyvies — he could at least tell Captain Athorpe plainly that he loved his niece, and that he was not stooping from his position when he asked his consent to the engagement. He would seek Captain Athorpe at once ; he would write a letter to Mr. Whiteshell—whose address he remembered to have taken, at the old man's request ; he would write to his mother also. He would seek Milly in the evening, and tell her that he was still a partner. Though it mattered little to him, he thought, if both uncles were to refuse him their sanction to the match— though Milly and he had, in reality, only themselves to study

17—2

—still it was a rule that should be honoured in the obser-
vance, and it would render all things satisfactory.

It was close upon three in the afternoon, when he resolved
to open proceedings with Captain Athorpe.

"Has Athorpe come up from the mine yet, Mr. Waters?"
he asked of the old clerk.

"I don't think that he has been down to-day, Sir."

This was startling news, Captain Athorpe being as regular
as clock-work in all his business movements.

"Not down! Who is in charge of his gang."

"The second hand," was the reply. "Captain Athorpe
was here rather late, and reported himself as late, Sir. I—
I don't know what to make of him to-day," he added, confidentially; "if I didn't know him so well, I should have
thought almost that he had been drinking last night—or
early this morning. I don't believe that he would have
spoken to *me* so rudely," he added, reflectively, "if he had
been quite right."

"Oh!—he is unwell, perhaps, Waters."

"Very likely. I excuse his eccentricities—he never was
the best of tempers, poor fellow."

"Where is he now?"

"I haven't seen him for the last four hours—he may have
gone down the shaft after all; but at all events, he hasn't
changed his dress."

"I will try and find him."

To discover Captain Athorpe in a bad temper was not a
pleasant quest, but Laurence was determined to begin his
confessions that day, and he thought that he understood
the man for whom he was searching, and that the man
understood, and even liked, him. If anything had gone
wrong, perhaps, the revelation that he was about to
make would have its effect on the mining captain's better
nature.

He made several inquiries of the surface-workers concerning Athorpe's whereabouts—being directed hither and
thither, according to the last person's glimpse of the man,
and wondering why Athorpe should have made the circuit
of the whole estate that morning, in lieu of following in the
track from which he had never seemed to deviate. Something was wrong with Captain Athorpe, it was evident; and
when he found him at last, he thought for an instant that he

would defer his statement, until a laugh at his own nervous-ness dismissed the thought into the background.

He found Captain Athorpe standing with his hands in his pockets, looking intently at the great wheel to which mention has been made in an early chapter—the motive power which turned many thousands of wheels, near and far, above and below, in the mining-grounds of Fyvie, Fyvie and Raxford. It was revolving now slowly and ponderously, the whole earth throbbing with its revolutions, and the water rushing like a cataract about it.

"One might look at it, and go mad," thought Laurence, as he approached the burly form of the man of whom he had been in search.

Captain Athorpe was standing on the very edge of the brick wall, looking down a hundred feet below him, to where the water was churned and lashed to foam, and looking gloomily into the dark depths, rather than with an artist's eye to effect at the prismatic tints into which the sun's rays had split the upper half of spray and mist.

"Good-morning, Captain Athorpe—I have been searching for you everywhere."

Captain Athorpe did not reply. He might have been struck into stone hours ago, for the movement that followed Laurence Raxford's salutation.

Laurence was by his side now, and laid his hand upon his arm.

"Captain—don't you hear me? Aren't you well to-day?"

Athorpe swung round at last, quickly and impetuously, and Laurence went back a step or two, fortunately away from the brink in the suddenness of his companion's move-ment.

"I'm well enough. Can't a man be alone for a few minutes, without being hunted up like this?" he asked, with a fierceness that was very new, even in him.

Laurence looked attentively at him. The face of Captain Athorpe was dark, angry, and rugged; it might be the face of a man who had been drinking, for what Laurence knew to the contrary—but he hoped not. He would be very sorry for the confirmation of such a suspicion as that.

"I regret to intrude, Athorpe," said Laurence, "if you have anything that disturbs you or requires your serious consideration. I wished to see you—but I can call at your house this evening."

"Yes—this evening. That's better."

Laurence was turning away, when Athorpe called him back.

"No, not at my house," he said; "I keep no company— damn people who come to my house disturbing me. What do you want?"

"Five minutes' serious talk—attentive hearing."

"What have *you* heard, man, that you come to me like this? Great God of heaven, if it's really worse—if it's the worst of all, after—after—all that she has sworn. Have you been to the Cleft to-day?"

"No, I have not."

"Have you seen my niece?—my wife?—Jonathan Fyvie?" he shouted.

"Neither of the three."

"Then what do you want with me?"

"I think, Athorpe, that I will defer my communication till another time. Something appears to have disturbed you."

"Appears!" he answered, scornfully; "something has, or I shouldn't carry my story in my face like this. I'm an open man, and can't look pleased when my soul's wrung—I never learned the trick of it, as you gentlemen have—what I feel here," striking his broad chest violently, "I show in my face, worse luck!"

"Come away, Athorpe."

"No—I like this place. Here I can talk to myself, and the row of the wheel keeps fools from listening to a greater fool than they are. Mr. Raxford," he said, with a shade less fierceness, "I'm ill at ease—ill in my brain—and I have been drinking raw brandy to cure me."

"Ah! that is not like you, Captain. I am sorry."

"It hasn't done me good—but it hasn't made me drunk— by God! it hasn't made me one atom's worth more mad than I was before I took it. I was mad enough for murder, before a drop had passed my lips, I swear!"

He clenched his great dark hands together, and his face became purple as he spoke. It was the face of a madman, Laurence thought at once.

"A trouble at which you will laugh presently, Athorpe.

You regard minor cares with too much intentness; or you have had too much your own way, and a little check has disturbed you. Don't stand so near the edge, man."

"Who would care, do you think, if I fell in ?" he asked ; "who wouldn't clap hands at the accident, and thank God that it was all for the best that I was swept out of the way ?"

"Every friend you have would be sorry, Athorpe."

He laughed scornfully at this, taking no heed of Laurence approaching him more closely—Laurence, who was full of doubt how this mad mood would end, and was now determined not to leave Athorpe in that place and that position.

"I haven't a friend in the world—I never made friends. So there's no one to be sorry for me," he added, moodily.

"Your wife—your niece—what are you thinking about?"

"I know what I'm thinking about," he answered; "and it's the truth, if I were to die this minute, and they were the last words that I ever spoke. If I were to die, Master, in a dash at the great wheel, and missing it, or clinging to it, pass from life to death — from misery to sleep—*like this?*"

"No! no!" shrieked Laurence, dashing at him with all his force, flinging his arms round him, and arresting him, just in time, from a madman's plunge at annihilation; "for God's sake, Athorpe—no !"

"Let me go, Sir! I have made up my mind to die, and this is easy and quick," he gasped, struggling with a vehemence that threatened death to both of them.

Laurence was a young and strong man, but he felt himself no match for the power which now exerted itself against him, which bore him back the few steps that his sudden impulse had gained, and faced him suddenly and awfully with a sense of the peril that he was in. The man had the strength of a giant, and he put it forth to the utmost, and Laurence felt but as a stripling in his clutch.

"Athorpe!—Athorpe!" he shouted, and then both men fell heavily to the ground—within a hair's breadth of destruction, where it seemed as if they must topple over into the gulf. Athorpe, panting and glaring like a wild beast, looked down upon the man who had proved too weak for him.

That glance saved both men, and Athorpe, by an effort that neither understood afterwards, stumbled forwards and away from the brink, dragging Laurence along with him.

"Keep still," said Athorpe; "don't make a scene of this, and a talk of this for life everlasting. I will do no harm—I am a child afraid of danger now—I am in your hands. I never thought to thank God again, but I do, that he has not let me kill you, Sir. There, it's all over, and I'm mad no longer."

He moved away from Laurence, and sat holding his head between his hands, looking at the marks of the recent struggle left upon the ground. Laurence drew a deep breath of relief, and then sat up also, feeling faint for awhile, but ready to make another fight for it, should Athorpe's determination to destroy himself once more become apparent. If he could only humour the madman until help was at hand to save him from his rashness.

But Athorpe had become suddenly sane. He seemed to have changed as by a miracle—the miracle that had preserved both their lives. It was a face of unutterable misery still, but the fierceness had all vanished therefrom, and the man was calm enough.

"You are not hurt?" he asked.

"No," replied Laurence; "and you—you will come away with me?"

"Yes, in a minute or two, when we are both cool," he said.

"That's well, Athorpe. It's a promise——"

"Don't try and humour me into keeping my word, Mr. Raxford," he said, gloomily; "I said Yes, and that's sufficient. It was only a fit, and it's over. But though I shall not attempt my own life again—though I'm afraid now," he said, with a shudder, "it would have been so much the best for everybody if you had not tried to stop me."

"I'll not believe it, Athorpe. I'll not believe that there's a real cause——"

"Don't argue with me," cried Athorpe, almost imploringly. "You don't know what a blank my life is, and I can't tell you yet. They will tell you down in Tavvydale presently, or you will find out for yourself, but I—haven't the courage."

Laurence felt that the man had encountered a great trouble then—a trouble, perhaps, that nothing could soften or change. A far-off suspicion that he had had, came back to Laurence as he sat there; he believed that he knew the story now, that it accounted for this wild demeanour, and was even an excuse for it; but he prayed, for more than Captain Athorpe's sake, that it was a false idea.

"I can only say," Athorpe continued, "that I'm a man alone in the world, and that very shortly I shall go away from here—go abroad, and be lost for good. For there isn't a chance—I don't believe, as I'm a miserable wretch, with heaven shut out of sight of me, that there's the faintest chance left. For, God help me, I can't believe *her* ever any more!"

He suddenly held his arm before his eyes, and sobbed long and passionately—a man wholly broken down at last. The reaction had been too much for him, and all the strength and self-will of the man could not save him from this wild abandonment to grief, which unnerved Laurence almost as much as Athorpe.

"Athorpe," said Laurence, "you will think better of everybody soon. I hope that there has been only some misunderstanding, which a few words will rectify. You, perhaps, have been hasty."

"I had better kill myself than commit a murder," groaned Athorpe, "and it will come to that if I drink again; and drink, Sir, I must!"

"No, you are too strong-minded, Athorpe, you——"

"There, there, *that* gives me no comfort—nothing can. What did you want with me, may I ask?"

Laurence thought that it would divert his companion's train of thought, and told him, briefly and plainly, why he had come in search of him that day. Captain Athorpe listened, or rather strove to listen, but the eyes wandered restlessly, and the old thoughts settled about him again, like evil spirits by which he was haunted.

"Do I make out—do I make out that you want to marry Milly?" he asked, absently. "I have tried to follow you, but you speak at a great rate, and I am dull this morning. You spoke of Milly, didn't you?"

"Yes—and of my wish to make her my wife."

"You had better think of hanging yourself than of

marrying." he said, shortly. "You would marry her, and be sorry afterwards that you had stooped so low."

"I have told you that my position is no better than Milly's."

"Have you?" he said. "Ah, I don't understand. It may be so. It does not matter—it is of no account to me. You will do as you like—and Milly will follow her own inclinations in this respect as in others. Why do you bother me with this, when I am troubled unto death?"

He asked this fiercely, as he rose and moved away towards that part of the ground where mining life was busy. They were laughing amongst the women as he passed them, followed at a little distance by Laurence, and he bade them, with a scowl, make less noise and do more work. He went at once to the outer gates, pausing there with his back against a huge oaken post, until Laurence came up with him.

"I am going now."

"You will go home, Athorpe?"

He shuddered, and shook his head.

"Not there again—I can't go into that house. I shall burn it down before I leave the place—mark that."

"You will come to work to-morrow, Athorpe?"

"Never again, Sir. I'm clean settled in this world and the next. I've gone astray, and the devil is driving me!"

He moved onwards, and Laurence stood and watched him down the high-road. Presently, becoming nervous lest he should commit some rash act in his recklessness, Laurence went into the office, took up his hat, and followed along the high-road after him.

On the high-road he met Bully Churdock, whom Athorpe had passed without a glance, and who was now standing and looking after Athorpe.

"Churdock, what is the matter there?" asked our hero; "have you heard?"

"A row with the missus. He was at it all last night, like a daft one. He turned her out of doors. I was in the Cleft, and saw him. But what's it to ye?"

"A great deal. He is a valuable man in my service, and I am sorry to see him like this."

"Everybody that knows him is sorry. Milly's sorry. So be I, o' course."

"Follow him, then, and see that he does not get into mischief, Churdock. He is not safe to be trusted by himself."

Churdock grunted, but did not move.

"He'll go and drink. I can't stop him—nobody can."

"You might see that he did not get into any danger."

"I'm seeing. I've come to see after him. I told her that I'd look after him to-day, and I'm a-doing of it now. Let me be, please."

He began to follow slowly in the wake of Captain Athorpe, and Laurence felt that he might trust him. Laurence was assured that he had no power over Athorpe, and that the man must drift on for a while, until his better, stronger nature asserted itself. That would be in good time, Laurence trusted. Athorpe was safer possibly in Bully Churdock's hands than his own; and with an injunction to the wrestler to be very watchful, for the watched one was dangerous, he went back to the counting-house, to reflect upon his next step—what he should say to Milly, and in what way he should advise her.

Meanwhile Athorpe went doggedly onwards, until he came within sight of his own cottage, standing out amongst the trees, like a sentinel, guarding the entrance to the valley. He stood looking at it for a while; then he brandished his clenched hand iu the air, and cursed it—striding away at last at a pace that put Bully Churdock upon his mettle, and halting not till he was in Tavvydale village, and had plunged, almost head-first, into the place where there might come forgetfulness in due course, if he drank hard enough.

"Brandy!" he gasped forth; then he sat down at a small table in a corner of the room, and waited almost patiently for the fiery waters of Lethe.

CHAPTER V

BEFORE THE STORM.

LAURENCE started for Tavvydale half an hour after he had left Bully Churdock. He could not rest within doors; he felt that there was danger abroad—danger in a variety of ways to Milly, and those connected with her. If the mad fit came on again, he could not foresee the consequences to any one with whom Athorpe came in contact. He must learn the whole story, and judge what was best for all, and where it might be likely that he or Milly, or both, could interfere with a prospect of success.

Making for Tavvydale, he was met by Bully Churdock once more.

"I be to wait for ye—she told me."

"Milly?"

"Yes. Ye're to go on down the Cleft, and she'll come to ye."

"Where is she now?"

"In her uncle's house—with him."

"Is Athorpe at home, then?"

"Yes—she managed it; she came after him to the 'Fyvie Arms,' and got over him somehow to come home. I thought he would hae hit her once, and then I should have fell on him, and smashed him. But, Lord, Sir!" bursting into sudden enthusiasm, and forgetting his late dislike to our hero, "she got round him, and told him lots of things to smooth him down like—and he's at home, and Milly's with him."

"It is scarcely safe," said Laurence, anxiously; "I will call there first."

"I'm a-watch there. If she were to skreek ever so little, I should hear her."

"I will go there," said Laurence, firmly.

"Well, as ye like. Ye've a right, I s'pose, for ye're the lucky gentleman she fancies. I guessed it somehow long ago, and now I know it all for truth. Wull, ye're a great man, but she's too good for ye, Mister Raxford."

" Ay, that's true."

" Better you than the long chap that's been up to mischief all his life—but better that never a one of ye came coorting here. I can't recken that it will come to good, though I hear good of you—aboots the place. I was in love wi' her first—long ago, before she heerd of you, and you spiled it all, though I was a poor devil that never had a chance," he added, irrelevantly; " but she likes you, and I makes it up with you for it—there!"

He extended his big hand, which Laurence took, wondering if Bully Churdock had been drinking with Captain Athorpe, for company's sake. But Bully was as sober as a judge, and this was a touch of sentiment on his part, and not the result of strong liquor.

" And Mrs. Athorpe, Churdock?—what has become of her? Did you not tell me that she had left her husband?"

" He turned her out of doors last night, and she went, all of a fright like, and crying like a child, to Milly's cottage, where she has been ever since—where, I think," he said, reflectively, " that she had better stay."

" But all this may be a mistake?"

" Likely 'nuff," responded Churdock; " but I never seed a man like the captain when he's off his balance—it's the devil hisself stopping for nothing. He's not right, you know!"

" And you have left Milly with him?"

" Ah! but he can't hurt her. She's different to you, or me, or his furrin wife. And all's right there, I tell you, even if he hadn't calmed down like a babby."

Laurence did not slacken his pace for this assurance; he walked rapidly towards the cottage, of which Captain Athorpe had been so proud, and met Milly—his Milly—at the door thereof.

" Oh! Laurence," she cried, " yesterday so full of promise and to-day with so much trouble to fight against!"

" Troubles to be conquered, I hope."

" Well, I hope that, too, now," answered she; " I think the worst is over, and we shall live the scandal down—even here in Tavvydale, where he has been foolish enough to magnify his grief, and let the world know how weak he is, as well as—Inez. You saw him at the mine to-day?"

" Yes."

" Come in and see him now, and tell me if you can hope
with me that we can make this strong but stricken man
happy in his home, and with his wife again—his weak but
not guilty wife, Laurence. I want you to assure me that I
am not scheming for his old life in vain—to scheme with me
and be interested always in what strikes at me and mine."

" You may be sure, Milly, that our interests are identical."

" Yes, I am sure of that—and so, amidst all this, and
with this thought, I keep very strong."

" You were always a brave woman."

" I was glad—very glad—when a chance word of my
uncle told me that you were still in Tavvydale. You will
not leave me now, Laurence, until we have done our best for
husband and wife in this house? You are one more friend
on my side."

" Mrs. Athorpe is at your cottage in the Cleft ? "

" Yes, for the night. To-morrow she comes back here, I
trust. You know the story ? "

" No."

" You guess it ? "

" I may have a suspicion of the truth—a faint one."

" The truth is not so much against her—she has been
vain and thoughtless, and you must not think worse of her
than that. I do not," said Milly proudly ; " I am her
friend still—I see her errors, and pity it and her. But she
can come back to this house, wronging him not by her
presence here—however bitterly he may have spoken against
her."

" I do not attribute any harm to Mrs. Athorpe, Milly."

" Forgive me. I am excited, Laurence, and unlike myself. See what a hasty woman you may have some day
for——"

She paused, blushing very much, and he caught her in
his arms and kissed her.

" For a wife," he concluded ; " on some early day, which
we will talk of presently."

" Yes—yes," getting herself free from him ; " when we
have a right to talk, unshadowed by the troubles of the
friends we love. Now it does not seem quite right."

Laurence, thus reproved, followed Milly into the front
room, where, heaped in the arm-chair by the window, sat

Athorpe, white faced and weary-looking, with his throat bare, his hair wild and tangled, and his eyes dim and lustreless, lacking the mad fire of the morning.

"Mr. Raxford has called to see you, uncle."

Athorpe glanced at our hero, clasped his hands, which appeared to have become thinner and more claw-like since they had fastened their clutch on him, Laurence thought—looked uneasily towards the door, and then said, with a short, hollow laugh,

"She has brought me home, you see, and I thought that I would never step into it again. I fancied that I was a stronger man until to-night—that I could stand anything."

"You will be better and calmer in the morning."

"Oh! I'm calm enough," he said with his old abruptness of reply, "though all the brandy has not got out of my head yet. This girl, Sir," pointing to Milly, "would persuade me that I have been a fool—very rash altogether, and perhaps I have. She makes it more clear and less dark, and I—I believe her. God forgive me!—perhaps it all may turn out better than I hoped. But," with a groan of anguish that he could not repress, "why should I believe it all after she has deceived me like this? Can I see her sit down before me again *there*, and fancy that she loved me—or can I trust her ever? I who have been a distrustful man all my life!"

"You have not heard the story, uncle, in its entirety. And if she tells it herself, you will forgive her."

"Not in my heart; I can't do that," said he firmly.

"Ah! but you will, for you have been very fond of her and she of you; and she will love you for that generosity that takes her back, forgetting all the foolish, miserable past."

"She has been very false."

"But she has been strong, too—and she has committed no fault deserving of a life-long separation from you. Think of her back again, uncle, as though nothing had happened. There, I will bring her back to-night."

"No, not to-night," he said quickly; "not till I am more sober, and can face the facts. Not till I am more prepared. Are you going now? You must not leave her alone in that place of yours too long, though I scarcely think he dares to enter the Cleft again. By God, if I thought that——"

He would have leaped to his feet, had not Milly's hands restrained him.

"He is in London now—he would respect her and you, I hope, even if he were in Devon."

"I shall have to kill him," he muttered ; "I don't feel that I can rest, without doing harm to him—where's Churdock ? "

" Outside the cottage."

" Ask him to come in and mind me," he said, plaintively , " to keep the brandy from me, and knock me down rather than let me touch it. If I could only sit here quietly till the grey morning came again—oh ! if I could but rest till then, creeping back by degrees to the old self that has gone."

" Shall I stay with you, uncle ? "

" No. See to her—tell her how I am—what she has made of me suddenly ; and if she's sorry—very sorry—let me know to-morrow. Mr. Raxford, you will see Milly down the Cleft. It is not safe for her to be alone, now—the place swarms with spies — and I suppose," he added, almost hesitatingly, " that I can trust *you ?* "

" Yes—I think you can."

They went out together ; and Churdock, after receiving his instructions from Milly, and bestowing a dismal look after her and Laurence as they turned towards the Cleft, passed into the parlour to keep watch upon the stricken man —stricken with an old disease, and a new one.

In the dusky twilight gathering about them, they went down the Cleft together—for the first, and the last time in their lives—a man and woman full of trust in each other, and even, in the midst of grief around them, rejoicing in their loves. Milly was more sanguine of success, and was more full of light and life in consequence.

"The stain will pass away for good," she said, " and Inez will go back to him a stronger, better woman. I'm sure of it, now, and the weight off my mind makes my heart lighter. There, Sir, I shall tell you nothing of this story of a jealous man, and his foolish little wife—I only ask you to believe that from beginning to end there is more romantic folly than real harm in it. I shall keep this little family secret as close as

I can, Laurence—for I am a proud woman, objecting to tattle—and if you hear anything against us—very much against us—don't believe it."

"Certainly not."

"I wonder why people who should be all-in-all to each other—people like my uncle and his wife—like you and me, may I add," she said, pressing his arm—"I wonder why they hoard up their foolish little secrets, when there must come an unguarded moment to betray all, some day ? Can men and women really love each other, completely, and yet have a secret that they dare not confess, shut up somewhere in their hearts ? That is not love that is ashamed or afraid to confide, Laurence."

Laurence winced ; Milly's words had struck home, for Milly had spoken warmly and earnestly. He thought of his own shabby secret, which he kept back for Hester Fyvie's sake—for Hester's father's sake—and it was on his lips to utter his confession, and break the promise only made that day.

"There are secrets that affect others rather than ourselves, and that we have a right to keep, I think, Milly, for their sakes," he said, after a pause.

Milly misunderstood him, and he did not undeceive her.

"Ah ! you are thinking of what I said just now about my aunt and uncle — you are very kind, Laurence. Yes, perhaps we have a right to hide them as much as we can—sometimes I am not quite certain of that. How thoughtful you are !—have you anything to confess to *me*, Laurence ? "

"Yes ; that I am not so poor—or rather, not so reduced in position—as I hoped to be by this time—as I prophesied that I should be."

"You have seen Mr. Fyvie ? "

"Yes—he was with me at the mine this morning."

"And—and you told him how foolish you had been to fall in love with a village girl ?—how bold I had been to fall in love with you myself, Laurence ? " she said, in a lower tone—so prettily shy, too, that Laurence's arms were round her before she could escape them.

"I told him what a proud and lucky fellow I was. I offered my resignation, too, as a partner, but he would not accept it at once."

18

"Oh, dear !" with an odd little sigh ; "then you will be a rich man, after all ; and for ever ashamed of me. You should not have tried to love me until you were sure of our being nice and poor together ! "

"The partnership will not bring a penny into my purse," he replied ; "and presently—very shortly—I hope, I shall be more of my own master, and less a slave to the promise that I have made him. He may call me his partner, Milly, but I am simply his clerk."

" I do not quite understand."

" Presently it will be all clear," he answered—" I do not think that it is worth further explanation now. If I seem a little mysterious, Milly, I must ask you to wait for the light that I will shed presently on *my* secret. There, you trust me ? "

" If I did not, Laurence, with all my heart, I would not think of you again ! " she cried. " I *would* forget that I had ever seen you."

" I wonder whether that would be possible," said Laurence more lightly ; and then the lovers drifted into a channel less despondent, and talked of their future, and looked at them-selves and their home in the distance together, like two selfish beings apart from that world wherein people were less full of joy than they. Even the troubles of Uncle Athorpe and Aunt Inez were not considered in those fleeting, soul-bewildering moments, appertaining only to lovers — true lovers with their hearts in their throats. The troubles of that day were likely to end with that day, Milly thought, for she had faith in her powers of intervention ; and now for a little while, with the idol of her girlish fancies at her side, she could pass into the neutral ground appertaining to dream-land, and yet which was a something brighter and more elastic than dreams.

For he spoke of his love for her—and it was the one romance of her life as well as his — and both were young, impassioned and true, with faith in their future together, and confident enough then—ah, then !—that there was not such a man, or such a woman, in the world.

What did it matter to Laurence, then, that society would call this a *mésalliance?* He could look into her bright face, as they slowly walked together under the shadowing trees, and thank God for the rare gift of this maiden's love — this strange girl whose beauty, grace and modesty rendered her a prize of which the world would envy him ! He made no sacrifice of position in giving her his name ; he brought happiness to himself and his home for ever afterwards, and the worldlings round him could not, in their hearts, condemn his choice. There was not one fault in Milly, he said to himself later that night, at which a finger could point, and say *that* would betray her origin, or disgrace himself—there was not one grace in women better born which Milly—his Milly !—did not possess !

And she was not *his* Milly when he rhapsodised like that— when he believed that perfect bliss was attainable by man, even in a world that preachers had told him was full of vanity and unprofitableness. He had faith in the world, and believed that preachers and cynics were too hard upon it !

CHAPTER VI.

RIVALS.

THE twilight had come, the sky had deepened very much, and stars were thickly sown in it when Milly Athorpe parted with her lover, and went up the green slope towards her cottage.

They had stood together in sight of the house ten minutes or a quarter of an hour, with Inez looking at them from the trellised doorway ; they had been unwilling to part, and put an end to the sweet music of their own love murmurings, as though a faint, far-away soughing amongst the hills around them was the warning voice of the future, wherein such bliss should never come again. This was the end of the idyl — the bright break in two lives—and they lingered side by side till the last, and were shamed not that Inez stood there witness to their parting kiss.

More witnesses than Inez, too, of which Milly knew nothing, or she might have been less demonstrative in her affection. And yet she was proud of her lover — her heart was very full of him—and no one, save his mother, perhaps,

18—2

had so great a right to kiss him as she had. If Inez reproved her, she thought as she went up the slope, she would defend herself with some such words as these.

She believed that Aunt Inez would reprove her, and with a show of justice in her reproof, for one woman's heart was as full of bitterness, anxiety, and mortification, as the other's was of hope and joy Still she was the bearer of hopeful tidings in her turn, and that had made her own heart light, and her thoughts able to turn to her lover. Things were not so gloomy at Captain Athorpe's house, and the worst, she felt convinced, was over. Husband and wife need not be separated longer than that night, and new lives—better and stronger ones—would date from it But the night was thick with events yet, and Tavvydale folk were to speak of it long afterwards.

"Milly," said Inez, an excited, but careworn woman enough, with two spots of fire burning on her cheeks, "here is a visitor for you—there is no peace even *here* for any of us."

"A visitor !—not Mr. Fyvie, Inez ? "

"No—no. But his sister, who is very anxious to see you. Oh ! Milly, I can only trust in you—tell her nothing that affects her brother and me. Soon enough they will know all, and I cannot, will not, bear this interview now. Mind that—I cannot bear it."

"What has she said ? "

"She has said nothing—remarked not upon my presence in your house — taken no notice of me in any way — but waited like a statue for you. Oh ! Milly, you will not satisfy such paltry curiosity as hers ? "

"You may trust me, Inez."

They went into the house together—two women mistaken in the motive for Hester Fyvie's presence there.

Miss Fyvie, paler than her wont, but looking more firm and hard and angular, sat by the window waiting for them —a lady richly dressed—a lady whose proud distant bow towards the new comer gave sufficient evidence at once of the difference in life between the two.

It struck Milly at once—and confused, even humbled her. She understood the grandeur of the Fyvie family, and their height above her ; she took no credit to herself for being superior to her class in any way ; teacher as she was in Tavvydale now, she was still simply a village girl in her own opinion, as well as Miss Fyvie's. She dropped her modest curtsey, and waited for the lady — the *ci-devant* patroness—to speak to her.

"I am sorry that you have had to wait for me, Miss Fyvie—if I had known that you were coming to me at so late an hour, I would have reached home earlier."

"My time is my own, and of no consequence to me, or to anyone else, I am sorry to say," she said, quickly, but very coldly; "I have been waiting here to speak as a friend to one in whom I have been interested for some years."

"And been a true friend, too, Miss Fyvie."

"In my way, perhaps," she added, "you will think that I am an enemy after this day, or you are less of a woman than I am. Mrs. Athorpe," turning to Inez, "I wish to speak to Milly alone."

Mrs. Athorpe coloured, but held her ground.

"We guess—both of us—what has brought you to this place, and we are ready to defend our name against any aspersions that may be levelled at us."

"I do not comprehend you," said Hester, looking with surprise at the last speaker, that cold, well-bred surprise, which defeats so well the lower and more impulsive character.

"It concerns *me*."

"Pardon me, but it is no business of yours whatever," said Miss Fyvie, becoming more stately every instant; "you are not connected in any way with what I have to tell your niece. It is private matter between her and me, concerning which she may seek your advice afterwards, if she is disposed to resent my own. I am here to speak plain truths—that's all."

"It—it concerns Milly?"

"Yes."

"I beg your pardon," said Inez, relieved by this assertion. "I will withdraw, Miss Fyvie, at once."

She passed into the inner room, and closed the door behind her, leaving the two maidens—the rivals!—together. Milly guessed what was coming now—what advice she was likely to receive—and whose name would be uppermost between them both. Already she felt more strong to resist the advice that would be proffered her—the advice which no one had a right to offer her out of her own family. Still she would listen respectfully, and answer respectfully, if it were possible. For the Fyvies were old friends of the Athorpes—they had saved her and her mother—when the father was dead, and the uncle had not come back to Tavvy-dale—from the workhouse, and had given them the very cottage whose roof sheltered her then ; she remembered the Fyvies in her prayers, and had been ever grateful for their patronage. Even without them she would have never known Laurence Raxford, and that was the last and newest tie that bound her to the family.

"Milly," said Hester, in the same cold, unsympathetic tones, which told against words that were not, at the outset, unkind in themselves, "we have known each other from children—I am only two years your senior, and we have met as children together. I have had great faith in you all my life, and resisted the slightest insinuation uttered against you."

"By whom, Miss Fyvie ? "

"By friends who have made some little effort to under-stand you."

It was on Milly's lips to say that their efforts were un-called for, and unfair, but she restrained the retort, and held her peace.

"I believed, Milly, that the suspicions that others had of your vanity, your craving for admiration, were based upon false assumptions, and I took your part, and called you modest, gentle, good."

"I hope that I am no worse than other women, and I thank no one who thinks me worse, or does not take my part against the slanderers. Thank God, Miss Fyvie, that I have my friends, and they have faith in me ! "

"True friends are hard to know, and it is the cruellest delusion to put your faith in false ones. You are doing that."

Milly shook her head.

"You resent my speech already, though it is intended for your good, and you have been weak, foolish, wicked enough to trust a gentleman above you in position—to scheme to gain him as a lover—risking your good name in the wild hope of becoming his wife, perhaps—a delusion that has ruined thousands of women of your class, and not helped one to her ambition. Girl, you, with more knowledge than your set, should have known better than this!"

Milly trembled for awhile beneath this sudden attack—this change of tone, from the ice that froze, to the fire that thawed the passion within Hester Fyvie's breast. She stood there blushing very much, but not very much afraid—conscious of her own strength, and ignorant yet awhile of the heaviest blow to be struck at her. That would dash her and her fresh young heart down at one blow, for it would shiver her faith in the idol she had reared.

"You allude to Mr. Raxford?" she asked at last.

"Yes, I allude to him," said Hester; "I presume that there is not a second swain who——"

"Miss Fyvie, you have defended me from the insinuations of the base, you tell me," Milly interrupted here, almost scornfully.

"Pardon me," said Hester quickly, "I am wrong—but I am a hasty girl, and this is a strange subject between us. I have a right to speak concerning it, or I would not have come here to-night thus officiously. I am here to tell all, as well as to hear all."

Milly looked nervously towards her; there stole to her mind the first doubt of the result, of what Hester Fyvie might say to her presently, and then it was dissipated again, as the image of her lover, noble and true, passed the track on which her eyes were fixed.

"Miss Fyvie, I will tell you what is no secret, and what I am very proud to own — that I love Mr. Raxford very dearly."

She hung her head as she spoke, but she spoke her avowal boldly and confidently, noticing not the deadly pallor that seized upon her listener.

"Well," gasped Hester, "what else?"

"That he is above me in position, I know," continued Milly, "not so much above me as you may imagine, perhaps, but more so than he would lead me to believe, and oh! immeasurably higher in mind and thought, and true nobility. I was sorry for this at first—but I think that I am becoming used to it, and proud of it. For I am very proud of his affection for me, which stoops to me, and will raise me with him, sharing his home and making me the happiest of wives! He sought me out and strove to win my love; and winning it, and having faith in him, knowing what an honourable man he is in all respects, I do not fear, and I do not accept, the warnings you have given me."

"You speak well," said Hester, "but it is a woman in a book, not a peasant girl on the verge of her ruin. For it must come to that," she hissed forth, "if you think and trust like this, and know so little of human nature."

"I trust with all my heart where I love, Miss Fyvie."

"Has he trusted you with all his, do you think ? "

"I am very sure of that."

"What has he said of—*me?*"

It was the jealous woman now, not the cold, stately lady who had begun the conference. The woman jealous of the man whom she loved, and who, she believed, had been false to her from the first—the woman who was not heroine enough to feel lacking in a desire for revenge.

"Of you, Miss Fyvie—nothing of you," stammered Milly.

And then the doubt flickered before her again an *ignis fatuus*, that was to last now till the end.

"Has he not told you, Milly, how he came to my father's house as a guest, was made my father's partner, and had riches thrust upon him ; how he spoke words of love to me, as he has done to you, and how I was, like yourself, weak enough to believe that he loved me, and believing that, to love him with all my heart and soul. Has he kept this from you ? "

"Pray go on," entreated Milly ; "I can believe you, I hope, for you have been always a truthful woman. Pray go on, please."

"He told me that he loved me, and we were engaged to each other with my father and mother's consent. *He is still engaged to be my husband!* "

"*What!*" cried Milly, losing her own self-command now, and swaying to and fro, with her hands clasped to her temples.

"He has never given me up. He has never expressed by a word or wish that our engagement should be cancelled. The last words that he ever spoke to me were, 'I love you!' He is bound in honour to marry me, and I will NOT resign him ! There, I have told all."

"But—but—oh ! Madam, this is so unlike him—so unlike anything that is fair and honourable, and manly—and, oh !

dear, oh ! dear—he is not likely to have acted so. How could he have been engaged to you, yet come to me—me who had never harmed him—with his story of his first, his only love ? No," she cried with vehemence, " he cannot be so shameful ! "

Hester tossed towards her, almost contemptuously, a small packet of letters—the few letters that Laurence had written to Hester when he was away from her, in his solitary lodgings at Wheal Desperation.

" I doubted if my word would be believed, and I brought my proofs with me," Hester Fyvie said ; " read them, if you wish."

" Yes, I will read them, if you will allow me," said Milly, opening the packet in feverish haste ; " you see," she added, half apologetically, " this is a serious case, and I have no one to advise me as to what is best."

She read them hurriedly, searching out their meaning almost at a glance, stabbing repeatedly at this new bleeding wound, which time would never heal in her. At the last letter— which with a strange sense of fairness Hester had added to the heap—she paused, and read more slowly.

" What does this mean ? " she asked, almost peremptorily.

" There had been a little quarrel between us, and he was anxious to make it up and be forgiven. You see, he writes to that effect. Well, I wrote back, implying that he was forgiven, and from that day we have not exchanged an angry word together."

" My God ! he is very false ! " exclaimed Milly, with a throbbing heart, as she thrust the letters together and restored them to the owner ; " and you will marry him, you say, despite all this ? "

" Yes—if he will have me. He shall break our engagement himself, and be a scorn to the world about him, or he shall be my husband."

" You can forgive him asking me to be his wife, then ?— you, coming of a high-spirited race, too ! "

" Yes—I can forgive even that. It was a cruel jest on his part, to make time pass less idly on his hands — but in time I will absolve him."

" For you love him ? "

" Yes."

" I thought that I loved him as no woman had ever loved before—but no, I could not forgive him the lesser injury of the two. But the wrong that he has done me —the *jest*, as you call it, that he has played with my heart, with a poor girl who would have died for love of him, had he never spoken to me — I must remember with all a woman's scorn. Miss Fyvie, take your lover back ! "

Milly Athorpe never looked more beautiful than in her pride which gave back Laurence Raxford to patrician hands ; and Hester Fyvie never felt so acutely miserable and mean. The jealous woman had triumphed — the false lover had been dragged from his idol ; but her heart was very heavy, and there was no sweetness at the last in the revenge — truly womanly—that she had taken. Laurence had humiliated her—cast her off contemptuously—won her love, and then spurned her almost from him ; but she did not feel so abashed as in those last moments when Milly resigned— wholly and completely—the lover she had gained. If she had not uttered one lie in all that heated conversation, she felt as a liar, that had destroyed the happiness of two lives, and not enhanced her own. And she knew, for the first time, how wrong she had been.

" She went out of the house swiftly and suddenly into the dark night, like an evil presence, that weighed upon people more artless than she was. She dashed upon some one waiting beneath the trees for her, as he had waited for two hours.

" Well, what the devil has it all been about, that I should lurk here like this ? "

" Oh ! are you here still ?—I had forgotten you," said Hester, to her brother ; " why did you wait ? "

" To protect you, to be sure."

" There is no harm likely to come to me. The carriage is at the top of the Cleft, I suppose ? "

" Yes."

" Then let me go alone—don't follow me—I am a wicked, miserable, covetous wretch, Jonathan."

" Ah !—and not the only one in the family," added the brother with a half-groan.

" Don't come with me."

" I will see you to where the path widens — just before

Athorpe's cottage—if I get shot for a dog by the way. So it's no good talking to me—I never cared for talk ! "

Hester said no more, and brother and sister went on together for the next quarter of an hour until the point was reached which the former had indicated. There Jonathan Fyvie stopped, and there was something in his manner—hard, and dogged and new—that even distracted his sister's thoughts from her own actions that night.

" You remain here ? "

" Yes—I am going back."

" Going back—where ? "

" To perdition ! " he answered, as he retraced his steps and left her watching him, until he disappeared in the shadows of the lower ground.

CHAPTER VII.

TWO WOMEN IN TROUBLE CONSOLE EACH OTHER.

MILLY was standing where Hester Fyvie had left her, when Inez Athorpe stole from the inner room towards her. She had stood there ten minutes at least—a figure struck into stone by the revelation that had been made to her.

Against such news there was no holding firm for ever—looking at it from Milly's point of view, believing every word, and having had proof to confirm almost every word that had been spoken, it was like a shock that swept away the hopes of a lifetime. This was no mistake—it necessitated no explanation from the coward who had deceived her—it was plain as Holy Writ, and she had but to live and suffer from that day ! Not a word concerning Hester, or his engagement to her, had he told her; he had whispered that she was the first woman whom he had ever loved, and when she had told him that there should be no secrets between a man and woman pledged to one another, he had kept his story hidden from her, and laughed in his sleeve at her simplicity ! Yes, it *had* been a jest; he was a rich man, a gentleman by birth and education, and gentlemen were allowed to destroy the happiness—the souls, if they were able—of poor, ignorant girls like herself. She was only a woman, to be led away by a few compliments, and who was likely to care what became of her, or what feelings she possessed? She was not of the "set" which society acknowledged; and a few, more or less, of unhappy ones troubled nobody in a decent sphere of life. "Simply a jest!" thought Milly, with her proud little heart bursting with indignation meanwhile. Inez touched her on the arm at last.

"Trouble to you too, my child—you, who were only building on your future this morning."

"This evening, as I came up the Cleft with him," said Milly sadly.

"But you will not grieve for a man like that, child?"

"You have heard all."

"Yes—I could hardly help it, with the room so close to this," said Inez, colouring at the question; "and you would have told me all, Milly, after she had gone."

"Yes—I must have done that," answered Milly. "Well, well—you must not laugh at me for once?"

"No," said Inez, "not now A week ago I might have done so, for I was jealous of your good looks, and what people said of them—I, who did not like any one to be admired save my wicked, wretched self! There, I am candid with you—I disguise nothing—I bare my inmost heart before you."

"If I had never known him!—oh! if he had never come to Devon!" said Milly, dropping into a chair, and covering her face with her hands.

"Milly—you, always so strong, mustn't give way!"

"I am not going to cry," answered Milly, without removing her hands; "but I am not going to say that I am not grieved—broken-hearted—to lose him."

"Is he worth grieving for, Milly?"

"Ah! that's not it. I grieve to lose him like this—to find out how base and mean he is, striving hard to win a love from me that he knew he could never value—that he did not think worth valuing. I could have borne up against his death better, but to bear up against the shame that he has cast upon me! Inez, I can't stop in Tavvydale any longer—I will go away at once—I must!"

"For ever?"

"For a time, till they have done talking about me—

laughing at me and my poor ambition. I think that they will give me a month's holiday at the school ; and if they will not, I can't help it. I must go away at once—oh! I must—I must ! "

She lowered her hands to beat them impatiently upon her lap, to wring them together till the joints cracked.

" And what will become of me ? " cried Inez, with a look of alarm—with the old selfishness predominant.

" You will go back to your husband, forgetting a romance more miserable and more full of folly than my own. You will go back with a higher sense of duty to him and yourself—and I think that you will be a different woman."

" He—he will kill me," said Inez, shuddering. " Oh ! if I could only trust him—if I could believe that he would trust me—I would go back so willingly and cheerfully, beginning afresh the better life you hint at. But that hard, unforgiving nature which I have ever feared."

Milly shook off the thoughts of her own troubles to reason with her. Here was a life on the verge of shipwreck, and hers would flow on smoothly enough in good time. She *must* think of this woman first—time enough for herself at a later hour, when she had delivered the news, which had made her more sanguine of results that night, until Hester Fyvie had appeared before her.

" Inez, I will tell you what I have been doing to-day— what my Uncle Athorpe has been doing."

" That's kind of you—that's kind, Milly," she said. " I am listening very patiently, dearest ; I am all attention now."

She dropped down at Milly's feet, crossed her hands on Milly's lap, and looked up at her, absorbed in Milly's next words—a dark-faced, beautiful woman, contrasting strangely —as an artist would have contrasted her—with the fairer English loveliness looking down upon her. If her nature— variable and selfish, and yet affectionate and trustful—peered out here, and jarred on the love troubles of the junior woman, Milly did not show it, and understood and felt for the terrible anxiety of her uncle's wife. After all, what was her distress to one with a name, home, and husband, trembling in the balance ?

" When my uncle found out that you had loved Jonathan Fyvie before your marriage, and had met him afterwards more than once—in all innocence, perhaps, but in all stealth, that was not worthy of you—he believed the worst, and turned you from his home."

" Ah ! shall I ever forget that ? "

" You came to me, and told all your story—what a strange one it had been ; how that man Jonathan had loved you after his own fashion, or told you that he had ; how your pity for him, your desire to see him a better man, and forget vou entirely——"

" Did I say entirely ? " asked this weak woman suddenly.

" Entirely ; why should he think of you any more ? "

" Ah ! why indeed ! But to be utterly forgotten by one whom we have passionately loved ! "

" I should wish to be forgotten by any one who could not think of me purely," said Milly, and Laurence Raxford crossed her thoughts at that time, and elicited a shudder, as though he was walking once more over the grave of her dead hopes.

" Well—my pity for him ? " questioned Inez.

" How your pity for him had led you to see him more than once," continued Milly, "and advise him to go away from Devon, and not imperil your good name. You told me this ? "

" All true—all true, every word of it, for I meant no harm, and would have done no harm, to my poor husband. All vanity, love of excitement, and—and love for the man who is going wrong through me." " Your husband ? "

" No—the other ! There, it is true—I can't tell a lie —I can't change my heart. I would not go away with him to be his mistress, but I love him all the same— just as I ever did ! "

" Hush ! hush ! you must not say this."

" Can you tell me that you will love Laurence Rax- ford less because he is false to you ?—No—you will love him the same, for all his baseness—you will remember him always as he was to you, as he might have been, if people had not interfered."

" I will not think of him at present, Inez. I am talk- ing about yourself."

" Well," said Inez, gloomily, "one misery at a time is enough ! "

" But this is a misery that has lasted but a little while, and is to pass away for good."

"It depends upon my husband—if *he* is charitable, and ready to trust me again. What did he say, Milly, when you told him all the story?—how I had struggled to do my duty by him, and keep Jonathan Fyvie from my thoughts?"

"He had been drinking early in the day, and was desperate in his grief. I lured him from the public-house to his home, and let him sleep awhile before I told him all. Then he listened, was unmanned, and was even hopeful, after awhile, that you would come back with a promise to be ever faithful, forgetting all that has separated you from him."

"Forgetting all that I can!"

"You can forget everything; you must!"

"Or he will kill me, I know that. I know, too, that he will be trebly suspicious after this; that I shall be watched, and that there will be no faith in anything that I say or do. But if he will take me back, with all my faults, I shall be glad and grateful."

"I am sure that he will."

"I will do my duty in earnest—I will love him more—making every atonement for the misery that I have caused him, Milly. He may change to-morrow, so I will go to-night and face him. I am not afraid—I feel very brave—brave enough to go down on my knees before him, and ask him to forgive me."

"I will return with you," said Milly.

"No, I will go alone, or you will think me a coward. I would rather be alone, trusting to myself for support. If he cast me from him, I can but come back here."

"Churdock is there."

"Then he is ill and wants help. I will go, and when I am found back again in my husband's house, the Tavvydale folk will believe it all a dream!"

"And this the pleasant waking!"

"Yes. And if they are too hard in their comments, or my husband is too proud—which he will be—to serve the Fyvies ever again, why, we can go abroad together," she said, thoughtfully.

She had forgotten Milly's distress completely, and Milly did not remind her of it by a word. Milly had already made up her mind what to do, and there was no occasion to discuss that matter at the eleventh hour.

Inez was ready to depart, draping her shawl about

her head and shoulders in a Spanish fashion, worthy of her foreign name.

"I am going now. Wish me joy, Milly."

"All the joy that should follow peace between man and wife, Inez. God bless you!"

"I am sorry that I was ever unkind and harsh, and jealous of you, Milly," she said, pausing, with the cottage door open in her hand.

"I never fretted for an instant, and I soon forgot our little bickerings—don't speak of them. You will hear from me in London. I shall write from Uncle Whiteshell's to you."

"Thank you," she answered, without realising the idea conveyed by this. "In the morning call upon me."

"In the morning! I shall be away early—very early. I shall be glad to escape for awhile from all this," Milly said, wearily.

"I will write to you, then. Now, I am really going—strengthened by you, and without a fear in the world—back to my husband."

" If I accompanied you, Inez——" began Milly.

"He would think that I was afraid of him—which I am not now. Will—will you sit up for me an hour?"

" If you wish it."

"He might send me back—I don't think that he will, I don't believe that he will, Milly; but sit up for me!"

"Very well."

"If he will half pardon me—if he will forgive me presently, years hence, I will stay. So I shall not come back."

"No—I hope not."

"Strong of purpose—fearless of danger—hoping to be trusted, with my niece's blessing on my steps, I go."

She passed out of the house, and Milly followed her to the door, and looked out after her. The moon had risen; in "the open" all was bright as noonday, and there were tracings of silver where the glen narrowed, and the trees met overhead. It seemed a path of promise for the young wife, leading straight back to her husband's heart, and Milly thought so as she watched and prayed that all good thoughts of her might come true, before the night was ended.

Inez looked back half-way down the slope, and Milly could see by the moonlight that her lips were moving.

"I shall not come back," Milly was sure she said, and she came back never again, as she had prophesied. So she passed from the pure brightness of the night into the darkness, lurking by the lower ground, and was lost.

CHAPTER VIII.

LAURENCE IS BEWILDERED.

THE next morning Laurence was debating within himself whether he should go down the mine, or have another turn at the books, or proceed in search of Captain Athorpe, who had not entered an appearance that morning, when two letters were brought in to him. They had both arrived by special messengers, within ten minutes of each other; the earlier missive from Milly Athorpe, the later from Jonathan Fyvie, junior. Acting to the rule of business first, and pleasure afterwards, he opened his partner's letter, in the first place. It ran :—

"My DEAR RAXFORD,

"I have been a long while making up my mind to face you with a full confession of the enormities of my extravagance—but I cannot do it. I have ruined everybody connected with me, I fear, and it is all over with your hopes, as well as with the rest of them. I am fated to bring misery upon every one with whom I come in contact. I am reckless, and may kill myself before this letter reaches your hand—or I may go to London, and plunge into the vortex, always ready to engulph such a poor devil as I am. I cannot ask you to forgive me—I cannot forgive, or understand myself—I have tried to do good, more than once, but evil has come of it; ill luck rather than a bad heart has made me a scamp. I give up !—so don't be surprised at anything I say or do, from this day. Strike me out of the partner-

19

ship, as out of the pale of good society, and think no more of me. I have written to my father, and told all at last. Yours,

"JONATHAN FYVIE."

"I don't know what to make of this," said Laurence, holding it at arm's length, and in that position reading it attentively again.

That Jonathan Fyvie had been extravagant, that he had probably ruined the prospects of the in-coming partner as surely as his own, that he had long been a source of trouble to his father, was apparent enough, but it scarcely accounted for the tone of this epistle. There was a recklessness about it foreign to Jonathan Fyvie's character—unlike the man who took good or bad fortune with equal complacency, and was very rarely moved to speak or write with anything like earnestness. There was something new in it ; more, there was something purposed by the writer when this line was penned, "Don't be surprised at anything I say or do from this day."

He laid it aside at last, and took up Milly's note. He was a bad hand at enigmas, and time must solve this one rather than he. Here, at least, in this dear letter ready to his hand, would be nothing to distress him.

He broke the seal, and read, with suspended breath and widely-distending eyes, the following lines, full of a deeper mystery, and a mystery that concerned himself more closely :

"I know all, and bear no malice. But I am going away, and if you have a spark of honour left in you, you will not seek to follow me. I must trust in other friends now that I have discovered your unworthiness. Miss Fyvie called last night, and told me of your engagement with her. That explains everything. God forgive you, Mr. Raxford. I do with all my heart, which you might have spared and left at peace. "MILLY."

Laurence did not hold this at arm's length, but spread it upon his desk, flattened out the creases, planted his elbows firmly, took his chin between his hands, and studied hard for the reasons that had dictated this new incomprehensibility.

As he had seized upon one line in Jonathan's letter as the key to all the rest, so he fixed upon one which showed naturally enough whence the mischief had arisen. "Miss Fyvie called last night!"—then it was Miss Fyvie who had stepped between him and the second woman to whom he had offered his hand since his stay in Devonshire. Well, it was a painful task, a task of bitterness, but it must be prosecuted for his honour's sake, and for Milly's satisfaction. He must see Miss Fyvie.

He gave up all thought of work for that day, and rode off at once to Tavvydale House—driving a little pony trap that appertained to the estate, and was useful for the senior clerk. He was half inclined to halt at the entrance to the glen, and call on Athorpe, or seek Milly in her own home; but Athorpe could tell him nothing, even if he was a different man from yesterday; and Milly was probably in Tavvydale.

At Tavvydale, the thought occurred to him that he would make an attempt to see Milly first, after all; his heart was wrung by her reproaches, and though he was sure that it was in his power to bring the sunlight back, yet every minute that gave her pain or kept her in suspense was a torture to himself. Yes, *this* was real love!

He drove at once to the school, and confronted Mr. Wells, the minister who, report said, had had an eye on Milly himself, at the front gate.

"Miss Athorpe—is she here, Sir?" Laurence asked.

"Miss Athorpe has taken a month's leave of absence—very unceremoniously, I may say," was the reply made, not without evidence of tetchiness, "and whether we shall fill up her place or not, depends upon the committee. Miss Athorpe, I think, might have waited until somebody was up in my house, instead of writing incoherent letters to me."

"Where has she gone?"

"Really, I don't know, Sir; London, I believe. Are you the gentleman from the mines who—who is engaged to her?"

"I am that gentleman."

"Then—then you should really know more about her movements than I. The school is in an uproar this morning—and I am very much confused, and can't give any further explanation if I remained all day. Good-morning, Sir."

19—2

And away bustled Mr. Wells, evidently very much put out by Milly Athorpe's eccentricity.

Gone to London. To her Uncle Whiteshell's, where it was easy to follow her, he having Uncle Whiteshell's address. A few more hours of suspense for her and him, and then all would be well again. To think, he said to himself as he mounted into his gig once more, that she should act with this impetuosity, hurling herself away from him, on account of a few words spoken by Hester Fyvie concerning an old engagement. He had not been frank with Milly there—but it was for Hester and her father's sake. And now Hester had forestalled him, caring not for the family pride that he had been asked to respect.

Some time afterwards—it appeared an age to Laurence— he was before the doors of Tavvydale House. The footman did not ask his business, but stepped back and let him pass with impatient steps into the drawing-room, eager to confront all aspersers without fair notice of his presence there. The room was empty.

The servant followed him.

"Miss Fyvie—can I see her? Will you tell her that I wish to see her, on very urgent business?"

"She is not at home, Sir."

"Where has she gone?"

"To London—she left here with her mother half an hour ago."

"Where is Mr. Fyvie?"

"Just come in, Sir, from the station."

"I will see him."

The servant withdrew, and Laurence, chafing at these disappointments, paced the limits of the room till the door reopened, and an old man tottered very feebly towards him —a man so old and bent and weak, that Laurence did not at the first glance recognise his friend and benefactor.

"Mr. Fyvie—what has happened to—to everybody?"

"I know what has happened to me, and that is sufficient," said the old man, with his customary curtness predominant; "I should have sent for you to-day, Laurence, if you had not called upon me. You have heard from Jonathan?"

"Yes."

"Well, he has confessed the worst, and the worst is—ruin. I can see no help—neither for you nor me now. We must give in, Laurence, and I, who would have advanced your fortunes, must drag you down to the level of my indigence. It is worse than I could have believed, and you must forgive me starting you in the world with the big ugly label of 'bankrupt' round your neck."

"Jonathan——"

"Has acted like a fool and a knave, and I can't pity him at present. A gambler, profligate, and betting-man—having no bowels of compassion for those who bore him, and whose grey hairs he might have respected a little more. Laurence," in a hasty whisper, "you will stand by me—struggle with me to the last—see that all our books are right, and that with us there has been nothing but honourable trading from beginning to end? I am coming to work myself to-morrow, and the creditors shall find me at my post whenever they appear at Wheal Desperation. Laurence, you will not desert me for an instant now?—I trust in you and your presence of mind for the last faint chance to save us."

"I will stay, Sir, if you think it absolutely necessary—if affairs are really so bad for you and me," said Laurence; "it is my duty, and I cannot leave it."

"I felt that you would not."

Laurence still thought more of Milly than the avalanche on its way to sweep off all prosperity from those with whom he was connected; all *that* might be borne up against, but the loss of Milly, and Milly's loss of faith in him, never! All this time he was revolving in his mind the course that lay before him. If to leave the business now, even for a day, was to add to the chances of Mr. Fyvie's ruin, why, he must hold fast to his post with Spartan firmness, and leave himself to be condemned unheard. Presently—very shortly —must come the time when he should meet Milly, and all would be explained. Milly was in no danger—only in sorrow. He would go back to the mine, find Mr. White-shell's address, write a letter to her at her uncle's house— where she was sure to be—following that up by his own presence there, if she did not believe in the earnestness of the epistle that he would write to her. But all would be well—all *could* not end like this—and he must have patience to wait.

"I called to see Miss Fyvie—she has been to Milly Athorpe and told all."

"Has she?" said he, unconcernedly; "well, it does not matter much now—she was too proud to keep her secret, I suppose. You will go back to the books, and, for God's sake, keep them clear as daylight! Let the creditors see that we are blameless in our business transactions. You will return at once—I will be with you to-morrow."

"I will go now."

"It is kind of you."

Thus they parted, and Laurence drove back towards Wheal Desperation, more bewildered than he had left it. Everything had clouded wondrously since yesterday, and everything had altered for the worse. He seemed groping in the mists—unable to grasp at anything tangible, and staggering like a blind man on his way. He prayed for patience to wait—for time to think, amidst all this turmoil that surrounded him—or else he should go mad like Captain Athorpe.

That prayer escaped him as he entered Tavvydale again; and found more confusion there—people running down the street towards the open country—men and women with excited faces, talking and gesticulating, and no one listening —a crowd of boys round a little shed, on which was written "Engine House," and a drivelling old beadle feeling in all his pockets for the key.

"What is it?" asked our hero, reining in his pony. "What has happened now?" he added, querulously.

"Not much, Sir," answered one man, with a grin; "only Athorpe's house on fire, and nobody a loser but himself."

"It is a judgment on him for his bumptiousness," said another. "He was mad drunk last night, and he's mad drunk now. Here's a man as seed him fire the place hisself, Sir."

Laurence waited to hear no more, but drove off towards the Cleft at the most furious pace the Desperation pony could be persuaded to adopt.

"Was the mystery deepening, or clearing up?" thought Laurence, as he dashed along.

CHAPTER IX.

ATHORPE'S REVENGE ON THE LARES.

"FOR many a long day" there had not been so much life and excitement on the road to Tavvydale. Men, women, and children were making for the Cleft ; the surface workers in the neighbouring mines had left off work, in flat disobedience to orders, and were already in the foremost rank of sight-seers ; the news had even got below ground, and men who could escape to the free air by any excuse, rose up, one by one, and ran for it.

When Laurence Raxford was on the scene of action, he was surrounded by many of his own men, all anxious to relate, at once, the full particulars of the accident, and each primed with a different version of the story. He forced his way through the crowd into the inner circle—with some difficulty kept free from intruders—and paused for an instant to realise this scene of confusion in the heart of the Devonshire hills, where the sudden twitter of a bird had startled him before this.

Captain Athorpe's villa was in flames ; it had been on fire two hours already, and was now burning itself out. The place was a lurid shell, with the roof fallen in, and a dense volume of smoke issuing from the gap. Some trees by which the house had been environed, had caught fire here and there, and their branches were crackling vigorously still. There were showers of sparks when they fell, or a rafter gave way in the house ; but the flames were low now, and quenched by the daylight. It was simply a scene of destruction, without any of the lurid picturesqueness which gives a charm at times to wholesale ravages by fire. There was more of the horrible than the beautiful in all this ; and women screamed when the pigeons, more faithful to their home than Captain Athorpe, flew round and round the remnants of the place, and, dizzy with the smoke and heat, dropped at last into the furnace.

Efforts had been made at an earlier period to form a chain of men from Athorpe's house to the stream winding through the Cleft, but the fire had already gained the mastery, and it was thought a useless task, and known to be one for which Captain Athorpe would not thank them. The house must burn itself away, and the better and more comfortable plan was to lie about the green turf and sloping banks, and see the end of it.

Those more interested in human nature than the scene before them, might join that group of anxious, stalwart men, surrounding some one who stood in the midst, sullen, and heavy-browed, and repellent.

Laurence pointed in that direction.

" Is Captain Athorpe there ? "

" Yes, Sir—sure he be. Take care, Sir."

Laurence was on foot, having left a boy in charge of his pony-chaise, and he walked rapidly towards the knot of men —the curious, gaping sight-seers encircling the ruined man. Nobody was speaking—all was stolid curiosity, that made no sign, but took a wondrous interest in every movement of the man in their midst. Athorpe, wearing the look of the preceding day, distraught and fierce, stood, with his coat and waistcoat at his feet, staring before him at the ruin which his hands had made. One sleeve of his shirt was torn, and trailed from his arm to the ground, and the muscular arm itself was bruised and bloody, as though a weight had fallen on it. There was a smear of blood across his face, too, from a wound above his eyes, and his tangled hair had been singed by contact with the flames.

A man of brute strength, forbidding and dangerous, whom nobody cared to approach too near just then—this was the Captain Athorpe that Milly had had hope of yester-night.

" Is he conscious ? " asked Laurence, of a man near him ; " how long has he stood like that ? "

" Half an hour, maybe, Mr. Raxford."

" Have you spoken to him ? "

" Bully Churdock has—here's Bully."

Churdock, looking almost as strange as Captain Athorpe, slouched towards our hero at this juncture.

" What is the meaning of all this, Churdock ? " asked Laurence ; " how did it happen ? "

" He drank hisself mad, and did it. What he did wasn't in his sober senses, mind you," cried Churdock with excitement; "I stands by that in any court of law, what-ever they may do to him. He's stark, staring, raving mad, and not accountable. Oh! good Lord! to think of this day, and all the harm he's done—poor fellow! To think of the trouble that's come to everybody belonging to him—to think of me in charge, and couldn't stop him —oh!"

And to Laurence's amazement, Bully Churdock tore out two handfuls of his hair, and then cast himself upon the grass. There was a roar of laughter at this from the miners and Tavvydale nondescripts—for Bully was not graceful in his movements, and fell noisily and clumsily.

"Bully got drunk with the Captain's brandy last night, and hasn't sobered down yet," cried a voice, and another roar of laughter followed the sally, until Churdock sat up suddenly, and looked savagely at his tormentors.

"You, Mr. Laurence, speak to him. Try and get him away—anywheres away from this place," he said, turning to our hero.

"I will speak to him."

"There's enough of us to hold him if he goes off again into a fit," said Churdock; "but he'll talk to you, if he will to any one."

Laurence approached his old servant.

"Why, Athorpe, old fellow," he said, in that friendly, earnest tone of voice which had a peculiar and winning effect on most people, "what's all this?"

Athorpe did not answer, but stared before him still. Laurence approached more close, and the men pressed closer with him, ready to hear all, or to tear Athorpe away from Laurence if he sprang at him.

Laurence touched his arm.

"This is a misfortune, but one which you will overcome in time, Athorpe; you, strong and hale, and with good sense to back you. There, you have seen enough of this place—come away now, Captain, and forget it."

Athorpe looked at him at last, turned upon him as though he would strike him, and then paused, almost quailed, before the unflinching eyes that met his own.

"You ask what this is?" he said; "well, it's death. Death to peace and honour—and all your fault."

"Mine?"

" You should have let me die yesterday of my own free will, and all would have been well. You are the man that stopped me at the wheel? "

" Yes, thank Heaven ! "

" You were a meddling fool, as you always have been. I should have died, and known no shame—now, they'll hang me."

" They can't hang you for setting fire to a house," cried Churdock, over the heads of his contemporaries.

" I would not have had a stone of it standing," said Athorpe, with increased excitement, " though I was to be hanged a hundred times. It was a mockery in my sight, a home blasted by a weak and wicked woman—you know she's gone, Sir ? " suddenly catching hold of Laurence's arm.

" If it be true, I am very, very sorry."

" She's gone—and there's an end of her foulness and deceit. Better, after all, that it should end like this."

" Young Fyvie met her in the Cleft last night," cried Churdock, " and coaxed her to go away with him. May he die by inches for the trick—may ruin seize him and his from this day."

" Ay, ruin seize him and his ! " cried an old man, " that's justice."

" Ruin to him ! " echoed half a dozen voices, like a Greek chorus to this tragedy, and there were women's voices mingled with the malediction.

Laurence shuddered at the intensity of hate, at the ominous coincidence in this. For ruin was on its way towards the Fyvies, and he could almost believe that the curse would give it impetus from that hour.

" You will come away now, Athorpe? " asked Raxford, again.

" Yes ; I will walk steadily away to hell ! "

" No—no, you will not," said Laurence ; " you will sober down, and become resigned to this, Athorpe. You are not a child to fret at the first trial which God sends to your patience."

" I have done, Sir, I have finished my efforts to be good. He who stops my progress must be a brave man. I have to find your friend Jonathan Fyvie, and then—then you may guess the rest, for, by Heaven, it's not difficult of comprehension."

"Coom away ! " cried Churdoek.

"Where's Milly ? " he said, looking round suddenly ; "I mustn't leave her, to be led astray like other women. I must take her with me—I promised her that I would when Inez was gone."

"Milly's gone to London," said Churdoek, in his ear, "will you coom now ? "

"Is the fire out ? " asked Athorpe, wrenching himself away from the group, and taking his place opposite the ruin again ; "is the place gone from the face of the earth ? Yes, yes—I can't see a room of it—not the little room where she waited to kiss me coming home, and to hope I wasn't tired—where she sang to me, and lied about her comfort, when that wretch was lurking in the garden, like a wolf—not the room where we slept, and she looked like an angel in her sleep. Oh ! Inez ! Inez ! "

"Hold him ! " shouted Churdock, and a dozen arms were round the frantic man at once. Whether he would have given way as he had done yesterday, or have plunged at the ruins, as his mad impulse would have plunged at the mining-wheel, is uncertain, for Churdock allowed no time, fearing the worst himself. Athorpe was struggling with the hands that fastened on him, the crowd was swaying to and fro, the women's shrieks were adding to the tumult, when four policemen from Tavvydale, and parts adjacent —mustered in great force for so startling an occasion— appeared upon the scene.

"Mr. Athorpe, you are our prisoner upon a charge of arson," said the Tavvydale policeman, respectfully—for he had known Athorpe in his better days. "I hope that you will come quietly away with us ? "

A pause of the struggling mass ; Athorpe glaring at the representatives of the law, with brawny hands upon his arms still, holding him from mischief.

"You want me ? "

"Yes."

"It's his own hoose ; mayn't a man do what he likes with his own ? " called forth one.

"And it bean't insured for a farden," added Churdoek.

" I dare say it will be all right when it's inquired into," said the policeman ; " but we have our warrant to arrest him."

" I'll go," said Athorpe ; " I'll go with you gladly. I'm sick and tired of life, Sirs."

And, to the amazement of the rest, who anticipated another stormy scene, Captain Athorpe walked quietly away with the police, the tag-rag of town and country bringing up the rear. As they marched into Tavvydale, and the few stay-at-homes left in the place turned out to see the cortege, the parish engine started on its forlorn hope.

Laurence went back with the mob, left his address at the police-office—a cottage of weak materials, with a rusty birdcage kind of grating before a window in the roof—stated his wish to be of service to Captain Athorpe in any way that might be required, and then, with this new incident to add to his bewilderment, went back to those books of business life, to which stern duty bound him.

But, though he chained himself to the desk, he could not work. There are times when the hand and brain will rest, however grim the necessity which calls for immediate action.

.There had been two days of wild excitement, mystery and suspense; all whom he had known for good or evil seemed to have been shaken together, inextricably confused, and then spread out before him, like the broken pieces of a child's toy. He did not believe that night that peace and rest would ever come to him again ; for the felicity which had seemed almost within his grasp, had passed from his view into a darkness that no light could pierce. He had had hope till he was by himself, chained to his business, which was a curse and clog upon him—now he thought that the misconceptions and falsities, which had sundered him from Milly, would only gather force as he proceeded.

He tried to write to her, and failed in the clear explanation that was necessary, for he did not know what explanation was needed yet awhile. He spent an hour in searching for Mr. Whiteshell's address, which he had mislaid somewhere ; then, in the quiet of his room, late at night, he set to work, begging Milly to tell him how he had offended her, and writing carefully and laboriously at the story of his first engagement. He was explaining how it was impossible that he could leave the mine for a few days, yet awhile, and begging Milly to come back to him; he was urging her to come back, also, for her Uncle Athorpe's sake, when the handle of his door turned suddenly.

Laurence was a brave man, but he could not resist a start at this shock to his nerves. He had locked his door hours ago for good, and was writing far into the night, or early morning. Only a few minutes since he had paused to consider whether two or three had struck last by the gaunt old eight-day clock on the landing, and hoped that it was only two, for there was much work before him still, and he needed rest after it was finished. Then the stillness of the house had suggested itself for a fleeting instant before he bent over his desk again—and now the click of the lock seemed to snap at his heart-strings.

"I have overtasked myself after a day of excitement," he said, with a smile at his own nervousness; "it's all fancy, or Waters has forgotten a message for me. Who's there?"

There was no answer; but as he kept his eyes upon the door, he saw the handle turn again, and this time the door was pressed, silently, from without.

Laurence rose, and asked again who was there.

"It is I," whispered a harsh, guttural voice, that was new to him—the voice of a man whom he now could hear panting on the landing-place. "Let me in."

"How did you get here?—who are you?"

"I came in by the counting-house window, and up the stairs—are you afraid of me?"

"Are you Athorpe?" asked Laurence, guessing the truth at once.

"Yes—you may trust me."

Laurence had grave doubts as to the wisdom of his next step, but he unlocked the door and admitted Captain Athorpe, who advanced stealthily into the room, with the marks of the morning's fray still upon his face, and with the exception of a jacket too big for him cast round his shoulders, the same man whom he had left in the policeman's hands.

He looked round the room cautiously.

"I thought he might be in this place—hiding like a fox."

"Of whom are you speaking?"

"The man who has worked evil, and made a devil of me —Jonathan Fyvic."

"He is not here, Athorpe—I pledge my word."

"I know that now—I have been to every room of the place—how that Waters snores—like thunder ! "

"You have escaped from the lock-up ? "

"Yes—it was not wise to stop, I thought, so I tore out the grating, and slid down the thatch into the garden. This is Bully's jacket—he's a good fellow in his way. I wish Milly would marry him—that is, if she could really like the fellow. For if she can't, it's damnation ! "

Yes, he was mad—very mad, Laurence saw. Whether a madness that would last, or would pass away after the first pangs of his misery were over, it was impossible to guess.

"I think that I would go and find Bully," suggested Laurence ; "I will accompany you, if you like."

"And give me up to the first man that passed. Do you think I trust in anybody, or anything, after this ? "

He reflected for a moment, then said,

"I trust you, though—for you are a man that has an honest face. I took to your face," he added, sadly, " when I was a different man to what I am now—when she hadn't gone away ! "

"Trust me then in saying that you are best with some one to take care of you for awhile—if I were you, I would even go back to the place from which I escaped."

"I am going abroad—I've money left—seven hundred pounds."

"Let me be your banker."

"Oh ! no——" with a madman's cunning in his face, " I don't trust you so far as that. But I want to trust you with Milly. Failing to find the devil I came in search of, I thought that I would ask you—if I was never to be heard of again—to keep your promise to her, and take care of her, and always love the girl. For she is honest and true, and knows her Bible by heart."

"I will love Milly all my life, Athorpe. And now come with me."

"No. Keep back. I'm in a quiet mood now, but a straw upsets me, and it is wiser—safer—to leave me to myself. Raxford," with a hollow, unearthly laugh, " I've had another look at the wheel, but it frightens me in the moonlight."

" Ah !—give up such a foolish thought as that, friend."

" I give it up because I am afraid.   Is there any brandy in the house ? "

Laurence answered in the negative.

" I treated you more handsomely when you called upon me," he said, frowning, " but no matter.   You will see to Milly, like a man of honour—now, good-bye for ever, Sir ! "

He stretched forth his horny hand, and looked hard at Laurence, who noted that his lip quivered.   If he were to give way—break down like a child again, it might save him, thought Laurence ; but as he thought, the face hardened and darkened once more.

" I will go out by the window.   I am as agile as a cat to-night.   Don't move."

He pushed back the window—already left ajar by Laurence, clambered through it, and dropped to the ground easily enough."

" Take care of her—remember she hasn't a friend who can help her now,' he cried ; and then moved away, striding along the high-road at a great pace, full, evidently, of a new purpose, that had stolen to his unsettled brain.

Laurence thought that he had better follow him, lest harm should ensue, but when he was in the high-road, Captain Athorpe had struck away from it, over the cold dank moor, towards the hills, whose shadows shut him out from all men.

END OF BOOK THE SECOND.

BOOK III.

———

CHAPTER I.

IN SUSPENSE.

THE nine days' wonder of the fire at Captain Athorpe's —of Captain Athorpe's escape from prison and mysterious disappearance—of Captain Athorpe's wife's elopement with Jonathan Fyvie, which was a great scandal, that gossips grew fat upon—passed away at last, and there was peace in the villages by the Dartmoor Tors.

Laurence Raxford put up with the difficulties — the suspense—of his position, working hard for the benefit of the firm, and praying for the hours to lessen between the dispatch of his letter and the answer to be received from James Whiteshell, of Milk Street. "Telegraph to me if she be with you," he added, in a postscript, but no telegram had been forwarded to the offices of Wheal Desperation, and he must wait the slow, dragging hours before the truth was evident.

Many men have two lives, it is said, but to bear with two lives of suspense—one of business with the affairs of the counter out of gear, and another with the affairs of the heart in confusion, falls at the same time to the lot of few mortals. All Laurence's trouble had come at once, and it was to the credit of his character that he grew stronger in the conflict. He felt that it was his duty to keep strong, and hold a faith in better times, if possible ; and save that he smiled very seldom, and was graver in his looks and manners, he was the same Laurence Raxford whom his friends had known.

He was an unlucky man, but he did not repine at his misfortune, or dream of giving way to it. If he had accepted but a partnership in difficulties with Fyvie and Fyvie, still his father's friend had meant to make him rich, and he would be grateful for the intention, and work with all his strength for "the house." If Milly had distrusted him at once—turning away from him before he could offer one explanation of his conduct—he was sorry for the rashness that had separated her from him ; but his love was ardent and intense, and he began to hope again that all would be well when they met. In the midst of all this uncertainty enwrapping him, that belief was a satisfaction to him. He loved her with his whole heart—he knew now that he had never loved before—and he could not see the barrier strong enough to stand between him and the girl who had been made happy by the assurance of his passion.

A cruel suspense enough, but in the good time to be cleared away, after a few reproaches, that would be even sweet in their way, murmured by the lips of the loved one. That suspense increased when no letter was received in due course from James Whiteshell. The old man evidently resented Laurence's anxiety to see Milly ; probably believed in Milly's explanation of the cause of their disunion, possibly had not given to Milly that hurriedly-written confession, at which our hero had laboured on the night Athorpe stole into his house. Oh! for a day of rest apart from the accounts, thought Laurence, that he might face the mystery fairly, follow it step by step, and demand its solution from Milly or Hester Fyvie. He sat down to write a letter to Hester, and then the result of his epistolary correspondence of late days deterred him. Hester had spoken the truth, he was assured —but it had been a woman's version of the truth, coloured, perhaps, by her indignation at his second choice after she had dismissed him. Had he been a vain man, he might have thought that Hester had really loved him—though he would have known nothing of that letter of pardon which had been burked in transmission—and that she had made an effort to secure him again at the eleventh hour. But he gave Hester full credit for not loving him at all, and he could not see in the first woman whom he had asked to marry him, any meanness of disposition that would stab in the dark at his peace. On the contrary, she was a proud,

20

high-spirited girl, and would have done him justice at all hazards.

The whole error had arisen by his silence, for her sake and her father's, and it was a pity that his heroine—his Milly—should have resented his want of confidence by a rash separation. Truly, she was more high-spirited and impulsive than Hester Fyvie, he thought—more cruel in her judgment of him even, and more unforgiving, he confessed, as the days went on and brought no tidings of her—it was his fate to meet strange women in his pilgrimage! But he did not resent Milly's want of faith in him—if he was grieved at her precipitate conduct, still he yearned with his whole soul to forgive her, and to be forgiven—he could not give *her* up, or tell her that he would allow her seven days to confess that she had acted unfairly towards him. For her confession he would have waited half a life-time, he thought —and all around him was stale and unprofitable without her.

Though he did his work well at the books; expedited the actions of the men, sinking fathoms deeper into the earth in search of a fresh lode—and upon the result of that lode depended the future fortunes of the proprietors—swerved not an instant from the manifold tasks which devolved suddenly upon him, still Milly was foremost in his thoughts, and no business application could set her from him. "When I get free of this—when it is honourable in me to step from this post in search of her, I will crush down all opposition that keeps her from my arms." He said this, or something like this, twenty times a day, and he set his shoulder to the wheel more sturdily, hoping for the best in the brighter days ahead of him.

He had a coadjutor suddenly appear at his side, to work with him night and day, knowing as little rest as he. This was the senior partner—the man who had built on making him his son. He came and took his place at the desk, with a business-like face; and he seemed to have shaken off—as though by a strong will, which had power to throw off physical weakness—the signs of the old age that had come to him.

Laurence had protested, but Mr. Fyvie had overruled all argument.

"When there was no occasion to work hard, I took my

case, Laurence," he said; "but with a wife and daughter to
support, I come back to my post, to do my share of work
with the rest. You will find me very punctual, and very
useful still."

And Laurence did so, though it grieved him to see the old
warrior donning again his suit of mail for the battle of life.
He feared that it was a false strength, which would have its
reaction when the victory was gained, or the worst was
known. It was the resolute will which had worked at the
mine in the old days, and in the face of despair—the will
which would fight on till the last. Mr. Fyvie was as early
at his post as Laurence—he left off at as late an hour.
When Laurence feigned fatigue, in order to lessen the
labours of his partner, that partner, in the room he had
chosen for himself at the office, would be poring over the
lists of his son's creditors—the letters from them which
flowed in with every mail—the letters from his son,
even, which Laurence knew that he received, although he
spoke not of them to our hero; until one day—three
weeks after the fire at Wind-Whistle Cleft—when he said to
Laurence,

"Jonathan is very penitent, but very wild in his penitence.
But I think that he is more sorry for the ruin that over-
shadows me, than for the ruin that stares him in the face.
It is late in the day to think of the father; but, Laurence,"
crumpling the letter in his hand, "it is better late than never.
And I'm glad."

"Where is he, Sir?"

"He is abroad—in Rome, now."

"With poor Athorpe's wife?"

"God knows," said Mr. Fyvie, sadly; "it is more than
possible. He has scathed many lives in his career, and one
more or less matters not to him. And I tried, Laurence, to
make a man of him—in all my life, I never crossed his
wishes!"

"And that was his destruction."

"Ah! you reproach me."

"Pardon me, Sir—I have no right to do that. He was
your only son, and you loved him well, and made a favourite
of him, acting for the best in your own judgment."

"Yes, yes; I did my best, and I failed to make him good,
and honourable, and true. And I was to blame when he

20—2

first went wrong. I was too easy with him, and too hope-ful of him. He resigns every claim upon the estate; he gives up the partnership; he leaves it in our hands to dis-pose of him and his effects, his chances—just as we consider best for our interests. Laurence, will you, a partner too, forgive an old man's pride, that has helped on this ship-wreck?"

"Helped it on, Sir?" repeated Laurence.

"Yes," he said, sinking his voice, "there were debts of honour—gambling and racing debts—which the law would not have recognised; and I paid them out of my own estate, and then out of ours—wiped them all off, and left his name free. We stand to pay the last farthing that is owing in our name, or in his, and we have nearly succeeded."

"So far as I am concerned, Mr. Fyvie, it matters little, for my position is not greatly affected, and I brought only my wish to be of service to you into the partnership; but had you a right to think of these debts of honour—debts due to men who are sharpers, and live by dupes like Jona-than—before the interests of your wife and daughter?"

"I consulted first my wife and daughter—I have not left them in the dark. It was Hester's wish, and Mrs. Fyvie's—they are both prouder than I am."

"You have all acted too generously, perhaps."

"I kept the word of my son, as well as my own—and a promise, if even made to a thief, is none the less a promise binding to an honest man. I do not beggar my wife; she has a little property that is strictly her own; and when I am gone—thank God!—neither she nor Hester can starve. As for me, why, if the worst comes to the worst, you know that I can do a good day's work yet."

"I hope the necessity will never arise for that, Sir."

"It is as well to hope for the best," he said, drily.

He was turning away, when a new thought struck him.

"Have you told your mother anything of this?"

"Not yet, Sir."

"I think that I would begin to prepare her by degrees. A sudden shock might be serious to her, and she is a mother whose heart is full of rejoicing at her son's prosperity."

"I would leave her at rest, Sir. I have not distressed her yet awhile with the story of my unlucky engagement to your daughter, and how it has ended."

" Why not ? " he asked, eagerly.

" Because a little excites her, and renders her despondent, and she has built upon this marriage."

" Perhaps you thought that, some day, it might come——"

" No, no, Sir, I am engaged to marry Milly Athorpe."

" Ah ! I had forgotten."

" I fancied that long ago I should have been in London, to detail all the particulars to my mother ; but events have transpired to balk me, and I have no faith in sending consolation by post."

" Well, you know best your own business," said the other. " Shall we reckon up how we stand with the smelting-houses ? "

" I think that it may be as well."

" And we will go on with the balance-sheet afterwards—that clear statement of affairs which, as gentlemen, we shall have to submit to all those who have had dealings with us."

" We *may* have to submit," corrected Laurence.

" Ah ! don't buoy me up with a fallacy, Laurence," he said. " I have strength, and to spare, and, shoulder to shoulder together, I think that we can stand the first shock of the storm. If I could only be as sure of you as I was once, —sure that you would be my son, to take poor Jonathan's place, and shield Hester in her coming loneliness. Only to be sure of that ! "

Laurence did not answer—it was beyond his power. He was to be the husband of Milly Athorpe, and he could not promise to return to his old position, any more than he could confess that it was gratitude alone that had originated the engagement. Mr. Fyvie turned away with a sigh, and very shortly afterwards the old and the young man were fathoms deep in figures.

Mr. Waters and the clerks in the office watched them with some interest. They scented the coming troubles, and were not at a loss to account for them. They knew that Tavvy-dale House was for sale, by private contract, and the sudden and constant presence of that gaunt old man at the mines told its own tale too well, despite the every-day manner with which Mr. Fyvie masked his anxiety. But, for a wonder, they were men to be trusted, and they held their peace, and worked with the rest, hoping for that change for the better which a few weeks might bring to them all. They could scarcely realise the ruin of the mining proprietors—the sudden collapse of a splendid fortune—and they believed that the whole affair would right itself. Believing that, they were wise or generous enough to hold their peace, and let things take their course without undue interference. And the men, women and children on the estate, took their Saturday wages regularly, and thought as much of the judgment as of Fyvie's mine coming to ruin.

A few hasty tongues had wished ruin to the Fyvies on the day that Athorpe set fire to his house; but the wish had been forgotten even by the denunciators, and it only rang like a knell, at times, in the ears of Laurence Raxford. In the outer world, far away from Tavvydale, some inklings of the truth were in circulation, and it was noticed that claims upon the estate came in with more rapidity than usual, and that creditors were anxious for settlements of accounts, and pleaded being pushed themselves. But in Tavvydale, in Tavistock, and round about the Dartmoor Hills, there was the security born of perfect ignorance.

Laurence was still working at the books one afternoon, when a message was brought in that a gentleman desired a few minutes' conference with him. Accompanying the message was the card of him who had solicited the interview —Mr. James Whiteshell.

Laurence flung down his pen, and rose with excitement at this break upon the monotony of business-work. Mr. Fyvie, working in the same room with him, surveyed him with amazement.

"I have been very unhappy at heart, Sir, concerning Milly's disappearance," Laurence explained; "and this man —Milly's uncle by her mother's side—brings me news at last. You will excuse me for half an hour?"

"Certainly. The worst of the work is over, Laurence— and half an hour, half a day, is not of any consequence now. I feel strong enough, boy, to do the rest myself."

"I will take Mr. Whiteshell to my own room."

"If you please. I daresay that I should be in the way here. And—oh! Laurence!"

"Sir."

Laurence paused at the door, and the grey eyes of his friend looked almost beseechingly at him over the books.

"Don't make any rash promise—be sure of the reasons for the disappearance of this village beauty—and—and so on, you know."

He stammered and blushed beneath Laurence's fierce stare at him; and, conscious that he had betrayed his anxiety too much, Mr. Fyvie ducked his head behind the accounts again.

"If this foolish romance—this out-of-the-way folly—were only dissipated," he murmured, as Laurence closed the door, and went up stairs to his room, where Mr. James Whiteshell had been already conducted.

The little man, very pale and nervous, clad in the old shabby suit of black that he had been seen in last—rose with a stiff bow, as Laurence entered, and closed the door behind him.

"You bring me news—good news—you will tell me that at once?" said Laurence, not heeding in his excitement the frigid demeanour of the dancing-master.

"Sir, I bring you no news at all."

"You refuse, then——"

"Mr. Raxford, whether I have a right to refuse or not, I might take into consideration if I were possessed of news, but being left completely in the dark by all of you, I have nothing to communicate."

"You received my letter?"

"Yes, Sir."

"And gave the one enclosed to Milly?"

"I have not seen Milly since I was last in Devonshire."

"Not seen her!—*you* have not seen her?" cried Laurence; "you tell me this?"

"Yes, Sir; and as James Whiteshell never tells an untruth, I will beg of your politeness to believe him."

"You have heard from her?—you know where she is? All this is an evasion."

"When I last heard from Milly, she was very proud of the new post of schoolmistress that had been offered her. That was the last sign from her, Sir, made to her old uncle, and I believed her at peace until your letter reached me."

"Why did you not answer *that?*" said Laurence; "could you not see that I was dying of suspense, and that it was your duty—that it was common charity—to have mercy on me?"

"Mr. Raxford, I am a cautious man," replied Mr. Whiteshell, loftily ; "there had been a sudden disappearance of Milly—you write to me like a demented lover, and I left her last your servant on the mines—you enclose a letter for her, believing her with me—she has evidently been afraid of you, or your intentions, and been anxious to escape—it was necessary that I should exercise great caution in this matter."

"You might have trusted me," said Laurence, moodily.

"I had faith in you, Mr. Raxford—before I left here, I esteemed you more highly than any man whom I had ever met. I think I told you so. But," he added, very sadly, "I am an old man, who has mixed a great deal with the world, and seen great deception practised in it—and when your letter came, and I learned that Milly had fled away from you, I thought that I might, after all, have been deceived again. In the hope—and it is a faint hope even now —that you can redeem your character in my eyes by explaining the relationship existing between my niece and you, I have come back to Devonshire. In the greater hope, too, of finding a clue to Milly."

"Mr. Whiteshell, in the first place, I love your niece," said Laurence; "there is no disguise concerning it. I am engaged to her."

"You a gentleman?" said he. "Well, well, gentlemen have married poor girls before this, but never with so much excuse for them. For—God bless her !—there never was a better, purer, or more lovable girl. I—I don't know that I am very much surprised, although you or she might have written to tell me all about it. Well?"

"And then, when we were all in all to each other, thinking of the time when we should be married—when she trusted me, and loved me most—she disappeared. That is the story."

"I don't think that she would go away without a reason— that's not very probable."

"Miss Fyvie, a lady to whom I had been engaged once, and who broke off that engagement at her own wish, saw her the night before."

"Ah! I see now," said Whiteshell; "and of course she tells all manner of lies, and Milly, hasty in her movements, is too ready to believe her, and away she flies ; but," with a half groan, "where can she have flown to ?"

" I cannot guess."

" She has not a friend in London, save myself," said Whiteshell. " Oh ! Sir, I hope that you are telling me all the truth, for this is becoming very serious to me."

" And to me," said Laurence, very pale now, " for I see no light before me. Mr. Whiteshell, if you only knew how I love her—how acutely I have felt this want of trust in me, and this readiness to believe that I am untruthful and deceptive ! "

" Did she go away without a word—a line ? "

" No—she wrote to me."

" I should like to see that letter."

It was ready to Laurence's hand—it was the first thing in that private desk—it had been Laurence's study in the night, when the long day's business was over. Laurence placed the letter in the hands of Mr. Whiteshell, who, after some preparation with his glasses, read the contents attentively.

" You have seen Miss Fyvie, of course ? "

" Not yet. Miss Fyvie is in London, and I am chained to business here."

" It is necessary—very necessary—that you should see her."

" Yes," said Laurence, gloomily ; " but she cannot bring me back Milly, or point out the way by which I can find her."

" It is very strange," mused Mr. Whiteshell, " for I do not see a reason for Milly hiding away from all her friends like this—it is not right of her. There is your letter from Milly," he said, returning that document, " and there, Sir, is your letter to Milly, which you enclosed to me. You will find that I have not tampered with the seal."

Laurence took the letters, and then looked hard at the old man.

" You are offended with me ?—you doubt me ? "

" No, I don't," replied Mr. Whiteshell, after a moment's consideration of their relative positions—" there, I don't, Sir. I think that you have told me all, but not all that has led Milly to conceal herself, for you are in the dark as well as myself concerning that. It is not possible, I suppose, that any wretch about here has run away with her ? "

" Great Heavens, Sir, no ! "

" I never liked this place, you are aware—a gloomy, cut-throat locality, where there is no protection for well-disposed beings, and where evil might sweep down upon the inno-cent, and nobody the wiser. You know what has happened to poor Athorpe ? "

" Yes."

" And poor Inez—Athorpe's wife ? I learned the news to-day in Tavvydale. If I had only spoken when I was here last—spoken with my usual kindness and gentleness to Athorpe, putting him on guard," he said, with his cha-racteristic conceit evincing itself for the first time; "if I had persuaded Inez to tell her husband the whole story, instead of promising to keep her secret, what a deal of harm might have been averted from them all ! "

" You knew the baseness of Jonathan Fyvie's character, then ? "

" Yes—his baseness, or his base weakness—I knew all that."

" And kept silent ? "

" For Inez's sake—for the sake of peace."

" You will not keep silent for Milly's sake even, when Milly comes to you," said Laurence, turning again to the one subject from which he could not distract himself—"you will write, telling me that she is with you ? "

" I will hear her story ; she will not prevaricate or ex-aggerate—she will tell me all the truth."

" All the truth she cannot know, Sir, or she would not have left me thus," said Laurence : "there must come a time when I can explain in my turn."

" You have explained all to me, then ? " Whiteshell asked, almost doubtfully again.

" Every word. Ah ! you distrust me, and will set Milly against me."

" No—I believe you. There, your pardon, Mr. Raxford, but I *have* found it a deceitful world ; there appears so much mystery in it, and beneath the mystery so much evil, that I can't hold fast to my faith in human nature. When I have found Milly I shall be myself again."

He rose, shook hands feebly with our hero, and prepared to depart.

" It will all be right in good time, I dare say. If there be no foul play anywhere—and I'll not think of that—we shall hear of Milly soon, and she will explain, to every-body's satisfaction, the reason for her disappearance from us. Till then, Sir, good-day."

"You return to London at once?"

"To-morrow. To-day I shall spend in Tavvydale, and in that horrible Cleft, making every inquiry."

"You will be careful in your inquiries," suggested Laurence suddenly, "for there is a world of tattlers in Tavvydale."

"To be sure," said Mr. Whiteshell in dismay, "and the fools will make a story about her next, and invent their own reasons for her absence and my anxiety. Won't it—won't it look strange—if I am seen in Tavvydale, after Milly has told her friends that she was going to London? For the dear girl's sake, I must be very careful."

"And you will write to me, whenever you see or hear from her?"

"Yes—unless——"

The bewildered old man again paused, and turned his vacillating face towards our hero.

"Unless," repeated Laurence.

"Unless I find you very false—which I pray I may not, Sir, with all my heart."

"You will write to me, Mr. Whiteshell."

"Yes, yes. I think that I shall have good news to send you presently."

But he went away sadly and disconsolately, as though the hope to which he had given voice had found no echo in his heart.

CHAPTER II.

IN THE CLEFT AGAIN.

Mr. Whiteshell went towards Tavvydale at a pace that increased in progression with the thoughts which spurred him on. He had dined early that day, and now the day was before him to make all the inquiries concerning his niece which he thought necessary. In those inquiries he would be very careful for Milly's sake, but he could not rest idle, whilst her absence from all friends was unaccounted for. He could but connect her disappearance with some accident that had befallen her—it was so unlike her considerate self to keep all friends in suspense, that he was certain Milly Athorpe was in danger.

He was not known in Tavvydale, he believed, therefore he could make a few inquiries with impunity. He repaired at once, as Laurence had done, to the dissenting minister's, trusting that that latter gentleman would not recognise the likeness between him and his niece—a likeness that no one had ever seen save Mr. Whiteshell himself. Mr Wells was not ready with his inquiries; on the contrary, he was disposed to be sulky, and to snub the old dancing-master for his trouble. Milly's sudden departure had not been forgiven yet by the minister, whom she had not consulted in the matter, and who, we may confess now, really had had a *penchant* for Milly, and a secret wish to make her his wife, and constitute her a second mother to his numerous progeny.

He could not furnish the inquirer with the address of Miss Athorpe; he only knew that she had gone to London, and he supposed that she would return when her month's holiday had expired, and she had thoroughly enjoyed herself, and——Good-evening.

Mr. Wells, who had opened his own street door—being a man of humble ideas, and one servant, who always waited to hear if her master was likely to respond to the knocks, before she stirred from her seat in the kitchen—shut it rather quickly in the face of his visitor, and went back to the composition of his sermon.

James Whiteshell took off his hat to the closed door, either in irony or from his old habit of politeness, and went in search of the schoolmistress in charge, from whom he learned no more than he was already aware.

"I—I hope nothing fresh has happened?" this lady ventured to say, after one glance into the sad face of the inquirer.

"Oh! no—nothing at all, Madam," replied Whiteshell, remembering our hero's caution; "but I thought that I would call and see Miss Athorpe. Gone to London, eh? and left no address. Good-evening, Madam."

He went away out of the village at once, and found himself half an hour afterwards staring at the ruins of Captain Athorpe's cottage. Here he sat down for a while, wiped his hot forehead and face with his handkerchief, and thought of Inez, and her flight from home—her temptation, stretching over many years, and ending at last, after a hard fight, in ruin.

"Poor woman!—always so childlike, thoughtless, and vain ; and yet trying so hard to do good. Why didn't the story end better than this ? "

He rose at last, and went down the Cleft in sheer absence of mind, fancying, in his abstraction, that he was staying at Milly's cottage, and going home to Milly. It was not till the duskiness of a premature night met him under the trees, that he recovered himself, and remembered that he was lodging at the smallest and most uncomfortable inn in Tavvydale. He was a nervous man, the reader is aware, and he looked round him somewhat scared at last.

It was a place that had always been full of mystery, he thought ; and crime and violence—the crime of a wife's flight, and the violence that had demolished the home from which she had fled—had now rendered the place absolutely hateful.

What did he want there now ?—groping in the darkness that had not stolen yet to brighter and more hallowed spots.

He shivered a little; then buttoned his old black dress coat to the chin, and stood reflecting on his next step. The Cleft was deserving of its odd cognomen that night, for the wind was whistling low and plaintively through the branches of the trees.

"I'll go on to the cottage, and see the place," he said to himself ; "I don't suppose that I shall ever see it again. I've been very much at home there in my time, and in my way, and I can't go without a look at it. There's nothing to be afraid of, for it's not worth anybody's while to hurt me."

Thus adjured, the old man went on, increasing his pace when the footpath wound its way amongst the darkest portions of the Cleft, and skipping lightly over every obstacle. When he reached the open ground, he found that it was not quite dark, even yet, for half way up the slope he could see the cottage that Milly had inhabited.

"It looks the same as ever—it's like the peaceful times

again," he said. "Now, to find Milly at her books, with those beautiful big eyes of hers, bent upon the wonders which she always found in print. If the last month was only a dream!"

He paused at the door, and knocked as though he expected that Milly's voice would call to him to come in; then he tried the door, and to his astonishment found it unfastened.

"She wasn't afraid of having the place stripped before she went away," he muttered; "but she never believed in thieves in Devonshire. Well, after all, there wasn't much to take."

He pushed the door back and looked in. It was dark within there; but he did not seem afraid to venture into the old home—the associations that were connected with it allayed his natural timidity.

"I'll look about me now I am here," were his next words; "after all, there may be a clue to Milly's flitting. She stepped from here into cloudland, and she may have left a clue to her whereabouts behind her. Now, if I could find that box of German lights which she always kept upon the mantelpiece! If nobody has been here since Milly went away, it will be at the corner behind the china shepherdess."

He crossed the room, stumbling against a chair in the way as he did so, stood on tiptoe to reach the high mantelpiece, swept off the china shepherdess with his nervous hand to the ground, where it split into fifty fragments at his feet, and found the little box of German lucifers where he had seen it last.

"Just like home still. All the same, and yet all so different!"

He struck a light, and looked round him for a candle, which he failed to find, whilst the thin slip of wood burned away in his hand. He walked about the room, striking his lucifers, and peering vainly for something to ignite by them. He passed into the inner room, and began lighting up again —this time discerning a chamber candlestick, with a wick still left therein, on the broad sill of the lattice window near the bed.

"Poor Milly!—here she waited till the morning before she went away from him who she thought had deceived her," he murmured ; " here I could swear—just here—she knelt and prayed for him—for me—for all whom she could think of, before she went away heart-broken. I see it all—I see it all plainly enough !"

He lighted the candle-wick with difficulty, and then set it down to sputter for awhile, and struggle for a few minutes of light before it died of inanition.

" And here I'll pray for her to come back, and clear up the mystery around us. Nobody prays ever in vain—Milly used to say—and I was a cynic who used to satirise her faith—a wicked old humbug that I was, for the tears were in my eyes all the time that I laughed at her."

Then this simple old man knelt down and prayed for his niece, rising at last, and rubbing at his knees, as though praying had not been a constant habit lately.

" Why, I fancy that I can hear the rustle of her dress already," he said, taking up the candlestick ; " and it's only those wretched noisy leaves behind the window there."

He passed into the sitting-room, shading the dying flame from the draught, and then paused, struggled for his breath, and tried to gasp forth a name.

For Milly—or something like Milly—was standing in the shadow of the room, with a shawl draped above her head, and her face—colourless as death—peering from its folds. The noise of Whiteshell's approach had held her spellbound, perhaps, for it was a face of fear that met her uncle's.

" Mil—Milly," he said at last, " it is you, then—say, for God's sake, that it is you !"

" Yes—it is I."

" You have come back, then, as from the grave."

" From the grave, where I should have been more happy —more at rest and at peace, uncle."

" I have seen Laurence—he has told me——"

" Ah ! no matter—some other time for that, when I have less upon my mind—not now. Why, uncle," with a faint and weary smile, " I have almost forgotten *him !* "

She dropped into the chair by the table, and covered her face with her hands, to cry silently and softly to herself. As James Whiteshell bent over her, to assure her of his love, his friendship and support, the light that he held above her head went out, and it seemed as if a darker, denser mystery had followed swiftly on their meeting there.

CHAPTER III.

THE CREDITORS FACE THE ACCOUNTS.

WHEN one waits patiently for failure, failure generally arrives. He is pretty sure of the *dénouement* who builds not on one hope of success.

Mr. Fyvie had been only anxious to put his house in order, to show a fair set of account-books, a business well conducted to the end, and a true and strict register of honourable dealings, from the opening of Wheal Desperation to its close. That being done, and he being able to retire with honour from the scene, he was prepared to ring in his creditors, and face them with an unblushing front. He had done his best, and they who knew him best would believe in his assertion. They would believe him more readily, as he was about to pay every farthing that he owed them, as the transfer of the mine to his creditors would enable him to pay every farthing, and leave him, as the phrase runs, with scarcely a shilling to bless himself. There had been one faint hope that, sinking deeper into the bowels of the earth, they would light upon fresh and richer metal ; but the best metal had been near the surface in Wheal Desperation, and the last shaft had but only added to the working expenses.

So a circular was despatched to all friends, and the "ringing in," to which allusion has been made, took place in the large coffee-room of a principal hotel at Plymouth.

This a week after James Whiteshell had called on Laurence Raxford, who was left to wonder whether the old man was still in ignorance, or was keeping the silence with which he had threatened him. All was guess-work, for the old man had not been seen again in the neighbourhood of the mine.

Now the climax was reached, and after the day of meeting, Laurence would be free to act for himself—to search for himself, and to hunt down the mystery that had rendered him unhappy. Had it not been for old Mr. Fyvie, he would have been glad even of the complete ruin of the business hopes that he had had once, for he would be his own master from to-morrow. Under any circumstances it was satisfactory to think that his freedom was close at hand—that having done his duty, and sacrificed much for duty, he could, with a clear conscience, think for himself next day. It would have been a matter for exultation if he could have rescued the ship from the wreck, steered it into deep water, and resigned the partnership for good, but to run it upon the shore, and escape with all hands, but with all honour, was, to him, at any rate, a relief. He scarcely knew how passionately he had loved Milly Athorpe, until this trouble, apart from hers, had stood in his way like a rock.

The meeting was called at Plymouth, where some of the leading creditors resided; and the meeting was small enough, not a dozen creditors, on the whole, but that dozen representing a colossal claim upon the estate. Every one knew that it had been Mr. Jonathan Fyvie's past extravagance that had brought the old man to ruin—and there was no occasion for the senior partner to offer any explanation as to the causes which had thus reduced him. There had been many cheques drawn by Jonathan Fyvie junior in the name of the firm, that had not been applied to the purposes for which the money lay at the bankers—the son had freely made use of the common purse for his own purposes, and had it been the purse of Fortunatus he must have emptied it. He had not acted dishonestly, according to the law of partnership, as it existed at the time—he had not even acted with a dishonest intention in his heart; but he had gone on with a recklessness that was the recklessness of despair, or with a faith in the resources of the estate that was the faith of a fool.

Still, had he been a wit less extravagant, the property would have been saved to the Fyvies—perhaps to the third and fourth generation—for at the last they had escaped prosperity by a hair's breadth.

Thoughts like these—and more thoughts than these—passed through the minds of the creditors, as Mr. Fyvie stood with his back towards the bay-window, behind which shimmered the blue sea in the light of the afternoon sun. Near to him—facing him as one of the principal creditors—Laurence was surprised to see Mr. Engleton, looking more wiry-haired and sallow in his new energy. He had been beating

21

up the manufacturing firms for a new philanthropic subject, had met with a good business man, and drifted into commerce as a sleeping partner—turning up as a Co., even to the surprise of Mr. Fyvie, who had neither seen nor heard of the gentleman since he had been a guest at Tavvydale House.

Mr. Fyvie, senior, had not a long speech to make. There were the books and the accounts to compare with the balance-sheet that had been forwarded to them last week—— there was Wheal Desperation at their service, and they would find their money, and good interest for their money, therein. There was himself, he added, with a slight French shrug of his shoulders.

"And where is your son, Mr. Fyvie?" asked one irascible gentleman—the only man who looked sourly at all these proceedings; "his signature is required to half-a-dozen documents before the mine can be formally made over to the creditors."

"He will be here," said Mr. Fyvie.

Laurence was astonished at this firm assertion; he had not expected that Jonathan would enter upon the scene again, and he had fancied that the matter would be arranged without his presence there.

"I don't believe that he will come," was the flat assertion made in this place.

"With all his faults, he has a habit of keeping his word," said Mr. Fyvie, drily; "perhaps that was the only good thing I taught him."

He gave a little sigh at this, and then coughed violently to smother it, fidgeting about with the papers heaped on the table.

Business matters in a novel are best kept out of sight, or passed over as rapidly as possible, if they form part of the machinery of action; the fair reader will be glad to hear that we are going to leave these creditors, and these solicitors who represent the creditors and the partners in the firm, to worry and tease over the agreements and other documents with which the room was full.

Mr. Engleton was the busiest man in the community, but gave the most trouble, as he referred but seldom to the solicitors, and kept starting the strangest ideas for the arrangement of affairs, after everything had been almost decided. At the very end of the discussion, he took Laurence confidentially aside, saying,

"Can I speak a word or two to you, Mr. Raxford?"

"Certainly."

"All this has made a very deep impression upon me," he said very rapidly; "I wouldn't have gone into commerce at all, if I had had an idea—the least idea—that I should have come into collision with my old friends. Won't they sink these debts for a little while, and let you begin again, and wipe the lot off by degrees?"

"I am afraid not," said Laurence, shaking his head; "the mine must be your security—must, in fact, be transferred to yourselves."

"Well, we will not let you starve, if we can help it. This is not bankruptcy, but an honourable break-down. That son was an infernal scamp and profligate, I am afraid. He'll never face us."

"I fear not," said Laurence.

"A daughter like an angel, and a son like a devil, and both of one family—how do you account for that?"

"I have not attempted to account for it."

"I shall start—put into working order—as soon as possible, an institution for honourable but decayed merchants. A first-class affair, where every man, *sans reproche*, shall have a thousand a year at least, so that no sudden drops to indigence can possibly occur. Don't you think that this is a very good idea?"

"I am afraid that it is not practicable."

"We'll see about that," said Engleton, with a knowing nod of his head towards our hero; "I don't sleep over my ideas—and you'll see."

Laurence saw that it came to nothing in due course, which was not the prospect *in futuro* to which Mr. Engleton had wished to draw his attention.

"Then it is settled that we take the mine for the debt," said a creditor.

"Yes—certainly," cried Engleton, "and a very good take, too. If it is not better than taking our money, I'm a Dutchman."

"And we purpose to allow two hundred and fifty pounds a year to the late proprietors."

"Yes."

2—21

" I think that we can venture to make it two hundred and fifty pounds a year each," cried Engleton ; " I mean for these two, of course—not that other one."

" Really, Mr. Engleton, I wish you would consider the feelings of the creditors more," cried the angry little man ; " if you can afford it, we can't. Mr. Fyvie has suggested this himself, and I dare say that he has done the best for himself that he could. Everybody does."

" I have not the pleasure of your acquaintance," said Mr. Fyvie, looking at him through his eye-glass very sternly ; " this is the first time that we have met, I think."

" The first time, Sir."

" Had you met me twenty years ago under similar circumstances, and hazarded the same comment, I should have opened this window and dropped you into the sea."

" Good God, Sir ! "

" As it is, I must ask my young friend Mr. Raxford to do me that invaluable service," exclaimed Mr. Fyvie.

As the junior partner was looking at him as sternly as the senior, the abashed creditor said hastily,

" I am sorry to have hurt any one's feelings—I spoke in the heat of the moment, I assure you. The accounts are very fair and square, and all that. Nothing can be fairer and squarer, Sir."

" Very good—we will dismiss the subject and accept your apology," said the debtor with becoming dignity. " I set down two hundred and fifty pounds a year, and my partner and I will not accept a farthing more until you have cleared off the debt, with compound interest. But all this is arranged."

" It is arranged that you should receive that amount, Sir," said one of the legal gentlemen, bending across the table towards Mr. Fyvie.

" That we should—Mr. Raxford and I."

" But Mr. Raxford told us——"

" That as he brought not one penny into the firm, so he will not receive one penny from it, Sir," interrupted Laurence ; " that," he added very firmly and defiantly, " *is* arranged, and no one can shake my will concerning it."

" Laurence, my wife has two hundred a year in her own right," whispered Mr. Fyvie, at whose side he was now.

"Don't vex me, Sir. I am young and strong, and the whole world is before me to make my fortune in."

"But——"

"Mr. Fyvie, I have sworn this," said Laurence, "and it must be."

"Well—well—it is generous. But we will talk of this another time."

Mr. Fyvie, who had kept firm throughout, winced a little at his partner's stronger will, fidgeted with the papers again, and finally drew forth his watch.

The action attracted attention, and he noticed it.

"Jonathan is not behind time, gentlemen—he said between four and five, and it now wants twenty minutes to the latter hour. You may rely upon him."

"If he should disappoint you, Sir," whispered Laurence, "he so thoughtless, and so little regardful of the wishes of others."

"Yes—but I told him that I had given my word—pledged *my* good faith that he should be present. And that boy was prouder of my honour than his own."

"A strange man. A stranger man still if he appear."

"You will not greet him as a friend?"

"No, Sir—I cannot."

"Because he has ruined you?"

"No—but because he has brought ruin to a home where there would have been peace without him."

"You don't know a great deal of the world, or you would look over that," said Mr. Fyvie coolly.

But Laurence's words appeared to suggest a new thought to the old man, for when the creditors were gathered in one group at the end of the room, and Mr. Engleton was gesticulating in their midst in a most excited manner, Mr. Fyvie's voice commanded silence and attention.

"Gentlemen, I have only to say that this is a business meeting, and that I hope you will not allude to private and personal matters when my son appears. I don't know," he added, repressing an expression of grief, which stole to his face despite him, "whether it will pain him or not, but—it will me."

"Mr. Fyvie," said Engleton, "we are friends of yours still, we trust. More, we are business men, and have met here

solely for business purposes. Mr. Raxford," turning to our
hero, "it has been suggested——"

"By yourself," said one creditor, more conscientious than
the rest.

"Was it ?—thank you—I had forgotten," said Engleton ;
"it has been suggested by myself—now. I think of it, I was
going to say so—and approved by the rest of the community,
that you should accept office under us as chief manager at
Wheal Desperation. You are from the Royal School of
Mines, with the best of characters," he said, affecting to
treat the matter lightly, " we can see that you have been of
immense service to the Messrs. Fyvie ; we know that you
are acquainted with the workings of the mine, and the men
who work it, and, assured that we can trust you with our interests as with your own, we beg that you will accept the
post we offer you."

Laurence recoiled from it, as though a bowl of poison had
been offered him.

"I am going away from Devonshire ; I am anxious—very
anxious—to be free."

"The salary we have fixed upon, by way of a commencement——"

"Sir—you must leave me free for a while," interrupted
Laurence, with almost passionate haste ; "in Wheal Desperation I have known nothing but misery yet, and I would be
quit of it ! "

"But a month hence—when the excitement of all this
is over, and you have sobered down again, urged Engleton, "you may think of this ?"

"Then there will be time enough to speak of it," said
Laurence, fretfully. "You are very kind, gentlemen, and I
thank you," he added, becoming aware of his own ungraciousness ; "but you cannot imagine how anxious I am to be
my own master for a while."

"Oh ! yes, I can," said Engleton ; "I think that sticking
to one shop, or one idea, is dreadful work, and softens the
brain. We will not speak of this again for a month ;
meanwhile, there is much to do, and I have a plan
of my own as to the working of the mine to submit
to you."

The gentlemen whom he addressed, and who were looking
disconsolate at Laurence's refusal of their offer—although a

few of them had objected to that offer in the first instance—made a wry face or two at this.

"Five minutes to five," said the solicitor for the creditors ; "I am afraid that it does not matter much about your plans and offers now—and that we shall have to hold another meeting to consider how——"

"Mr. Jonathan Fyvie," announced a waiter at the door, and the tall figure of the man for whom all had anxiously waited, came into the room.

"I am thankful," murmured the father.

CHAPTER IV.

THE MAN WHO KEPT HIS WORD.

JONATHAN FYVIE looked taller than ever as he came into the room, for he was thinner, and more gaunt and angular. He was well dressed—even carefully dressed, as a man should be who is about to face men ready to pick holes in his coat ; but there was, despite that, an utter carelessness of walk and look and manner that struck Laurence as he bowed slightly to the people looking at him, before dropping into the seat which a hand more friendly than the rest had placed for him.

It had been a task almost beyond his strength to come there ; for he was a man that disliked facing his responsibilities, and had never cared for the society of crowds about him—and a crowd of creditors is never pleasant company. He had been walking the streets of Plymouth, and prowling round the hotel till the last moment, before he had summoned the courage to enter the room ; but there he was at last, a haggard, listless man of the world, seeming to care for nothing so that the part he had to play was not too long for him, and affairs might be wound up at once, and leave him free to go his miserable way again.

He had glanced furtively at Laurence sitting by his father's side, and then, meeting but little sympathy in the franker face before him, had glanced at his father, who had said in a low tone,

"Well, Jonathan; you have not betrayed me in this."

"No, Sir," he had replied, before turning his attention to the withdrawal of a pair of gloves from his hot hands; which operation having been accomplished, he sat patiently waiting for any communication that might be made to him.

"Mr. Jonathan Fyvie, I presume," said one of the solicitors, to whom Mr. Fyvie, junior, was a stranger.

There was a general murmur of assent, which saved Jonathan the trouble of replying.

"We presume, too, Sir, that you are fully acquainted with the terms of the agreement between the firm and the creditors, and are prepared to affix your signature with your father and Mr. Raxford's."

"Fully acquainted with everything, Sir, and prepared to sign anything that you have handy there."

"If you will allow me," said the solicitor on the mining side—the losing side, "I will read——"

"If I tell you that I am fully acquainted with all the details," said Jonathan, "you will perceive that there is no necessity to read any documents for my behoof. The whole thing has been brought to ruin by me—utterly to ruin. Surely that's enough!"

"Your father will receive two hundred and fifty pounds a year; that is all the estate can afford at present. Mr. Raxford has stipulated that you and he should not participate in that amount—and it being barely necessary——"

"There, there," he said with a visible shudder, "it is simply starvation for the old man."

"No, it is not, Jonathan," said that old man of whom the son had spoken as though he was not present there.

"And," Jonathan added, with a short unpleasant laugh, "I hope that even you don't think so badly of me as to think that I would put in my claim for any part of it? By Heaven, gentlemen, I would sooner put a pistol to my head!"

He struck his hand with a sudden passion on the table, and sent the pens out of the inkstand, and some splashes of ink over Mr. Engleton's shirt-front; then the passion died away again with the echo that had made the window-glass vibrate, and he was waiting patiently for all that might be asked of him.

"Then we may complete the transfer of the property—the dissolution of the partnership between these gentlemen—and the other little matters at once."

Then began all the signing, sealing, and delivering—the fussiness of law—and presently the whole thing was a fact accomplished ; and two young men were cast upon the world, and one who had been rich remained but poorly endowed. It was all over, and the creditors were passing from the room, shaking hands with the three partners, wishing them better fortune—renewed prosperity—and everything else not likely to come to men who had dropped so surely and heavily from their high estate as they had.

The creditors, Mr. Engleton excepted, shook hands impartially with all three. If Jonathan had been a black sheep that was not their business ; if it was reported in the world that he had run away with somebody else's wife, at least their wives were safe, and the mine was equal to a dividend of twenty shillings in the pound. Sanguine men amongst them thought twenty-four shillings in the pound might be looked to with a certain degree of hope, and they shook hands more heartily with Jonathan than the rest.

Mr. Engleton bore Jonathan Fyvie no malice, and had been but lately a guest at his father's table ; but he was a staid, strait-laced man, running over with crotchets concerning the morality that there should be in the world ; and he could not face as a friend the man who had outraged society by his guilt and duplicity.

He walked out of the room without a word to Jonathan, and went into the street, pausing opposite the house, to tap his forehead with a new idea, or to let a new idea escape thence.

"If we could pronounce such men as young Fyvie dangerous to society, and lock them up in one nice large institution, what a world the rest of us would make of it ! "

Meanwhile, the man who was dangerous to society had sat in his place, languid and indifferent, until the last man had gone, and left the *ci-devant* partners together—for the first time alone together in business conclave since they had put one common name at the head of their circulars.

Then Jonathan's indifference, or hardness, or whatever it

was, melted away, and he turned a flushed and agitated face towards his father, and to him who had been his friend.

"Heaven knows I did not dream that it would be so bad as this!" he cried. "If that is any excuse for me, take it both of you. If not, why curse me sitting here."

"No, we will not do that," said his father.

"You cannot curse me worse than I have cursed myself," he cried.

"I do not think all this is worth raving about now," said Mr. Fyvie, drily; "the mine has changed hands, and here we are at the very end of our commercial enterprise. What do you mean to do?"

"I don't know, Sir," was the gloomy answer.

"And don't care?" added his father, interrogatively.

"Not much—not at all!" Jonathan answered, desperately.

"That is a foolish recklessness, which can't lead to any good, Jonathan," Mr. Fyvie said; "surely this might teach a lesson to you. Is it quite impossible—even at the eleventh hour—to begin afresh?"

"Quite!"

"You know that there is a small income belonging to your mother, from which she would be glad to allow you sufficient for another start."

"No, I'll not touch it."

Mr. Fyvie looked earnestly and wistfully at him as he sat there, with his head bent downwards, listless and crestfallen, and his hand idling with the pens upon the table.

"What will you do?"

"I shall hide myself away from you," he said. "I am an unlucky man, bringing ill luck to all who come in contact with me. So I will steer clear of the few for whom I have respect yet. You know, you will try to believe, both of you, that I am sorry for this break-up and that I take all the blame upon myself?"

"It's of no consequence now who takes the blame," replied the father.

"Oh! but it is," said Jonathan quickly. "And I don't want to evade it. If ever I get rich," he added, as though he had, despite his past reckless airs, a prospect ahead of him, in which a hope was flickering yet, "I will make good my words, Sir. I ventured here to-day, anxious to make a long statement, to tell the whole story of how I came to grief, to ask the pardon of you two, if not your sympathy. But I can't do it—and, after all, it does not matter."

" Quite right," said the firm father.

" I am very glad to see that you bear your losses well, Sir, he said to his father ; " you are an old man in a thousand."

" He is a fool who frets at the unalteralbe, Jonathan."

" You, Laurence, are young, and strong, and clever ; you will succeed in life, I think—I hope."

Laurence slightly inclined his head. He might succeed —he might fail — he had his own opinion upon his chances of success, and he did not care for Jonathan Fyvie's.

Jonathan having offered this little encouragement to his late partners, and disturbed once again by the coldness with which it had been received, idled with the pens once more. He was conscious of looking all that was mean and despicable in their eyes ; he was as sorry as a man of his nature could be that others had suffered with himself for his improvidence ; he was anxious for their forgiveness and sympathy, and he believed that he was not a bad fellow at heart, but the creature of unfortunate circumstances that had surrounded him !

" I'm not fond of preaching," he said, with more excitement, and in tones that were more genuine in consequence. I'm not a man with a strong will, and I have met with great temptations all my life ; ah ! and tried to fight against them, too. God knows I have !—though He knows, too, how miserably I have failed ! "

" You have thought too much of yourself, and too little of others," said Mr. Fyvie, coldly, " and the result is not satisfactory to anybody. Try and amend."

" It's no use trying now," said Jonathan ; " every bad habit is burnt into me ! "

" Then, God help you, my son ! "

Mr. Fyvie packed up a few papers before him, twisted a piece of red tape round them, secured them with a neat bow and ends, and then rose, as though weary of his subject. Laurence looked anxiously towards the old man, whose calmness of demeanour he doubted, but whose struggle to be unmoved and philosophic to the last he admired. Mr. Fyvie stood beating the papers against the palm of his left hand for a while. Jonathan took up his hat from the carpet, and rose with him.

"I shan't go back with you, Sir—I can't face *them*," he said.

"I think it is as well, until you can face them with a better story than to-day's. It is as well that I should go alone to your mother, leaving you to return to the adulteress."

The sting, sudden and sharp, was almost too much for Jonathan; he was not prepared for it, and he went back a step or two in an uncertain, awkward haste, as though his father had struck him.

"Sir—Sir," he repeated twice.

"Is it possible that you can blush now?" said Mr. Fyvie. "Well, then I have hope of you."

Jonathan Fyvie's heightened colour disappeared as quickly as it had come, and was replaced by a strange, death-like pallor.

"I will go now," he stammered forth.

"What has become of that poor woman?" asked Mr. Fyvie.—"Is she with you still, or have you cast her off yet?"

"Don't ask me," he cried, with excitement; "I have much to bear."

"Yes, I agree with you," returned his father; "there is her ruin and her husband's to your share, as well as the ruin of our house. You are too heavily laden for heaven, Sir."

"I have no hope of it," was the despairing cry, "though —though I did not take her away from her husband. There, I did not—I did not—*I did not!*"

For the second time that day his hand smote the table passionately, and then he went with a rush to the door, pausing thereat to look towards them with a bewildered face.

"What have I said?" he asked, vacantly.

"A lie—simply," was the terse reply of Mr. Fyvie.

"Don't you know — anything?" he inquired; "you have not heard — you have not seen — why, where is Athorpe?"

"Gone away—a madman."

"A madman, of whom it is best to beware," said Laurence, speaking to him for the first time.

"Yes, I know that," said Jonathan ; "he would have my life if he could, and he may have it if he likes. He has blasted it almost from beginning to end, and I had more right to Inez than he had, for I loved her first of all, and she, I am sure of it, loved me."

"Two such loving souls should be very happy in their fallen state," said Mr. Fyvie ; "but there is always something in the way of perfect bliss, especially bliss *à la Française.*"

"Sir, I will not have this !" shouted Jonathan, standing at bay at last—"reproach me as you will with your ruin, and I bear it, but with hers—I can't. For she was pure at heart ; no one is more glad of it than I am now. She stood her ground when I became a coward, and tempted her — she was at her best and brightest when Athorpe killed her !"

"*What ?* " shouted Laurence and old Fyvie in one breath.

"Not his accuser—I am no man's ; but he had no mercy, and *was* raving mad with hate of her. He killed her, Sir, but I am more her murderer than he is. Why did I come here to suffer the torments of the damned before my time ? "

He dashed from the room before an effort could have been made to stop him, had that thought occurred to either man left staring at each other there.

"Is this—this possible ? " said Laurence.

"I don't think that it is," replied Mr. Fyvie, after a moment's thought—" it's too much like melo-drama. It's an allegory, or something, and as Jonathan has not stopped to explain, and as we have other matters to attend to, I don't see any occasion to trouble our minds further with his rhodomontade."

"I will make inquiries," said Laurence, thoughtfully.

"We don't deal in murders down in Devon," said Mr. Fyvie, "and Jonathan is quite as mad as Captain Athorpe, and I'll swear is equally as destructive with property— only, with him, the property, unfortunately, is not his own."

Laurence again looked attentively at Mr. Fyvie. This airy and light manner was, to a certain extent, part of his senior partner's character, but it had been a natural part of it in prosperous times, and when the troubles came it had been simply his disguise. Laurence was sure that his partner's gay words were all forced now, and was at a loss to see the necessity for them, in the presence of a man who had been ruined with him.

"Shall we go now, Mr. Fyvie?"

"With all my heart, Laurence. It's after office hours."

They went out of the room, and down the broad stairs together. Flitting about the hall were half a dozen waiters, anxious to be in the way when Mr. Fyvie departed. The mining proprietor was well known there, and had always been liberal with his douceurs—the lackeys had even hope of him in the days of his decadence.

Mr. Fyvie shook his head at them as he reached the bottom stairs. He was quick of apprehension still, and realised facts at a glance.

"We have nothing to give away but our blessing on this occasion, gentlemen," he said; "will you kindly make the best of that, and share it, as well as you can, between you?"

"Oh! Mr. Fyvie, we don't want anything from you," said the head waiter, suddenly seized with contrition on the spot. "We're very sorry to hear of the business going wrong, Sir. What are all you chaps hulking about here for?—isn't there *anything* to do?" he said ironically.

"Good-day, good-day," said the old man.

"Good-day, Sir, and good luck again, Sir."

"And good luck again," quoted Mr. Fyvie, when they were in the streets of Plymouth, "in the good time, for the honest, and true, and *young*,"—passing his arm through that of Laurence's—"why not?"

"Why not for all, Sir?"

"I am not so energetic as I was," said Mr. Fyvie. "I don't know that I care for any more good luck. I only hope to be strong enough to keep *them* strong."

"With God's blessing, I hope that, Sir!"

"You will come home with me to-night?"

"I—I thought of leaving at once for London."

"I want you to see my new home in Tavistock—a little quiet villa, on the road to the old mine. Not so large a place as Tavvydale House—which Engleton has bought, by the way, my agents tell me—but a place wherein it will be easy—I hope it will be easy—to feel content. As for myself, why, Laurence, I am content already."

"Your wife and daughter will be—women are more quick, I think, to adapt themselves to circumstances, and make the best of everything."

"Hester will, for she's a brave girl. But the poor old lady has some pride of her own still, is an invalid, and has been used to the gratification of every wish. Still, the Fates be good to us," he said, dashing again into the light vein that was particularly objectionable to Laurence that day, "we'll pump up the sunshine, and all three of us be jolly. Come with me to-night?"

"You are alone there?"

"No, I am not alone. My wife and daughter came back yesterday, and I want you to see them—just as you used—for I think they understand you now, and they know that you have been a friend to me. I have been singing to your praise and glory with no end of energy lately."

"Miss Fyvie is at home?" said Laurence, eagerly.

"Yes. And though there may be a little confusion at first meeting, it will wear off, as it should do. You don't object to being our friend, our every-day friend, to look in upon us, and cheer us now and then with that good-tempered face of yours? Why, I may want cheering myself sometimes, and for the sake of the old man you will come?"

"I will come to-night, Sir. I am very anxious to see Miss Fyvie—she saw Milly last."

"Ahem—I would not begin talking about Milly Laurence. That is rather a vexatious topic to introduce to the poor girl."

"Ah! you do not understand me—you cannot comprehend my great suspense, for I have not intruded my deepest trouble on you."

"Thank you for that," said Mr. Fyvie; "I appreciate the motive for your reticence. Well, come home with me, and talk to Hester even of your sweetheart if it please you, and you have—the courage!"

"I will come, Sir," said Laurence firmly.

A few minutes afterwards, and they were in the train, bearing them from the bustling sea-port towards the quiet any pretty town of Tavistock. They travelled third-class as befitted the new condition of things, and in the crowded compartment in which they were ensconced there was but little opportunity for conversation. Both men sat very quietly facing each other, and both became very full of thought— stern, hard thought that would be kept down no longer— as they were whirled away to Tavistock.

CHAPTER V

THE EXPLANATION COMES AT LAST.

LAURENCE did not think much of the embarrassments natural to the position of facing a girl to whom he had been engaged to be married. Had he not possessed deeper and graver thoughts, he would have reflected on the delicacy of his own position, rather than of the feelings of Hester Fyvie.

Looking from his own point of view, at the antecedents of their courtship, he could but estimate Hester as a girl sorry for her engagement, and glad enough of an excuse to get rid of him—a girl who had known her own mind for the first time when she had made up that mind to dismiss him. He had not the remotest idea of any love for him having a place in her heart—for she had treated him badly, he considered, and cast him off, in the old days, almost with scorn. All this for the best, for they had not understood one another, and had never been in love with each other ; had he not been impulsive and foolish, they might have remained the best of friends all their lives.

Both glad to be free from a false position, they might be friends, he had thought very often—almost brother and sister in good time. For he did not believe that Hester had exaggerated a single fact in her frank confession to Milly—that confession had only come with a shock to the village girl, and he had been to blame to withhold it from her.

Hester and he *must* speak of Milly, for Hester might hold the clue to Milly's disappearance; if Mr. Fyvie's daughter were generous—and he felt that she would be—she would tell him all, calmly and coldly, as though it was a story that he had a right to hear, albeit it was of no great moment to herself.

It was not the thoughts of his coming interview with the old love that made his face so grave then.

All *that* had been considered long ago, but of Milly he could never tire of thinking. She had gone away from him without a word—she had not cared to hear him in defence—she had torn herself rashly and foolishly from his arms. It was his fate to be distrusted, and he was not lucky in his loves. But where was she?—that was the crushing thought which brought the furrows to his brow—where had she flown, telling no one of her flight, and holding aloof from the friends in whom she might have put trust? When he found her, would she offer to explain her absence; and had he not a right to know where she had been, and in what company? He was enveloped in mystery, and he detested it. He was a man who loved the light of noonday on mundane matters, and though he would take Milly to his heart and forgive her all her doubts of him yet he would ask her in return for all her confidence, and to have for ever afterwards a greater faith in him. He would tell her that she did not love him yet, as he loved her—and the last thought of that meeting—of her face before him, bright and radiant in its entrancing loveliness, suddenly cast a brighter gleam upon his own.

Mr. Fyvie leaned across and touched his knee.

"I wonder what you smiled for, Laurence?" he said.

"At the future, with all the misconceptions of the present trodden under foot."

"I wish that I could smile with you, then," he said; "as I get nearer home, I don't feel *quite* so lively as I did. I can't keep that boy out of my head."

"Jonathan?"

"Yes—I must tell his mother something about him. I must make the best of it somehow. It's a great deal to say," he whispered, "that he denies all knowledge of that woman."

"Yes."

"I'm inclined to believe that there is some mistake there. You will make inquiries for me, you say?"

22

" I will try and find Churdock, whom I last saw with Athorpe, on the night that it was supposed Athorpe's wife went away with Jonathan."

"He must know something," said Mr. Fyvie.

No more words were exchanged until they were in the main street of Tavistock, and then Mr. Fyvie said,

"Now for home, Laurence. After all, there *is* nothing like it ! "

They went the whole length of the street, and a short distance along the country road before the new home was reached—a pretty little villa, standing in its own small patch of garden ground.

"This is the old place reduced—according to scale," he said, as he led the way along the garden-path towards the house. A trim servant-maid opened the door in lieu of the stately footman of old times, and Mr. Fyvie remarked that *that* was an improvement for the better, at least. Then along the narrow hall to a front room on the left—a well-furnished room in its way, with a few of the ornaments belonging to the drawing-room of Tavvydale House doing duty in their low estate. At the table, busy with her needle-work, the daughter who had been crossed in love !

" Hester, I have brought Mr. Raxford to say good-evening to you," her father said, as they came into the room.

Hester looked at him shily, almost nervously ; she changed colour as his name was mentioned, and said,

" I am glad to see you and to thank you for all your kindness to my father."

She extended her hand towards him, and Laurence was aware that it trembled in his own. It was strange, he thought, that she should be more nervous than himself.

" I have but done my duty to your father—and that is a poor return for his generosity."

"We make a great man of you here," said Mr. Fyvie, warmly; "for we are just beginning to understand you. This is the fellow, Hester, who would have given up the partnership when affairs were brightest, but who held fast to us in the storm and shipwreck."

"Yes—yes," said Hester, seeing that Laurence was dis-comfited by these encomiums ; "and it was his duty, as he said just now."

"Take a seat, Laurence, and consider yourself at home.

You are as welcome here as you were in the big house," he said, dropping into an easy-chair himself; "where's mamma, Hester?"

"She is not very well to-night."

"Dash it!—not fretting?" said Mr. Fyvie, with a scared look.

"No—she is resigned—I think that she is resigned to the change," corrected Hester; "but she said that she was very tired, and would go to bed."

"Better that, than sitting up full of anxiety as to the result of to-day's meeting."

"And the result?" asked Hester, looking full of anxiety herself for an instant.

"Is that we retire with dignity and honour from the mines," replied her father; "everybody satisfied, and nobody with anything to complain of—what can be better than that? Everybody content—Hester?"

"I hope so—I am."

"That's well—after all, a big house is not much to be proud of. I only want you and your mother to think that it has not been a very great drop."

"We could have dropped lower and not have hurt ourselves much," she said with her old crispness of speech predominant.

"Exactly so."

Then there was a pause, after this little effort to sustain one another's courage, if it was an effort on Hester's part at all. For she had spoken naturally and cheerfully—and had evidently settled down to her surroundings already. Laurence looked attentively at Hester again; she might be resigned to the change; it might have improved and strengthened her character, as such changes will with the true breed of man and womankind, but it had not improved her personal appearance.

She was paler and thinner, and there was a greater degree of angularity about the features. Very graceful, and lady-like withal—and the subdued sadness of expression a new charm, that he had not expected to see there, and which took away from him the last faint feeling of resentment at her change of mind towards him. Had she met him coldly and proudly, he would have been a very iceberg in return; had she appeared before him the gay, spark-

22—2

ling woman whom he had known in their early days together, he would have resented her demeanour as a piece of coquetry, that was a jest at himself; but she had altered—she was subdued—and he was glad to see it, though he was sorry for the cause that had produced it. He was not sorry that he had come; he felt that he and she could speak seriously of Milly together, and that she might even feel an interest in his love story. He was not sorry, also, when Mr. Fyvie rose, stamped his foot upon the ground as though he were cold, and said,

"I think I will go and speak to your mamma for a while. Put away your needlework, Hester, and try if Mr. Laurence be as good a chess-player as he used to be. Find a glass of wine for an old friend, too; we are not without a good glass of sherry yet in the cellar—or the cellaret," he added with a half-grimace over his "quantities."

He hastened out of the room, and congratulated himself on having made his escape easily and naturally—and as the door closed behind him, the hearts of both man and woman beat more rapidly, for all their outward gravity.

There was a long silence; the moment had come for explanation, and Laurence sat and thought how it was best to begin a painful subject. Despite the double pulsations—which were a nuisance at that juncture, for they made him husky, and he was certain that he should croak like an old crow,—he was firm and ready to speak of their past engagement,—why he had kept it a secret from Milly, and why Hester had not—to speak of Milly, even to the woman sitting there, as one whom he loved best in all the world. Hester Fyvie was not equally firm; for she was a woman, and she was doubtful of the turn which he might give to the conversation. She could scarcely account for the presence of Laurence that evening; he had been a friend to them lately, and she was grateful, and forgave him in her heart all his trespasses against her, just as he thought that he was entitled to the glorious privilege of offering his forgiveness. But she became very nervous, and she trembled very much at last.

"I don't think that you or I care for chess this evening, Miss Fyvie," he said suddenly.

Yes—he was as hoarse as any raven in the country!

"No—I don't suppose we care at all."

One effort at her old quickness of reply, spoiled by the faltering accents of her voice. But the ice was broken, and they were soon more firm.

"I have been waiting long and anxiously, Miss Fyvie, for the opportunity of speaking to you, and I am very glad that it has come. I am sure that you will listen to me patiently, and if I pain you at all, that you will forgive me, and set it down to my natural anxiety."

Hester bowed her head. She was not certain what he was going to say next—he had been very noble and earnest lately she was aware, and oh ! if he had but brought back his truant love to her, to beg her to accept it and forgive him.

"I am about to speak of Milly Athorpe—and of that night you called upon her in Wind-Whistle Cleft."

"A memorable night for us," she answered, "and for more than you and me. Mr. Raxford, I acted cruelly on that night—unmaidenly—and I am sorry."

"I will beg you to relate to me the particulars of that interview between you and Miss Athorpe; for your visit has parted us—it has sown the seeds of suspicion between us, and she is very dear to me."

Hester's heart sank, and her colour changed once more. He confessed it; he had the cruelty to confess it to her, as though she had never been to him more than a common friend! She believed that misfortune had quelled her pride, and rendered her more womanly, but her spirit rose at this, and it was beyond her power to subdue it on the instant.

"Mr. Raxford," she said quickly, "I told Milly Athorpe the truth—but I was not gentle in my way of telling it. If for some purpose or other you kept that truth from her, I am not answerable for the mistakes that have arisen since. I am sorry—that is all."

"I did not tell her—pardon me for alluding to this— the particulars of our past unfortunate engagement. It was your father's wish, and there were reasons for respecting it."

"His wish ! "

"I was wrong to keep that secret from her—I see that now," he said. "You, with more fearlessness, took that task upon yourself. Miss Fyvie, what do you say ?—in what way did you tell her ? "

"Don't ask me!" she entreated. "You can guess; you must know, Sir."

"I thought that I could guess every word—for there are not two versions to the story—but your manner alarms me. I will ask you as a friend—even as a friend who was very dear to *me*—to tell me all, and set me on the track of Milly."

"I cannot do that; I know nothing of her movements. I told her all," she said, looking at him steadily; "but I told it like a spiteful woman, jealous of her conquest."

"You told her all."

"Everything."

"You told her that I asked you once to be my wife, Miss Fyvie—that you and I were engaged to be married, until you tired of me, and cancelled the engagement? That it was a folly on your part?—a girlish folly of which you afterwards repented; and took in consequence the wisest, kindest step for both of us—a step backwards from your promise to me?"

"No, Sir," cried Hester, her eyes flashing now with all the fire inherent in them, her bosom heaving with its resistance to his injustice, her white hand clenched, like a man's, upon the table at which she sat, looking across at him, proud and imperious as a queen. "I did not lie to preserve my womanly dignity, or spare myself one pang. I told her that you had grown tired of me, and were too ready to leap at the first excuse of a petty quarrel, and stand apart from all the love I had for you. That you did your best to win me—and, winning me, to cast me off!"

"Miss Fyvie, I did not perpetrate an act so dastardly. You could not have told her that?"

"I did."

"It was not honestly spoken," said Laurence, warmly. "Oh, Miss Fyvie, it was unworthy of you. You were right—it was cruel and unmaidenly!"

For an instant she shrank from these bitter words, as though they scared her; then she shook herself away from them, crying—

"I spoke the truth—I had a right to do it! For you had treated me cruelly—you had crushed me with your intensity of silence, when I was yearning for one word from you. You were unforgiving and hard—for it was you who had grown tired of me, whilst I—whilst I——"

She paused, and looked towards him with her gaze softening, and the tears stealing up to quench the fire with which her eyes were glowing ; then she rose, trembling at the confession which had hovered on her lips, and stood by the mantelpiece with her back towards him, crying for very shame at the love which even then she could not hide.

"Miss Fyvie," said Laurence earnestly, and more kindly, "what does this mean? How could you thus have misinterpreted my actions?"

"I—I will say no more."

"Pardon me ; but this is no explanation ; and if you impressed Milly with your wrongs—it explains her honest indignation at my seeming treachery. For I was *not* false."

"If it consoles you to believe that you were true to your word—if you can believe it—why there the matter ends. They tell me that you are generous," she said ; "where is the generosity that prolongs this discussion?"

"You have not told me all?"

"Not quite all," she said, shivering at the reminiscence— "all to the purpose, save that she gave you up."

"Miss Fyvie, I cannot be generous when a charge against my honour is made—that would be cowardly to submit. I gave you up, you told her?"

"Yes."

"When we quarrelled in the garden I gave you seven days to consider."

"Yes."

"Before that time expired, troubled by your silence, and scarcely able to reconcile it with your character—your love for me—I wrote to you."

"Yes," said Hester for the third time.

"And you returned me no answer—at least, you sent me word that there was no reply."

Hester dashed the tears from her eyes, and looked at him intently. She could scarcely comprehend what he was saying yet, and she let him proceed, whilst she held her breath and listened.

"Your silence was a ratification of that previous dismissal, which, as an honourable man, I could not receive in a fit of petulance, born of a jealousy that was not worthy of you. But after a week's consideration, to let me know that there was no answer to my letter, was to remind me again of your wish to give me up, and I retired."

"Laurence, do you tell me—do you dare to tell me that I did not write to you?" she gasped forth.

"Not a line."

"That I did not ask you to come back to me, and take your place at my side again?—that I did not do all that was in my power to get you back?—and from that day to this we never met again. You—you must remember that I wrote to you?"

"I received nothing but a message, that there was no answer to my note," said Laurence, "and *you* tell me that you wrote!"

"There has been treachery at work to separate us!" cried Hester, wildly; "we have been deceived, then—there has been an enemy in our midst, for I wrote to you to come!"

Her hands dropped to her side, and she stood there with her head bent down upon her bosom, a figure that was touching in its new misery—the misery that saw at last how she had been balked of her prize. It was a strange position, and Laurence felt it acutely. He saw that she loved him—that she had always loved him—and now his heart was beating for another woman, and there was no power on earth to bring him back to Hester. He had sworn to be true to her or to his promise until she gave him up, and she had never done so!

"Miss Fyvie, who is this enemy?" he said.

"I will find out," was the reply. "I can guess."

"He or she has worked irreparable harm," he said, scarcely knowing what his words might imply to Hester, "and we must find the foe, for our own truth's sake. I am very sorry."

"I am very glad," answered Hester, so quickly, that Laurence started in his amazement.

She saw his look of surprise, and blushed crimson at it. She hastened to explain.

"I am very glad, Mr. Raxford," she repeated, "for it removes the stain upon your honour,—and it lay like a foul brand between us. I am very glad that you did not lightly cast me off—however much your—your affection is centred on another ! Believing that I had acted lightly towards you, you were justified in seeking your happiness away from me, and I—I do not blame you now."

"We acquit each other of all blame," said Laurence, "but I am sorry for the pain, the suspense, the mistakes that have followed our separation."

"Mr. Raxford, I have more to tell you," said Hester, speaking, too, with more confidence, as his embarrassment became more evident, "for I have not yet spoken of my cruelty to Milly. I told her that—that I had not resigned you, and that you had never offered me your resignation. That *was* unmaidenly," she continued, speaking with great rapidity as she looked down at the carpeted floor, "and I was grieved at it, and at the anger which had given voice to it. I—I told her then that I would consider this still an engagement until you set me free by confessing your love to another woman—you have confessed it, and I set you free, Sir, and wish you—my father's friend and ours—with all my heart and soul, every happiness in life."

She stretched forth her hands towards him, and he took them, and wrung them long and warmly in his own. He had not the heart to say a word to her in reply, for every word must carry its sting with it.

"If, judging you falsely, I tried to mar that happiness— why, now I will do my best to promote it. You must not be," she said, rallying her forces very quickly, and speaking in her natural tone of voice, "the only generous being in Tavvydale. I have done wrong—and you must ask Milly to forgive me presently, and be a little generous also."

"Thank you, thank you," he said hurriedly ; "if I can only find her."

Hester felt a stab at this wish, but she hid all signs of the pain that his words had caused. She must learn to bear well such "little slings and arrows of outrageous fortune."

"I would ask one more question, Miss Fyvie—only I am troubling you very much."

"Not at all, now. I have confessed, and am at peace."

"Milly did not speak that night of going away ?—of any steps that she might take consequent upon your avowal ? "

"Not a word."

"I will go now—I think that I had better withdraw without seeing your father again."

"You will not forget him sometimes, Mr. Raxford," she said ; "he will be very lonely in his retirement here—and very dull."

"I will not forget my friends," he answered.

Then he went away slowly and thoughtfully, but full of his one purpose, to find Milly. He had discovered at last the clue to her indignation against him, and the means were to his hand to turn it once more into love for him. One shade less of mystery before him, and he rejoiced at it, and forgot in his exultation the woman whom he had left sorrowing for the loss of him.

She was in tears again when Mr. Fyvie came down stairs to rejoin his friend.

"Why, where's Laurence?—why, what's the matter Hester ? " he exclaimed.

"Nothing," she said, " only that I am very happy."

"Happy! Why, surely he hasn't——"

"No, no," she cried impatiently, "don't guess like that, for I cannot bear it to-night. I am happy in the thought that he *was* worthy of me, and that it was my fault, not his, which brought about an end to our engagement. And that's a bright thought, which will not grow dim with years."

"And he told you that, and didn't ask you to try him again ? "

"Not he. Why he," with a little sigh, " is in love with Milly Athorpe now."

"Ah ! I shall never understand you women," remarked Mr. Fyvie, sinking into his arm-chair ; "you had better go up stairs and tell your mother all about it."

CHAPTER VI.

FOUND AT LAST.

LAURENCE slept at the inn at Tavvydale that night, or rather he tried hard to sleep and failed. The day's bustle crept into his brain and kept him busy—and the revelation which had followed the day, mingled with his thoughts and added to his confusion. Lying on his back, staring at the window at his bed's-foot, he could imagine that he was going mad like Oliver Athorpe—that there pressed too heavy a weight upon his mind to keep him sane. His own future was uncertain, but that was of little moment then ; his mother he had neglected lately, but that was an omission which she would readily forgive—he felt like a child now, who would like to tell his story to his mother, and feel his mother's arms round him, comforting him in his troubles. He had seen Hester Fyvie, heard the whole truth, and it had scared him.

If he could only have lain there and thought of one thing, he could have borne better the night's restlessness ; but though his meeting with Hester was ever foremost, there dashed across it all the day's business anxieties, and all the misty speculations of the morrow.

He was hearing Hester's confession ; he was becoming assured again that she loved him very dearly ; he could see her flushed face, her eyes full of indignation at her charge, and then full of love at his denial of it ; and yet they were talking of accounts, in that room at Plymouth, looking on the sea, Mr. Fyvie was sitting at the table, Engleton was busy with the creditors, and Jonathan Fyvie was coming into the room, tall and haggard. It was Jonathan Fyvie sitting with his father and himself shortly afterwards, raving of his best intentions, and his poor performance of life's duties, speaking of Inez Athorpe as of a woman who had not fled with him, but had been killed by her jealous husband ; and after that it was one stretch of trouble, with Milly vanishing further and further away from him—a speck of light upon the desert he was traversing.

If he could only sleep, and wake up in the morning with a clearer head, to prosecute his search for Milly ; if he could but rest for a couple of hours, and forget the turmoil of the day ! But he was intensely wakeful, and everything was a trial to him ; the waiters in the inn wore creaking boots, and went up and down stairs in them, and vexed him with the noise they made ; people at the inn came home late, blundered about the passages in search of their numbers, and talked in loud voices to each other, talked even to themselves in their rooms, for the mere sake of talking ; there were dogs yelping in the streets without, and then, just as Laurence was losing himself, some wretch made a clattering row with a horse and cart in the inn yard, and drove off to an early market with his pigs.

It was three o'clock when he went off to sleep at last, and dreamed of the day's incidents, only confusing them a little more, and having the meeting of the creditors in Wind-Whistle Cleft, with the cascade splashing over the account-books, and Hester and Milly running in and out amongst the trees, pursued by Captain Athorpe, as raving mad as he had seen him on the day the house was fired.

He woke up tired and unrefreshed, and went down stairs to the coffee-room, where he attempted breakfast before setting forth in search of Bully Churdock. He had resolved to find that gentleman next, to hear the particulars of what had happened in the Cleft on the night Milly stole away, to ask if Milly had called upon her uncle to bid him good-bye before she started on her journey, and if she told him, or any one, in what direction she was tending. He began to think that he had not been quick enough in his conjectures, and that Churdock was the man to add his mite of knowledge towards the dissipation of the mystery. Milly would have seen her uncle, that was most likely. Seeing Churdock, too, would throw a light upon Jonathan Fyvie's story —for Churdock had been left in charge of Athorpe, and could answer at once as to the strange explanation that Jonathan had offered concerning Inez Athorpe. Was it possible, he thought, suddenly, that Inez had gone away with Milly, instead of with the tempter?—two women acting upon impulse, one flying from a husband's wrath, and the other from a lover whom she had been taught to doubt.

Laurence asked the waiter if he knew a man of the name of Churdock.

"Wrestling Churdock—Bully Churdock, Sir?'

"Yes, the very man," said Laurence.

"It'd be odd to live in Tarvydale, and not know him, Sir," affirmed the waiter. "What I call a pop'lar man is Bully. And not proud with it, Sir."

"No, I have never remarked much pride in him. Where does he live?"

"Up on the hills, at the back of the Cleft, Sir, he and his mother and his little brother Johnny. It's a long pull up there, and you're more likely to find him in Tavvydale than at home."

" He works at one of the mines, too—which mine ? "

" Well, I think he's given up the mining profession, Sir," remarked the waiter, twirling his napkin in his hands ; "and it was rather lowering for a pop'lar man, you see. And Bully's won a match at Cornwall lately, and a gent from London who was there has offered Bully a capital opportunity of trying his luck in the ring. Did you ever see Bully fight, Sir ? "

" I have not had that pleasure," said Laurence.

" He's uncommon clever with his fives," said the man, warming with his subject ; "there's regular genus in Bully. Ah ! it'd be a fine thing to say some day that a Tavvydale man was champion of England. I'm real Tavvydale, my-self, Sir."

" Oh ! are you ?   Let me have the bill, please."

"And if you particularly wish to see Mr. Churdock, I'd advise you, Sir, to wait here till he comes into the town. It's a long pull up the hill for nothing."

" I may meet him coming down," replied Laurence ; " should I miss him, will you say that I will be back here at one, and that my business is of great import-ance ? "

" Yes, Sir—I will say so.   Mr. Raxford, I think it is, of the Desperation mine ? "

" Yes."

Laurence paid his bill and went out into the High-street. It was a bright morning, and the place was as lively as the absence of its thousands of mining population could make it.   All the women too old, and all the children too young for work, all the shopkeepers who were not busy behind their counters, and all the dogs that had made the place resonant with noise last night were at the open doors, or on the pebbly ridges of the footpaths.   Laurence walked briskly down the middle of the road, and when out of the village, stepped from the beaten track, and made at once across the moorland for the hills beyond.

On the summit of the hill forming one side of the Cleft, he should be able to look across the higher ground, and see the Churdock cottage, he thought, and he pined for the fresh air that would meet him there, and drive his headache away. On the wild land that he was crossing, he came upon an old man with sheep, and hailed him.

"Churdock's cottage—is it up the tor, there ?"

"Ay !—ay !—up the tor—the one by the Cleft—a long way over, Sir. Nobody goes to see Bully very often," he added, with a grin upon his withered face ; "but it's a fine air up there, and that's made Bully such a wonder ! "

Yes, Bully Churdock was evidently a popular man—a man who was respected in the country.

Laurence ascended the hill-side, finding it warm work after awhile, and pausing to take breath now and then, as the ascent became more steep and arduous. The view opened out to him as he looked upwards, and it was a fine stretch of Devonshire country, that rewarded him for the labour of his ascent, when he was standing on the summit of the hill, and the wind was rioting around him.

"Dear old Devon !" he murmured ; "I should have been happy here, had I not been precipitate and foolish."

He looked towards a patch of woodland a few miles away on the plain beneath, but seeming as if he could throw a stone into it, and spoke as though he thought from Tavvy-dale House there had arisen all the misconceptions of his life ; then he walked a little way onwards, and gazed from the high steep side of the tor into the mass of foliage shooting upwards, and far beneath which was the Cleft where Milly had lived.

Around him on every side was a fair landscape, and he could take hope again to his heart—hope born of the beauty of the scene, and the freshness of that autumn morning. Within a little circle, comprising but a small part of that fairy land beneath him, and in the course of a few months, he had met all the romance of his life, and all the joys and sorrows born of that romance. It might make a story for an idle hour or two some day, with readers to pity his career, beginning so fairly and ending in the mists—or readers to rejoice with him at the brightness which followed the dilemmas, and the reward which came to him with the last chapter, when he should be married, and lady-readers would care no more about him.

If it would only end as he wished—if he could but guess the end, and find the village girl with love and faith in him again. But he had a search to make, and he was not lucky in his quests—why, he could not see Bully Churdock's cottage even now !

He walked on across the table-land thinking of Milly, and exulting at least in his freedom from "the books" at which he had toiled so long. No more accounts—no fighting more with figures—no sitting down to desk-work, or supervising of shafts, and miners and samples of copper ore, until his path ahead wore less perplexity. He was free now, and his own master, and he trod with an elastic step the short, crisp carpet which Nature spreads over her downs. Free at last ; free to go where his thoughts directed him, with no one to remind him that his duty lay in a diffcrent direction ! Free as the winds of heaven that rioted on the high hills on which he wandered. Yes, surely the worst was over, and the bettcr times were coming !

Far off, some distance across the downs, Laurence's quick eye detected some smoke curling upwards in the clear sky. He was approaching the place rapidly; he could see the roof of a small house or shed peering above a slight dip in the surface—a hollow which the sheep knew well, for here they nestled at times, out of the way of the wind. The place was stony hereabouts, however, and the scanty herbage struggled hard to live.

Laurence, when he had reached the outer ring of this hollow, discovered that he had descended a little way, and that the other side concealed the cottage from his view once more. He was about to make a short cut across this hollow, when he became aware of a man lying complacently on his back at the bottom of this natural basin, with two huge hands crossed on his chest, in monumental effigy style, and with a felt hat cocked over his eyes, to keep the sun out. The length of limb and solidity of form suggested Bully Churdock on the instant, and Laurence called his name.

The figure moved, took the cap from his face, sat bolt upright, and stared sleepily at Laurence standing on the brink of the hollow beyond. Yes, it was Churdock, red-eyed, red-faced, and sinister.

Laurence was at his side the instant afterwards.

"I am very pleased to find you, Churdock. I have come from Tavvydale in search of you."

Churdock's face did not light up at Laurence's appearance —it might have assumed a shade or two of greater stolidity even, for the giant was not pleased to see the gentleman. That last fact was evident when he replied, with a low growl,

"I don't see what you want with me."

"You *will* see that."

"I don't know what business of mine is business of yours, Mr. Raxford— it never was—and it can't never be."

"I think that I may interest you in my own, at all events."

"I'm dorned if you can, though!" he said; "for you're nothing to me."

"I thought that we were better friends than this, Churdock," said Laurence; "but you speak as an enemy might speak to a man who had injured him."

"You've done that fast enough. You turned the gal's head by making love to her; and I ain't blind enough not to know now that you was making fun of her all the blessed time."

"You are alluding to Milly Athorpe—I wish to speak of her, Churdock."

"She's given you the go-by. What's she to do with you now?"

"She is everything to me. I hope that she will be my wife, Churdock—that's all."

"You hope so. Well," with an oath that escaped him in his surprise, "gin you get her, you're a cleverer man than I take you for."

"When did you see her last?—you must have seen her since that night I left you in charge of Captain Athorpe at his cottage?"

Bully did not answer. He thrust his hands into his pockets, and looked at Laurence contemptuously.

"You must have seen her, or your words could not have a meaning to me," he said. "Well, I *will* ask you, Churdock, to tell me when you saw her, how she was looking, and what she said of me? She is unhappy, and the cause is easily removed. She is the victim of a great mistake, and I would rectify it. There, I am talking to you, as I would scarcely talk to another man in the world. For you may know where Milly is; and if so, you will be my friend, Churdock, I am sure."

Laurence spoke earnestly, and Churdock was not proof

against this genuine outburst. He kept his eyes fixed on
Laurence, swayed uneasily from side to side, swallowed something in his throat, which came up again and had to be re-
swallowed, finally burst forth with—

"Nobody's told me much—all I know I guessed myself—
and that's that you and Milly was sweethearts, and now isn't.
That's your fault, not her'n."

"It is all a mistake—Milly has been deceived, Churdock."

"As it may be," said Bully Churdock, quite argumenta-
tively, "possible like, though you're out o' my style quite,
and I don't know. And you ain't like that dorned sneaking
sarpent who has done such harm about here. Sorry all the
same, mind you, that you ever knew her—that you couldn't
a-found somebody in the big places to take a fancy to, instead
of one of our'n—but having happened so, and you all square
—why, there's an end on't, if you *is* all square. You talk
as if you meant it—and though *I* didn't think till jest now
—why oo !"

Bully Churdock took his hands from his pockets to snap
his thick fingers in the air, then he rose to his feet and shook
himself violently, like a great dog—and a great and faithful
watch-dog this Devon wrestler had been of late days.

"You've turned up lucky like," he said. "A week ago
and I mightn't have done nothing, save pitch you down into
the Cleft ayont for poking and prying in this part of the
hills. But things is better, and p'raps they'll be glad to see
ye."

"*They*—is Milly here, then? At your cottage?"

"She was this morning. Here she be now, with the rest
of 'em."

Laurence turned quickly to look in the same direction as
Bully Churdock—to look with intense bewilderment at the
strange cortege coming towards him from the house upon
the hills. Whatever happened in the future, the mystery
was at an end at least, and for that let him be thankful. The
reality was better than the suspense—even if the former
hewed down that tree of promise planted in the brighter
days. He thought so then, before he knew all—before
that pale-faced, beautiful girl had faced him with her
strength of will.

It was a strange cortege, then ; a woman at death's door
still—lingering yet on the threshold, clinging hard to life,

23

and praying night and day that she might live a little longer
—a woman led between James Whiteshell and Milly, who
were careful of every faltering step made towards the dip in
the land whre the air was less intense. Following behind
them little Johnny Churdock with a stool, and a gaunt, ropy
old woman, evidently Churdock's mother, with pillows in
her arms. The woman in the centre needing all this care
changed very much from the dark-faced, Spanish-looking
beauty whom Laurence had known as Athorpe's wife—the
shadow of her past self, who might steal away like a shadow
from them even yet, so weak and helpless seemed she.

Laurence made a step towards them, but Churdock's hand
was on his arm immediately.

"Don't fluster her who's ill, Mr. Raxford. *She* sees you
—they see you—that's enough!"

Yes, Milly had seen him; the colour had mounted to her
face, and was lingering there still, though her eyes were
fixed upon the ground now. Mr. Whiteshell had seen him,
and was holding up his head defiantly, as though appearances were against him; but he should clear himself
presently, and overwhelm his adversary completely. Inez
Athorpe was looking at him with a piteous, beseeching expression, that implored him not to speak to her just then,
but to leave her to herself.

Her lips moved, and Milly bent down her head to hear her.

"Yes," he heard her say, "we will send him away at
once."

"I will see to that," Whiteshell added; then he beckoned
to Churdock, who changed places with him as they came
down the slope towards the bottom of the ring.

"You will step back, Mr. Raxford," said Whiteshell, iu a
tone verging on peremptory; "you don't want to excite Mrs.
Athorpe, whom an angry word would kill just now?"

"I will step back, of course," said Laurence, retiring with
Mr. Whiteshell, as the rest approached; "but I will nqt
lose sight of Milly till I have spoken to her. It looks as
though I have been treated badly by you all," he added,
with some little signs of vexation in his voice.

"Or all of us—all who know and love Milly—have beeu
treated badly by you."

"I was not trusted—aud I deserved to be heard in a
serious charge against my honour, Sir."

They were out of hearing of the rest of them, but Laurence, from the higher ground, could see Milly still bending over her aunt, and arranging the pillows and cushions for her.

Mr. Whiteshell glanced upwards at his taller companion, put his fingers nervously to his lips, and said,

"If—if—you shouldn't be so bad now, oh! you don't know, Mr. Raxford, how pleased I should be, for one!"

"You, knowing all this," said Laurence, warmly, "where Milly was, and with whom, could come to me with your false excitement and your lies, to add to my misgivings, when a word would have saved me weeks of agony!"

Mr. Whiteshell changed from white to red at this reproach, at the sudden manner in which the tables had been turned against him, and he compelled to stand upon defence.

"I did not know, Sir, what had become of Milly—I was full of trouble concerning her when I came to you. Afterwards, on the same night, I found her at her house, whither she had stolen for some things she wanted. I—I hope that you may be able to answer with as clear a conscience as that, Sir."

"You told me that you would write to me."

"If I thought you honest—which I could not think afterwards."

"It is all easily explained."

"Then——"

"I will explain to her who has a right to hear me first," said Laurence. "I am waiting for her very anxiously."

"I will send her to you at once," said Whiteshell; "it is better over, perhaps. You see now why she has been absent from the Cleft?"

"Yes, I think that I see it all," said Laurence. "Express my regrets to Mrs. Athorpe at meeting her like this."

"Poor woman!—struck down when she was at her best —when she had the strength to turn away from the villain who had tempted her so long—and struck down by her husband. He always was a little rough!" he added.

"Yes—yes—will you tell Milly that I am waiting here?"

He was not curious concerning the story of Inez Athorpe; his own fate was trembling in the balance, perhaps, and Milly still distrusted him. He was sorry for Mrs. Athorpe

—he would be glad to be of service to her presently, if it were in his power ; but every minute away from Milly now —with her before him, and with those cruel thoughts of him which Hester Fyvie had sown within her mind—was torture.

"I will go at once. And you *can* clear yourself ? "

"Or I should not have come," said Laurence.

"I—I believe you again. Somehow, I can't look at you, young man, and see any harm in you," said Mr. Whiteshell. "And there really was no engagement with that Fyvie minx, and——"

"Mr. Whiteshell, I am waiting for Milly ! "

The old gentleman bustled away, and Laurence stood, with the fresh breeze playing round him, waiting very anxiously, and yet very hopefully, for the old love and trust to come to him again.

Milly was at his side before he was aware of it. He had looked down for an instant to consider how he should commence his explanation, and conclude it as quickly as he could, for the sake of the after bliss awaiting him, and she had come across the dip of land, and was at his side when he looked up again.

"Mr. Raxford," she said, very firmly, and not flinching from the loving, sorrowful gaze directed towards her, "you wish to speak to me again, then ? "

"Yes, Milly. I think that I have a right."

Then they walked together, side by side, silently for awhile, till they were away from the group near the cottage, and there was only heaven to hear them.

CHAPTER VII.

FOUND IN VAIN.

Yes, Milly was looking very firm. If he had been bold enough to seek her out—why, she must face him, for once more in life. He *had* a right to ask the reasons for her

separation from him, he might explain part of the mystery
which had baffled her, remembering what he was, and how
truthful and earnest he had ever seemed to her ; and though
it could not alter her determination to be quit of him, it
would be pleasant to think that he had not jested in his love-
making. There was the hope, too, that he might explain
all away, and shine before her with that undimmed lustre in
which her loving heart had placed him—that would add,
that would complete, the sweetness of the reminiscence, and
comfort her throughout the life she had resolved upon. It
would not draw him nearer to her ever again, alas !—but it
would render her content for ever afterwards.

All this, which was passing in her mind, he could not
guess at. He believed in his power to shiver with his love
the brittle wall of glass which circumstances had raised
between them ; there was not anything could stand the
shock of the truth, now that he was face to face with her at
ast.

Possibly it was good policy to begin with the old half
reproach, it prepared Milly for a better judgment of him.
Had he been wholly unworthy of her, they could have parted
without an explanation, and she would have been wretched
all her life. But his first words brought back to her the
hopes that she had had of him—hopes that had seemed
based on nothing, amidst the suffering iu which her new lot
was cast, and the sterner, deeper thoughts that were dis-
tressing her.

" Milly, you might have listened to me, instead of writing
me that letter," he said ; "the veriest wretch before his
judges is asked what he has to say in his defence."

" I was hasty, perhaps," she confessed, "but I was heart-
broken, and it all seemed unanswerable to me. It seems
so now."

" I will explain at once," he said.

" I shall be glad to hear that you were not false to—to
Miss Fyvie," she said, after a moment's hesitation ; "and,
Mr. Raxford, though no explanation that you can offer me can
place us in our old positions towards each other, still it will
take a great weight from me to believe that you did not intentionally mislead me."

Laurence did not like her reply, or the coldness of the
tone in which it was conveyed. There was a hardness in

her manner that was new to him, and that warned him all might not end as he desired.

He dashed at once into his explanation. He told her all that of which the reader is aware, and which he would not thank the narrator for repeating *in extenso*. It was the story which has taken us two-thirds of our journey to relate—the rash engagement out of gratitude to Hester Fyvie—the quarrel between the lovers—Hester's missing letter, that was to bring him to her side again, and which had never reached the hands of him to whom it was addressed—the love for Milly starting forth in the days of his new liberty —their engagement—his promise to Mr. Fyvie to spare Hester's feelings—the consequences that had followed his silence.

It was told very rapidly, and very briefly, and Milly listened patiently, and with her form trembling more than once as he went on, firm as she had determined to be throughout their interview. For he spoke much of his love for her, and without a word it would have been evident enough to Milly. He could tell her again that he had only loved her, and that without her he left his life a blank ; he could dwell upon the misery that she had caused him, until Miss Fyvie had thrown a light upon the mystery ; he would have flung his arms round her, and begged her to have new faith in him, from that day knowing how true he had been to her, and how well-meaning was the error which had parted them —had she not suddenly stepped back from him.

"Milly !" he cried, "have I erred beyond all hope of pardon ?"

"No, Laurence," and the mention of his Christian name was to make his heart leap again with joy ; "the little that there is to pardon, I am very glad and grateful to forgive. But we stand—both of us—beyond all hope of ever being— the—same—to—one—another ! "

Her voice sunk lower as she uttered that sentence against him, and she paused between every word that escaped her ; but she was very firm still.

"No—no, Milly—I cannot believe that unless you have wholly ceased to love me."

"May I speak of you before I speak of myself ? " she asked ; "I have not much to say."

"Speak to me all that is in your thoughts against me, and

let me combat it with my love for you, which must break down everything opposed to it."

Milly shook her head sadly, and then went on—not meeting his face, and not speaking perhaps so firmly.

"Laurence—I will call you Laurence," she said, in explanation, "as I would a dear brother or true friend—you do not consider that you asked a woman of your own station in life—a woman more fitting for you than ever I should have been—to become your wife? You asked her—you bent her thoughts towards you, and away from others who might have loved her better, and been, pardon me, more faithful—you gave a colour to her whole life and life's thoughts—you led her to love *you*, at least. Well, are you not bound in honour to her?—are you justified as a gentleman in setting her aside?"

"I do not love her."

"But you told her so," said Milly; "you pledged your word that you did love her, and you were engaged to her. I think that if I—if I—had been a man to say what you have said, even feeling now as you feel towards her, I would have *forced* myself to love and cherish her, rather than wholly crush her by casting her away."

"I do not love her," repeated Laurence, gloomily; "and I should make her unhappy by a marriage with her. I was to blame—I have not forgiven myself—but I should add to my mistake and hers, if I renewed this rash engagement, or she was foolish enough to give me her assent to it. Milly, it is unnatural to reason thus, for I have set my soul on you. And you would force me into the arms of another woman!" he cried, passionately.

"I was thinking what I might do if I was in your place," said Milly, less resolutely; "I may be wrong—I have only just thought of this—and you have never loved her, you say?"

"No. I see that—I know that, now," he answered.

"She was badly treated," said Milly, thoughtfully.

"But, Milly, I have explained all this—how gratitude for her father's kindness——"

"Rendered you unjust," concluded Milly; "yes, you have explained that. We will not speak of it—I am not her champion—I am glad, at least—there, I own it," she added, quickly, "that you were not false to me, and that one bitter memory the less passes away from this day."

" To be replaced, Milly——"

" Oh ! Laurence, you must let me speak—speak of myself, whilst I am strong and resolute ! "

He met her imploring look, and was silent. He had less hope after meeting those earnest, sorrowful eyes—less hope, now the great barrier between them was broken down for ever.

" Had you not been engaged to Miss Fyvie, had you never seen her," she corrected, as Laurence stamped impatiently upon the turf, " I should have asked you this day to forget me, to make up your mind, Laurence, to consider me as standing apart from you for ever."

" It cannot be done. You have accepted me. You have told me that you loved me, Milly ! "

" You must not think of that any more," said Milly, sadly ; " but go back to your own sphere, and find the wife more suitable for you. It was an unsuitable match from the beginning, and my heart sank at it, for I was *not* fit for you, and your friends would have ridiculed your choice, and stung your pride at every turn, making me miserable with you."

" We have spoken of this before," said Laurence, " and I have shown the folly of this reasoning."

" Perhaps I need not have mentioned it again," said Milly, humbly accepting her reproof. " I bring it back to say that now in the end—facing the end of our romance together, Laurence—the match is *entirely* unsuitable, and would, by its continuance, end but in misery to us both."

" I do not see that."

" I could have brought into your family——"

" My family ! " he cried scornfully.

" I could have said to that mother who loves you, and is very proud of you, that I brought for my dowry a name that was spotless, and that my uncle and aunt—well known in Tavvydale, and very much respected—could speak for me, and say that I was worthy of her son. Now—the blight is on all of us, and there is no cutting it away."

" There is nothing in the world that can stand between you and me for an instant."

" Ah ! but there is, Laurence," said Milly. " They are talking in Tavvydale of my Aunt Inez, and how she ran away with Jonathan Fyvie."

"That is false. It can be proved——"

"It can be proved, perhaps," said Milly, "that she did not run away, because her husband met them in the Cleft, and tried to kill them both."

"But she?" asked Laurence.

"*She* was urging Jonathan Fyvie to leave her, and was returning full of faith—full of her sense of duty to her husband's home, when my uncle, mad with passion, full of his past suspicions, dashed upon them. That is her story, which I believe—but which the world would laugh at. The world has heard of this long intrigue, and has condemned her."

"The world has condemned unjustly many times—why should you and I study the world?"

"We are living in it, and have bread to earn," answered Milly; "and it takes time to live down a slander like this."

"It is neither yours nor mine."

"I share it with her—I am an Athorpe," said Milly. "But I share with her a greater fear than that even—the fear that she should die, and that my uncle should be called her murderer."

"You have lived up here apart from the world, until your mind is full of disordered fancies, Milly," said Laurence. "I will hope still—I will never surrender you."

"Inez was carried up here by Churdock, at her wish, out of the way of my uncle, who believed that he had killed her. In the morning, when I was ready to go to London, when I had returned from making arrangements at Tavvydale school, Churdock came to me, and told me that Inez was dying at his mother's house. She had only one wild hope to die there, unknown to anyone, and save her husband from arrest; to give him time to get away out of England before the news went down into the village that he had slain her. Better be it said for a little while that she had gone away with Jonathan Fyvie, than that her husband should suffer, she thought. She forgot herself, and thought of him, at last. I remained with her—I nursed her night and day—and she is better now. The doctor, who has kept our secret well, says that she will be always very weak—always require constant attention, and unceasing watch; and I have taken that task upon myself, for I am the one friend left her."

"If I——" began Laurence, when she interrupted him again.

"It is a hard task—I do not deny that," said Milly; "but I have begun it cheerfully, and I shall not shrink from it, I am sure. My duty, Laurence, is to part with you, for my own sake—for yours—for hers!"

In his bitter disappointment—in the first agony of his baffled hopes to win her—stung, as it were, by the assurance that Milly would not swerve from this new duty—he cried impatiently,

"You have no right to sacrifice your life for that woman's —she was always selfish, vain, and weak—and she will make a slave of you."

"She is the wife—the honest wife, after all—of my poor uncle. Would you advise me to desert her?"

"There is Mr. Whiteshell," suggested Laurence—"he——"

"He is a very poor man; and if he was a very rich one, he is not fit to be a weakly woman's nurse. I shall be in my old place as school-mistress, I hope; and with that salary, and my little savings, I will take care of Inez till my uncle comes."

"He will never come back."

"I will pray with all my might that he may—pray with Inez, who will die very unhappily should he keep away."

"He is mad."

"His better thoughts will come back, for he is a thoughtful man. He will not go wholly to ruin, and when he knows all the truth he will not wholly despair."

"Still, all this need not separate us," urged Laurence; "you must not make every sacrifice for your aunt, you must let me share all your sorrows, and your trials, as I should have done if we had been married."

"No, no, it can't be," cried Milly. "I will never bring my husband a single care to the altar. I will be all joy to him, or I will never marry. And I shall never, never marry now, Laurence!"

"Ah! Milly, you will love me—you *will* love me still!"

"Yes, I will love you Laurence," she sighed forth, "with a far-away affection, that shall keep you apart from me, and yet ever in remembrance. For I can't forget—I never shall forget you. But as surely as I love you, as I am very glad that I have not loved unworthily, so surely must you say good-bye to me now, and feel yourself, from this day, free of any promise to me."

˙ She held out her hands towards him, and he seized them and drew her at once into his arms, where she remained for an instant, and let him kiss her passionately. Then she sprang away from him, and was crying very much, and sobbing forth "Good-bye" again.

"No, no, it *is* not good-bye," cried Laurence; "it is not a parting to which I can consent—it is not right! For we love each other, and should have hope in the future together."

"That would unsettle me," said Milly, turning quickly to explain, and dashing her tears away amidst her explanation; "that might render my duty irksome, after awhile, and *she* would see that, and fret at my selfishness. I have promised to take care of her for life. I will go down with her to Tavvydale, and tell them all there that I am her friend, because she has been true to her husband; and though they will not believe that at first, I will, in time, force the truth upon them. Though she has ever been a strange and jealous woman, she has loved me I know now, and I will show my gratitude for it. And, should she get stronger—which she may, in good time, and with God's help!—and we should hear in any way of my uncle, we two women will set forth in search of him, to tell the whole truth, and make his heart more light by it. And if he never comes—if we never see him again—why, then I must comfort her through life, in the best way that I can."

"Can I say anything to all this, save that I will wait for you?" said Laurence; "that year after year, taking pattern by your patience and unselfishness, I will bide my time for Milly?"

Her lip quivered again, and she wrung her hands silently together, as though that was a check upon her tears.

"You must not," she murmured.

"There may come an early sequel to this discomfort," said Laurence; "strange are the ways of life, and full of changes. I will wait!"

"If I thought that you were waiting for me—that I was shadowing your life like this—it would make me very, ery wretched. Laurence, you will marry some one better than myself—a lady, well bred, well born—and not think of me any more. For I will never have you!"

"Milly!" he cried.

"There, I have said it! I will never have you, Laurence —I could never come to you without some drawbacks to my name and *theirs*—and I have mapped my life out to the end. You shall not burden your mind with thoughts of me —me, growing old before my time, and thinking from this day no more of you."

"Only a little while ago, and I was to be kept ever in remembrance," Laurence reminded her.

"There, there! you torture me—you are not kind," said Milly; "ever in remembrance as a hero of my books, then —the hero of my one romance! But to think of you as— as—as I *have* thought of you, Laurence, why, never again, as I am a woman who has suffered."

"I will wait," repeated Laurence, firmly.

"For the true wife whom you will meet in your own circle, and be happy with," said Milly; "for here we say 'Farewell!'"

If her cheek had paled still more, she had assumed all her old firmness. Would she soften ever again towards him?—was it the girl who had let him enfold her in his loving clasp?—or was it the woman, cold and grave, whom he was henceforth to meet?

Should he meet her again?—were they to be friends or strangers? That last question he put at once.

"I may stay in Tavvydale.—I may go back to my old post at the mines. Shall we meet at times by chance, and may I speak to you?"

"I hope that you will not. I ask you in all charity towards me not to seek me out. It will not be fair or kind to do so. You will go please," she urged; "I have been long away, and Inez is very weak and nervous. You will say good-bye, Mr. Raxford, now?"

"Ah! no longer 'Laurence' to you! For you are as unfaithful to your word, as I was to Hester Fyvie."

"And the last parting comes with a reproach!" said Milly—"well, think that I have treated you badly—it is best for both, perhaps."

"God bless you, my own unselfish Milly!" cried the repentant Laurence. "I am a villain, and you must not mind me. I am in despair, and know not what I am saying, what is happening around me, save that you are going away for ever, and that all the love you had for me—that you confessed to me in the Cleft—goes with you. Good-bye."

"Good-bye."

"Good-bye, Milly—for the last time you will call me Laurence in return ? "

"Yes, Laurence, good-bye."

Yes, this was true love, not the every-day article passing for the same in every-day life, but the love which belongs to real life sometimes, for all that—to the very young, and the very true, who are born with poets' souls in them, perhaps, and know but little of SOCIETY—the love of which true poets have spoken in verse, and to which verse gives a tinge of reality when prose labours hard for effect. The love that has the wings of the angel, and hovers between heaven and earth, fluttering between the pure thoughts of heaven and its worshippers, but rendering earth, whilst love lasts, a Garden of Eden.

It was a wild moment of bliss, even on the verge of separation, when this strange couple, parting thus strangely, gave up for the instant their hardness, their resolves, and met in one close embrace, to kiss each other for the last time as lovers. If, looking back upon it, it added to the grief of their disunion, still it was a fair retrospect, that made their hearts thrill, and kept them green and young. Fate had separated them—not themselves.

She watched him down the slope of the hill, going back to a new life, which she could never share with him. And, like a true woman, she prayed that her hero would be ever happy without her!

END OF BOOK THE THIRD.

BOOK IV.

THE OLD LIFE.

CHAPTER I.

A NEW BEGINNING.

LAURENCE left Tavvydale for a week. He was unsettled
and troubled—he had been disturbed so long by the anxiety
which affected others as well as himself—he had struggled
so hard towards the end of mystery, and, attaining it, had
been so utterly cast down, that he craved for change, for
isolation from his old world, as a life prisoner·in a dungeon
might crave for liberty.

He set off, with a small knapsack at his back, across the
country, tramping from South to North Devon in a day,
and arriving in the middle of the night, tired, weary, and
footsore, at the old village of Hartland. There he rested
for the week, lying all day in the shadow of the gaunt
sea-cliffs, watching the play of the waves over the sunken
rocks, and looking out at sea long and steadily, as though
at his future beyond the line where the sky and ocean met.
Here no one could step from his post to meet him—here,
free from his old world, he felt that it would be a pleasure
to dream away his life. This on the first day after his
arrival! on the second more calm in mind, looking out at
sea more gravely and intently, as though life's duties were
coming back to him with a sense of their importance, and
would be in the bay presently.

If Laurence Raxford was romantic, still it was not the
romance of the fool ignoring real life, and conjuring up
phantoms at every step. He was philosophic in some

respects; he could make the best of circumstances, and he was not a slave to one grief.

He felt that he was a part of the world in which he must live, and, if possible, prosper; he had business ideas, and they were not likely to rust long in inaction. The rest at Hartland did him good—for it was a complete rest, and when the week had expired, he could shoulder his knap-sack, and trudge back to Tavvydale, all the better for the change and all the stronger in his purposes and in himself.

He would accept Mr. Engleton's offer—if it were still open for him to accept—and go back to his old post at Wheal Desperation; he would try and be a son to the old man who had given up, in all honour, his great possessions, and a brother to the woman whom he had not treated well —who was the only one in all the world that could accuse him of a broken promise, and who had, for all that, readily forgiven him. He would summon his mother to Devon-shire, to make that home for him which he had never found there; that home wherein he would settle down, thanking God for the true friend, adviser, and sympathiser left him in the world yet, and to whom though he had written once or twice, he had never related the story of his love for Milly. He would work on patiently, doing his duty everywhere, and from the distance he would watch Milly Athorpe with all his heart, trustful of better times, and, failing them, to grow old and grey-haired with her, but loving her to the last as fondly as when the magic of her beauty first entranced him.

He would say nothing of that last resolution, for it was stagey, and no one—save Milly, perhaps—would understand him; but he would keep to that, as to all the rest of the plans which we have set above, as part and parcel of his resolutions. He wrote to his mother on the first day of his return to Tavvydale; he wrote to Mr. Engleton; he called upon Mr. Fyvie, and saw that gentleman, his wife, and daughter—the gentleman still buoyant, and more than re-signed, outwardly, to all the changes which had come to him— and he walked over to Wheal Desperation in the evening, looked at the old place, and wondered if his lot was to be cast there after all.

The answers to his letters arrived in due course—they were both answers in *propriâ personâ;* Mrs. Raxford and Mr.

Engleton appearing within half an hour of each other before the startled Laurence.

"I couldn't stay a moment, Laurence," said Mrs. Raxford, "after your letter. I have been packed up this last month, and ready to fly here at the first signal—which you have been a long while making, my dear."

"Ah! that is easily accounted for, mother. I told you in my last, I think, of the failure of the firm—the run of ill-luck that followed the advent of the new partner."

"Yes, my dear boy—very terrible—and that accounts for your rambling letters, full of little hints of coming changes, which you said would be all for the best, which they can't be, surely."

"Patience, we shall see, mother. Everything is for the best, I suppose."

"That's my own son. Glad to see you, Laurence, contented with everything. Well, have you found a little house for me, in which I shan't feel myself quite lost after your marriage?"

"I have found a little house for you and me, mother—for you alone, if I have to seek my fortune elsewhere—and for both of us to settle down in, if an offer made me by the new proprietors is once more renewed."

"To settle down in?—both of us?"

"There's the riddle that I am going to solve," he said, attempting a smile at his mother's perplexity; "now, sit still, and listen to my love-story."

Then he told her all for the first time—all that he was just acquainted with himself, and which had separated him as far from Milly Athorpe as from Hester Fyvie.

The mother listened patiently—open-mouthed, in fact—shed tears over all the pathetic pictures, like a tender-hearted woman as she was, and wound up by flinging herself headlong at Laurence, putting her arms round him, and patting his back with her little fat hands, as though he was choking.

"How the girls have been worrying you, my poor boy!" she said; "I suppose it's quite natural at your age—poor Hester!—poor Milly!—what a mix-up to be sure, and nobody to blame!"

"Yes—I am to blame."

"But you did love Hester at first—I'm sure I never saw

two young people take to each other more—and now Milly
has given you up, like a sensible young woman who knows
her place, and wants to keep it—it may all come round
again, just as Hester's father and myself prophesied it
would."

"No—that can't be. I beg you not to think of that—all
I ask of you is to leave me to myself."

"Of course, I shouldn't attempt to interfere."

"Then we'll go and look at the house that there is to let
within a stone's throw of Mr. Fyvie's," said Laurence.

"Ah! that will be nice—nice," she added, detecting
Laurence's suspicious look towards her, "to have a neighbour not quite a stranger to us."

"Yes."

"And if you never marry, Laurence, it is not for me to
complain—me who will have you all to myself, if you don't.
We shall be very comfortable, and with you on my mind
instead of my house property—it's in the hands of a most
respectable agent, Laurence, who will not deduct much for
repairs—I shan't know a single care."

"That's well."

They were going away arm-in-arm to see the little house
at once, when Mr. Engleton arrived and delayed the excursion. He was full of bustle and excitement, as usual, and
his pockets and his hands as full of papers.

"Glad to see you—glad to see you in Devonshire again,
Mrs. Raxford," he said, upon entering; "and glad, Raxford,"
turning to our hero, "to receive your letter, which I should
have answered before, had I not been very busy about some
model cottages I intend to build in Tavvydale. You remember my old ideas about the cottages?"

"Ye—es," said Laurence, hesitating a little; "I remember something about cottages, but the details have escaped
me."

"I'll just give you a sketch."

Then he sat down, and dashed into the subject of his
model cottages, which, now that he was firmly established
as a Devonshire celebrity, he should certainly build in Tavvydale forthwith. Laurence and his mother listened for half
an hour or so, until the speaker detected some signs of weari-
ness in the lady, who had come a long journey that day.

"But we're getting too dry and business-like, and

24

fatiguing Mrs. Raxford," said Engleton, suddenly; " and, besides, there's your business to attend to, in the first place. Well, I have settled all that—I'll have you at your own terms. How much ? "

" My remuneration must be left to the proprietary."

" Oh ! hang the proprietary. We had a meeting last week and a quarrel—some objections being raised to expending a few thousands on my new principle of ventilating mines—for it's as stuffy as possible down there at present, and how the poor beggars can keep on breathing, I can't understand—and so I made them an offer, and bought the lot of them out. What I hadn't got myself, my bankers were good enough to find me ; and so," with a pleasant laugh breaking in upon his rapidity of utterance, " I am sole proprietor of Wheal Desperation, and you must try and make it pay a fellow."

" It will pay a fair per centage on the capital," said Laurence ; " there is no doubt of that."

" Well, I hope I'm not greedy—a fair per centage will do," was the reply ; " and to show my principle of conducting business, I should like your salary to depend upon the profits too. If you like a fixed sum, name it."

" I think that I would prefer a commission, Mr. Engleton."

" All right. That's settled. I wish I could make every man Jack of them work on commission, and keep them all at concert pitch. I've been trying to knock off a new scheme about wages, but it don't come exactly right at present, and is devilish intricate—excuse me, Mrs. Raxford—carried away by the warmth of my subject, and naturally excitable."

Mrs. Raxford accepted his apology very graciously, for he was their new benefactor, and her son's master. He had always liked her son, too—and, who knows? there might be another partnership in store for her Laurence.

" My friends tell me that I shall never stick to the mine," he said—" that I never stick to anything. Ha ! ha ! that's a good joke, when I'm always hard at work, too. And, hang it ! if I don't stick to the mine, it's all up with me, for all my money's there — except what I have got in the smelting-house. Why, I hold firm to my ideas like a barnacle to a ship's bottom—I never change. Where I seize

an idea, take a fancy, or see the being whom I would like
to call a friend—the idea is carried out, the fancy is realised,
the being is my friend for life ! Now, I always admired
your straightforwardness, Mr. Raxford, and you're my
friend, I hope, as well as my right-hand man. And I always
liked the Fyvies, Jonathan excepted, and shall like them to
the end. By the way, Miss Fyvie's looking very ill," he
said.

" Do you think so ? " said Laurence.

" I hope that she does not feel the reverses very much—a
sensible girl like her ought not to chafe a great deal at them.
Money, after all, isn't everything, and if my father had not
died a rich man, and my uncle had not left me all his property, I don't think that I should have cared a great deal.
I should have only cut the tails short of my hobbies," he
said, laughing again, " that's all—do you think that Miss
Fyvie has anything else to fret about ? "

" Nothing at all."

" I suppose you and she will marry shortly."

Laurence winced.

" That is not very likely," he answered ; "our engagement was ended some time since."

" Dear me !" said the astonished Engleton, "you don't
mean that ? Why, the Llewellyns never told me—and I
met them only a fortnight ago at Torquay."

" Mrs. Llewellyn must have been aware of it, too," said
Laurence drily ; for Laurence had his suspicions as to the
lady who had stood between him and Hester, playing the
part of spy with considerable success.

" Nice people the Llewellyns," said Engleton, who saw
few faults in the human nature with which he came in contact ; " I expect that they'll be down here in the course of
a few days."

Laurence stared at this unwelcome piece of news.

" A flying visit—in fact, I'm going to give a kind of house-
warming to the estate which I purchased of Mr. Fyvie—my
sister who is my good housekeeper there, and I together.
Mind, I insist upon the company of Mrs. Raxford and
son."

Laurence hastened at once to offer his excuses. He was
going to apply himself earnestly to work ; he had been ill
at ease lately—oppressed in his mind, as it were—and he

24—2

would prefer for a while pursuing without interruption his own quiet way.

"Then I'll make a dinner-party of it. You must eat, you know, somewhere, and you and your mother may as well have dinner with me as with yourselves."

"I am sure that we shall be very happy to join you on the occasion you mention," Mrs. Raxford hastened to say, greatly to the discomfiture of her son.

"Thank you—thank you," he said twice. "I want as many of my own friends round me as I can — the old friends that always made my stay at Tavvydale House a pleasant one. I think of starting now. To-morrow I hope to see you at the mines, Raxford."

"I'm ready to begin, Sir."

"That's well; that looks like energy, and an eye to the commission. Good-morning."

At the door he stopped.

"Are you fond of mystery, Mr. Raxford?" he asked.

"God forbid!" said Laurence hastily. "I have had enough of mystery these last few months for all my life."

"Very good. Then I suppose there's no secret connected with the reasons for the termination of the engagement between Miss Fyvie and you? You will excuse my curiosity, but I was a little interested in that match for a bystander; and upon my word, I cannot make out why it has been broken off. Why you were so admirably suited for each other!"

Laurence felt that Mr. Engleton was a trifle too curious—presumed, perhaps, a little on his superiority of position. Still there was no secret connected with the story now; he was intensely grateful that he had not a secret in the world.

"Miss Fyvie and I were engaged in too great a hurry," said Laurence; "before we understood each other's character—each other's feelings. I am to blame for all; and Miss Fyvie, in cancelling that engagement, has acted well and sensibly."

"Exactly," said Engleton; "she would always do that—a sensible young woman, lively without being frivolous. In the old days, when we three were guests at Tavvydale House, I used to think to myself what a model couple you were. I suppose it is possible——"

"It is not possible," cried Laurence quickly, and almost angrily forestalling the supposition.

Mr. Engleton quite startled.

"Ah! you were a little too hasty, perhaps, for her. I remember how you used to cut me short in my explanations, and only half look through my papers. That will not do at the mine, Raxford."

Certainly a pleasant habit of darting away from a delicate question, and setting himself and everybody else at ease— certainly not the worst task-master whom Laurence might have found in authority over him.

Laurence turned upon his mother directly the employer had vanished.

"Whatever made you accept that man's invitation to dinner?" he exclaimed. "How is it possible to back out of it?"

"My dear, we must not back out of it! I haven't come down to Devon to be buried alive; and though reverses have occurred, I think," holding up her head quite proudly, "that we are well-born enough to take our place anywhere."

"We should know our place now."

"I hope we do, Laurence."

"And I am totally unfitted for society. I wish to be at rest for awhile, till I am better—stronger!"

"No one ever got stronger by moping, Laurence," she said; "and I want to see you your bright, cheerful self again."

"In good time, I will begin to drift back to that character."

"And as you can't begin too early, we'll dine with Mr. Engleton at Tavvydale House."

"We'll talk of it again when the invitation comes."

But the invitation came when Laurence was at Wheal Desperation, and Mrs. Raxford answered it at once in the affirmative.

CHAPTER II.

LAURENCE had begun work at Wheal Desperation, and all things were progressing fairly there, when the invitation to dine at Tavvydale House was accepted by his mother.

He was not pleased to hear of its acceptance, but he did not utter one more protest against a visit to the old quarters. His mother seemed disposed for a little life and bustle—and surely, for one night, he might form her escort, and face people whom he disliked, or whom he did not know, passing away from them in a few hours, and letting them, with all their vanities and inanities, pass away from his remembrance also.

He was certainly in no mood for dinner-parties, or parties of any description; he had become grave and thoughtful—more reserved, in fact—and he would have forfeited a fair sum to be allowed to stop away; but he said no more in opposition to his mother's wish. That mother, it may be added here, was an amiable schemer, too, artfully feigning an interest in evening-parties, in order to draw her son out of his one morbid groove, to cast him into society that would distract him a little from what she called his "maunderings after business." For she was distressed about him, though she disguised her trouble well, and deceived him; this new grave-faced young man was not her Laurence, and "that Milly"—however good a girl she might be—had certainly bewitched him. It would all come right in time, she believed; the village girl would fade away, or marry, or something, and Laurence would marry Hester Fyvie—*she* would take care that Laurence and Hester should meet more often than either bargained for; and although Hester was not a good match for Laurence now—"not good enough for him," thought this doting mother—still, she loved Hester next to her own son; she had always regarded her as her daughter-in-law, and she felt very keenly, and as a proud woman might feel, that it was a question of honour that a Raxford should not swerve from his word. True, Hester and Laurence had cancelled the engagement between them, but they had made it up, and were like brother and sister almost, and she was not in her right senses, if Hester did not still love her Laurence very dearly. When they were out of hearing, she and Mr. Fyvie had many long talks together, keeping their consultations and their results under lock and key. These two old fogies would conspire when they got together for the future felicity—or that which they believed would be the felicity—of their children.

"If I could only be sure that your boy would marry my girl, after all," said Mr. Fyvie, in one of these secret councils, "I could really be content, for I should be sure of her future, and of a worthy husband for her. Laurence dines with Mr. Engleton, then?"

"Yes."

"Then I'll take Hester and her mother. It's rather uphill work to go back to the old place," he said, "though I don't pretend to care a button for the change. I fancy that we're all three thundering hypocrites sometimes."

"Each supporting the other—just as it should be."

"Ah! yes, and I'm as strong as a lion, and nobody sees through me, at all events. I'd rather Engleton have had that place than any man of my acquaintance—though Engleton will knock it all to pieces, with his new ideas, and fool's-head alterations. I dare say I shan't know the house."

He groaned as he said this, and he groaned again in the verification of his prophecy, when he found fifty men coming from work at a new wing that Engleton had considered would be an improvement to the establishment.

"I never liked the fellow," grumbled Mr. Fyvie, "a harum-scarum man, with no gravitation in him."

"What do you think of this idea?" Engleton asked of him.

"It will make the house large enough for you, at any rate, was the sour reply; "I dare say you felt yourself cramped a bit here."

"I thought that it would add to the effect," said Engleton, "I always thought that the house wanted width and solidity; you remember a little suggestion of mine, that you pooh-poohed—well, this is it!"

"Oh! you carry out some of your suggestions, then?"

"A few of them. And I would beautify this place in every way in my power, out of respect for the good friends

that first made me welcome here, and gave an old bachelor
an idea of what a happy home was like."

"Well and gracefully put, Engleton," said Fyvie, seizing
his hand, "and I'm a crabbed old wretch, envious of those
who are better off than myself. You must make allowances
for a man as broken down as I am."

"This Engleton's a good fellow, Laurence—I took to him
from the first," said Mr. Fyvie, later in the evening. He
had reversed again his opinion of the man who had sup-
planted him—he was not so firm and persistent as in the
days when he sank his last shilling at Wheal Desperation.

Mr. Engleton's dinner-party was a success—most dinner
parties are, so far as the dinner is concerned, when there are
plenty of waiters to hand round plenty of good viands, and
to see that the glasses always sparkle to the brim. This
was a success, whilst dinner lasted, with the guests, too—for
they had been well paired off by a shrewd little lady, who
possessed a knowledge of character, and was as good
tempered, and witty an old maid of five and forty, as Charles
Engleton deserved to be blessed with. The people who
could talk about books were together; the people who were
fond of gay life found themselves side by side; the Tavvydale rector and curate were with district lady visitors, who
thought clergymen should always be "shoppy," always talk
as if they had their surplices on, and were thumping velvet
cushions; Mrs. Llewellyn was with an old gossip and
scandal-monger, secured expressly for the occasion; Mrs.
Raxford was with Mr. Fyvie; Laurence was by the side of
Miss Llewellyn, and Hester Fyvie was on the left of the host,
who certainly might have paid more attention, with
advantage, to the married lady whom he had escorted into
the dining-room.

Laurence had shaken hands with Mrs. Llewellyn upon
first encountering her; he had endeavoured to avoid that in-
fliction, for his instinct assured him who had worked long
and laboriously against his peace; but Mrs. Llewellyn had been
demonstrative, and he was not inclined to make a scene upon
mere suspicion. She had separated him from Hester after
all, and remembering the bright face that had succeeded his
first love's—that was ever before him, for his heart to yearn
for—he could forgive her the deed more readily than the unworthiness of the motive that had prompted it.

He found that he was in the thick of the Llewellyn family at dinner—a fact which certainly did not speak well for Miss Engleton's judgment in selection, at any rate, for Laurence would have preferred being in the thick of a street fight. Miss Llewellyn, mild, and placable, and stupid, was on one side; Mrs. Llewellyn, fierce and implacable, and bony, was on the other; facing him was the bumptious Treasury clerk, bristling with more importance than ever.

"Do you intend to remain in Devonshire for any time?" Laurence inquired of Miss Llewellyn.

"I don't know—Miss Engleton has been kind enough to ask us to remain as long as we please here. It will be like the old times over again, Mr. Raxford," she said with a sigh.

"Were they happy times—with you?"

"Yes—I think so—I'm sure they were," she said, blushing; "and though the house don't belong to our family now —still I—I think that I shall like to stay here."

"Jane, don't you hear that Mr. Engleton wishes to take wine with you?" said the mother sharply; "how stupid you are, my dear, to be sure!"

"I—I didn't hear him," said Miss Llewellyn; "I was talking to Mr. Raxford."

Mrs. Llewellyn turned upon Mr. Raxford with a sweet smile, that curdled every drop of blood in his body.

"I'm afraid that you're a sad flirt, Sir," she said, and the jingling ornaments in her hair—she had a chronic passion for jingles, evidently—danced as she shook her head at him; "I have heard many strange tales about you lately."

"It is as bad a habit to put faith in all you hear," said Laurence, meeting her hard smile with a cold, steady stare, "as it is to put faith in every one you meet."

"Certainly it is," assented Mrs. Llewellyn; "that is the reason why I turn a deaf ear to all insinuations—however much they may look like truth—until I have faced the man or woman at whom the shafts are aimed. You follow me?"

Laurence nodded his head.

"*I* hear that you have broken off your engagement with my niece, Hester, Mr. Raxford," she said in a lower tone; "but I don't believe it."

"Why not?" asked Laurence, curtly.

"Because it would not be like you," she replied ; "because I am sure that you are too honourable and steadfast a man, Mr. Raxford, to give up Hester on account of the misfortunes that have happened to her family. She is the same girl to whom you offered your hand, and I feel sure that it was not for her money—her father's money—that you sought her."

"I am thankful, Mrs. Llewellyn, that you do me that justice in your thoughts—it was not for her money, or her chance of money."

"Then if you are still engaged, why do you let so dangerous a rival as Mr. Engleton monopolise all her attention ? " she said, with that demonstrative tetchiness which always betrayed the scheme she had in view ; "why didn't you take her down to dinner ? "

Laurence saw clearly through this shallow, but obtrusive woman of the world. He remembered all at once her anxiety to throw Mr. Engleton into the society of her daughter, her manœuvring for that end—her jealousy of the many young women who had set their caps at the rich bachelor. He had been at a loss for a reason for Mrs. Llewellyn's wish that he should marry Hester now—until he read the fear that Mr. Engleton would fall in love with Hester himself, now Hester was free to accept a second offer. A partnership with Fyvie and Fyvie for her son, and Laurence ousted from his place for his fickleness, was no longer on the cards—the firm was a ruin, and Laurence had been fickle to some purpose.

"I am not engaged to Miss Fyvie now," said Laurence.

"Not engaged ! " she cried. "Is it possible ? "

"I am so far free from any wish to make Miss Fyvie my wife—and yet so deeply interested in her well-being—that it would afford me an intense pleasure to see so worthy a man as our host marry so excellent a girl as Hester is. I wish that any power of mine could bring that to pass, Mrs. Llewellyn."

"Well—I am astonished ! All *is* true, then, that I have heard," she said, looking rudely—even fiercely—at him ; "you did fall in love with the mining wench, and Hester found you out, and resented your low tastes by dismissal."

It was a harsh speech, but he had not expected mercy from Mrs. Llewellyn. It made his face flush to the roots of his hair, and his blood tingle unpleasantly to his finger-ends, and the tips of his ears. But he stood his ground still.

"Yes, it is true that I fell in love with the mining wench —and I shall never get over that fall, Madam."

"I would not glory in my treachery to Hester, Mr. Raxford. It is in bad taste—spoken to the face of her aunt, too."

"It was the treachery of a little-minded being, whose soul was narrow enough to stoop to the commission of a theft, that separated me from your niece, Mrs. Llewellyn—not my treachery, I beg you to consider."

Then it was Mrs. Llewellyn's turn to blush till the colour of her hair was pale by contrast. This was a deadly thrust of the rapier on Laurence Raxford's part, and he believed that his adversary deserved it—though she was a woman, and it was etiquette to spare her. We are of opinion that she deserved it, too.

"It is all very fine to invent excuses," said Mrs. Llewellyn after a pause. "I don't know what was stolen, and I don't want to know. All that I am aware of is, that you were not justified in breaking that engagement."

She did not seek to prolong the conversation; she turned her attention to her neighbour, for she was afraid of Laurence, and of what next he might say, now that he had lost all respect for her sex. She was glad when he was talking to her daughter, and those clear, fearless eyes were not probing to her very soul, reading her guilt as it had never been read yet. She hated this Laurence Raxford, but she did not wish to make an enemy of him; she had a faint hope that he might be led to marry her niece, and leave her daughter free for Mr. Engleton. She knew that Hester had loved Laurence very deeply—that she loved him still, in all probability—and her faith in true affections did not lead her to believe that Laurence cared a great deal for the " mining wench." That was a fancy such as men have very often, and which so very, very seldom comes to marriage—the fancy that fills the streets, nothing more than that !

She was vexed at her own craft now, for she was aware that she had over-reached herself. She had sinned grievously, and in an unwomanly fashion, to separate Hester from the upstart partner, and now Hester was free to become her daughter's rival. She was sure that Mr. Engleton had paid

Jane a certain amount of attention, and that Jane had encouraged it and exulted in it, in her quiet way; and now
when she had come to Devon to finish matters, and hook
this goodly fish, lo! he was talking earnestly to Hester
Fyvie, and looking at Hester as he had never in all his life
looked at Miss Llewellyn. If she had let things take their
course, and had never interfered, how much better it would
have been. She would have got her fool of a daughter off
her hands, and made her a rich woman—now the foothold
that she had gained was slipping away from her.

Mr. Engleton was certainly attentive to Hester that evening; it was remarked in more than one quarter before the ladies
had risen to withdraw, that those attentions were certainly
"marked." And when the ladies had retired, and the decanters were circulating more briskly, it was noticed that Mr.
Engleton was particularly thoughtful.

Once he moved his chair closer to Mr. Fyvie, as though
full of some important communication, and then he began
suddenly upon a plan of his concerning hospitals, that was
for once a "turn off," and not in any way interesting to the
planner. For he had made up his mind to ask Miss Fyvie
to be his wife, as he would have asked her some months
ago if Laurence had not been too quick for him. Laurence's
rapidity of movement had staggered him then, though he
had swallowed his disappointment, and disguised it admirably well. And now Laurence was apart from her,
and Hester was free, he thought that the great plunge
might be made, and that there was no time like the
present.

He had his doubts—his very grave doubts—as to how his
offer would be received, but he was no student of womankind, and his sister—who knew all about this love affair—
had assured him that no woman would say No to him.
Hester Fyvie had always been kind, gracious and sisterly—
she had been more kind, if more sad, than usual that night.
He took that as a good omen—not thinking that she might
be grateful in her heart towards him for having been a good
friend.

Suddenly, and when the wine was low in the decanters, a
new idea seized him. He was a man of impulse, and his
impulses were more than ordinarily generous.

"Raxford," he said, in an aside, "don't join the ladies

when we rise, but step into the garden — under the old tree on the lawn."

Laurence looked surprised, but assented by a nod; and when the gentlemen rose a few minutes afterwards, and Engleton led the way towards the drawing-room, our hero passed through the window into the garden—now cold and gloomy with the late autumn, and with the leaves thick about the lawn and gravel paths, despite all the gardener's care.

In a few minutes Engleton joined him, passed his arm through his, and led him away to the very spot where he had quarrelled with Hester Fyvie.

"Now, Raxford, tell me the plain truth, like an honest fellow," he said. "Do you love Miss Fyvie—or do you not ? "

CHAPTER III.

ANOTHER LOVE AFFAIR.

The question put by Charles Engleton startled Laurence Raxford. He was not prepared for so leading an interrogative after dinner; he was not quite certain that the dinner, or the wines which accompanied it, had not been too much for the composure of his host.

Still it was a question easily answered, and requiring no evasion ; and the gentleman before him might be actuated by the best of motives.

"No, Mr. Engleton," he replied, "I do not love Miss Fyvie."

"Thank you," he said sitting down on the rustic seat beneath the tree. "I am glad to hear it, for I have come to the conclusion that I do."

He sat down, crossed his arms, and stirred the fallen leaves around him with his feet. He was sober and serious enough, as befitted a man thinking of a wife. Laurence sat down beside him, saying,

" I am glad to hear that, too, Mr. Engleton, for it is good news."

" That depends how the matter is likely to end," said Engleton ; " for Miss Fyvie is a girl of determination, and if she has made up her mind not to marry, or to have you after all, why, it's all over with the couple of us. I thought that I would put the question to you, Raxford, for this reason—that there might be a hankering after her in your heart—a consciousness that you had not acted up to the letter of· your engagement—a wish even to renew the old ties. Then I would not have stood in the way ; not so much out of charity to you," he added—"for no man studies another when a woman is in the case, perhaps—but out of consideration for the feelings of Hester, who, woman-like, would have known, by instinct, all that was in your thoughts. But you tell me frankly that Hester is nothing to you ? "

" Nothing."

" Then I shall briefly lay my plans before her," he said. "Ahem—not my plans exactly, but my suit, and you, as a friend, will wish me success ? "

" With all my heart," said Laurence, shaking hands with him.

" I—I should like to know what you two quarrelled about," said Engleton, after a moment's consideration ; " for she possesses a good temper, and yours, I take it, is pretty equable. Why you could not agree, is quite a mystery."

" And I hate mystery," said Laurence. " Well, there was a mistake about a letter first, and that separated us. In the meantime, I fell in love with another woman."

" Impossible ! " said the enthusiastic Engleton.

" A woman who was unlike anyone whom I had ever seen—who was clever, original, and beautiful, who——oh ! but you'll not care to hear me go on like this."

" And when shall you be married ? "

" Never," said Laurence, gloomily ; " it's all ended be-tween us."

" What ! a row in that quarter, too ! Why, Raxford, you must have a frightful temper, after all ! How I have been deceived in you ! "

" I am an unlucky man—that's all," said Laurence.

"Had we not better go in? Sitting out here bare-headed, and in dress-coats, is not a wise step."

"Or complimentary to the rest of the company. Rax-ford, I shall propose to-night, if there's a chance."

"I would not be too hasty," suggested Laurence.

"I never sleep on my projects; and that's a good joke of yours about being too hasty. Ha! ha! a capital joke!"

"I don't see where the point of the jest lies."

"Why, when I was watching my opportunity to propose to Miss Fyvie the last time we were together, old Fyvie came down one morning and told me confidentially that you had made Hester an offer of your hand; and you had only been in the place three or four weeks."

"I *was* too hasty," Laurence confessed; "though I did not warn you for that reason—or think of that mistake of mine. I wished you to consider whether time and place were suitable — whether a better opportunity might not present itself at Tavistock."

"I hope that I shall not frighten Miss Fyvie very much," he said. Then the two walked into the house.

Laurence wondered a few minutes afterwards at his own anxiety to see Hester Fyvie engaged to Charles Engleton— was it for her sake, or for his own? He leaned against the corner of the piano in the drawing-room, and watched her from the distance with Mr. Engleton hovering about her, and manœuvring for the first vacant chair on either side of her, and he wished very heartily that this might be a match. It would raise Hester back to the old position, which she had adorned, and set her in her proper sphere—it would give Engleton a good wife, as surely as it gave her a good husband.

This for her sake!—what would it do for his own? Well, it would take a load from his conscience, for he felt that he had darkened her life by his seeming duplicity— that he had taught her to love him, and then passed away from her to make love, with all his heart, to Milly Athorpe. He could not shake from his mind the impression that their engagement was scarcely at an end; he felt as if his promise to her had never been broken, for she had told Milly that *he* should give her up, and that unless he did so, she would hold firm to her engagement. In their explana-tion together Hester had told him that he was free, but it was a hurried explanation, born of an excitable meeting, and he could scarcely remember all that had passed on that night. They had met very often; they had spoken coldly and dispassionately; they were good friends, who understood each other's thoughts, perhaps; they could never in all their lives be more than brother and sister; but he should be glad to hear that Hester had accepted the offer of Mr. Engleton. That would free him from his ideas—concerning the old compact — ideas which would have troubled him at times, even if he had married Milly Athorpe, or if Milly had not spoken of his duty to the woman whom he had innocently deceived.

He had combated Milly's reasoning successfully; he had laughed at his mother's; he had almost scoffed at Mrs. Llewellyn's on that very evening, but he could not completely master his own. There was a drag upon his freedom, for he felt that there was a wrong or a sorrow that Hester Fyvie nursed, and he feared that it concerned himself. There was a staidness and quietness about her which was new—more, there was a firmness which showed itself frequently in her lower condition of life, now that she held the reins of management at the little villa where the Fyvies lived. He should feel more happy in his mind if Hester accepted Mr. Engleton; he should feel wholly free, which he scarcely did now, though he was waiting for Milly —though it made his heart more light to think that he was waiting for her patiently and trustfully.

Mr. Engleton proposed that very evening. He had made up his mind, and he was prompt and business-like about it. He found the vacant seat, making quite a race for it between himself and Mrs. Llewellyn, who would have kept him out of it, if possible, and Hester, innocent of her host's intentions, smiled a welcome to him. When he had sat by her side ten minutes, or a quarter of an hour, she had her doubts, for the first time, of Mr. Engleton's thoughts, and wished that she was away by her mother's side instead of in that suspicious recess by the window, where nobody could hear them, and where they might be taken for lovers by those who were curious enough to look after them. Mrs. Llewellyn was curious, and on the watch — Miss Llewellyn, also, perhaps, though she was turning over a photographic album with Miss Engleton; the rest were talking, laughing, sipping coffee, or thinking it was time that their carriages were called round to the front door.

Mr. Engleton watched his opportunity, and dashed suddenly into the subject.

"I hope your visit here, Miss Fyvie, has not given rise to many painful associations."

"A few—not many," said Hester, with a sigh.

"I want you to get used to coming here," he said, in tones that put Hester completely on her guard at once, "just as if it was the old home, where no changes had occurred."

"It would be hard to believe in that," said Hester; "but I hope that I shall get used to visits here—though the first step has cost me an effort."

"If I could only hope that you would consider it as your future home, Miss Fyvie," said Engleton, rapidly getting up the steam for the occasion, "your home for good. If you would only give me a hope to claim you for its mistress presently, I should be the happiest fellow in all the world. For I really love you very much—and I want you to try to love me, a little, some day!"

It was an eccentric confession, that might have elicited a smile from one less interested than Hester. But Hester, on the contrary, felt inclined to burst into tears; she was distressed in mind at this avowal, and though she had had an idea once or twice in life that Mr. Engleton was inclined to be fond of her, yet the confession had come upon her with a genuine surprise; for the time and place for the confession had not been chosen well, or even with consummate delicacy. Still it was a well-meant offer, and Engleton was in earnest.

"I don't want to hurry you with an answer," he said. "I feel that I have been too quick, perhaps, with my offer; but I thought that it was best over, and that you might like a little time for consideration. Please don't answer me tonight—I would so much rather that you wouldn't! I won't have an answer now."

For he had already read his answer in the deepening gloom of her face, and he felt sure that second thoughts were the better for him.

"You are very kind to make me this offer, Mr. Engleton," said Hester, astonished at her own firmness, now that she

25

had found her voice at last, "and I thank you for the great compliment that you have paid me—me who can bring you no beauty, no money, no love, Sir."

"Love will come in time," cried Engleton. "Why, it must, Miss Hester!"

Hester shook her head.

"I am sure that you will not pain me by any further discussion on the subject—that you will accept my answer now as final—that you will let me think of you as a friend again."

She spoke as if, for the last few minutes, he had been her enemy, and he ran his hands through his wiry hair, and looked utterly crest-fallen.

"There isn't a chance, then, for me?" he said dismally.

"No," Hester answered. "And it is the best for you, too, that there should not be. I could only marry you for your money," she added, with asperity.

"I wish that you would marry me for something—I don't care for what!" he replied; "for there never was a girl I cared for except yourself."

"Not Miss Llewellyn?"

"Oh! bother her!" cried he. "I liked her because she was a relation of yours, and something like you about the nose; but I couldn't marry her because she had your nose, you know!"

This was turning from sentiment to burlesque at a jump, although Engleton did not see the humour in his speech, and thought Hester was somewhat unfeeling to smile at him. He went back to sentiment again, however, and turned Hester grave enough with his next words.

"I loved you long before I knew it myself, or you knew Mr. Raxford. I wondered why I was constantly inventing excuses to come down to Devon—and I bought this house because it had been yours, and I thought that I should not like strangers to live in it. If it hadn't been for Mr. Raxford coming here—that was your father's fault!—I think that I might have persuaded you to have me?"

"You are a very lucky man to escape me," she said bitterly; "for I am vain, exacting, irritable, jealous and unjust. You know how soon this Mr. Raxford found out my failings and tired of me."

"Pardon me—but he says——"

"Ah! no matter what he says," she interrupted; "he would do his best to clear me with honour, I dare say. And yet, after all, he was true and honourable until he thought me false. You will go away now, Mr. Engleton—I am distressed and excited, and don't know what I am saying. Surely," she said impetuously, "you will spare me?"

"I—I am very sorry that I have given you pain by my addresses," he said, springing to his feet; "you will forgive me, I am sure. I—I only wanted to make you a happy woman."

"Yes—yes, I know that, but you will meet with a better wife than I could have made you—you are deserving of a better one."

"I don't want a better."

And with this flat assertion of his wishes, and denial of her assurances, he walked out of the room, and was not seen for half an hour afterwards. When he returned, the guests had thinned, and his sister was apologising for his withdrawal, and telling everybody that he was subject to these sudden "rushings."

"No, I'm not," he said flatly, "but I was a little upset to-night, gentlemen—too much drink, shall we say? That's the best excuse."

"Charles!" exclaimed his sister, "how can you?"

"Has Mr. Raxford gone?"

"Yes, he and his mother went away five minutes since."

"And the Fyvies—oh! here they are! Miss Fyvie, will you allow me to escort you to your carriage? Thank you."

"To our hired fly, he means," said Mr. Fyvie jocularly; "and capital flies you can get at the Lion, if it wasn't for the screws they put between the shafts. We have one to-night, Engleton, that I'll swear I sold fifteen years ago as incapable—a grey jibber, with one eye out."

Engleton escorted Miss Fyvie to the fly, Mr. and Mrs. Fyvie bringing up the rear. He did not address a word to Hester until her father and mother were in the carriage with her, when he leaned forwards, shook hands, and said,

"Tell them all that I have said, and all that I have been disappointed in, Miss Fyvie, and then—and then forget all about it, if you please!"

Hester did not answer, and she remained very quiet in the corner of the carriage for a while. Mr. Fyvie, having re-

25—2

covered his astonishment, spoke to his wife, congratulated
her on the way in which she had gone through the fatigues
of the evening—thought that a lower estate agreed with
her, take it altogether—remarked on Mrs. Llewellyn's vigour,
and her lord and husband's abruptness, and fancied that both
of them might have preached less at him about imprudence,
and so forth—finally, came to a full stop, leaned across, and
looked into his daughter's face.

" I am not asleep," said Hester, mistaking his movement,
probably mistaking it intentionally.

" My dear, I never thought that you were."

Another pause, then he said—

" May a curious old man ask what Mr. Engleton meant
to-night ? "

" Nonsense—that's all."

" Has he asked you to become Mrs. E.—and have you
snubbed him in consequence, like a well-conducted young
lady as you are ? "

Mr. Fyvie was a sharp man yet, and jumped at conclusions
with considerable perspicuity.   Hester had made up her
mind to postpone her revelation till the morning, but her
father had been too quick for her.

" Mr. Engleton asked me to become his wife—and I refused him, papa," she said ; " for oh ! I had no love for him,
and I did not want to share his high position without it.
He was very kind and very earnest, but—he has made me
very miserable."

She would have spread her hands before her face, but her
father suddenly took them in his own.

" We can't have any crying about this, Hester ; there's
nothing to cry about, unless you're sorry that you didn't
say 'yes.' "

" Sorry ! " said Hester scornfully, " if he had been king
of England, I would not have married him."

" Right enough.   Nobody wants you to marry him—some
of us might be sorry to have you married at all.   What do
you say, old lady ? " to his wife at his side.

" It was a good offer," she replied ; " and Mr. Engleton's
of very good family, and quite a gentleman in himself."

" Pooh !—a fellow that's always talking about drain-pipes
and sewage," said the sire, lightly ; " a nice fellow in his
way, barring his nasty talk, but not good enough for our girl."

"Too good for me—a fretful and dissatisfied woman ! "

This was the second time that night that Hester had called herself names ; and she did it with a vengeance, as though she thought that she deserved every epithet thus self-bestowed.

"Ah ! we'll find a first-rate husband for you some day, Hester."

Hester did not smile at her father's jest.

"I hope—I hope that you'll never talk to me about marrying," she cried passionately. "I will never marry ! "

"Hester, my dear," said the mother languidly, "you're not thinking anything about Mr. Raxford now ? That's not showing a proper respect for yourself."

"He is free—he may marry whom he pleases. I set him free myself," said Hester wildly ; "but I love him ! There, I am not ashamed to own it. I am true to my first promise to love him always, and I shall never—never think of anybody else."

"Whew ! " said Mr. Fyvie ; "it's out at last ! I knew it."

That is what Laurence had known too, and which rested on his hopes distinct from hers, like a weight that there was no upraising. This was the shadow that had fallen on him that night in the drawing-room of Tavvydale House. This was the burden which Hester had to bear, and which she had borne well, until the current had grown too strong for the flood-gates. Then suddenly she had ceased to resist— for they had spoken of marriage, and giving in marriage, and this was a young woman who had lost her lover by her own self-will.

But he had never given her up ; and in her heart she held fast to her engagement. She had set him free ; but he had never by a word, even at so late an hour as this, when he confessed to a love for another, accepted his freedom, or told her that she was *not* engaged to him. It was an odd reasoning, and it only rendered her more miserable to brood on this, though face to face with Laurence she was an admirable actress.

"Courage, Hester," said her father ; "the storm is over, and it is late in the day to fret concerning it. Presently another and a brighter day for all who are young and pure as you are. Leave the old to complain."

"No, I will keep with the old; and they shall not complain whilst I am with them," was Hester's ready answer.

～～～～～～～～～～～～

CHAPTER IV

MILLY'S NEW HOME.

MEANWHILE, it behoves us to see how Milly Athorpe was bearing the absence of her lover. Here was a woman in the same position as Hester Fyvie, loving the same man, and set as far apart from him. A woman who had the advantage in Laurence loving her in return—if that be an advantage rather than an aggravation of despair, when the certainty of separation is arrived at.

The younger, and the stronger, as she was the more lowly woman—bore up better, for she had other cares to fight against, and that kept her from brooding. She set that one particular care as much aside as possible—for that belonged to the past now. In her own room sometimes, when Inez was asleep, and did not require her attendance, she could sit down and face it, even shed tears over her loss, as a girl has a right to shed tears over the loss of a sweetheart true and affectionate, and yet sundered from her by unavoidable circumstances—torture herself by drawing the vivid picture of what might have been, had she thought more of herself, and less of the duties that had devolved upon her.

But in the every-day world she was content—even cheerful. She possessed a strong will and it bent her into the new channel, and trained her thoughts aright; she was a religious girl, who could find a consolation for all worldly troubles in God's Book, and when the troubles were at their thickest, she was calm and brave and strong withal.

Milly had come down to Tavvydale with Inez. For the convenience of having Inez near her, she had taken a little house in the mining village itself, and given up Wind-Whistle Cleft for good. She had found a tenant for her little cottage there and it was pleasant, when Inez was strong enough to be left, to go in search of her rent through all the spots that were home-marks which she loved. We believe that the rent was only eighteen-pence a week, and *that* she had thought at one time of offering to Mr. Fyvie, now that he was in reduced circumstances, but her common sense had deterred her from wounding the old man's pride by the offer.

She had come down to Tavvydale with her uncle's wife then, and the story had been quietly told of how Inez had not been to blame, and how Captain Athorpe had been unduly jealous of her, and what a sad result had followed the mistake. Tavvydale listened to the recital, and believed what it liked about it, and thought, take it altogether, no better of Mrs. Athorpe. Tavvydale knew the world, and put this and that together, and was not to be hoodwinked at its time of life. It was a neat story, but Tavvydale had its own version of the facts, and set it side by side with the more authentic narrative. Mrs. Athorpe was only hindered from running away from home by her husband's stepping in to stop her—the charitable, who had never liked Captain Athorpe, pitied the result, and were sorry for the wife's affliction; but they were nearly all of one opinion, that Mrs. Athorpe would have eloped with Jonathan Fyvie, if she had not been prevented.

"He will believe this, too—he will never take your word and mine, should he ever come back, Milly," sighed Inez.

"He will believe us—when he returns," said Milly assuringly.

"But you don't think that he ever will come back—in your heart, Milly, you don't," said Inez anxiously.

"Every night I pray for his return."

"Ah! for your own sake as well as mine—that you may be quit of all my fretfulness, and wickedness," said the captious woman; and then Milly had to assure her that it was not for that she prayed.

Thus it may be seen that Milly had no light task in this quarter—Inez being very weak, and in her weakness very irritable and jealous. Affliction, if it had improved the character of Mrs. Athorpe, had not transformed her into a heroine—it was not in her nature to develop any heroic traits, or to be meek and angelic with her moral change.

She was an invalid—she might remain an invalid all her

life. She had been snatched as from the very jaws of death ; for Athorpe had left her for dead, and Churdock had not thought her living when he had carried her up the steep sides of the Cleft to his mother's house.

All her strength had departed, and she dragged her limbs about the rooms, holding chairs and tables in her progress, the wreck of the woman that she had become, the ghost of the handsome wife whom Captain Athorpe had taken to himself, and trusted in.

She was fully alive to the dangers to which her vanity had led her ; she did not spare herself one reproach, on the contrary, she magnified her sin, and despaired of mercy in this world, and the next. Though she *was* returning to her husband's home, full of resolution to make that home a happy one from that night, though she had defeated Jonathan Fyvie, her tempter, and bade him depart from her for ever, and leave her guiltless in her husband's eyes, it was only Milly who could console her by those assurances, not herself. By herself she was a woman wholly wretched—and she quenched the sunlight from the home she dwelt in by the force of her morbidity. Add to this that she deplored the loss of her beauty, though she took it as a judgment against her for her vanity ; that she was ever on the watch for signs of Milly tiring of her, and fretted at signs that had never had existence ; that she was beset by a craving to see her husband, and tell him that he had judged her wrongly at the last— that she was cross with Milly, and then sorry that Milly had been pained by her capriciousness, and the reader will not envy our heroine her charge.

Milly had not gone back to her school at once. She was behind time ; she had taken an extraordinary lease of holidays, and Mr. Wells was deeply offended, and had suspended her. He had gone very much out of his way to secure Milly the appointment, and then Milly had absented herself within a week or two after entering upon her duties. He had half-engaged a substitute, when Milly had returned to the village, and every child in Tavvydale had gone half mad with the news. Then he thought it over again—called on Milly, heard the whole truth, and nothing but the truth, and softened at once, like a good-hearted, sensible old gentleman that he was.

In the autumn, then—in the clear October months that

one finds in Devonshire as a rule—everything was in a state
of rest, and there was no sensation to stir the little world of
Tavvydale. Milly was teaching regularly at her school
during the day—teaching Inez regularly in the evening, or,
trying, perhaps, to teach her patience and submission.

Coming home from school, she would find Inez watching
at the door for her—a large-eyed woman, with a sallow face,
that had become lined before its time.

"What a time you have·been, Milly—how you must have
been loitering, and I all alone like this, too !" Inez would
say sometimes.

"I have been to the Tavvydale library for a book that I
think will suit you."

"Ah ! you are always considerate, and I'm an ingrate
that is not deserving of a thought."

Sometimes Inez would mourn the absence of James
Whiteshell, once again in London for the winter season,
teaching a crowd of little ones to dance ; she would have
been happy with Mr. Whiteshell, whose reminiscences of the
dancing days—the theatrical days—almost took away the
sting of present pain—the horror of present isolation. Poor
Inez was full of regrets and reproaches, and therefore not
pleasant company—as who is with half the strength gone
away from him, and with all the hopes of peace or of advancement in the background for ever ? It was a marvel, that a
girl so young as Milly—a girl unused to face sorrow and
suffering in others, having a sorrow of her own, too, that
less thoughtful girls would have made much of, having an
aunt looked down upon by Tavvydale respectability, and an
uncle wandering in the world friendless and alone—it was a
marvel, we repeat, that a girl so young as Milly should have
settled down to all this, and shown no traces of the "wear
and tear !"

Was she well and strong with all this ?—or would she
fight on to the end, like a thoroughbred, and then collapse ?
She was looking well and strong, at all events, and the
colour had stolen back to the cheeks of the Devonshire
rose.

She was absent on school duties, and Inez had curled
herself into an arm-chair, and was dozing away the afternoon—looking not unlike a dead woman in her sleep—when
a knock was heard at the outer door.

"Come in," said Inez.

The knock was repeated, however, and Inez gave vent to a scream of "Come in!" at this. She was weak, and to move to the door was an effort just then;—why could not people touch the latch and enter?

The latch was touched at the second adjuration, and a plump, round-faced, rosy-cheeked old lady, with silver ringlets hanging in bunches on each side of her head, came into the cottage.

"I hope that I am not disturbing you?" she said.

"I was going to sleep—I am an invalid," said Inez, in reply; "but I am used to being disturbed now. What is it?"

"You—you surely are not Milly?"

"No, I am Mrs. Athorpe," was the answer here; "you have heard of me, I dare say?" she added, with a curling lip.

"I cannot say that I have," said the old lady, in a bewildered manner. "I may have heard, and forgotten, for I have not a good memory. Are you—are you Milly's mother?"

The slight figure in the chair writhed uneasily at this, and two thin hands were beaten impatiently together.

"My God! have I changed so much as to be taken for Milly's mother?"

She sat and thought for awhile of this great alteration in her, then she said,

"I am only a few years Milly's senior—her uncle's young wife, just recovering from a violent illness. I don't think that I am six years older than Milly,—certainly not more than six."

"Dear me! you must have been very ill indeed," said the visitor. "I should not have thought it, now."

"May I ask your name and business, Madam?" said Inez.

"My name is Raxford, and I wish to see Miss Athorpe."

"Is your business particular?"

"Well—not very particular, perhaps," Mrs. Raxford confessed; "but I was curious to see Miss Athorpe for myself. I have heard a great deal of her."

"From your son?"

"Partly."

" Your son, I hope, has not sent you here ? "

" He has not sent me—but why do you hope that ? "

" Because—it is better that we all keep apart—that he should not come, or send any messages, to unsettle my niece again. He has his duties to fulfil, and she has hers, and I don't see any occasion myself why they should ever meet."

" Oh ! I am quite of the same opinion," said Mrs. Raxford, unable to resist a toss of her head at this ; "quite of the same opinion as you are."

" That is good news," said Mrs. Athorpe ; "will you take a seat ? Milly will be home in half an hour, or there-abouts."

Mrs. Raxford took the seat indicated, by the window full of geraniums and fuschias—as flower-burdened as the window of the cottage had been in Wind-Whistle Cleft—and waited patiently for Milly. She had come out of curiosity, partly ; she had come to analyse Milly with her woman's shrewdness, and even sift, like a jealous mother, for facts against her, that should assure herself—perhaps Laurence—how wise a step it was to keep away from her. She had other little schemes in her head, too, and the reader will guess all about them before the chapter ends.

Her first appearance at the cottage had been inauspicious ; she had met with one member of the Athorpe family, and a very tetchy, odd, foreign-looking, old kind of a young woman she was. Probably Milly would be like her, and she, Mrs. Raxford, would be one more mother to throw up her hands in astonishment, and mourn the perverted tastes of her son. Young men had strange tastes, and dashed strangely at their fancies—Laurence had been under a spell here !

She sat and thought of this Milly, and of a hundred things akin to her and connected with her—of Hester Fyvie and her Laurence in particular. The weak woman stared at her for awhile, and then went off to sleep again, breathing with difficulty in her sleep, and panting more like a dog than a woman. The motherly heart of Mrs. Raxford softened as she watched her. She rose and bent over her, fancying once that she was choking in her sleep.

" Poor thing !—how ill she looks," murmured Mrs. Raxford ; " how ill she must have been ! "

" Ah ! you may say that, Madam," said Mrs. Athorpe,

suddenly opening her eyes; "for three long weeks I looked death steadily in the face, and prayed God not to take me."

' Were you afraid to die, then ? "

' Yes—bitterly afraid," said Inez; "for my husband mistrusted me, and I was anxious to see him again and tell him that I was not so bad—not one half so bad as he believed—as the people about here believe to this day. To see him once more—and *then* to die, Madam !"

" Oh ! dear," sighed Mrs. Raxford. This was a strange family into which her son Laurence would have married —all manner of things spoken against the Athorpes in the village, evidently, and one woman with whispers circulating against her fame. What a lucky thing for Laurence that he had escaped this doutbtful lot ! Still the woman's excitement touched her sympathy—she might be a woman unjustly suspected, as any woman might be in a world so apt to think the worst of everything. She was a woman more sinned against than sinning, or she would have not spoken with that earnestness.

" I am keeping you from sleep," said Mrs. Raxford.

" Oh ! I shall not sleep again—the least thing disturbs me, and I knew that you were standing over me. What made you do that ? "

" You were breathing heavily, and I thought that——"

" That I was going to die," added Inez, quickly ; " I always sleep like that. And I am getting stronger every day I can walk the whole length of the street with Milly's arm to lean upon."

" I am glad to hear that you are recovering."

" Why, you are a stranger—why should you be glad to hear that I am getting well again ?—what am I to you, Mrs. Raxford ? "

Mrs. Raxford was embarrassed by these sharp replies. She coughed, and stammered, and felt that Mrs. Athorpe was a trifle too much for her. She made an effort to stand her ground, though.

" I think that it is common charity to be glad when a woman recovers from a long illness—just as it is charity that makes us pray at church for all in misery and affliction."

" I wonder how many really think of what they are

praying for," said Inez; "it is common-prayer—common-place prayer, like your commonplace condolence. You must excuse me if I speak abruptly," she said, less acrimoniously; "I am an invalid, and have been humoured lately. A little while ago, I was the life of my home—almost the only one who could make poor Captain Athorpe smile. You will excuse me?" she added, gesticulating with both hands, in that foreign manner which Laurence Raxford had not liked.

"Pray do not mention it."

Mrs. Athorpe had had her say, and was inclined to be more courteous. She felt better now that she was thoroughly awake; she was not in pain, and Milly would be home directly.

"Will you take a seat again?—my niece will not be long now," she said. "Your appearance here will be a great surprise to her. I hope that you will not disturb her—she is disturbed enough by me, poor girl! and would be all the better for more rest."

"Is she your only nurse—and friend?"

"The only friend in the world, save one poor old man, living in London," Inez answered. "Why, without her I should have died long ago, and yet I am not grateful. I worry her—and tease her with my humours, till anyone but Milly would wish me in my grave. Madam, she stands as near the angels as she can."

Inez woke up to enthusiasm, and Mrs. Raxford sat down once more, bewildered at the variable moods of this sick woman.

"I don't know what you have come for—you haven't offered me a very fair explanation," said Inez; "but I trust it is not to unsettle her by any thoughts of your son. She has got over that—and the matter had better rest. I am sure that she would not marry him if you were to go down on your knees, and beg her to become his wife. If he were dying, and marrying him might save him, she might do that, perhaps—that's all. You perceive how ill I am," she added, with characteristic selfishness, "and how impossible it is for her to leave me!"

"Yes—I see," said Mrs. Raxford absently.

"And she would not—even if I wished her, which I do at times, when I am full of pain and aggravation. They

say women are patient in affliction—well, I am not, Madam.
It was never my nature to be patient."

"I shall not ask Milly to become my son's wife," said
Mrs. Raxford, by way of assurance to her companion;
"that has not once entered my thoughts."

"The idea has shocked you, perhaps? It is an unequal
match?"

"Well, yes—a little so, possibly," stammered Mrs. Raxford, at a loss for an answer.

"Why so?" demanded Inez imperiously, and with fresh
excitement; "what are you Raxfords, I wonder, that you
should lord it over Milly Athorpe. Her grandmother was
a lady, and her father's father was an honest man. Can
you go back even as far as that with *your* pedigree? Can
you show in all your purse-proud circle, Madam, a face and
figure like our Milly's—a more gentle-hearted, purer, better
girl? Why, I was a beauty myself, but I was jealous of
her face—and if I had had but the shadow of her virtues,
I should not have been a woman stricken down to helpless-
ness like this!"

She burst into tears, and turned of a stony grey. Mrs.
Raxford rushed to a water-bottle on the table, filled a glass,
and placed it to her lips.

"My dear woman, how excitable you are."

"Yes—and I have been worse since my illness," she
whispered. "Let me see, what was I saying?"

"Oh! never mind—don't try to recollect. Please don't
say any more."

"It doesn't matter what *I* say, at all events—I'm a poor
dependant here. I have not a penny in the world but what
I am indebted to Milly for. How many nieces would stand
by their aunts in marriage as that faithful girl has stood by
me?"

"Who's talking about Milly?" said a cheerful voice
behind them.

"Oh! here you are at last. What a time you have been,
to be sure, and I tormented by this woman here," she said.
"Well, well, there's nothing in the house that's worth
hurrying home for."

"I don't know that, when we have a visitor waiting for
us," said Milly, with a graceful bow to Mrs. Raxford.

"You are Milly, then?"

"Yes, Milly Athorpe. Did you wish to see me?"

"I have been curious to see you for a long time. My name is Raxford."

"His mother!" murmured Milly, as she sat down and faced the visitor. "Well, Mrs. Raxford, you are welcome here."

CHAPTER V.

THE DAUGHTER THAT MIGHT HAVE BEEN.

YES, she was very beautiful, thought Mrs. Raxford; in all her life she had not seen a face like that—a face that told its story well, and thrilled with its earnestness those who gazed too long at it. She was not surprised now that Laurence, with his love for the beautiful in nature, should have loved this girl before her. Her only wonderment was, that he should have had strength of will to put up with the loss of her—to become resigned to a separation from her.

She could have taken Milly in her arms, folded her to her heart, and kissed her then and there; but she resisted the impulse, lest the girl should take fresh hopes from her sympathy, and think that she was the bearer of glad tidings to her.

She was looking at Milly still, when Inez rose from her chair, and began to toil towards the stairs in one corner of the parlour.

"Are you going, Inez?" said Milly. "Surely," turning to Mrs. Raxford, "there's no necessity for this?"

"Not any," said Mrs. Raxford. "I have scarcely a motive to allege for this intrusion."

"I would rather go up stairs, and lie down for a little while," said Inez. "Mrs. Raxford has not let me sleep much this afternoon, and I must have rest, Milly."

"You will not be able to get down stairs again to-night."

"No matter. That will give you more room till bed-time," she answered.

Milly went up stairs with Inez, conducting her carefully

from stair to stair, till she had landed her in the upper room.

"What a trouble—a life-long trouble—I am to you, my child!" the invalid said as they went up stairs together.

"Nonsense! What a companion, Inez, saving me from my Robinson-Crusoe like existence in the Cleft."

"Hush! don't speak of the Cleft, where murder might have been done, Milly," she whispered. "I have been dreaming of the Cleft this afternoon, only I didn't tell that woman down stairs about it. An awful dream—with everything like reality before me."

"Ah! but this is reality, Inez ; and the worst is over."

"I will try to think so."

Milly was in the parlour again. She had removed her bonnet—she had taken to bonnets since her rise in life—and the beauty of her face was more apparent without it.

"Now, Mrs. Raxford, I am at your service."

Mrs. Raxford, however, was at a loss how to begin, or what to begin about. This was not the Milly whom she expected to find, and to whom she could have spoken words of kind, well-meant advice. She had expected a pretty, round-faced, high-complexioned maiden, with country clumsiness in everything she did and said, and with that unmistakable Devonshire accent, from which we have endeavoured to spare our readers, and which Milly had very faintly possessed at any time, and seemed latterly to have entirely dropped. Here was a girl, very beautiful, and graceful, and grave. She had heard that Milly was a nervous girl, but her timidity was not apparent on this occasion, and the mother was at a disadvantage even in deportment.

"Are you very much surprised to see me here?" she asked.

"I am surprised, of course," answered Milly ; "but I always thought that I should see you some day."

"You have been anxious to see me, perhaps."

"I was anxious *once*," said Milly, in a lower tone, "anxious to know whether you were like your son, or if you would think me deserving of him—the girl that under the circumstances he should have chosen. You will pardon me speaking like this—for I do not think that you will misjudge my motive for thus speaking."

" No, I don't think that I shall misjudge you," said Mrs. Raxford.

" If—if things were different, I could not have spoken so calmly, and with so little hesitation. As it is, I can speak of you and your son, and not shrink much—at least, I can speak to you of him ! "

" Why to me ? "

" Why, are you not his mother ?—the mother who might have called me daughter, and forgiven, for her son's sake, my poor life and calling, if it had been ordered otherwise ? He used to tell me that he was sure his mother would not look down upon me, but love me for myself, just as he loved me. Well," with a shy glance towards her, through the tears that had stolen to her eyes, despite her self-command, " I think she would ! "

" My dear, if it had been ordered otherwise, as you say, I'm sure she would," burst forth the old lady, " for my Laurence's happiness is mine. I should not know any comfort without I did not share all the joys of his life ! "

" Yes, yes, you are the mother that he sketched to me," said Milly, hurriedly ; " and the daughter that might have been, and that would have loved you very, very dearly, ventures to kiss you in all reverence."

This was too much for the good lady, as it was for Milly, and both women cried in concert, as though their joys and sorrows were one already.

" Ah ! I see now," sobbed forth Mrs. Raxford ; " I understand Laurence better than I have ever done before. I think, Milly, that it was, perhaps, a very wise choice of his."

Milly shook her head.

" You must not think that, Madam."

" I wonder what you will think of me when I tell you that I came here to ask you to send some message to Laurence, that should render him more resigned to your loss ? "

" Why, that a mother's love brought you to ask me that —not any enmity to me ? "

" God forbid that I should bear enmity towards any one who has loved my boy ! "

" I can tell you, Mrs. Raxford, almost without a blush, what I might have never found words to tell to him—the

26

depth of my true love for Laurence. It is not like the love
that I have ever read in books—I don't know what it is
like, Madam ! "

" You love him still, then ? "

" Why, yes, with all my heart—with a love that I shall
never be ashamed of, though it sets me apart from him for
good."

" I—I can't tell him this."

" Oh ! no to be sure not," said Milly ; " I will think of a
few words for him, and you shall tell me what you think of
them, and if they are applicable. My love for him is a
secret between you and me—may I speak of it again ? "

" Yes, if you like," said Mrs. Raxford.

" I like—because I want you to understand me. If you
and Laurence think the best of me, I shan't mind what anyone else says, now. Well," drawing a deep breath, " I loved
him first, before he ever thought of me—when he came
into the Cleft carrying my uncle's bag. I never thought
that he *could* think of me ; but I made him my hero in my
heart, and shut him up there, treasuring my idol like a
romantic school girl. I knew how high he was above me
—he was like a demigod to my poor village fancies—and
when he came to earth to tell me that he loved me, why, I
felt raised to heaven."

She clapped her hands as though applauding her own
rhapsody, and the face was aglow with fire, and still more
beautiful.

" Are you self-taught ? " gasped Mrs. Raxford.

" Partly so. Why do you ask ?"

" These are strange words of yours."

" Ah ! the fault of the books I used to read in the Cleft
—they spoiled me with their poetry," said Milly. " I will
be less high-flown, and more precise."

" I did not ask you for the reason you think," murmured
the old lady.

" When I fancied that he had tried to deceive me, I was
more sorry for him than myself—I was heart-broken,
Madam. If troubles affecting my family had not come at
the same time to distract me in the first moments of my
bitterness, I think that I must have died. For there had
not stolen to me a thought of his unworthiness. And when
we met again, and I knew that I could never be his wife,

I was as glad that he could free himself from every stain against his honour, as though it placed him at the altar with me. And that is my comfort now, Madam—that he *was* the hero worthy of my picture."

"I—I wish that you did not think of him so much, Milly," said Mrs. Raxford, laying her hand upon the brown braids of hair caressingly. "I am sure that it would be better for you."

"I never speak of him to my aunt," replied Milly; "only to you have I confessed everything, for you are his mother, and understand me. Because I can never marry him —because I feel it my duty to say that I *will* never marry him—I can't love him the less, though I would, for his sake, make him believe so."

"Your duty lies with your aunt, you consider?"

"Yes—for her husband, my uncle, befriended me when I was left an orphan in the Cleft. My duty may take me in search of that uncle at any moment of my life, for I am on the watch for news of him—and my duty to my old lover is to keep away from him. For these reasons, and for another which casts a slur upon our name—oh! for many reasons, all unutterable—I gave up your son and begged him to marry the girl to whom he was first engaged."

"You begged him to do that?"

"I thought that he would be happy with her, and make her happy. And it appeared to me at first that it was his duty."

"It is—we think it is," said Mrs. Raxford.

"Is he—is he much altered?"

"He is a graver man, and he has lost that pleasant smile which won upon us all."

"I remember," said Milly.

"And it seems a pity that, as he can't marry you, and as Miss Fyvie has never forgotten him—as they were first engaged, and all that—it seems a pity that he doesn't make up his mind to have her."

"If he does not love her?" asked Milly, with his indignant tones ringing in her ears again, as they had rung out on the hills.

"He would love her again in time," asserted Mrs. Raxford; "he would make an affectionate husband and father!"

26—2

"Ye—es," said Milly, with a heavy sigh that she could not keep back ; "and I think it would be the best for us all. What message shall I send him ? "

She rose and stood deliberating with her finger to her lip. Suddenly she turned upon Mrs. Raxford, and said hurriedly,

"I have it—tell him that you have seen me, and that you have found me very happy. That you spoke of him to me, and that I said very calmly and dispassionately—very dispassionately—that I hoped that he was going to marry Miss Fyvie, shortly, for her sake, and for his word's sake. Will that do ? "

"Yes—it will do," said Mrs. Raxford, thoughtfully ; "but how—how can you find the heart to send that message, loving him as you do ? "

"Because I love him!   If I can't have him myself—if I am sure that *that* is utterly impossible, do you think that I would have him mourn for me all his life, when he might be happy in forgetting me ? No, Madam, I may wince a little when they tell me that he is married, but I will be glad to hear it, and I will pray with all my heart for a blessing on his future."

"God bless you, Milly. I think I understand you—and your nobleness and unselfishness. You would have been a daughter to me indeed ! " she could not help asserting as she kissed her.

"And I might have known a mother's love again—sharing it with Laurence. But, let it pass away. I have lived many years without it."

"I shall come very often now, and——"

"No, you must not come again," said Milly, firmly ; "it has been a great satisfaction—a great pleasure to me—to see you, but you would unsettle me for active life, and you and all belonging to you must not cross my path."

"We two women might be good friends.   Why not ? "

"You would speak of Laurence to me, and I might get dissatisfied, and repent my firmness. I have told you that I love him—and I am only a woman ! "

It was an entreaty not to come again, and Mrs. Raxford accepted it, and bade Milly good-bye, as though it was for ever.

"You do not regret the message that you send **to**

Laurence ? " she whispered ; " if so, my dear, I will not say a word about this meeting."

" I do not regret it," answered Milly.

So they parted ; and Milly, the daughter that might have been, stood very white and firm at the open cottage-door, and watched the messenger proceed upon her way.

CHAPTER VI.

AN AWKWARD POSITION FOR A HERO.

WAS the reasoning good of all these friends of Laurence Raxford ? Was the correct solution to this riddle of love's perplexities offered by the good folk interested in our hero ? Given two women in love with one man—with a man supposed to have been in love with both of them—one woman standing apart from him, maintaining that it was for ever, and pointing to the other waiting for him patiently—to find if it was better for Laurence Raxford to marry the woman who wanted him, than to mourn for the maiden who was beyond his reach ?

Milly had also wished that he should marry Hester Fyvie—had talked again of his past promise, and seen, as she thought, how a peaceful life would evolve from the union that she recommended, and end all doubts for good. When he was married, everybody could settle down, feeling sure that the best had come to pass, and to make the best of the result was surely everybody's duty.

Laurence knew what Mr. Fyvie's wishes were, though Mr. Fyvie had grown despondent concerning them of late ; the old gentleman—the old friend—would have preferred the clerk for a son-in-law, to Mr. Charles Engleton of the great house. He did not want a rich man for his daughter's husband ; and though he respected Mr. Engleton, and believed that he would have done his duty by Hester, still his heart was set on Laurence. Mrs. Fyvie, when she had time to arouse herself from her customary apathy, was almost of the same opinion, though she thought a little more of the great house, and a little less of Laurence, after Engleton's proposal. It would be comfortable to know that the old place still belonged to the family, and if Hester could only make up her mind to like Mr. Engleton, why it might be the beginning of better times again. But she kept this wish to herself, and agreed with everything that her husband said; she would not have uttered one feeble protest against Laurence becoming Hester's lord and master; if it was to be—so be it—there was an end to uncertainty at least, and the smiles would be back again on Hester's face. She would have preferred to talk the matter over with her strong-minded sister, Mrs. Llewellyn, but that lady kept to Tavvydale House, with her husband and daughter, as though no relations by blood were close at hand. Mrs. Llewellyn had resented their fall in life as an insult to herself and a slur upon the family. Mr. Fyvie was a parvenu, and he had come to grief, as parvenus will sometimes; she had often thought that he was far too extravagant for his means. So she remained at Tavvydale House, and Mr. Engleton began to wonder when the Llewellyns would go back to London. They never talked of going; they gave him Miss Llewellyn to walk with and to take rides with as often as they could conveniently manage it, and him; they clung affectionately to what Mrs. Llewellyn called "the home of their forefathers," as though Mr. Engleton was in unlawful possession of the same. All this, added to his recent disappointment, kept Charles Engleton depressed in spirits; it drew his attention to government affairs, too, as connected with the Treasury department, and he sketched out a plan for saving more money to the state, by allowing more time for business, and giving Treasury clerks fewer holidays during the year. By Heaven! they seemed to have all holidays, of Mr. Llewellyn's time must have been up weeks ago!

He sought refuge at Wheal Desperation, where the old stereotyped idea of what was best for Laurence was suggested from a new quarter.

"Upon my honour, Raxford, it's no good everybody being miserable," Engleton said one day; "you had better marry Miss Fyvie, and have done with it. We shall all be comfortable, then, I am sure."

"If I were certain that Miss Fyvie would have me, I

could not so insult her as to offer her my hand, with my heart full of love for another."

" Yes—but the other—you know——"

" Well—what of the other ? " asked Laurence, sternly.

" She can't have you," replied Engleton, stammering a little ; " it's not the correct thing to have you."

" I wonder that you can recommend me to adopt this course—you of all men, professing to admire Miss Fyvie."

" Upon my soul, I never shall admire another girl ! " cried Engleton, enthusiastically ; " but she won't have me, and she's miserable—everyone can see that. And you *were* engaged to her—that makes all the difference."

" Would you mind coming into the mine to-day? I want you to see the effects of this new powder," said Laurence, shutting the door suddenly in the face of further argument.

" I shall be most happy ; and about the new shaft for air, that I fancied might answer. Has the design come back from Mertram's ? "

" Yes. They sent it back by return of post."

" What did they say about it ? "

" That it was thoroughly impracticable."

" Oh ! did they ? " said Engleton, looking somewhat surprised. " Well, we'll go into the mine now. Have you seen the plan ? "

" Not yet."

" Look at it to-night—you'll find it as simple as it can be. The fact is, they can't make enough out of the job, to render it worth their while to undertake it. I hate selfish people ! "

He was unselfish himself, at any rate, or he would have never placed Hester Fyvie's felicity so far apart from his own. He was ready, like Milly Athorpe, to make a sacrifice for the common weal.

At home Laurence had his mother to charge him with the old story. He grew angry at last, and one evening shut up his book, leaned his arms across the table, and prepared to do battle with her, and end this worry for good.

" What is the objection of all my friends—my kind, but over-officious friends—to leaving me as I am ? Whom I marry concerns myself, rather than other people."

" Well, Laurence," protested his mother, " that is no

reason that you should fly into a bad temper about it. You never used to have any tempers at all—and I'm sure, in all your life, you never gave me a cross word."

"I hope that I never shall," said Laurence, softening. "I'm cross with myself, and with your arguments, perhaps, but not with you. Why, you are the one friend left me!"

"You will not listen calmly to me," said the mother.

"There, I have put away my books on purpose to listen to-night; let us settle the matter by a long talk concerning it—a long last talk, mother, and then the key turned for ever on this abominable skeleton."

"I don't know what you mean about skeletons," said the mother, "unless it is that you're becoming nothing but skin and bone. It's no good thinking of Milly, now—harassing yourself about a girl who has a sick aunt to nurse, and all that."

"I am content," said Laurence. "I stand apart from her—I am trying to forget her. I respect her wish that I should never cross her path, to disturb her by a sight of me. I have not seen her since she told me that she should never marry me!"

"That's something to say—but it is not all."

"What more can I say or do?"

"Forget her, and remember Hester."

"Hester Fyvie is nothing to me."

"You asked her once——"

"I know," cried Laurence, "don't remind me of my great folly. I was a blackguard, a scamp, a liar, everything that was vile, to make love to a woman without reflecting whether I could be true to her for life."

"There you go again!—firing off at the slightest word."

"All this, mother, I have heard before," said Laurence, lowering his voice again; "you will tell me next that we were engaged, and that I had no right to give her up."

"You never gave her up, Laurence."

"What makes you say that?" said Laurence, nervously.

This was his own thought, or the thought that he believed to be in Hester Fyvie's mind.

"You told her once that you did not set her free— that it was not your wish, you listened to her assertion that she resigned all claim upon you, and released you from your word — but you never accepted your freedom, and your silence, Laurence, may have left a hope with her."

"We thoroughly understand each other," said Laurence; "I could not coolly tell her that I did not want her for my wife—she set me free, and wished me happiness apart from her."

"But you *were* silent."

"How do you know all this?" said Laurence; "surely Hester has not related this story to you?"

"She told her father — her mother—the particulars of that first meeting between you when you came back to Tavvydale; she has told them since, on the night of Mr. Engleton's dinner-party—that in her heart she still felt herself engaged to you—there, I promised Mr. Fyvie that I would never say a word about it to you and now it has all escaped me! And he promised her that he would never mention it, too! Oh, dear! and now it has got round to you."

"I thought Hester Fyvie a more sensible woman than this," he said, his brow contracting; "she gave me up—she set me free by her own words."

"Yes—but you——"

"I know—I know," cried Laurence; "Heaven's mercy on us, mother, you are not going to begin again!"

"And you're never cross with me, you say. Well, Laurence," wiping her eyes with a corner of her handkerchief, "that's not quite true, now."

Laurence did not refute this statement. He might acknowledge by his silence that he had lost his temper, or he might not have heard the accusation. He sat staring at the great oil lamp upon the table, with his hands clutching his chin, and his brow lined and scored like a railway map. He was touched by Hester's devotion to him — her faith in him, though he looked so stern and hard that his mother was afraid to say anything more upon the subject. He could not bear the thought of a woman being truer to him than he had been to her — of her loving him through all his want of love.

"Why cannot I be left to myself?" he said at last.

"Because you are unhappy."

"I ask again where is the objection to leaving me as I am?" he said; "for I am *not* unhappy."

"Ah ! we all know better than that."

"Is Milly unhappy, I wonder ? "

"No—she is happy."

" You know something about her, too," he said, betraying again no small excitement ; " what is it ? Who has told you that she is happy ? "

"Herself."

" You have seen her, then, at last ! Well, was it very strange that I should love her, mother ? "

"Not very strange, perhaps."

" Tell me all about her," said Laurence ; "how was she looking ?—did you speak of me ?—what did she say ? "

Mrs. Raxford entered at once into the particulars of her interview with Milly Athorpe—abridging the narrative of Milly's love for Laurence, but giving him the message that had been sent him at the last.

"Tell him that you have seen me, and that you have found me very happy and content. That I hoped that he was going to marry Miss Fyvie shortly, for her sake and for his word's sake !"

This the message which she sent to him—which she had begged his mother to remember that she sent " calmly and dispassionately."

" She wishes that too, then. After all that I have told her—after all that has passed between us ! And I respect no one's wishes but my own," he said bitterly.

He opened his books, and feigned to commence a diligent perusal of them. The old subject was dismissed—he had discussed it deliberately ; it had been worn threadbare, now and for ever afterwards let them hold their peace concerning it. What the discussion had ended in his mother did not know—he did not know himself. There was no good result to follow ; she had given up all hope of good result. Everybody would remain miserable, of course.

Laurence went early to bed ; left early for Wheal Desperation before his mother was up.

At the office, he found Bully Churdock waiting for him. This man was a friend of Milly's—a staunch and true one— even a lover of Milly's, as he was aware, and he shook hands with him.

" Well, Churdock, is there anything that I can do for you ? "

" Ees—if you wull "

"What is it?"

"You can take me on the mine, and I'll work for ye, twice as much as e'er a' one in stock yonder."

"We can find a place for you, Churdock. When will you come on the works?"

"Oh! I'll go at it at wunst, Sir. I want to get reg'larly into work afore Sunday."

"Very well."

"You see," with a sudden scratch to his head, "I'ze married on Sunday; and she wants to see me settled, and give up wrustling and foighting. So I settle down as I said afore, at wunst."

"Who is the happy bride, Churdock?"

"Poll Raffles. She was allers arter me, and she's as good as gould, and as purty a Devonshire lass as ony in the county—barring Milly, o' course. You know that I wor fond o' that gal, Mister Raxford?"

"Yes—I have heard so."

"But it was like being in love with a grand lady you couldn't get near to, and who didn't care for you a bit," he said; "though I axed her to have me, for I worn't going to lose even that chance. I thought that I'd never marry, but I altered my mind, for Poll was precious cut up aboot it, and had been swect on me so long! I didn't see the good of fretting about it any longer — and keeping everybody in a stew, and myself like an owl. So I said, 'Poll, here I be, if I be worth anythink to you.' And Poll jumped at me straight. And precious glad I am that it's all squared."

"I congratulate you, Churdock. Will you put yourself in Captain Peters's hands, and tell him to find you the best place that he can."

"Thank'ee, Mr. Raxford. I wull, and cheerful."

Laurence went back to his office, and thought of Churdock and Churdock's reasoning. This was a case not unlike his own, and in Churdock's philosophy might he not read his lesson? If, after all, he could make one woman happy, and brighten her father's home, as well as his mother's, might it not be well for him? He had a promise to keep, they all said—even Milly had sent him that message again, and it had rendered him more resolute in consequence — or more desperate—he scarcely knew which.

Let it end so. He was tired of striving against every-body's wishes—setting his puny will against an army that opposed him.

"Mr. Waters," he said five minutes afterwards, "I am going back to Tavvydale."

"Very well, Sir. All things moving on very comfortably Sir, and no necessity to return, if there's anything of importance to keep you away."

"Do you think that it is a matter of importance, then, Mr. Waters," asked Laurence, " that takes me from business to-day ? "

"You are looking very grave, Sir," was the reply ; " and as I have missed for a long while that old bright look of yours, I fancy that there's something in the wind. Excuse me mentioning this — it *is* every bit fancy, of course — for there has been nothing new for weeks to talk about, and yet you've been getting graver every day."

"This is a crisis," said Laurence. "I shall return with a lighter heart, I hope."

" I'll wish you joy," said the old clerk.

Laurence departed in the horse and chaise which was at his disposal as general manager of the mines. He drove direct to his stables at Tavistock, and returned at a rapid pace through the town, meeting Miss Fyvie on the out-skirts.

"The very one I wished to see," he said after shaking hands with her. "Are you very busy ? "

"No—I was going to market for papa."

"Will you walk with me for five or ten minutes first ? " he said. "I have come from the mine to ask your advice."

" Yes—I will come with you, Laurence."

They turned back into the town, leaving it presently on their left, and passing to that lovers' walk by the side of the deep river, where the Tavistockians had made love from ages remote—all very still and picturesque that calm morning, with the leaves not all gone from the great trees, and the stream, like molten silver, crossed and recrossed by the shadows of the branches.

They sat down side by side on the second rustic seat, and then Laurence and she looked steadily at each other again, and hers was the longest and most unwavering gaze.

"Hester," he said, in a low voice, "my friends remind

me that I have not acted well by you — as if I had need to be reminded of that! But I had your forgiveness—and I thought myself absolved."

"All that there was to forgive — freely forgiven, Laurence."

"We were engaged to one another — you were the first woman to whom I ever confessed an attachment. I promised to be true to you."

"And I freed you from that promise."

"You promised to be true to me, and I never freed you from that. You have been true—more true than the object of your faith deserved."

"I have been true," was the answer made, with all her characteristic quickness, "because I could not help it."

"But——"

"But I was not acting wisely or generously to you. For you have felt of late days hampered by that resolution, which I thought that I had hidden pretty well. Who told you that——"

She paused, and left Laurence to guess at the inquiry that she might have made. He understood her and answered,

"My mother."

"Ah! my poor secret was ill-kept by my friends. My father and your mother have laid their wise heads together for our benefit, and that amiable conspiracy has done us both good, and set us acting for ourselves. Well, Laurence," she said, speaking very rapidly, "shall I ask you to take pity on me at last, and make me your wife?"

"No, Hester," he answered, in a suppressed voice—"not yet!"

She was strong and brave, and did not flinch at his denial.

"Shall I ask you to set me free from the promise that I made to you? The promise to be true and faithful to the end?"

"Ah! yes," he answered quickly, "ask me that, and take the last load away from my conscience! For I love Milly —pardon me saying this—as I love no one in the world. I can't give her up, though they tell me that she can never be my wife. I would resist all the foolish but well-meant advice of the friends around me, and leave them without one reason for their arguments. I would ask you to forgive me and absolve me, Hester — to give me strength *yourself* to wait for Milly. There, I am very cruel—I am but thinking of myself, and acting unmercifully towards you—but I have been driven to this, and my last hope of her I cannot let escape."

Hester touched his arm quickly. She was paler perhaps than her wont, but there was no anger, disappointment, or mortification in her glance.

"Well—give me up, Laurence! It is late in the day to ask you, but it was a foolish promise, which a vain and obstinate girl made to herself, perhaps to spite herself, or to foster a dream that had long passed away with her — and you. There, I ask you to give me back my promise to keep true to you."

"I give it back," he murmured.

"Released from my word, I feel more free," she said, "free to think of you as a brother, Laurence—to advise you like a sister. May I advise you now ? "

"Yes—if you will—if you can, Hester. For I feel utterly cast down."

"Keep strong for Milly's sake," she said; "she loves you, and you rank her first of all women in your thoughts. Wait for her like a man. If you should never marry, why, you will be happier, knowing that you have been true to each other ; then, if she or you were forced into marriage with another for pity's sake—wait for her—pray for her ! "

Before he could reply Hester Fyvie was gone. When he came to himself, as a man out of a swoon might come, he was sitting alone on the bench under the trees, gazing at the bright water.

"Yes, I will wait for her," he said; "I will wait for her for ever ! "

END OF BOOK THE FOURTH.

BOOK V.

THE FIFTH ACT.

——

CHAPTER I.

WAITING.

FIRM to one purpose, Laurence Raxford became a better man ; more like his old self. He had not wavered in his love. He had never been a weak man, although the weakness of others caused him pain. Had the letter which Hester Fyvie wrote to him long ago reached his hands, he would surely have married her — keeping firm to his word, and trying to think that he had never loved Milly Athorpe. Now all was settled ; he was wholly free to think of Milly, and to wait for her. There was a pleasure in thinking that he was young, with years of life before him, and years of life before her. There might come a time when she *would* be free to love him again. Their paths, diverging so much now, might meet in the after time, and if they went on and on, and further apart, till they passed beyond earth's boundary, still she would be faithful and true to the last, he was assured.

He gave no thought to the weak state of Mrs. Athorpe— he framed not one wish that death should sweep her away, as an obstacle that stood between him and his love ; he believed that she would grow strong again, and he only hoped that her husband might come back, hale and strong too, and take her away to his new home. That fact accomplished, the world placing more credit to the account of Mrs. Athorpe, Jonathan in Tavvydale as an important witness to her fairer fame, and Milly alone in the world—then his chance might come again. He was waiting for strange events to happen, but he waited patiently, and his mother was glad to see a change in him.

Engleton, knowing not that Laurence had already followed his advice, said to him one day,

"I say, Raxford, *is* it really single blessedness all the days of your life?"

"I have proposed to Miss Fyvie, and been rejected."

"Eh?—nonsense—what's that?"

"The day after you badgered me last, I told Miss Fyvie that I was ready to marry her — that is, I would have told her, if she had allowed me. But she nipped my offer in the bud, and would not have me."

"Really!" said Engleton, rubbing his hands together, "really now, I don't know that I am very sorry. How difficult it is to understand these women!"

"Very," asserted Raxford.

"If she had a chance of having you back again, and would not have you, why, she could not have cared a great deal about you, after all. That's how I put it."

"I hope that that's the correct version."

"It's not flattering to your vanity, though."

"Never mind that."

The two young men laughed at this, and were closer friends from that day. Engleton had offered Laurence the best advice in his power, but he was not sorry, as he had confessed, that it had turned out unprofitably. He had always liked Laurence Raxford, but he liked him all the more for leaving the path open to Hester Fyvie still. He had been once rejected, but he, in good time, would make another venture, after preparing the way well beforehand, and offering stronger proofs, if possible, of his affection for her. Meanwhile, he was perplexed concerning other ladies who had become difficult to understand, and he was inclined, by way of return, to seek advice from Laurence.

"Have you much to do to-day?"

"Not a great deal."

"Just come outside the office with me. I'm in a regular fix at home."

"Indeed!—how is that?"

They went out of the office together, and walked up and

down the broad space of ground before the house—Engleton full of excitement as usual.

"I don't know what to do with the Llewellyns," he said dismally; "they won't go home! It's a most absurd situation, but there they are, and, so far as I can see, there they are likely to remain."

"You are tired of your guests, then?"

"Well, yes. How old Fyvie used to stand it, the Lord knows—perhaps relationship had something to do with it."

"What does your sister think of it?"

"Oh! she laughs, and makes a joke of it all, which is rather aggravating. You see, she takes things coolly, and I am naturally of an excitable disposition. She says—it's very ridiculous, but it makes me nervous, for all that—that they will not quit the house until I have made an offer of marriage to Miss Llewellyn."

"Why do you not?—and get rid of them."

Mr. Engleton was not a good hand at a jest; all his life he had had a habit of regarding things with decorum. He stared hard at Laurence, and then said,

"I don't suppose you mean me to take that seriously, Raxford?"

"Well—no."

"Then it was not worth treating the matter flippantly. I never regarded your affairs in that light."

"I beg pardon, Mr. Engleton," said Laurence.

"Very glad to see you so lively, and all that," said Engleton; "a pleasant change, that shows a better frame of mind. You can't tell me, I suppose, how many holidays are allowed to principal clerks at the Treasury?"

"I cannot."

"Two months seem nothing for them. That old Llewellyn talks about two months' leave of absence as if it was two days. And government losing his services all this time!"

"Government gets on without him, at all events."

"I'm obliged to invent all kinds of excuses to escape these people—especially Mrs. Llewellyn and her daughter. Now, I have no earthly object in coming here to-day—but here I am, in self-defence."

"Some months ago, I used to fancy that you were a little attentive to Miss Llewellyn."

27

" Common politeness—a respect for her relationship to the Fyvies, that's all. But the old woman — that's Mrs. Llewellyn, I mean—talks as if I really had been very polite to her daughter."

" What does Miss Llewellyn say ? "

" My opinion is," lowering his voice, " that she's half an idiot, and that the family is trying to disguise it till she's married. She hasn't a single idea of her own upon anything —and she's ready to marry anyone her mother points out, at a moment's notice. She has received her orders to look after me, and I assure you it's becoming hard work to escape her vigilance. You cannot suggest an idea to get rid of them gracefully, Raxford—I want a new mind to assist me, and I don't care to act churlishly in any way, of course. I asked them in the first instance because I thought Hester would call to see them now and then, and she calls not. What shall I do ? "

" You have not a plan, then, of your own ? "

" For once," he confessed, " I have not a single plan ! "

" I can only recommend that you should take Mr. Llewellyn aside, and ask him to go."

" My dear Raxford, I could not do that ! "

" Or suppose that you receive an invitation from a friend to spend a fortnight somewhere ? "

" They would mind my house till I returned, and perhaps I should have some trouble to get into it, when I came back. Besides," said he, " I wish to remain near Tavvydale for awhile—and," with a stamp of his foot, " I'll not be driven out of my own house by a Welshman."

At this moment a four-wheeled chaise, occupied by the Llewellyns, appeared in the yard, to the dismay of Mr. Engleton.

" Thought that we would fetch you, my boy," cried Mr. Llewellyn, waving his whip triumphantly round his head ; " jump in, Engleton—they're going to see the Lydford Fall, and drop me here by the way. If you don't mind Mrs. Llewellyn driving—she's a good whip—you can sit behind with Jane."

Miss Llewellyn, on the back seat, began to draw her skirts together to make room for Mr. Engleton.

" Mr. Raxford," said Engleton, with a wave of the hand in Laurence's direction.

The Llewellyns had up to this time ignored the presence of that gentleman.

"Oh!—ah! how d'ye do, Raxford?" said Llewellyn; "still at the old game, I see. Nothing daunted by making a mess of the last undertaking."

"Neither daunted by difficulties, nor — impertinence," said Laurence; "the ladies are well, I trust? — good-morning."

"Very abrupt—very abrupt, indeed," said Mr. Llewellyn, as Laurence marched into the counting-house; "he'll ruin your business, Engleton, if you keep him long here."

"He don't take orders—so he don't frighten the customers," said Engleton, drily.

"I never can understand what people see in Mr. Raxford," said Mrs. Llewellyn; "there's a want of polish about him, which betrays his origin. Still, I *suppose* that he's a man to be trusted."

"I have an idea that way," said Engleton; "between ourselves, rather than lose him, I'd give him a partnership in the mine again."

"Good God!" ejaculated Mr. Llewellyn.

"But you need not let this go any further," said Engleton gravely.

"You may depend upon me, that it shall *not*," said Mr. Llewellyn, with decision.

"You would repent the step to your dying day, just as my poor brother-in-law will," said Mrs. Llewellyn, with a dismal shake of the head; "but he was no judge of character, and I think that you are."

"Ah! I may be," said Engleton, sententiously.

"And as for partnership," remarked Mr. Llewellyn, on whose mind Mr. Engleton's hints had made a serious impression, "you had better keep a fine property like this to yourself, or take some sensible, middle-aged man, with a knowledge of the world, into your confidence."

Mr. Engleton looked very much alarmed.

"I think we'll start for Lydford at once."

"Very well. Jump in, then," said Mr. Llewellyn. "I am disposed for a day's shooting in the preserves myself. I can ride your horse home, I suppose?"

"Mr. Llewellyn, you'll come with us, I hope. You've brought us out."

27—2

The voice was metallic and sonorous; Mr. Llewellyn succumbed to the warning.

"Very well, Madam," he grumbled; "but I hate water-falls—you know that. I got my shoes full last time I was here, and nearly caught my death of cold. You pushed me in," he said, venomously, to Mr. Engleton, now ensconced at the back, with Miss Llewellyn.

" Yes, I think that I remember something about it."

"Ah! you would have thought 'something about it' if you had been in the water instead of me," he said, lashing his host's horse unmercifully, as they drove away.

As they whirled by the counting-house window, Laurence looked from his desk at the *cortége*, and saw that Mr. Engleton was making a grimace at him.

"I hope that they'll not catch him for a son-in-law," was Raxford's fervent wish. "I trust that he is too sharp a man to walk into their trap."

Laurence went home early that afternoon. The nights were long now, and he had begun the wholesome and friendly practice of reading aloud to his mother. He was home early every night in the week but one—where he went to that night, or whether he stopped late at the office, he never told Mrs. Raxford. Once or twice he had been seen in the village of Tavrydale, it was murmured, and though Milly had not seen him, the rumour reached her ears, and scared her. Scared her with the assurance, too, that he might not be re-engaged to Hester Fyvie—which was not wholly dis-heartening, though it told her that he was single and "un-settled" still.

Laurence began reading to his mother that evening a new poem of Tennyson's. He had been always fond of poetry; since he had come to Devon he had been more than com-monly poetic, and his mother would have preferred a sensible fiction, or an exciting book of travels—which is about the same thing—to being deluged with verse night after night.

However, she always expressed her delight to hear him read; and it never occurred to Laurence that too much poetry might be objectionable. If his mother grew weary, and closed her eyes—"Just to rest them a bit from the light, my dear!"—Laurence, absorbed in his theme, paid but little heed to his companion, and went on to the end of the legend, where the lovers clasped hands, and everybody was in a state of bliss—or where the lovers, friends, and relations went all of a heap to the cemetery. For poems have uncertain *denouéments*, and poets kill off their surplus stock with less compunction than novelists.

Laurence was reading—and reading well. But the night was far advanced now, and Mrs. Raxford, with her chin on her bosom, and her needlework trailing from her lap to the floor, had withdrawn herself into dream-land, and was at that present moment bargaining for a pair of fowls in Tavistock, with the shopkeeper talking in a loud, high-flown voice behind the counter at her.

Peace and general satisfaction in Laurence's little house then, when a loud and prolonged knocking, of a fancy description, stopped Laurence in the middle of a verse, and frightened his mother into an upright position, with hands clasped together in supplication.

"Good gracious!—what is it?" exclaimed Mrs. Raxford.

"It's a knock," said Laurence, tetchily, for he objected to be stopped in his reading.

"I hope that nothing is the matter anywhere," said Mrs. Raxford. "Whenever I hear a knock at odd times of the night I always fancy that something's going to happen. And the fancy very often comes to me, Laurence."

"This is not an odd time of the night, mother," said Laurence; "it is only nine o'clock."

"I hope that Mr. Fyvie is not ill," said the lady, still oppressed by gloomy ideas; "he has not been full of spirits lately; and he was telling me only this morning, that he felt very anxious about Jonathan."

"If you please, Sir," said the little maid-servant entering the room, "it's Mr. Whiteshell from London."

Mr. Whiteshell from London again!—then something had happened to bring that old man to Devonshire. Mystery and trouble always accompanied him.

"Show him in at once," said Laurence; and before he could place a chair for his guest, James Whiteshell was in the room.

He came close to Laurence, griped his arm, and looked up very anxiously into his face.

"Have you seen him?—has he been here, Mr. Raxford?"

"Nobody has been here. Whom did you expect?"

"Captain Athorpe!"

CHAPTER II.

THE MOON AT THE FULL

MR. JAMES WHITESHELL sat down, and after his customary habit wiped his forehead with his great silk handkerchief; rose upon becoming aware of the presence of a lady, and executed his most elaborate bow, resumed his seat, and rubbed his hands nervously up and down his knees.

"This is the last place that I had a hope of. I can't think now what has become of him."

"He is found, then?" said Laurence with excitement.

"Oh! dear no; he's lost again."

"But you discovered him?"

"No; he discovered me."

Mr. Whiteshell did not mean intentionally to be aggravating; he was disturbed in mind by arriving at the end of his search, without a profitable result, and took time to collect his ideas.

"I shall be glad when you are more explanatory, Mr. Whiteshell," said Laurence severely.

"I'll trouble you to give me time, Sir," replied Mr. Whiteshell, exhibiting his usual dignity of demeanour beneath reproof; "I have come from London to-day, and have been running about Tavvydale, and the Cleft, and everywhere else, since five o'clock this evening. As impatient as ever, Mr. Raxford!"

"Pardon me, but I am naturally excited," said our hero; "if Captain Athorpe is in this part of the country there is no telling what may be the consequences."

"He is perfectly harmless."

"Is he sane, then?"

"Yes; save when the moon's at the full."

"God bless me!" cried Mrs. Raxford, "and it's a full moon to-night; I read it in the almanack!"

"Yes—that accounts for it," said Mr. Whiteshell, wiping his forehead again. "I'll trouble you for a glass of water, with a dash of brandy in it; and then I can manage to impart my information."

Mr. Whiteshell had evidently been disturbed by his journey, and its unprofitable result. It was not till he had imbibed the liquid that he had mentioned that he assumed a certain degree of composure.

"You will excuse my asking for brandy and water in a friend's house," said he, "but it *is* a friend's, I think?"

He looked inquiringly at Laurence, who answered—

"Yes; a friend's."

"We have had our little differences; we have not always understood each other; but I think that we are friends at last. Now, let me tell you all I know concerning Captain Athorpe."

Laurence nodded his head impatiently.

"Two months ago Captain Athorpe came into my rooms in Milk Street, and asked me to take care of him, just as if he had been a lost child. I did not know him; he walked so feebly, and his hair was so grey. He was very weak in intellect, but he was not dangerous; he had remembered my address, he said, and as he had no friends in all the world but me, he had come to ask me to take care of him. He gave me six hundred and fifty pounds to mind—all in notes, which he had sewed in the lining of his coat."

"Where had he been?"

"Wandering about the country for awhile, then laid up in a workhouse, where they took all the nonsense out of him, by giving him lots of leeches every day, till he was shot out of the place quite cured, and as bloodless as boiled veal. He's a ghost to look at, and until you're used to him, it's rather startling. When he looked at me first, through the parlour window, with his white face pressed close to the glass, I was as near having a fit as ever I was in my life."

Mrs. Raxford executed a slight leap in the air, and then proceeded to close the window-shutters for the night.

"He was not stronger than a child when he first came to me," continued Whiteshell. "You may guess how weak he was when he came to *me* for moral support—me, whom he used to call a driveller and potterer! He put trust in me at once, too, and told me of the notes, which the workhouse people would, he thought, have been very glad to find."

"He was not recognised?"

"Oh! no. He was very taciturn, too, and not likely to

betray himself. When he first came he did not recollect all
the past."

"That was a mercy to him."

"He told me that his wife was dead, and that Milly had
left the Cleft; but he did not appear to remember the circumstances that had occurred on the night before he burned
his house down. He was taken ill again at my place, and
when he came back, as it were, to life again, he was weaker
than ever, but more sane."

"Did you tell him that Mrs. Athorpe was living?"

"No. I was advised not by the doctor, whom I took
into my counsel," answered Whiteshell. "Athorpe never
spoke of the cause of his wife's death, and it was not
considered safe to mention the story to him. But when
the moon came round to the full he remembered it, and
accused himself of having murdered her. Then I told him
that Inez was alive, and he cursed me for attempting to
deceive him. And as the moon waned, so he fell back into
the old man, remembering nothing of the past."

"Is Milly aware of the charge that you have under-
taken?"

"She is now. I have been with her to-night, to put her
on her guard, and prepare Inez, if she think it necessary. I
thought that he would go to Tavvydale, after eluding me,
but he has not been seen there."

"You have been to the Cleft?"

"Yes."

"And to Wheal Desperation?"

"No; not there. That is a good thought."

"The old habit might take him to the place."

"And pitch him down the shaft," said Mr. Whiteshell,
starting up. "Let us be off at once. I'm as strong as a
lion—and nothing tires me."

"You would not like to rest here, and leave the remainder
of this task to me?"

"No; he is my charge," said Mr. Whiteshell proudly;
"and I think that I can only manage him. He has given
me a new object in life, and I feel as if I should not like to
part with him—much less to part with him like this. And
it is very odd to see that man of all men trustful in me.
He's a better judge of character *now*," he added conceitedly,
"than he ever was when he was strong!"

" You will be very careful, Laurence," said Mrs. Raxford. " I don't much like your going off in search of madmen in the moonlight."

" Captain Athorpe is not strong, Madam," said Mr. Whiteshell. " When I tell you that I can hold him down there is no fear that he will master this young Hercules. Indeed, there is no fear of him offering any violence at all."

Thus assured, Mrs. Raxford did not enter any further protest against Laurence's departure. She knew the history of the Athorpes, and she took hope to herself, rather than fear, at the news which James Whiteshell had brought. A little darkness—a shade more of mystery, perhaps—but afar off the glimmer of the dawn where there might be hope for Laurence. She was a sanguine woman—and this might be, she thought, the beginning of the end.

A quarter of an hour afterwards, Laurence and Whiteshell were driving along the high-road towards the old scene of action. Amongst the Dartmoor hills, Laurence had met romance first; here had ensued the joys and sorrows of his life ; here in one short year had been matter for melodrama almost—love, jealousy, and murder—the staple commodities for transpontine establishments—had followed his presence at Wheal Desperation.

The sky was cloudless, and the road to the mine was as light as day. Even the sulky Dartmoor tors became a silvery grey as the moon rose higher in the heavens.

" Yes ; the moon's at the full ! " said Laurence.

" That is the worst of it," replied Mr. Whiteshell, shivering a little with the cold ; " I can't depend upon what gets into his head, when the moon's like that. And yet the last three weeks have given me great hopes of him."

" He may be still in London."

" No ; I made inquiries at the London terminus, and one guard remembers assisting him into a third-class carriage, and another scolding him for not showing his ticket with the average degree of promptitude. They described him accurately enough."

" And at Devon ? "

" The train came in at night, and no one appears to have noticed him at Tavistock. But we shall find him presently —I don't despair myself."

They were silent for awhile; then Mr. Whiteshell, full of his subject, said—

"If you could but imagine how Athorpe has disappointed me, Mr. Raxford. I had arranged quite a pretty scene of reconciliation between Athorpe and Inez—of lifting the weight of misery from the minds of both of them. *That* lifted, I believed that Athorpe would be stronger again in mind, and Inez in body; and that with time and care they might be to each other a support and comfort. I had noticed last week that he was stronger in himself—remembered the past—the best part of the past, before Jonathan Fyvie upset everybody. Only a day before he took this freak into his head he asked me what had become of the violin that he had given me early in the summer."

"If we could find him there would be hope of him," said Laurence, becoming sanguine himself at these reminiscences.

"Yes, I think there would," said Whiteshell; "poor old gentleman, where can he have got to? He's twenty years younger than I am, at least, but I feel somehow like a son to him; it's very odd. What do you propose doing at the mine?"

"Searching the place."

"I'm no hand at that," said Whiteshell; "for I don't know the locality, and shall very likely kill myself. If we could only find somebody in the grounds that knew every turn of it as well as you do. Who's that walking up and down before the office?"

They were close upon the place now, and Laurence reined in his horse. It was some one who knew every turn of the mining ground better than Laurence Raxford, and she came towards them as they stopped.

"Milly!" cried both men in a breath.

"Yes; I could not rest. I did not tell Inez; it would have but kept her more anxious about him than I was. When she was asleep for the night I thought that I would come on here; I have asked a neighbour to be watchful till my return."

"The same idea that your uncle might come to the mine has suggested itself to Mr. Raxford—a gentleman whom you remember, perhaps?" said Mr. Whiteshell, caustically.

"Mr. Raxford is very kind," murmured Milly, looking at him.

"I hope that you are well, Milly?" he asked.

"Yes—very well," she answered.

So the lovers met again, with one thought common to both of them. When Mr. Waters had shuffled down stairs, and expressed his astonishment at the late visitors, the search was begun, each taking a separate route, and each meeting, after an hour's time, in front of the office, baffled and disheartened.

"No success?" said Laurence.

"No, he is not here," replied Milly; "it seems as if we were never to be successful again."

"I wonder if he has gone down the mine, now," suggested Mr. Waters, who, interested in the search, had been wandering about with Mr. Whiteshell, totally oblivious to the fact that he had his carpet slippers on.

"I will go down," said Laurence.

But before he could put his resolution into effect, and whilst Mr. Whiteshell was explaining that Captain Athorpe's strength would not have allowed of the descent, a man on horseback rode through the gates, that had been left ajar—so suddenly and swiftly, that the searchers there, whose nerves were highly strung that night, started at his appearance in their midst.

"You—you have been sent here for me?" cried Milly.

"Yes," he answered—"if you are Milly Athorpe, I have."

~~~~~~~~~~~~

CHAPTER III.

THE LLEWELLYNS ARE SURPRISED.

It is not an unnecessary aggravation of the reader's feelings to change the scene to Tavvydale House. It is requisite for the proper development of the little plot that is left us in the few chapters between us and "FINIS."

It may be remembered that Charles Engleton was borne away triumphantly by his captors to the Lydford cascade,

and that the task devolved upon him during the journey
of making himself agreeable to the fair maiden by whose
side he found himself ensconced.   This was never a task
of any magnitude, for Miss Llewellyn did not require any
great amount of attention, and it was fortunate for her
peace of mind through life that anything amused her,
although nothing excited her.   Her mother had endeavoured to teach her to behave herself in society, and
the result was tolerably successful to Mrs. Llewellyn, if
not to society in general.   Mrs. Llewellyn, figuratively
speaking, had sat on Jane's impulses, Jane's wishes,
Jane's little early tempers, till she had flattened all
character out of her.   She had employed strong-minded
governesses to do the same, and Mr. Llewellyn—a man
who had always objected to nonsense—had assisted with
a "clincher" now and then, until the subject had arrived
at perfection.   It may be said here that the same experiments had been tried on Master Llewellyn, who flitted
through an early chapter or two of this book ; it was in
process, and the Llewellyns were sanguine about that
period, but no mention was made of the son now.   He
had run away with his mother's lady's-maid first, and
then out of the country afterwards, glad to be rid of his
family, at any price—even at the price of a reward,
which his stern father had offered for him for successfully
imitating his signature to a cheque for five hundred
pounds, that he could not conveniently spare from his
" balance."

But the Llewellyns had been very successful with Jane ;
she was quiet and ladylike, and not liable to vulgar
surprises—the fall of a rain-drop, or the fall of a thunder-
bolt, would not have made much difference in her expression of features.

Charles Engleton felt disagreeable after a while.   He
sat at the back of that pony-chaise, and thought of his
wrongs, until he arrived at the conclusion that these
Llewellyns were going a little too far, and taking too
much advantage of his good-nature.   If he had run
away from them, they had no business to follow him to
Wheal Desperation, and make a prisoner of him.   They
betrayed their motives too quickly, and those motives
were objectionable.

Still Charles Engleton was a thorough gentleman, and though he did not start many topics of conversation, he answered politely all questions which Mr. and Mrs. Llewellyn put to him, and he even tried to interest his companion in a ruin on their right, which, being the flattest and blankest ruin in England, was not calculated to arouse to enthusiasm so quiet a young lady as Miss Llewellyn.

The whole task of making this journey to Lydford successful devolved, therefore, upon Mrs. Llewellyn, for her lord and husband had entered his protest against the expedition, and was already sulking at having been forced to join the party; and how Mr. Llewellyn could sulk, his wife, and daughter, his servant, and his maid, and all the unlucky subordinates in his own particular branch at the "office" in London, knew to their cost. Mr. Llewellyn was inclined to give up the idea of arresting Charles Engleton as a son-in-law; he had, after all, more common sense than his wife, whose manœuvres were as clumsy as a common mind could make them, and he saw that their host was now fairly on his guard. But Mrs. Llewellyn saw ahead of her nothing but success.

So they went to Lydford Fall—where many of us have been before them—put the chaise up at the farm-house, and slipped and scrambled down the path, towards the bed of the stream, Mr. Llewellyn, who objected to slipping, cursing all the way, as he dragged his better-half after him and upon him. Jane, of course, was left to the care of Mr. Engleton, and had to clutch him spasmodically at dangerous curves. Then they had stared at the water rushing down in no very great quantity from the rocks above them, and Mr. Llewellyn had expressed it as his opinion that the waterfalls in Devonshire were an utter sham, absurdity, and nuisance, and the sooner less fuss was made about them the better. He would lay a wager to any amount that there were not ten gallons there altogether, and *that* the miller at the top had turned on from his stream in order to make a display—he knew all about those dodges—he wasn't born yesterday! Finally, and to everybody's amazement—even to his own, for he had been particularly careful—he backed himself into two feet of water in his excitement, and stood in the stream shouting:

" There—I told you so ! It's always the way. This isn't the first time I have had to risk my life in these damned places !"

The expedition was not successful, and when they were back at Tavvydale House to dinner, and Mr. Llewellyn would not speak all dinner-time, the promoter of the excursion was fain to acknowledge the fact herself.

" I think that I shall go home to-morrow," Mr. Llewellyn said to his wife, *sotto voce* in the drawing-room, where he found his voice again.

" Llewellyn—I would not think of it yet awhile."

" You can do as you like," he said. " I don't ask you and Jane to come with me."

" But I cannot see any excuse to stop if you talk of going. And it would be, Llewellyn, such an admirable match for Jane."

" Ah !—but it won't do."

" And you and Mr. Engleton are becoming great friends."

" I don't see it myself, Madam," contradicted Llewellyn. " I don't like him. He's much too bumptious and opinionated for me."

" But Jane——"

" He don't care a fig for Jane—and I'm not astonished at *that*," said Mr. Llewellyn. " Besides, is he not looking after Hester ? "

" Oh ! that's all blown over."

" That's all you know about it," answered her rebellious spouse.

But he mentioned not again his intention to leave Tavvydale House, and though he would not, in his present temper, have confessed that Mrs. Llewellyn's remarks had had any effect upon him, still, tacitly, he had abandoned the project of returning home in the morning. He would stay and give his daughter Jane every chance ; it would be a capital thing to get rid of Jane, moping and puking about the house like an animated rag doll ; and the ties of relationship might give him a share in the mine, or put him in the way of some good thing or other, which would add to the income he received from that beggarly Treasury.

He was an envious man, and coveted other men's goods. He was not an amiable character ; no one was ever glad to meet him in the streets, or at a dinner-party; he looked down terribly upon people who received a less salary than himself—gauging their merits by their money —but he envied, and almost hated, everybody who had incomes above his own, and kept the horses and carriages which were never likely to become part of his appurtenances. He even looked upon Mrs. Llewellyn as his great mistake in life—possibly he was right, poor man! He had married her for birth—on account of the purity of the blood running in her veins—and he should have married for money, and been as well off as other people. And as for the purity of her blood—in all his life he had never known a woman come out so strong in pimples!

He was very tired after dinner, and thought that he would go early to bed, and prematurely nurse the cold that he felt certain was coming on. He never got his feet wet in his life without suffering for it, and he had been fool enough to go floundering into a rivulet, when a baby might have known better than that. Mr. Engleton had asked him if he had done it on purpose; and well he might put the inquiry, considering the stupidity of the act.

He swallowed a cup of coffee, and went early to bed dragging his unwilling wife after him. He did not want to sit up late, and play whist, and lose his money; he repeated that he wanted to nurse his cold in its early stages, and he ordered gruel and hot water into his dressing-room.

Mr. Engleton and his sister, not being partial to late hours, were willing to follow the example of their guests. They had adopted a country life, and were glad to fall into country habits whenever occasion presented itself. Before ten o'clock Tavvydale House was locked up for the night, the servants were in their rooms, Mrs. Llewellyn was asleep, and Mr. Llewellyn was in the dressing-room adjoining, sitting close to a bright fire, with his dressing-gown round him, his feet in hot water, and a basin of gruel on his knees.

He had been a quarter of an hour in this position, despite the prior remonstrances of Mrs. Llewellyn from the inner room; he was not going to hurry himself because his wife wanted to drop off into her first sleep; he knew perfectly well that she would go to sleep without him, if he left her to herself long enough. He had a cold to nurse, he shouted at her, and he was not going to be hurried for anybody.

He worried himself like a miserable, cross-grained fellow, as he was. He sat glowering at the red coals, and thinking of his own injuries—a red-haired man, with his back up like a cat's. He was in a mood to anathematise Tavvydale House, and all belonging to it; he had never liked the place or the people, and though he had saved a few pounds in house-keeping by his long stay with the Engletons, still he had put up with a great deal for the sake of economy.

If it was not for the chance of getting Jane off, he would not stop another day in the house; and though he could not see the probabilities of that event occurring, still his wife had spoken with confidence, and women understood those things better than he did. He did not tell her so, lest it should make her conceited, but that impression fixed itself on his mind, after his fourth or fifth spoonful of gruel. The warmth of the gruel, and the soothing effect of hot water, gave a milder turn to his thoughts after that, and he pictured Jane as Mrs. Engleton, with a very handsome annual income settled upon her—an income from which he could borrow a few hundreds now and then.

"It would be a capital catch," he said, aloud; "and I'll say that that snoring old woman in the other room is a genius, if she manages it. Not that she ever managed anything very nicely yet, Heaven knows! Hollo! what's that?"

Mr. Llewellyn paused, with his spoon half-way to his mouth, and listened. There was a strange noise outside his room, a sputtering kind of noise on the other side of a door on his left, that was never opened—that was not unlike the crackling of wood.

"It's the house on fire, possibly!" said Mr. Llewellyn, his red hair bristling somewhat with the idea; "that's a nice thing to happen, I must say. Running about stone passages, and into the garden, after his foot-bath. I hope it's somebody else's house!"

The thought occurring to him that the house stood in several acres of its own ground, and the fact of the crackling noise being on the increase, took Mr. Llewellyn from his bath, and across the room to the door.

The key was in the lock, and turned with difficulty. He opened the door cautiously at last, and peered out into a dark lobby.

"I don't smell anything," he muttered ; "but that's the cold coming on, confound it. If that noise continues, I shall alarm the house, and let other people look for it. Good gracious, it may be thieves, and there are Mrs. Llewellyn's jewels on the table!"

He was about to shut the door hastily again, when it was thrust suddenly upon him, sending him backwards a few steps at the same time, as a strange being came into the room, and closed the door cautiously behind him.

"If you make a noise, man, it may cost you your life," said the new comer; "sit down, and let me ask you a question."

"Ye—ye—yes! but, good God! who are you?"

"A murderer."

"O-o-o-oh—a murderer!—indeed, Sir!—really!"

Mr. Llewellyn sank into the chair that he had quitted, and burst into a cold perspiration—to think that he was closeted with a murderer, and no one near to give him help!

The intruder stood by the door, a man in a dark suit of clothes, torn and jagged in several places, as though he had been climbing over many obstacles in the way to his purpose—a man with a face that death could not have added a shade more ghastliness to, with white hair, moustache and beard tangled, matted and wild. A strange figure, that, coming at that hour thus suddenly upon the scene, might have scared hearts more courageous than the Treasury clerk's—for it was not an every-day face, and might not have belonged to this every-day world.

Mr. Llewellyn, in his fear, did not observe that the man leaned against the door for support after he had entered · he saw the movement only, and attributed the action to a settled resolve to bar his exit.

"I am Captain Athorpe—of Wheal Desperation—the man who killed his wife. You know me?"

"I—I can't say that I have ever had the pleasure of meeting you before," said Mr. Llewellyn, "therefore, *I* could not have done you harm in any way, you see."

"No," said Athorpe, gloomily, "it is not your life I want I am not so mad but what I can tell one face from another"

"Well, that's a comfort, anyhow," said Llewellyn—"*that's* fair."

28

" Where is Jonathan Fyvie?—this is his father's house, and I have been hiding in it all day, in the hope of meeting him. I shan't be happy, or like myself, until I have killed him, Sir ! "

" Lord save us ! " ejaculated Llewellyn, " how shall I get rid of this bloody-minded vagabond ? "

A vague idea of conciliating Captain Athorpe, of agreeing with him in everything, and humouring his inclinations, suggested itself to Mr. Llewellyn—that was the course to adopt he had read somewhere, and was grateful for recollecting at that juncture. He would humour him, if his presence of mind would allow of the process; but his knees were knocking together with fright still, and his difficulty in articulating was enormous. His feet had become stone-cold by this time, and he cast one bewildered look round for the slippers that he had left in the other room.

" I wish no man harm, but him who injured me," muttered Athorpe—" that's all."

" I'm sure that's very fair indeed, captain," said Llewellyn, assuming a brisk and lively tone ; " that's hon—hon—hon-ourable and manly. Can I offer you anything ? " helplessly taking down the basin of gruel from the mantelpiece, " not anything in this way, I mean, of course, but anything out of the cellar—sparkling champagne, for instance ? I—I can fetch it in a minute."

" I'd rather die than break bread, or drink in this house. This is the Fyvies' house."

" It used to be. They have left."

" What's that ? "

And Athorpe leaned forwards eagerly.

" Don't excite yourself, my dear friend. They have gone away—they came to ruin, and sold this house to Mr. Engleton. You remember Engleton—you'll be glad to see him. I'll just step out and tell him that you've called."

But Captain Athorpe made no way for him ; he still stood against the door staring wildly over Mr. Llewellyn's head at the opposite wall.

" Gone away," he said at last, " now, that's as black a lie as ever was uttered."

" I assure you that it's a fact, Sir."

" I say that it is not," cried Athorpe, " and I am sure that he is in the house. He took my wife away from me—he blasted as honest and peaceful a home as ever made a man's heart light, and I have a claim to justice on him."

"Most decidedly," asserted his auditor, assuming the conciliatory tone again; "I don't dispute the point at all—well, shall we try to find him?"

"Yes—yes—I think we will."

"Perhaps you would not have any objection to wait till I put my stockings and boots on?" said Llewellyn; "I find it rather chilly after a hot bath."

"I'll wait."

"Thank God!—thank you, Sir—will you take a seat?—I'll not keep you more than a minute—depend upon it we shall find him, Mr. Haycock."

Mr. Llewellyn passed with winged steps into the bed-room, and fell into the arms of his wife, standing rigid and stony, with a shawl round her, in the middle of the room.

"Don't leave me, Llewellyn—you took me for better, for worse—and you must not for—forsake me! He woke me up in a fright, and I've only just found strength to crawl out of bed."

"Hush!—don't make a noise—don't excite him, or he'll murder the two of us. Why don't you lie down till I come back again with assistance. He's perfectly harmless."

"He's raving mad!—I know him—I've heard of him—he did kill his wife nearly. Oh! what shall we do?"

"We'll alarm the house—that's what we'll do, if you'll only hold your jaw!" said this uncourteous helpmate.

"Shall I go?" in a stage whisper; "he don't know that I am here—and you might go back to him, and talk to him whilst you put your boots on."

"Go back to him!" cried her husband; "I'd sooner face the devil himself. Unlock the door, unlock the door, and we'll scream our hardest when we're in the passage."

They stole to the door together, opened it with difficulty, as both hands grasped the key at once, rushed into the passage beyond, and tore along it for their lives, screaming "Thieves!" and "Murder!" as none but frightened people *can* scream.

The house was soon astir, and men and women with pale faces began to look from doors and over balusters, and gasp forth inquiries, to which no one answered. From the stillness of death to the noise of Babel was but one step.

28—2

" Llewellyn, what is this ? " cried Engleton, appearing upon the scene, collaring the frightened man, and striving to shake an explanation out of him ; " Mr. Llewellyn, will you explain, please ? "

" There's a mad—mad—madman in the house ! " gasped Llewellyn, at last ; " in my dressing-room—and all the razors on the table—Captain Hayband——"

" Athorpe—here ! " cried Engleton ; then he led the way back to the dressing-room, followed by everybody in the house, and found Athorpe, still with his back to the door, sleeping at his post, from sheer exhaustion.

He opened his eyes as they approached him.

" Where's Whiteshell ? " he asked, vacantly ; " why has he left me like this ?—he who promised to take care of me ? "

" Athorpe, will you let me take care of you till I find your friends ? "

" Yes—if you will, Sir.   I am dead beat ! "

He tottered towards Engleton, pausing midway.

" Whose house is this ? "

" Mine."

" Ah ! it was *my* mistake, then.   I am not so clear-headed as I used to be."

He took Engleton's arm, and the young man, with ready tact, gave orders for a messenger to start at once to Miss Athorpe's house in Tavvydale.

" You'll—you'll never keep this dangerous lunatic here ! " cried Llewellyn ; " you'll send for the police, I hope, at the same time ! "

" He is very weak, and can't do much harm, poor fellow," answered Engleton ; " I know the man, and will take care of him."

" It's not safe."

A bright idea suddenly seized Charles Engleton.

" Captain Athorpe is my guest till he is strong and well again.   He only needs careful nursing.   See that the next room on the right of Mr. Llewellyn's be prepared for him."

" Mercy on us ! " exclaimed Mrs. Llewellyn.

" I'll not stop another hour in the house ! " cried Llewellyn ; " he's made a dead set at me, and he'll murder me, if I remain.   Lend me your carriage, Sir, and we'll try and catch the two o'clock mail train from Tavistock.

You—you can send the luggage after us—if we stay here, we shall all be killed. I would not remain till morning for a thousand pounds!"

"My carriage is at your service—John, put the horses to, at once," said Engleton; "sorry to lose you, but if Captain Athorpe has got an impression on his mind that you are his enemy, it may be safer to depart."

"We'll—we'll go, Llewellyn," said his wife from behind the bed-curtains, in which for modesty's sake she had now en-wrapped herself; "we'll go at once."

And away they went from Tavvydale House, long before the messenger had reached Milly's cottage, four miles away. They never revisited Mr. Engleton, and Tavvydale knew them no more.

"Captain Athorpe," said Engleton, as he led him to his room gently, "you have done some good by dropping in here. Upon my word, I am very glad to see you!"

CHAPTER IV.

THE MEETING.

INEZ ATHORPE was sleeping soundly, when the messenger from Tavvydale House aroused her, and the main street, with his summons at the door. She had gone to bed well-pleased with herself and Milly she had felt stronger, and, for an unaccountable reason, more hopeful of the future; she and Milly had talked long and earnestly of that past of which she had repented, and she had felt that night less querulous and jealous than she had been since her illness.

Once or twice a vague suspicion had seized her that Milly was anxious, for some reason or other, to lead the subject round to her lost husband—but she did not put her doubts to the test, lest Milly should think her weak and fidgety. Milly could not have heard of Athorpe, or she would have been the first to speak of him—the first to break the news. She was only more hopeful, like herself, for she had spoken that night of the probabilities of the stricken man once more coming before them, as from spirit-land.

"How he comes—or in what fashion—I do not seem to care, Milly," Inez had said when they were in their room together, and Milly was still sitting dressed upon her little cot in the corner, when Inez was in bed, "so that the chance is offered me to see him."

"You would not be afraid of him ? "

"No. Not if he was angry with me even, and unmerciful —which he will not be again."

"Which he will not be again, we pray. Good-night, Inez."

"Good-night. Ah ! " with a quivering sigh, "what a good friend you have been to me—and what a tax upon your time and patience I have been to you. I think that your reward will come, Milly, even upon earth."

"My reward is in your better health, Inez."

"I don't mean such a reward as that. But the great prize on which your silly heart was set once—you know ? "

"Ah ! I know," said Milly. "Now, good-night again."

"Good-night, my dear."

She fell off to sleep after that, into so deep and peaceful a slumber, that Milly felt courage to leave her and proceed in search of Uncle Oliver. That he might have gone to Wheal Desperation, had suggested itself to her as well as to Laurence, and she was anxious—intensely anxious—to find him. So she had departed—first warning a neighbour that Captain Athorpe had been heard of, and that she was going in search of him whilst Inez slept, if the neighbour would be watchful for a little while.

Then all at peace in Tavvydale, until the noisy message from Mr. Engleton.

Inez struggled out of sleep, crying—

"Milly—Milly—do you hear that ? "

But Milly made no reply, and the weak woman paused to consider if it had been one of her own disturbed dreams, and whether it was kind to wake her niece, tired out with school duties, and attendance upon her. Inez did not usually reflect upon the inconveniences to which she subjected others—in her illness she had been selfish enough. This was a good sign of convalescence, of bodily and mental improvement, when Inez thought that she would lie down again, and say nothing till the morning concerning the fright that she had had.

Then the knocking was repeated, and Inez could hear the shrill voice of her neighbour—one of the few who knew her story, and believed in it—begging some one without to make less noise.

"Milly, dear—some one *is* knocking!" she cried.

The room was light with the full moon that shone in through the latticed panes, but Milly's cot was in shadow by the wall. Still, sitting up in bed, Inez could define the outline of that cot, and there seemed a something new and strange about it, which, coupled with the silence, made Inez tremble very much.

"Stolen away, or dead!" she whispered to herself— "tired of me, or tired out with me. Or—thank God for that thought—shut out in the street, having gone for a moonlight stroll after I was asleep."

She left her bed, and crossed the room to Milly's cot. Empty!

They were talking still in the street, and she opened the window at once, and asked who was there?

"I've been sent to tell Miss Athorpe to come on to Tavvydale House."

"Didn't I ask you to be quiet?" cried the old woman next door. "It's nothing, Mrs. Athorpe — only Milly's wanted."

"But where is Milly?" inquired Inez.

"Gone for a walk—that's all," was the reply.

"What time is it?"

"Eleven."

"Ah! then there *is* something wrong!" cried Inez. "Milly would not leave the house so late as this."

"I'll come in to you, Mrs. Athorpe, at once—I've got the key," said the neighbour. "I think that I can explain it all. Don't distress yourself—all's well! You blockhead! Why don't you go on to the mine?"

"The mine—the mine!" cried Inez; "then Captain Athorpe has been found?"

"Yes, Ma'am," answered the man; "he's up at Tavvydale House—waiting."

"Well, or—ill?"

"Ill, I should say, Ma'am, certainly."

Inez fell back from the window, and the old woman, coming in with a light, found her lying in a swoon upon the floor.

" Here's my work cut out, surely," she muttered, bending over her.

But Inez very rapidly recovered, and began with feverish haste to dress herself.

" I will go to him at once."

" You—dear heart—why, it's impossible ! "

" No it is not—I am a strong woman now—I will go ! "

" But it really is imp——"

" Did you not hear that he was ill ? " cried Inez, turning upon her with a fierceness that made her recoil a step or two. " If he were to die now, and I never to see him again ! Think, woman, of his going from the world with all his old dark thoughts of me ! "

" Milly will be back shortly."

" She may go at once to Tavvydale House."

" Then she can tell him——"

" I will tell him myself ! "

Inez was dressed. She was tying her bonnet firmly on her head, and was pacing the room in her excitement, like the strong woman that her years might have warranted. She had been slowly gathering strength ; it was possible to walk half a mile without the aid of a friend's arm, if she walked slowly and carefully, but the change in her on that night was startling.

" I will go with you, then, if you are determined," said the neighbour, shaking her head at her friend's obstinacy, as she went out of the room and out of the house for her bonnet and shawl. She was not absent more than five minutes, but on her return, the door was open, and the house deserted. Inez had started on her way.

The old woman set forth at a trot after her, pulling up suddenly to recover breath the instant afterwards, and arriving at once at the conclusion that her galloping days were over. She walked on rapidly about twenty more yards, and was then seized with a stitch in the side, that incapacitated her from further service.

" She must go," said the woman, as she leaned against the garden-fence of one of the Tavvydale cottages. " I can't kill myself for anybody, and it's no business of mine. How she must have walked! I wonder if she has been shamming all this time!"

Pondering on this supposition, the woman who had meant well walked homewards slowly, giving up all further chase of Inez Athorpe.

Meanwhile Inez, borne along by one idea, was out of the village, and making towards Tavvydale House. Her pace had not slackened yet ; she felt strong enough for her task ; her footsteps were not faltering, and her breath was good ; she should reach there, and tell him whose life she had marred—that she was better than he thought—that she had been innocent of wrong towards him. Only to reach him—only to see him again, and ask his forgiveness for the secret that she had kept from him !—to relieve his mind from the weight that had oppressed it since he had condemned her, and struck her from his path.

He must be sorry to think that he had killed her ; if he were mad still, he would be sorry for that, surely, and joy would come to him again with the consciousness of her stepping back to life. Never a woman more sanguine than this of the good results to follow a meeting with her husband—and never a woman more repentant.

All her life she had been narrow-minded, secretive, selfish ; she was no heroine even in her better estate, but she was resolved, sternly resolved, to do her duty by her husband, and let nothing from that day forth stand between him and her. She did not fear that he would attempt her life again—after she had told him the whole truth, he might, if he liked, kill her, she thought. She was tormented by the conviction that she had driven him mad, and she knew how truly he had loved her, and put faith in her. Of Jonathan Fyvie she thought no more ; he was a dark figure that had passed away for ever. When he had met her in the Cleft — on her way to good, and needing friends to support her first faltering steps, he had sought to lead her away with him to evil—and she remembered him as the villain that he was. But that strong-hearted, trusting man whose life was bound up in hers, and whose life had thus been clouded at the first suspicion of her duplicity—if she could only be his friend, his slave—if she could only teach him to believe in her again !

A little faith in her—that was but wanted to bring back the past sunshine on them both, and then, with God's help, to begin life afresh.

These thoughts kept her strong for nearly one half of her journey, and then the reaction came suddenly upon her, and she swayed to and fro, and clutched at the hedges to keep herself from falling.

"It is too much for me," she gasped. "I shall never see him again! I am doomed never to see him!"

She groaned heavily. She sat down on the sloping hedge-bank to rest herself—to pray for a little more strength that should carry her to the house where he was —she wrung her hands together and wept, moaning piteously over the weakness which held her there a prisoner.

"I must see him!" she shrieked at last; "it is not just that I should be kept away from him!"

Then, with another effort, she dragged herself into the middle of the road, along which she ran until she fell there, and lay like a dead woman in the moolight.

Well for her that the moon was at the full that night, or her own friends might have killed her. They came dashing along the road from Wheal Desperation presently, and Laurence was the first to see the heap of dark clothes in the roadway.

"Some one is lying in advance of us—across the road," he called to the groom galloping by the side of the chaise; "do you see?"

"Good Heaven! it's a woman, Sir!"

"Inez!" cried Milly at once—Milly, who was sitting by the side of Laurence, and had been listening to his hopes of better times, and trying in vain to check his sanguine utterance. For she could not see any better times that would be the means of bringing them together.

Mr. Whiteshell, from the back of the chaise, leaped into the road at the same time as Milly, and they were bending over Inez the instant afterwards.

"Yes—it is Inez!" cried Milly. "Oh! what is to be done now?"

The hand of Inez closed upon Milly's, who bent her head towards her.

"Do I understand you—shall we go on to him?"

Another pressure of the hand, and then the head fell heavily back in Milly's lap.

" Now, if she is dead—dead like this, Laurence, after her long wish to see him ! "

" I can feel her pulse," said Whiteshell ; " let us lift her into the chaise, and drive back as fast as we can to Tavvy dale."

" No, let us go on," said Milly, " she wishes it. If she recovers, and finds that she is at home again, it will really kill her."

The groom volunteered to return to the village, fetch a doctor, and bring him on to Mr. Engleton's. He was a good-tempered man, with no objection to late hours. His services were at once accepted, and then, Inez having been lifted into the chaise, away they sped at full speed towards Tavvydale House.

As they passed through the open gates, and went along the broad carriage drive to the house, Inez, to the surprise of all of them, lifted her head from Milly's lap, and looked wildly round her.

" Are we at the house at last ? "

" Yes—yes. Are you better, Inez ? "

" Oh ! what a weary journey it has been."

" But we are at the end of it, and hope is with us," said Milly. " When you have rested——"

" I will not rest," cried Inez, struggling once more strangely back to life ; " take me to my husband, those about me who are merciful, for God's sake ! "

Inez was assisted from the chaise, and conducted to the hall, where servants, red-eyed and half-scared, were still lingering about. Mr. Engleton's sister met the party, and looked with surprise at it, dashing at Laurence for an explanation.

" Oh ! Mr. Raxford, what does this mean ? "

" It means, I hope, that we are going to clear up all mystery, and settle down for good now, Miss Engleton ! "

" But—but," in a whisper, " this dying woman ? "

" Not dying, Madam, God forbid that ! " cried Milly, who had heard the words. " She has been very ill, and has overtasked her strength in coming here. This is Captain Athorpe's wife—an invalid. She would have died of suspense at home, and so she has ventured to your house in search of her husband."

"Where is he?—can we not see him at once?" demanded Inez.

"Is it any good? He is——" began Miss Engleton, when Inez interrupted her.

"He is mad—I know it!" she said, hastily; "but I, who drove him mad, may bring him back to life. Where is he? I feel strong—very strong again! Don't hold me—I can walk alone."

But they continued to support her, and the procession, silent and thoughtful, went along the corridors, and up the stairs, like ghosts by which the house was haunted. On the first landing they were met by Engleton, who looked as surprised as his sister at the numbers.

"You have heard the story, Mr. Engleton," said Laurence. "This is Mrs. Athorpe and her niece."

"I can't make much out of the old gentleman, Raxford," said Engleton; "but he's an interesting study. If ever I sketch out a plan for a lunatic asylum, I'll have a different mode of treatment for——but it may be as well to talk of this another time."

He led the way to a large room on the first floor.

"I thought that he would be more quiet here," said he, "and out of the way of Mr. Llewellyn, whose red hair seemed to excite him a little too much—as well it might. Raxford, they've gone, by Jove! Athorpe's frightened them clean out of the house!"

"Considering the serious nature of our errand," said Mr. Whiteshell, "this is frivolous talk—and out of place."

"Hollo!" said Engleton, "who's this? Not my dancing-master—the only man in England who saw the real advantages of my ragged-school system? It's very odd all of you turning up here to-night like this."

"I say it's very serious!"

"There's nothing very serious about it, unless you have brought it with you," said Engleton, with a glance towards Inez. "Athorpe's quiet enough—and will come round well enough, if you humour him. This way, ladies and gentlemen."

Engleton's easy manner was assuring. But he was not mixed up in this tragedy; he scarcely knew the details of the plot, **and** he was wholly unaware of the motives which had impelled Inez Athorpe to his house." There was a fair amount of philosophic composure in Charles Engleton that night, and it was at variance somewhat with his natural excitability. But he had seen the Llewellyns out of the house, and even this new influx of strange visitors was simply a relief to him. He was on good terms with every-body now, and a madman or two on his premises did not make the least difference to him.

When he was in the room, however, his interest in the story deepened, and he put several questions to Laurence, who was too absorbed in the scene before him to reply. For the wife, as though she had risen from the dead, had passed across the room unassisted to the side of the white-haired man resting in the large arm-chair by the fire-side. The change in him—the age which had descended on him since their parting—she did not appear to notice; it was the same man whom she had seen last.

"Athorpe—Noll—I've come!"

Athorpe started, and shivered at the voice. He looked at her, and then at the background of faces in a new bewilder-ment.

"Who is this?" he muttered.

"It is I, your wife, who was not guilty of going away from you—who was coming back to you full of hope in a new life together, when you met me."

"My wife is dead."

"No, no—living—living, and at your side here. Don't you know Inez?"

"My wife deceived me, and I killed her. I have been hiding from the gallows ever since—though she deserved to die—though it was better that she should die. You, woman," pushing her aside, "are an impostor."

"Don't believe that—at the last!" she implored, "for I am Inez, and you must know me, Athorpe. Oh! look at me, and try hard to remember who I am."

He tried and failed.

"You don't belong to me!" he said.

Milly stepped forward with her Uncle Whiteshell.

"You will know us all in time," she said; "we have all come to fetch you home—and make you happy."

"You—ah! you are Milly," said he, his face brightening

very much, " the one true woman whom I loved—the dear
girl who stood by me, and will do so to the end now.   Yes,
you are Milly of the Cleft."

" And I ? " said Whiteshell.

" Oh ! you're the man who took care of me in London,"
with a furtive glance towards him as he spoke—" James
Whiteshell—*my* friend."

" And I ? " asked Laurence, who read hopes of Captain
Athorpe's recovery in these flashes of memory.

" You—you are Raxford, of Wheal Desperation, and are
going to marry my niece.   God bless both of you ! "

Milly and Laurence both started at this, and Milly shook
her head, as if in silent protest against his prophecy.

" And this—who is this, Uncle Noll ? " asked she, once
more indicating the woman, pale and trembling at his side
still.

" I never forget a face," he said, looking at Inez again,
" and I don't know her.   She belongs not to me."

" Wholly forgotten ! " murmured Inez, sinking to the
ground ; " Milly—take me home—and—let me die away
from him ! "

*   *   *   *   *   *

But Inez Athorpe did not die—though in the relapse
which followed her rash journey to her husband, the chances
against her living were many ; and the wise men who came
to see her were doleful in their looks, and hazarded no loss
of reputation by speaking of her recovery.

It was her old illness over again, lasting some months,
and aggravated by a want of consciousness—a stupor, from
which it was difficult at all times to rouse her.   She might
pass from this to death, it was surmised ; but she passed
from it to a sense of rest that was not death, but a coming
back to life again.

She was in Milly's cottage—where Milly had long ago
insisted upon carrying her—when she stole back to this new
life, and looked very anxiously at two figures bending
over her, and watching her.

" Milly," she said, " Heaven bless you ! you are there
still—and ever faithful to me."

" Hush ! You are not to speak too much," she whispered.

" Who is this ?—can it—can it be——"

Captain Athorpe bent over her and kissed her.

"Yes, it can, Inez," he said; "it is quite possible. Possible to believe that we have seen the worst of everything. Thanks to you, girl," turning to his niece.

"Thanks to God!" was the wise correction here.

~~~~~~~~~~~~~~~~~~~~~~~~~~~~

CHAPTER V.

THE NEW CLERK.

MILLY had two pensioners now in lieu of one at her cottage; that was the only difference that Captain Athorpe's coming had made to the fortunes of Laurence Raxford.

A man more morbid than he might have accepted that difference as one more obstacle towards his love, but he drew therefrom strange hopes, which he kept to himself, lest the world should say that he had turned castle-builder.

Was he living only for the present, and taking therefrom as much enjoyment as he could?—finding excuses to call at Milly's cottage now, and not balked by any gravity of demeanour on the part of Milly herself, who became, however, nervous at his frequent visits.

Still it was natural that he should call three or four times a week, to ask after Mrs. Athorpe, who was getting well again—and likely to get better than ever, the doctors ventured to say now—to make sure, too, that Captain Athorpe was steadily improving, keeping step with the woman whom he had learned to trust once more. When the moon was at the full, as Mr. Whiteshell had warned him, it seemed necessary to watch Captain Athorpe closely, and Laurence was always at the cottage at that period, doing his best to amuse them all. He would have preferred full moons three or four times a month himself—even when full moons, at last, put no check upon the progress to recovery of the mining captain.

Mr. Whiteshell was back again in London. He had spent a month in Tavvydale as custodian of Captain Athorpe, doing him good service, and seeing him a long way on the road to recovery. From London he wrote to Laurence, with

the news that he had lost all his pupils in his absence, and
that a retired harlequin had set up an opposition shop over
the way. Still, he had saved a few pounds, and next season
—perhaps at the fag-end of this one—he should be doing
well again. He never despaired in London—there was so
much to keep him lively—it was only in gloomy places, like
the Cleft, that he felt his spirits leaving him. He knew that
something would happen in the Cleft one day, and sure
enough every one knew that he was right. So, with love
to Milly and Inez—who were to know nothing of the slack-
ness of trade, lest they should be solicitous about his prospects—and with kind regards to Captain Athorpe, and Laurence, he was very truly, James Whiteshell.

"Is there any bad news in that letter, Raxford?" Engleton asked.

He was in the counting-house, doing his fair share of work
with the rest, when Laurence read the missive.

"Well, poor Whiteshell has stopped in Devonshire till all
his London pupils have deserted him."

"It's time he left off dancing," said Engleton ; "what
sort of office-keeper would he make for a Mechanics' Institute,
do you think?"

"An excellent one, no doubt."

"Well, why didn't you say so before?" cried the master.
"Here have I been advertising and corresponding for my
model place at Plymouth—and nobody likely to suit me.
You haven't heard of my Soldier, Seamen, and Mechanics'
Arcadia, have you? It's a fine idea, and as it's the first
thing I have really carried out in all its details—it has been
backed, too, by no end of big people—I expect your congratulations. Where's Whiteshell's address? I'll write to
him at once."

"Tell him that it's in a cheerful locality, for he detests the
country."

"I see."

So James Whiteshell was startled with an offer by return of post, and in less than a week was office-keeper to
Mr. Engleton's last idea. The idea was a success, and James
Whiteshell is office-keeper there still. After office hours,
and when less eccentric people are in their beds, the strains
of Captain Athorpe's yellow backed violin may be heard
from the back windows of the Arcadia.

Engleton was a man of many thoughts ; to the last day of his life it may be said that he was a restless man. They were thoughts for the well-being of "the masses"—far-fetched, and impracticable most of them—but they were always thoroughly unselfish, and they made him some stanch friends. And though he took broad views of the people, agitated for their benefit, made innumerable mistakes, and met with a certain amount of ingratitude, by way of counterpoise to his enthusiasm, he thought also of those more immediately connected with him.

"Raxford," he said, one day in the new year, "this mine is likely to be a good thing—a steady paying thing."

"Yes ; a quiet, money-getting mine, that will for ages pay a fair per-centage on the capital you have embarked in it."

"The shaft sunk last—just before the Fyvie smash—was a bad spec. But I shall have another try at a lower level—my *own* idea this."

"I think that I would remain where I was."

"Go further, and fare worse, eh ? Well, it is not a bad motto, though 'nothing venture, nothing have,' is a better one. A trifle more courage, too—and I admire courage. Now, about our partnership."

"What ? " asked Laurence.

"Oh, haven't I told you ? I thought that we had almost settled that little affair. If you take a commission on returns it is just the same as a share in the business ; and I— I would prefer that your name followed mine in this Wheal Desperation."

"For Heaven's sake, Engleton, leave me a clerk. Mine is an unlucky name, and brings bad luck to others. Besides, I would not be a partner just yet for all the world."

"Why not ? "

"It's my only chance ; I must keep myself down, Sir. Don't worry me about it, and presently, perhaps—if you really wish it—I will accept a *little* share. But not now."

"Only chance—keep yourself down ! You don't mean to say that Milly is at the bottom of this, then ? "

"Yes ; she is."

"Oh ! I see. Can't we manage to make you in the enjoyment of a salary of ten shillings a week ? It's a splendid plan ! Say you have had a rise to twelve, and want to get married on the strength of it."

29

"You'll not make a joke of this, Mr. Engleton," said Raxford, half-imploringly. "When I think of Milly Athorpe, I never jest."

"I beg your pardon ; this is the first joke I have ever made in my life, and it is not a bad one. I think," suddenly slapping Laurence between the shoulders, and sending a penful of ink over the accounts, "that we understand each other pretty well."

Mr. Engleton went to town a few days after this, returning in a great bustle, after his usual fashion.

"Make room for another clerk here," he said to Laurence —"a junior skipjack, who will have to work his way upwards, and who, if he don't behave himself, goes out as unceremoniously as he comes in."

"We scarcely want another clerk in the office," said Laurence ; "but as you have engaged him, I dare say we shall find something for him to do."

"I've no doubt of that. You'll look after him. This is my last idea."

The last idea, in the shape of Jonathan Fyvie, junior, came into the office a few days afterwards—a gaunt, thin-faced man, who looked as though fortune had not been propitious to him lately.

"Take no notice of me, Mr. Raxford," he said ; "let me have this trial, and be hard upon me if it is a failure. Leave me to my work—which I understand—and treat me as one on probation here. I have not much faith in myself, but I'll do my best, for the old man's sake."

Laurence took no notice till Engleton arrived. Then he expressed his surprise to him at Jonathan Fyvie's presence there.

"I found him in the streets as ragged as a colt," said Engleton, "and I felt for a fellow who had been once so high in the stirrups as he had. He was dispirited, and without a hope in himself—which was a bad thing. So I gave him a long lecture, and then I offered him—for his father's sake, not his own, I said—a clerkship in this office."

"It was a generous offer."

"You'll see after him, and make a little allowance for a man who has been master here. We mustn't let a Fyvie go wholly to the bad, if we can help it."

But Laurence saw nothing to extenuate in Jonathan

Fyvie's conduct, and Jonathan worked patiently and quietly at the books, taking little heed of things passing around him.

"Am I doing my best?" Jonathan asked once when Laurence passed him.

"Yes; no doubt of that."

"It is for the old man's sake, then. If it will please him to hear that I am at work again—and you don't think that I am in the way here—I'll remain."

"For your own sake, too, Jonathan, I hope."

"Presently for mine, perhaps. For the work does not *drag*, as it used."

When he had been a month at the office the Fyvies learned for the first time that he had settled down to work. Mr. Fyvie, who had been dull of late days, seized the hands of his informant, Mr. Engleton, and shook them warmly in his own.

"How can I thank you for this?" he asked.

"Well, there is a way."

"What is it?"

"Talk your daughter into taking a fancy to me," he replied; "it's about the best thing that could happen to her."

"I begin to think that it is myself," said Mr. Fyvie, laughing.

Hester Fyvie certainly greeted Charles Engleton more warmly the next time he called at her father's house—but whether it was on account of her father's "talking" to her, or in gratitude for his interest in her brother, this history is unable to declare. But there was a difference in her manner towards him, and Engleton took a new lease of hope from it.

When the winter had gone, and there were spring flowers in the Devonshire valleys—the Cleft was golden with the primroses—Captain Athorpe came through the gates of Wheal Desperation. He walked with his old brisk step to the past scene of action, as though he was coming to his work again, and stopped not until he stood at the mouth of the shaft which led by a hundred ladders to that part of the mine which had been under his supervision.

He seemed as upright as ever, but he had wasted very much, and the storm that had passed over him had lined his face, and whitened every hair upon his head.

29—2

Laurence, who had seen him from the office window, hastened at once to join him—for he had almost his doubts of him again, when he noticed his intent, almost gloomy looks down into the mine.

"Good-morning, Sir," he said upon seeing Laurence—and his first words assured our hero that all was well; "I was thinking if I should venture down there, and see how the old place looks."

"There are many below the surface who would be glad to see you."

"I think there might be," he replied; "for if I was hard with them—rough with them—I was always fair. But my mining work begins in Mexico."

"Mexico!" repeated Laurence.

"That is a climate that will suit me—Inez and me," he corrected, "better than this; and as Captain Peters is going out to this new venture, I have offered to go with him. I think that I have rested long enough."

"If you feel strong, Athorpe, you need not go so far as Mexico for work that is fitting for you."

"I could not work in England," he said with a shudder. "I want to be quit of all this—to begin a new life in a new world. Away from here, I think that I shall be a better man."

"I hope so, Athorpe."

"A year of trouble and crime it has been," he said—"a long grinding year, that has tried most of us. Why, it is close on twelve months ago since I drank your health in that office."

"We will pray that the next year may be luckier than the last."

"Amen to that!" he cried. "I think it will."

"Is your wife strong enough to undertake this journey?" asked Laurence; "she is improving very fast, but she is a weak woman."

"She will take Milly with her," said Athorpe, looking down into the pit again, "for a year or two, until her health is thoroughly established."

"Take Milly!" cried Laurence—"take her away to Mexico?"

"Well, we can't do without her, Mr. Raxford," said Athorpe, "and she is willing to go with us. She will be a part of any home that we may have together—it was never my wish, for that matter, that she should be separated from us."

"Take Milly to Mexico!" repeated Laurence.

"It's no good pretending that I am ignorant of your attachment to Milly, I suppose," he said—and it was the old abrupt Athorpe that spoke here—"it's not my way to fight shy of anything. But we have talked it over, and made up our minds, and Milly is not likely to alter hers, I fancy. She thinks that we want looking after yet—and go she will."

"She knows best what is her duty," said Laurence gloomily. "When do you go?"

"It is uncertain. Captain Peters resigns his old post on Saturday, I think."

"I am sorry to say that is correct."

"After that—we are under orders to be ready to join our ship at Plymouth at any moment. It may be a week before we go—it may be three months. It depends upon our employer—I shall be glad to be gone for one."

"You will give me fair warning of your going, Athorpe?"

"Certainly."

"May I call to-night and see you—at Tavvydale?"

"With pleasure, Sir. If you can persuade Milly to stay, you're welcome."

Laurence did not relish the uncle's confidence in Milly's firmness; and he knew himself how intensely resolute Milly could be. She would see her duty plainly marked out for her, and she would vanish away from him for years —perhaps for ever! It was evident that everything had been arranged—arranged, he thought a little bitterly, without any consideration for him. He did not believe now that this year would be any brighter than the last.

He was standing by Athorpe's side still, when a third figure came between them, startling Athorpe by his propinquity.

"You—you in this place too!"

"Yes, Captain Athorpe—trying at the eleventh hour to be a better man, and finding it not such hard work as I thought it would be. I have no right to trouble you by my presence—I dare say that I do no good by coming here

—but if you will let me tell you how sorry I am for all the past, and for all the evil that I caused in it, I shall take it as a favour."

"Anybody might be sorry for that," said Athorpe bluntly, "and not be much the better man. You'll never amend."

"I'll try."

"It's ingrained in you, and must damn you, man," said Athorpe with greater fierceness; "I don't want to hear a word that you have to say."

"As you please," said Jonathan; "I have told you that I am sorry—I will add, that your wife was not to blame—and that at the last she acted nobly in despising me."

"It is a lucky thing for you that we did not meet some months ago," said Athorpe moodily; "but I don't want your life now. I only pray that I may never meet so cold-blooded a rascal ever again."

"I can offer no excuses for my conduct," said Jonathan Fyvie, still humble; "if I knew her first, if I loved her first — I had no right to seek her out after she was married."

"What do you want with me?" demanded Athorpe; "to drive me mad once more? What are your excuses to me?"

"If you could say to me, Athorpe—if you could even say to me, from her—I overlook the past, and forgive your share in it, I should feel more free."

"Sir, I have no forgiveness to offer," said Athorpe sternly; "a man never forgives such treason against his peace as yours has been. Stand aside."

Jonathan Fyvie made room for him, and Captain Athorpe strode away.

"There," said Jonathan, "when I try to make amends for everything, I am balked in my purpose. I can't stop here; I can't face all these people, who know my share in that man's ruin. I must find another berth somewhere."

And he did. For the curse of unrest was upon him, and pursued him, despite all his resolves to amend. He went from the mines to the smelting works, where he stayed three months, and then changed for service in a merchant's office in London, till the American war broke out, when he went soldiering in earnest, and was made prisoner by the Confederates, till the war was ended.

His last letter is dated a month ago, and therein he states that he is settled down in Washington, and likely to get on in life, he thinks. At all events, he can say that he is steady—and that pleases the old man, reading his son's letter very carefully under the garden porch of his villa.

He calls Charles Engleton his son now, and is very proud of him, as a good husband to his Hester—but his heart is faithful to his first-born; it has forgiven him all his trespasses, and is more full of hope in Jonathan Fyvie's future than yours or mine may be.

CHAPTER VI.

HOW IT ALL ENDED.

LAURENCE went to Tavvydale that evening in an aggrieved spirit. He was prepared, at a moment's notice, to grow eloquent upon his wrongs—to upbraid Milly for that new resolution which would separate her more than ever from him.

But Milly was looking very pale and ill, as though her own firmness had tried her very much, and he remained with them till a late hour, saying nothing that could wound her. It was a painful task to sit there and see Athorpe and his wife build their castles in the air, and hear them talk of their future together, with Milly for a friend and counsellor, as though Milly had not a will of her own, or—Laurence sighed at the thought—had never had a lover to study.

It was all over between Milly and him; if he had not known it till that night, he was assured of it then. They spoke as if the love story was ended, and the book shut away from them for good; he was their friend; he had a claim upon their kindness and hospitality, for he had been of service to them; but he had no claim on Milly.

Milly had told him so long since, and he had replied

that he would wait for her; he would wait for her still
for the matter of that, or set forth after her in due course,
and bring her back from Mexico some day; that was
what he hoped to tell her before he bade them all good-
night.

Captain Athorpe was almost his old self again—rough
and positive, if less conceited—and Inez, though very pale
and far from strong, was not the fretful invalid on whom
Mrs. Raxford called. But if she was happy, and happiness had worked its usual miracle upon her, still the
character had not wholly changed, and amidst all its im-
provements for the better, the fault of selfishness remained.
Laurence thought so, at least; but then he was unsettled,
and it was Mrs. Athorpe's influence and entreaties, he was
certain, that had exacted a promise from Milly to accompany them. He made no allowance for her weakness,
and he thought that she might have considered his loneliness a little. She knew that he had striven hard against
a hundred obstacles in his way to her niece—and yet she
had set the reward for his perseverance almost beyond
his reach, for he was a man whom they hardly understood yet. He was knitting his brows and thinking of a
journey to Mexico as he sat there—and as he went away
that night, the opportunity came for him to tell Milly his
thoughts.

They were standing together at the door, and he told
her at once that if she went to Mexico, in good time he
should follow her. She might have dashed him down
with the old replies that he was nothing to her, and that
she would never acknowledge that he could be more than
he was then, but she did not. Tacitly she acknowledged
that their positions were changed—that she was aware
of his love for her, and had faith in him, for she
answered,

"That would be rash, Laurence—your fortunes will be
made in dear old Devon."

"Not without you."

"Perhaps you will change again," she said, and, despite
the sadness of her voice, there was a ring of the old arch
tones in her reply; "Mexico is a long journey, and there
may be years to wait yet."

"I will wait, Milly."

"You think that the clouds are floating from us, then?"

"All floating fast away, I hope," he answered; "and yet you are going to leave me!"

"To take care of them," she answered, "till they are better able to take care of themselves. Then——"

"Then I may come and fetch you back for good, Milly."

"Yes—Laurence—you may."

He took her in his arms and kissed her there, as he had not dared to kiss her for long months, and with her face against his own, he forgot that Mexico was in existence.

He went back with her into the parlour, and sat down facing Athorpe and his wife, to tell them of the new promise that they had made together, and which, God knew, they were not likely to break.

Athorpe expressed his satisfaction, and smote his hand upon the table with his old heartiness. He thought that it would come to that promise, although Milly had told him that Laurence was not engaged to her, and might possibly marry Miss Fyvie.

"Milly!" cried Laurence, and that was his one reproach of the night.

Mrs. Athorpe said that she was glad, also, and that she would try to get strong more rapidly, for both their sakes; although Laurence must not hurry Milly, or expect to call her his wife for many years yet. They were both young, and could wait, she said, and they both knew how Milly was everything to *her!*

Laurence went home in good spirits, to tell his mother all the news. For the next week there was but little poetry read in that house, for Laurence kept late hours, and went courting every night, making the most of his time before they took Milly away from him.

He thought with a shudder of Mexico when he was not with Milly—of what a blank the years would be until he could set forth to claim her. And no one, not even her husband, was more gratified to see how rapidly Inez Athorpe improved beneath the thoughts of her new life, than Laurence Raxford was.

One afternoon, a few minutes before he had closed his books, and just as he was thinking that he would start early, and have a long evening with Milly, a note was brought to him, a note hurriedly written, and by a special messenger. He opened it, and glanced at the signature— James Whiteshell.

"What has happened now?" he muttered; then he glanced over the lines, and let the letter drop in his dismay.

Had the parting come at last?—and had it come like this?

He took the letter up again, and read it, as though it was his death-warrant. It ran,

"DEAR MR. RAXFORD,

"They could not bear—any of them—the pain of a formal leave-taking; they are not strong, and that, I am desired to say, must plead their excuse. They were aware of it last night, but had not the courage to tell you. They leave Plymouth this afternoon by the *Maximilian*, and they depute me to say for them, 'Good-bye—God bless you!'

"Yours truly,
"JAMES WHITESHELL."

It was a strange epistle, in the Whiteshell style, but Laurence did not stay to consider it. He could only realise the fact that they had all left him without a word—that last night Milly had said "Good-night" to him, and let him depart in ignorance of the morrow's intentions. He could remember that she was more kind, more loving, yet more timid in his parting embrace, and he knew now the cause. But it was not kind to cast him adrift in this fashion—it did not spare them much, and it cost him a great deal.

Still there was a chance that the ship might be delayed, and he would go at once. He had so much to say to Milly —to remind her how often she was to write to him—how truly and patiently he was to wait for her. The letter was still in his hand, when some pencil writing on the back of it caught his quick eye.

It was Milly's handwriting—he could have sworn to it:

"Come to Plymouth," it said—an injunction that need not have been given him.

Still the request, or command, gave comfort to him, on

second thoughts. It told him that though Milly had acquiesced in her relations' silent movements, still *she* was anxious to say good-bye to him, and had not the heart to go away without a word. There would be time, he felt sure now, to reach the ship, and clasp his Milly to his heart once more — the special messenger was a hint to that effect. Thank Heaven that Milly had rebelled a little at the last, and had not been entirely a slave to her relations' fancies.

He was driving furiously on the road to Tavistock five minutes afterwards; the messenger had begged a lift in that direction, but had scrambled down again in fear of his life, Laurence had proceeded so recklessly upon his mission. His mother and Mr. Fyvie saw him rattle past, and looked with horror after him; they went on towards Tavistock to find out what had become of him, and came back wondering more than ever—for the horse and chaise were outside the railway-station, nobody in charge of them, and Laurence gone.

Meanwhile, Laurence was on his way to Plymouth—was presently running along the Plymouth streets with his hat in his hand, as though he had stolen it.

He was on the quay making inquiries about the *Maximilian* long before the rest of the railway passengers had found their luggage and departed; but he might have waited with the other travellers, for the news was given him that the ship had sailed an hour ago! This he would not believe—he *could* not believe—until it had been reiterated twenty times, and shouted at him by loud-voiced seamen, angry at his obstinacy.

"You may see it from the Hoe, now, if you like," said one; and Laurence went his way up to the higher ground, to look out at sea for the ship that bore his heart away. A fisherman followed, and when they were on the Hoe, he took the trouble to point out the ship, a speck upon the glistening water in the distance. He waited for a fee for that kindness, and asked three times before Laurence heard him; then Laurence put money in his hands mechanically, staring out at sea with all his eyes still.

"Never mind," Laurence groaned; "it has saved her many tears, perhaps, and it would have been a parting full of bitter sorrow She knew what was best."

" What was best for herself, as well as for my dreamer
here," said a voice behind him, and he turned round to face
Milly and her Uncle Whiteshell—to catch Milly in his arms
for joy !

" The ship has not sailed, then—and I was right.   Oh !
Milly, it would have been hard to go away like that."

" The ship has sailed, Laurence—but without me."

" You—you remain ! "

" Yes—I could not find the courage," she whispered, " to
go away at the last !   I told them so last night—I reminded them that they were getting well and strong, and
could support each other, and that friends were going with
them, on whom they might rely.   I told them—and they
believed it, and knew that I was right, Laurence—that I
had done my duty to them both, and that there remained
now my duty towards you, which was the first and highest
task before me in the future.   For I was a little silly,
Laurence, and could not give you up again ! "

" My own dear girl—I did not think my happiness was
so near at hand as this ! "

" And you'll forgive me my little deception, Laurence,"
said Whiteshell, after discreetly turning his head away for
an instant ; " my third person plural did not include my
niece."

" He has mixed with theatrical people, and likes surprises," said Milly, laughing ; " but I foiled him with
a pencil-note, that should have prepared you for the
truth."

" Which it did not," said Laurence; " but I forgive
him."

" Thank you," said Whiteshell ; " that forgiveness ac-
corded, I'll—ahem !—sit down here a little while, while
Milly shows you the way to my chambers, where tea is
waiting for you.   Nothing like a pure fresh breeze from a
hill !   Besides, I have a passion for sunsets, and this is a
bright and ruddy one, that I take as a good omen for
the voyagers."

" Which we will take also as good omen for ourselves,
Milly," said Laurence, as they walked away, " speaking of
the brightness of the morrow."

So they sauntered down the hill together—she leaning
on his arm, and looking at him with her trustful eyes, as

she, his fairy wife, and the mother of his first little girl, looks at him in his Devonshire home now.

So with the glow of sunset on them they pass from the pages of this history, and the echo of Uncle Whiteshell's blessing on them lingers with us for awhile.

THE END.

PRINTED BY W. H. SMITH AND SON, 186, STRAND, LONDON.

15—12—68.

www.ingramcontent.com/pod-product-compliance
Lightning Source LLC
Chambersburg PA
CBHW022016110726
47901CB00006B/1543